LISA STRØMME

Lisa Strømme was born in Yorkshire in 1973, and studied at the University of Strathclyde in Glasgow. She has lived in Norway for over twenty years. Her first novel, *The Strawberry Girl* was published in thirteen languages worldwide. *The Hall of the Mountain King* is her second novel.

www.lisastromme.com

ALSO BY LISA STRØMME

The Strawberry Girl

LISA STRØMME

THE HALL

OF THE

MOUNTAIN

KING

The Hall of the Mountain King
Published by Atticus Woolf

ISBN 978-82-303-5574-9

Cover Design: Jason Anscomb

For Janet
a true champion of creative souls

To live is to war with trolls in heart and soul
Henrik Ibsen

PRELUDE
The National Theatre, Bergen 1905

The music waits in my stomach. I inhale as my head takes aim at the first note. An E finds its way into my mind and I force it to stay there, making it wait until I need it. The stage is pristine, new and varnished. The plush curtains hang together, overlapping to conceal me as I stand here alone. Out there, I hear the mangled sound of the orchestra yawning and stretching, limbering up: the wail of the brass, the whine of the strings, the odd ping of a xylophone; all of it accompanied by the mumbling of the audience who sit restlessly in their hard-won seats. A ticket to the opening was difficult to procure. Most of them are esteemed guests. Nina is there in the front row. The king and queen are seated in the royal box.

Everything is new; the theatre, the royalty, even the country itself. How proud we all are of our newly independent nation; how eager we are to give it a voice. Change is in the air, on everyone's lips. There's a national need for rebirth, for us to form a distinctive character, to stand up and be recognised for who we are. Questions are floating through the collective consciousness: *how do we want our country to be? Who are we as a people?* Free from Sweden's governance we finally have a chance to paint our own picture, play our own tune. It's time to find out who we really are when we pull back the curtain. When we remove the costumes and make-up, when we stop singing other people's songs and are free to sing our own, who are we then?

I close my eyes, see flashes of Jacob's feet. His toes and the paleness of his skin, and the grub and muck smeared all over his ankles. It eases my nerves and I smile to myself. I will take four steps. No more. When the curtains pull back I will be blinded and if I walk too far I'll topple over the edge of the stage – not quite the opening night spectacle I would want people to remember. I focus on the E. It resonates inside my head and I whisper the lyrics: *The winter may pass and the spring disappear, the spring disappear. The summer too will vanish and then the year, and then the year.*

From the wings Herr Hansson gives me a wave and a nod. The director is a large round man with short flat hair that he plasters to his scalp. He has a squinty eye and a tufted moustache. He's rubbing his hands together nervously and his spectacles glint in the light. The orchestra's piping begins to fade and a hush descends. It's time. I glance at Hansson for half a second, catch the smile on his blubbery lips, then there's applause, loud applause. Another glance to the wings. Hansson is gone. He is on the other side of the curtain now, out there.

The audience welcomes him enthusiastically, clapping so vigorously the palms of their hands must sting: *slap, slap, slap*. When it dies down, I hear Herr Hansson's opening but even his thunderous voice is muffled by these thick velvet curtains and I don't catch every word. 'A fine night like this...honoured to be celebrating...'

Later there will be a reception at the Grand Hotel. Kristian said he would come with me but he shies away from this light into which I am about to step and I don't blame him. He thinks it is keeping me from him and I have let him believe that. The endless touring, the rehearsing, the late nights, the audiences, the parties, the glamour of it all. He thinks it's the Dagny Jensen *out there* who is holding me captive, keeping me at a distance, but he is wrong, it's the Dagny Jensen *in here*. He is pressing me for an answer and I must tell him. I've been stalling, kept him waiting for too long, but now my time is up. I must tell him the truth. It's always so simple when I think about it. Doing it is harder. I lose my voice, get stuck.

I see Jacob's feet again, running before me, the mud on his heels engrained into the skin the way this music is engrained in my soul. 'An independent Norway, a country with a rich cultural life, thanks, not least, to the work of Edvard Grieg who preserved and cherished the music of our people.' That word again, *independence*. Our nation has gained it, yet I am about to lose mine. 'Norway's leading opera singer, who, as a protégé of Nina Grieg, was the first to...'

I retrieve the E, get the feel of it in my head, in my face and airways, imagining a long thread extending from the bridge of my nose. *But this I know for certain you'll come back again, you'll come back again*

'...proud to have her here at the opening of this elegant new theatre.' I lift and drop my cheeks, tense and release my diaphragm, pop my lips together: *bah, bah, bah, pah, pah, pah*. It could be the last time I do this; the last time I grace a stage as fine as this one or headline a concert as important as this. When they discover the truth about Dagny Jensen, their opera-singing darling, it will all be stripped away from me. It's already dust slipping through my hands, a note I am trying desperately to hold, but I'm running out of breath.

'Your Royal Highnesses, distinguished guests, ladies and gentlemen, please welcome...' Jacob's muddy feet skip by, flecks of dirt dapple his calves and shins. I breathe. *And even as I promised you'll find me waiting then, you'll find me waiting then.* I hear my name. 'Dagny Jensen!'

There is a roar of applause. The curtains draw back majestically and the lights hit my face. Four steps, no more. Step by careful step, I emerge. The room opens up to me but I see nothing. I am aware only of the lights, the jingle of the brooch at my throat, the buckles on my belt and the sashes that hang in straight lines over my apron. No glamorous gown for this piece. I'm in Hardanger clothes. That's my Norway: Hardanger. My costume is becoming the

5

symbol of this new nation. Even Queen Maud herself has had a bunad fashioned to fit her.

I hold the E with every fibre of my being. Out here, all eyes are on me, standing before them in the clothes I wore as a child. I wonder if they can see who I really am? Or is it only the façade they see? Is it only the façade that matters?

The clapping peters out and for a few seconds there is absolute silence. Not a breath. Every single one of us is held in a spell, and no one knows what will happen next. But then the music rescues us and we take its hand as it leads us into its story.

Strings. The beautiful drag of bows on strings melts away the remainder of my nerves and awakens the raw boundless depths of my inner world. Another breath and I have access to it, the part of me that holds the music. The opening notes of the strings burst with sorrow and longing and I am taken back to the time I first heard them. How Nina sang, how she opened me up and placed the music there inside me, tucking it in gently with such love and care, like a babe wrapped in fur.

The bass echoes the call of the violins and the flute brightly signals the beginning, telling the audience to listen carefully now, something special is coming, something profound is on its way, complex in its simplicity, powerful in its subtlety. Listen. Listen and you'll feel it.

Four counts. Four people: Nina, Grieg, Jacob, Kristian.

I inhale, extend the thread further so that the music will reach the audience, penetrate their hearts, get under their skin and burrow into their souls as it did with me. This is Solveig's song. She is waiting, waiting for Peer Gynt to return. Waiting, as we all are, for that day.

I summon the E. It must come out and be heard now.

The fourth count introduces it.

Jacob's feet, filthy and muddy.

Nina, in the front row.

The king and the queen in the royal box.

6

And Solveig, waiting.
Andante.
Slowly, I open my mouth to sing…

FIRST MOVEMENT
SOUND

1

We believed in trolls. It wasn't a childish notion, some fairytale fancy that only children could accept. The belief was a fact of life, a rule. In the Hardanger fjord, where the mountains towered like gods all around us and we were nothing but tiny specks of human life at the mercy of nature itself, *everyone* believed in trolls. The mountains held many inscrutable mysteries and the stories had been told for generations, passed down with care and caution. Mothers warned their children of the creatures that inhabited the mountains. Sometimes you'd even catch a grown man quiver with unease at the mention of a troll. We trusted the ancient stories and lived alongside these beings knowing only this: that they were out there, and they were to be feared.

Living as close to nature as we did, it was important for us to be able to distinguish between what was harmless and what was poisonous, what was dangerous and what was safe. Knowledge of berries, plants, mushrooms, wild animals and trolls all held equal importance to our survival.

We lived in Utne, a cluster of houses at the tip of the northern peninsula of the Hardanger fjord. The mountain that soared up behind us was our playground, and inevitably it was only a matter of time before we encountered a troll.

It happened in the spring of 1875, when I was thirteen. Jacob and I were changing then. No longer the childhood playmates we had always been but not quite adults either. Children grew up quickly in communities like ours and we were no exception. This in-between time found us suddenly, and it both excited and frightened us. We were reluctant to let go of the stories we had grown up with, yet scared to face the harshness of life and all its painful truths. With no one else to guide us through our adolescence, we navigated it together, looking to each other for answers that would help us make sense of it all.

He had dared me to go with him, up to the top of the mountain, territory that was strictly forbidden. I followed Jacob everywhere and never stopped to consider the consequences. Whatever he did, I usually did too, and this challenge was the same as any other.

I was chasing after him, following his feet. The craggy mountain tracks were narrower this high up and I concentrated hard on his heels. My Far said I had to stop and turn when the streams froze but Jacob didn't care about that. Barefoot, he skipped across icy brooks and shaded ditches, places the sun was yet to find. The temperature was plummeting, mists creeping in. My toes were getting cold and I was wearing socks and boots. But not Jacob. He was as happy in his skin as a mountain goat – didn't feel the sharp edges of the rocks or the sting of the ice and snow beneath his feet. It was as though he was made from the mountain itself. He was a Fjellheim. *Fjell:* mountain, *Heim:* home. If anyone belonged to this mountain, Jacob did.

'Come on, Dagny!' he shouted, still sprinting ahead of me, even after the steep hike from Utne, now just a smattering of matchbox buildings way below us. He was pointing higher, up to where the gradient altered and the rocks were piled up vertically like a wall. We would have to climb up with our hands and feet. I had never climbed anything like it before, not even with Far and the boys.

'I can't,' I said, hesitating, staring at the cliff.

'Oh, come on! Stop being such a girl.' Jacob looked back at me, his eyes positively beating with adventure. 'Mats Ellefsen says trolls live up there. That's their staircase. They come down at night and eat girls like you for supper.' He winked at me and I couldn't tell if he was joking or not.

'Mats Ellefsen has lice,' I said.

'Bet he could climb those rocks though.'

'Bet he would wet his pants.'

'Bet *you* would.'

'All right,' I said, defiantly, 'let's go then.'

Jacob gleamed at me. His teeth flashed in his sun-kissed face. He pushed his hand back through his blonde hair. All of the children in Utne had blonde hair but Jacob's wasn't mousy blonde like mine, it was a pure white mop that became even whiter in the sun. No matter how dirty Jacob got, his hair always stayed as white as chalk.

He was laughing. 'Dagny's goin' up the troll's stairs! Dagny's goin' up the troll's stairs!'

I pulled a face, growled at him.

He turned and sped off again and I followed his feet. I fixed my eyes on his mucky heels and stepped where he stepped. Through the marshy slop of snowy mush and over slippery rock surfaces I placed my feet exactly where his had been. In some places the snow was still deep and he sank into it halfway up his bare shins without flinching. I put my feet in the holes he made, pretending I wasn't scared of the trolls or the mist or the cold that was descending.

At the foot of the troll's staircase Jacob stopped and turned to me again. 'I'll go first,' he said.

My stomach sank. 'Have you been up here before?'

'No,' he grinned, 'but I should go first. It's girls they eat, so if they get hold of me it won't matter.'

I gazed up at the steep rock face. The climb looked impossible; the rocks were perpendicular to the mountainside and shot straight up, as if they had been laid with pointing, like a wall. I couldn't even see where the giant wall ended. It was somewhere up in the clouds. Jacob was already seeking out footholds and crevices, places he could get some leverage. 'Come on,' he called, 'up here, follow me.'

Naturally, I followed him.

He pressed his body against the rock and hitched himself up onto the first boulder. 'Round here,' he said, 'see that bump? Put your foot on that.' He was grabbing onto something above him with one hand; what, I couldn't see.

13

With his other hand, he hauled me up. I gripped the stone and pushed with my feet. Jacob crawled up skillfully, finding ledges and slits and chinks and clefts, tufts of grass, clumps that were strong enough to pull on. Three, four rocks we climbed, five, six. The stone was freezing, wet in places. The air was damp and cold. We reached the steepest part – a mighty boulder with a flat smooth face that was taller than both of us and didn't have so much as a ripple across its surface. I clung on to the rock below while Jacob forged ahead, trying to find the best way around it.

'There is a way,' he shouted down to me, 'but you're going to have to reach high.'

I shivered. My fingertips were clinging to a thin ledge above me and my arms were already at full stretch. I was balancing on the tips of my toes. It wasn't a secure grip, I was slipping.

I made the mistake of looking down. We had climbed so high that the mountainside was too far below us to jump back down again now. It felt as though I was dangling from a shelf in the sky made of nothing but paper. The tension in my fingers was getting harder to sustain.

'Jacob!' I said. 'I can't hold on.'

'What?'

He was somewhere above me to the right. I was trembling. My voice was so shaky he couldn't hear me.

'I'm slipping,' I rasped. 'Jacob, I'm slipping!'

'Dagny, I can see something!' he shouted, 'it's big and grey, like a big boot. Could be a troll, a giant troll. Could be his foot!'

'Jacob, I'm falling,' I said, angrily. The game had gone too far; it wasn't funny anymore.

'There's a way around,' he said, 'I've got it now.'

'Hurry,' I said, as my fingertips slid a little more and I shifted my hands to find a better grip.

'There are two of them, Dagny!' he shouted, 'It's his feet all right.'

'Help me!' I said. At least I think I said it. I can't be sure if it actually came out of my mouth. I gave up. I lay my head against the wet rock face. My cheek turned cold. My breath was shallow, like silt seeping through my entire body. I was frozen. I couldn't move forward or back, up or down. I thought about my father, how angry he would be. *You're not to go higher than the first rocky ridge.* I had passed that some time ago. It was mid-afternoon now. *If the trees thin out, you're too high.* I couldn't remember when the trees had started to recede but the landscape up here was rocky and barren. *And stop if the streams are frozen, then you'll know you've gone too far.* We'd crossed plenty of icy streams. Jacob sprang across them so freely he made it all seem safe. Now I knew it wasn't. I was clinging perilously to a rock face in the sky. I had followed Jacob to my death.

'Dagny!'

I could hear his voice but I couldn't respond.

'Dagny Jensen, you're such a *girl*,' he said, hanging again with one hand and reaching down to me with the other. He grabbed my wrist. 'Follow me,' he said.

I was rigid.

'Relax your body,' he said, 'make it go soft.'

I looked up at him then, saw his white hair flopping about his brow and his deep blue eyes looking hard at me, half-laughing and making light of it all.

'I can't move. I'm going to die,' I said, annoyed.

'And you said Mats Ellefsen would wet his pants!'

'I'm serious, Jacob. I can't move!'

'Come on, girl, I've got you,' he laughed. 'Hand here. Foot here. It ain't that hard.'

I don't exactly know what he did but somehow he moved my hand to a stronger ledge and my feet seemed to follow as if they actually were climbing stairs.

'It's around this way,' he said, clutching my arm. 'See! It's easy.'

15

Jacob made everything look easy. My hands followed his feet and I scrambled after him gritting my teeth.

The rocks began to flatten out and soon the sheer wall had given way to a softer slope where, in parts, it was possible to walk upright again.

'Up here,' Jacob said, pointing ahead, 'I saw his feet up here.'

He turned to me and lowered his voice. 'Stay behind me, Dagny,' he said, 'if that giant troll sets his eyes on you, he'll have you, like that.' He clicked his fingers and I blinked at the snap.

I tried to pretend it was just a stupid story that Mats Ellefsen had made up, but out here on the forbidden mountainside, with my body shivering and the misty air thickening, and Jacob snapping his fingers in my face, I had never been closer to the trolls and the hulderfolk, the beings who took wicked children away in the night. I started singing to myself, humming a tune to pacify me.

'Quiet now,' Jacob said, marching ahead stealthily as if he were stalking deer. 'I saw his feet, he's here somewhere. No loud noises. You can't sing here.'

At the top of the ridge, there was a mound where the mountain plateaued and then gently rose to its peak as if to forgive those who had made it this far. Beyond the rocks, the mist cleared and we could see more snow stretching out towards the summit. I sighed with relief when I saw it.

'We can't go up there, not with—'

'Shhh,' Jacob said, pressing his finger to his lips. 'I heard something. It's him.'

We plodded on in silence.

'Jacob,' I whispered, 'have you ever actually *seen* a troll?'

'Course I have,' he whispered back.

'In real life?'

'Yes.'

'Where?'

'I crawled out on the Troll's Tongue when I was three years old. Ask Bestefar Jørgen.'

'Troll's Tongue's a rock,' I said, 'not an actual *real* troll.'

'It used to be real,' he said, looking at me, his expression hard and serious. 'The tongue turned to stone when the troll was slain. Don't you know that?'

I heard a noise, a cracking sound. Startled, I looked behind me but saw nothing.

Jacob proceeded to tell me one of his stories. He enjoyed frightening me and embellished the tales he knew for dramatic effect. 'That troll was a giant too,' he said, 'an ugly great giant who ate grown men, not just girls. There were disappearances, men went missing. All along the fjord they found them...bodies. Some say their bones had been snapped off, arms and legs. He liked to crack them with his teeth. And the smell. They knew they were close when they got the stench of him, that giant great stinking troll. They knew he was near. He came often, not just at night but in broad daylight. There were sightings of him. Big and ugly he was. Bearded, with evil yellow eyes. You can't look in their eyes you know, Dagny, or else you'll turn to stone.'

'So how did he die?' I said, still glancing about nervously.

'They summoned the strongest men in all of Hardanger,' Jacob said, 'men from Utne and Odda and Lofthus and Ullensvang came, armed with swords and knives and torches. They waited until nightfall and followed the stench. They say it's like rotting flesh.'

Jacob stopped then.

'And what did they do? How did they slay him?' I said.

'Shhh,' Jacob said, looking across the mountain.

'What is it?'

'Over there,' he held his hand to his brow and screwed up his eyes. 'Do you see it?'

'See what?'

'There,' he pointed, 'over there!'

'What is it?' My heart began to pump.

17

'It's smoke,' Jacob said.

'Smoke? Where?'

'Over there, a plume of smoke. See it? It must be coming from the other side of the mountain.'

After we saw the smoke there was no going back. Jacob was like a dog with a scent. He picked up his pace and sprinted off. I shouted at him to wait. My legs were heavy and I couldn't keep up with him even though the terrain was flatter now and we only had to cross the rubble of stones and scree. Jacob was flying ahead of me, running as if he'd been wound up and set down again like a toy. Then he stopped abruptly. It was only when I caught up with him that I discovered why.

On the other side of the mountain, down a sharp ravine, was a cabin.

'There,' Jacob said, out of breath, 'it's his house!'

I looked down to see a dark timber cabin with grass growing on the roof. Its chimney was puffing out smoke. 'You think a troll lives there?' I said, coming to Jacob's side.

'Smoke's a sign. Probably cooking his victims.'

'Do you think he can see us from there?' I said, edging away.

'No. Trolls are stupid,' Jacob said, authoritatively, 'even if he saw us, he wouldn't know what we were. He wouldn't know you were a girl until he could smell you.'

I stood still, not wanting to risk being seen. 'What if he has a telescope?' I said.

'Trolls don't have things like that, Dagny,' Jacob said, 'they're too primitive.'

I considered it. 'He could have stolen one.'

'Even if he did have one, he wouldn't know how to use it,' Jacob smiled, 'he'd probably be stirring his pot with it.'

'Do you really think he's cooking his victims?' I said.

'Wouldn't be surprised,' Jacob said. 'We have to get nearer.'

'Why?' I said. 'Then he'd smell me and know I was a girl.'

18

'But then we'd find out if it's him or not. Don't you want to see him, Dagny? Don't you want to see a troll?'

I stood there thinking about it, staring down at the cabin, which was unusually pretty for a troll's house. I'd never seen a troll before but he couldn't be a giant if he lived in that cabin. I looked at one of the windows, thought I saw something. I focused my gaze, there it was again. It was disconcerting and it worried me but I tried to put it out of my mind.

'Magnus Jevnaker has a telescope,' I said, after a while, 'in the sitting room.'

'Why does he have a telescope? He's a pastor, not a sailor.'

'Don't know. It sits in the bay window and they all look out at the passing ships and the gulls and the mountains, and Pastor Jevnaker always comments on everything he sees, like he knows a little bit about everything, enough to show off. And the three girls always sit on the sofa and beam at him and say, *oh, Far, how clever you are!* And Lillian looks at him like he's God Himself. Then he blesses everything and blesses them and says we're all blessed to live in the heart of the fjord where God's magnificent creations can be seen at their best.'

'I hate those stupid girls,' Jacob muttered.

'So do I.'

We stood there looking at the cabin, watching the smoke billow up and make shapes in the sky.

'Hey,' I said, looking again at the window, 'what if *we* had a telescope?'

'What for?'

'Then we could see into the troll's house from here. We wouldn't have to get close. We wouldn't have to risk anything, but we'd still see him.'

'How would we get hold of a telescope?' Jacob said, studying his nails. 'Bestefar Jørgen certainly doesn't have one. What use would he have for that?'

19

'We could borrow Pastor Jevnaker's,' I said.

'Don't be such a girl! As if he'd let us have it.'

'We could ask him.'

'We couldn't ask him, Dagny.'

'Why not?'

'Because then we'd have to tell him we've found a troll and the whole town would go mad with fear. We couldn't do that to them. This has to be a secret until we know what we're dealing with.'

'What about Mats Ellefsen? Can't we tell him we've found the troll's house?'

'We need proof. He wouldn't believe even this much. We need to see that troll with our own eyes, you and me.'

'And he'd probably tell Knut,' I reasoned, 'none of my brothers can know I was here, this high up. Lars would kill me.'

'Then we have to keep this to ourselves, Dagny, until we know the size of it.'

We shook on it as we always did. Jacob and I had many secrets, some were even sworn in blood. I had two of his and he had two of mine, the rest were joint secrets, things we had done together. Like the time we filled Hannah Jevnaker's satchel with fish heads. Bendik and Bastian Ellefsen took the blame for that. And when we snatched Grete Bremnes' bonnet from her peg and tied it to the Ellefsen's scarecrow in the middle of the night. No one wore bonnets in Utne. Veslemøy Bremnes reported it as a theft and Rolf Qvale was forced to take the case seriously. He reluctantly opened an investigation. When the bonnet was discovered at the back of the field a few days later, hanging daintily on the straw man's head, people had their suspicions, but Jacob and I avoided capture or recrimination. Rolf Qvale couldn't prove anything. He had one of the Dahlberg boys go and untie the garment and it was returned to Grete, pecked, ripped and stained with bird droppings. Angry that so much of his time had been wasted, Rolf Qvale blamed Grete herself and gave her a lecture about taking better care of her personal property. Veslemøy was affronted and started telling tales that Rolf Qvale had a wife in Bergen that he never saw. There were plenty of other mischiefs and misdemeanors but Konrad Olsen took the blame for most of it. Everyone made excuses for him.

This secret was different. It wasn't a crime as such, we hadn't done anything wrong, apart from going further up the mountain than was allowed. But there was something sinister about it. I could sense it. Whatever our discovery would lead to, it wouldn't be good. Being the ones who had discovered the troll's cabin somehow cursed us, and I had an ominous feeling that we were doomed from the moment we'd set eyes on it.

I dreaded the descent. Down is worse than up because you can see where you're going and you know how far you'll fall. We scampered back to the troll's staircase and I approached the rocks tentatively. Jacob went first and held his hand up to me. In the scariest places, he carried me. I don't know how he did it but he actually held me in both of his arms and lifted me from one rock to the next.

'Close your eyes,' he said, 'relax your body, make it go soft.'

Then it happened. That spring it kept on happening. The mood would change in an instant and suddenly we would become very serious and react to each other in a way that neither of us understood. It made me nervous. My chest fluttered as Jacob held me, the feel of his hands on me changed, the meaning of it was different. He wasn't just helping me climb anymore, it was something else. It wasn't entirely bad, but it frightened me. Jacob had held me, carried me, teased me and fought with me a thousand times before, it's what we did, what we had always done. But now things kept shifting with no warning and I was afraid. Did all this seriousness mean we couldn't be friends anymore? Jacob was my best friend, my only friend.

21

We reached the bottom of the rocks and he set me down on the grass but he didn't release me. His arms were still wrapped around my body and I clung on to him.

'There, you're down,' he whispered.

His arms slowly slackened and I clung tighter, pretending I was still afraid of the descent.

'Jacob, there's something I need to tell you,' I said, gripping his shoulders.

'What's the matter?' he said.

I felt all choked and hot, and feared I'd start crying but I couldn't be a sissy girl no matter how much I wanted to be, so I stared right into his eyes, locking him to me with the strength of my gaze.

He looked back at me with curiosity. 'Dagny? Why are you looking at me like that?'

'The mountain...'

'You're down now,' he said, 'there's nothing to be scared of anymore.'

'The troll's house...' I said, '...the cabin.'

'What about it?'

'I saw something there. Didn't you see it too?'

'The smoke?'

'No, at the window.'

'You saw something in the window?'

I nodded.

'What was it?'

I squeezed his hand.

'Dagny? What was it?'

I kept staring at him. 'It was the face of a woman,' I said.

His eyebrows twitched together as he processed the information and I waited for an answer. Jacob always had an answer. But this time he didn't say anything at all. He continued to stare at me, as though a veil between us had been lifted and he could see something revealing in my eyes. When he broke away, he held my hand firmly in his and we headed back down the hill to Utne.

We walked for a long time, holding hands. Neither of us said another word about the cabin, or the woman at the window, or the electrifying tingle of our bodies when we touched.

2

People say there are no words to describe the Hardanger fjord. It provokes such a complex brew of emotions that you can't pick one over the other and trying to describe it is futile. When visitors see it for the first time it terrifies and astounds them, pleases them and impresses them, makes them happy and fearful all at once. There's something about the hulking mountains rising straight out of the water that shrinks a mere human down to a speck of insignificance. By their sheer presence these dominating giants force us into a respectful silence and make us talk in whispers. Yet at their peaks they invite you to open your arms and sing out with all your heart. The clear blue water snakes the rocks and stretches over vast expanses with the endless sky and the clouds and the mountains all reflected back in it, like the world is folded over, above you and beneath you at the same time and whichever way you go, you'll sink into it. There are lush green hills, cliffs with intimidating rock formations, ledges that poke out boldly over plunging ravines, and thunderous waterfalls cascading in boisterous frothing waves. Untamed. Unfazed by habitation. Powerful. Magical. With nature as gigantic as the Hardanger fjord, it is impossible to find enough words to fill it. I had only one word for it: *Mother*.

She raised me to be free, like her. Wild, like her. I respected her and feared her, loved her. Loved the smell of her, the way she tickled my cheeks, played with my hair and got underneath my fingernails; she bathed me, dried me, warmed me, played with me. Far was a fisherman but it was Mother who supplied the fish. She gave us fruit and berries; valleys brimming with luscious apples, plums, pears, and black cherries so sweet and succulent they'd melt inside your mouth and the juice would dribble down your chin. Mother worked hard all year round, quietly performing her little miracles and we had to work with her. Whatever she gave us: snow, ice, temperatures so low they'd make your lungs freeze, winds that could rip a roof clean off, churn up the water and smash boats against rocks, rain that could flood the entire valley, it was all a way of life to us. Yes, she was cruel sometimes, but Mother never lied. She was always honest and she was always right. You can't question nature. Can't make up stories about her. She simply is.

Far could see that I was like her and it frightened him. I was his only girl, and what did he know about girls? Nothing much, only that they didn't grow up to be fishermen. I didn't have the same value to him as the boys. He expected me to know instinctively how to be a girl and thought that if he left me to it I would work it out on my own. But I wasn't showing any signs of it, with my messy hair and uneven plats, my unkempt appearance, my lack of interest in dolls and ribbons, my aversion to housework, my fighting and brawling with Knut, and my roaming in the mountains from dawn to dusk. Far had a picture in his head of the girl I should be but I knew I did not resemble her in the slightest. I was neither a boy nor a girl to him, and that baffled him to the point of permanent exasperation. I had done nothing that Lars Jensen could be proud of. The only thing I had ever done was a wicked thing, an evil thing: I killed his wife. Emma Jensen died of puerperal fever the night that I was born. Far lost a grown woman who knew how to be one and gained a baby that he couldn't begin to teach.

My mother had been an angel, everyone said so. She was gentle and kind and softly spoken and she had delicately sloping eyelids that expressed her infinite patience. There was one picture of her in the house, a photograph of her in profile, sitting at a table in a pose that seemed perfectly natural. One of her hands was resting on the handle of a basket of flowers, the other lightly skimmed the base of her chin. Her head was tilted, her hair wound around her head and tucked under her headscarf. She was smiling, as though

25

listening to someone who might have been sitting opposite her on the other side of the table, out of the picture. I liked to imagine it was me sitting across from her with my hand on the other side of the basket, emulating her pose. Me, the baby who had killed her.

Emma Jensen was the reason I was fascinated by souls. Mainly because every time her name was mentioned, it was followed by *God rest her soul*, in a hushed voice and with a bowed head. I wondered if her soul had never found peace, because people were always asking God to rest it for her. What was a soul? And what happened to us after we died? Did our souls linger between earth and heaven, waiting to find tranquility? And if so, what would help them to rest? I often asked Jacob about these things and he said that our souls were the deepest part of us, and that they continued to live on even after we die. He even suggested that part of Emma's soul was living in me, through me. But that only made me feel guilty. Was I the reason her soul could never find peace? Because I wasn't a typical girl, I wasn't calm and angelic as she had been, and because I was the one who had killed her?

As a result of the terrible misfortune of having a murderess for a daughter, the town took pity on my father. Old Mathilde Olsen told me Lars had gone cold after Emma died, hardened like the rocks in the fjord. He took no comfort in his children anymore and could barely bring himself to look at the baby girl who reminded him so vividly of what he had lost. When it became clear that I was not getting the hang of being a girl, Lillian Jevnaker, the pastor's wife, offered to take me every Wednesday afternoon to teach me how to be *feminine*. Magnus Jevnaker must have put her up to it because Lillian didn't have any interest in me. They all thought that if I sat there squashed into the corner of the sofa with Hannah, Selma and Lovise, listening to Lillian recite passages from the bible and watching them all at their stitching, it would provide some kind of learning by example and that one day I would emerge, glorious, like a butterfly from a chrysalis – a girl.

That day was not showing the slightest flicker of arriving. I loathed my afternoons at Pastor Jevnaker's. I deliberately ignored the needle and thread, asked no questions about the bible, couldn't care less about Romans, or Paul and his letters to the Corinthians. I had no interest in the things Lillian Jevnaker enthused about, or the merits she placed on female activities. *You've got to learn how to sew, Dagny,* she would say, *what kind of a wife cannot sew? Heavens!* She rolled her eyes and tutted at me, and all the girls nudged each other and giggled, and Lillian never once chastised them. I sat through it for two hours every Wednesday, this ridiculous attempt to turn me into a girl.

There was only one redeeming part of going to the Jevnaker's house, one single thing that appealed to me: the piano. More than just an instrument, the beautiful Steinway was a prized piece of furniture, which sat opposite the sofa, temptingly out of reach. The dark surface of it positively gleamed, it had a mirror-like quality – it was cleaned more than it was played. Lillian had Konrad Olsen in to polish it regularly. I'd seen him working at it, kneeling on the floor, rubbing it vigorously with his rags until he broke a sweat bringing a shine to the wood and the casters at its feet. Sometimes the lid was propped up and if I arrived early, I'd steal a glimpse at all the strings inside it and think about the music they secretly held. I often thought about climbing in and hiding there. I imagined I'd tuck myself in with the sleeping music, curl up on top of the strings and hum to myself the songs I longed to hear.

The only time I ever paid any attention to Lillian Jevnaker was when she played the piano. She played it with mechanical precision rather than any great passion. I was used to hearing her play austere hymns at church, where she sat with her back rigid at a functional upright chimeless piano, thrashing out notes like it was Lillian herself who was

27

delivering the sermon. But the beauty in the sitting room made a different sound altogether. The keys bounced softly down like cushions, they didn't clang like the piano at church, and the melodies Lillian played on the Steinway always sounded hallowed and glorious, as though it was determined to be magnificent, no matter who played it or how it was played.

Once, at Christmas, we all gathered around it to sing carols. I got so close that I could see myself in the rim and, when no one was looking, I secretly caressed the shiny ivory keys. They felt heavy, even beneath my fingers. They were smooth like velvet, deceptively gentle, concealing their power and strength, riches that lay beyond my reach. I sang out that day, singing of stars and kings and shepherds and miracles. The notes came bursting from a place hidden within me. I made them gracious and wondrous, as if I owed it to the piano to sound exalted. Lillian and the girls twitched their eyes towards me as I sang and I caught glimpses of myself in the surface of the Steinway, saw my mouth opening wide as the music sprang from me and my lips stretched tight into my cheeks. *Very good, Dagny,* Lillian said to me, *you actually have a very pretty voice.* It was the only time she ever complimented me and the only time I'd ever really seen myself. That Steinway piano somehow reflected who I was.

The first Wednesday after Jacob and I found the cabin, I was fixated on something else in the Jevnaker's sitting room, distracted, not by the piano, but by the telescope that sat on a tripod stand in the window. I gazed at it, wondering how far its range was.

'You'd better not touch that,' Hannah Jevnaker said, coming into the room. It was early, and the po-faced maid, Berit Lindeman, had already shown me in. I looked at Hannah and then looked away again, returning to the shiny brass telescope. 'It belonged to my Grandfather Jevnaker, he was an admiral in King Karl Johan's navy,' Hannah said, snootily. She did not rile me, although she was trying hard to make me snap. 'His name is engraved around the eyepiece.'

There was a gasp at the door as Selma came prancing in. 'You're not touching that, are you?' she said. Her hair was scraped back and braided, identical to her elder sister's. Her skirt and apron were spotless, her red bodice was finely edged, her shirtsleeves clean. I marveled at how impeccable the Jevnakers always looked. Selma was swinging a china doll in her hand.

'We're not allowed. It's sacred.'

'How is a telescope sacred?' I said.

'If you twist it here,' Selma said, pointing to the neck of the telescope, 'you can see for miles and miles. Far says you can see all the way to heaven.'

'That's nonsense,' I said. 'No one can see heaven.'

'I'll have you hold your tongue,' Hannah said. 'You are in a pastor's house. If my father says he can see heaven, then see heaven he can.' She brushed past me and reached out for the telescope.

Selma gasped again. 'You're not going to pick it up?'

'Why not?' Hannah said, 'I'm old enough. Perhaps I will be able to see heaven too?'

I stepped back as Hannah lifted the telescope from its stand. Selma looked as though she had stopped breathing. Hannah raised the telescope to her eye. She squinted and pointed the thing at the window.

'Well?' Selma said, excitedly. 'Can you see God? Twist it! Twist it!'

As Hannah turned the telescope it made a rattling sound and the lens came loose. The thick circle of glass dropped with a thud and rolled onto the rug.

Selma stared at it. Her face turned white.

'Pick it up!' Hannah said.

Selma crouched to the rug and reached out for the lens but pulled her hand back when she heard her mother and younger sister, Lovise, at the door.

'Get up! Blame her!' Hannah whispered, hurriedly returning the telescope to its stand.

'What in the name of our Dear Lord is going on in here?' Lillian said, surveying the scene. She was a thin, hard woman, finely tailored, as though every morning she had been sewn into place. Her white headscarf was stiff and starched, her bodice was deep cranberry and its insert was made from calamanco, richly embroidered with beads and metal ribbons. Despite her finery, Lillian's face often appeared masculine due to its severity and sometimes her eyes seemed translucent, as if every emotion inside her had fled.

'Dagny touched the telescope,' Selma blurted.

Lillian's glassy eyes turned on me. 'She did, did she?'

Lovise hid behind Lillian's skirt.

I shook my head. 'It wasn't me,' I said. 'Hannah wanted to see heaven. She lifted it up and the lens fell out.'

'Liar,' Hannah spat, searching for the lens on the rug. 'She's lying. I came in to find her meddling with Far's telescope, she had taken it off its stand.'

'I told her not to touch it,' Selma said, absolving herself, 'but she wouldn't listen.'

Lillian continued to stare blankly at me. She sucked in her cheeks and her jaw sank. 'Sit down girls,' she said.

The four of us went to take up our usual positions on the sofa.

'Not you, Dagny,' she said. 'You will stay at the window.'

'I didn't do anything!' I protested.

She ignored me.

The three Jevnaker girls sat in a perfect line opposite their mother on the sofa. Lillian drew up a chair and took out her bible. 'Stealing. Touching things that do not belong to us. What does the bible say about that, girls?'

Hannah thrust up her hand. 'Leviticus. *Do not steal or cheat or lie.*'

Lillian lifted her chin and stretched up her neck as Selma cut in. 'Exodus. *If anyone gives a neighbour silver or goods for safekeeping and they are stolen from the neighbour's house, the thief, if caught, must pay back double.*'

'Pay back double,' Lovise echoed.

'Corinthians,' Hannah said, '*nor thieves nor the greedy nor drunkards nor slanderers nor swindlers will inherit the kingdom of God.* Dagny won't inherit the kingdom of God, will she, Mor? It says in Ezekiel, *the soul that sinneth, it shall die.*'

I glanced at her, pressed my lips tightly together.

'It is up to us to warn the sinner, so that the sinner may save his soul, and if he does not stop sinning, even after our warnings, well, he, or she, will die a sinner,' Lillian said. 'I myself was thinking about Luke, *But Zacchaeus stood up and said to the Lord, 'Look Lord! Here and now I give half of my possessions to the poor, and if I have cheated anybody out of anything, I will pay back four times the amount.'* Four times the amount, girls. What is equivalent to four times the amount of Grandfather Jevnaker's telescope?'

I looked out of the window and pretended I couldn't hear them. I saw Konrad Olsen crossing the street, his bulky body shuffling along and his long wavy hair shooting up from his head. His expression was always the same: worried, troubled. He was a grown man with the mind of a child. Old Mathilde would be out soon, searching the streets for her baby. I saw Hedda Lilleberg smile at Konrad as he trundled past but he didn't stop or say anything to her. He continued on, wandering straight up the road towards the mountains. Soon he was out of sight. Over by the pier, old Mor Utne was leaning on her stick, waiting for the steam ship to arrive and bring her more guests. She liked to welcome them straight from the boat. That kind of service helped the hotel and more foreigners were coming each year. I wished I could get on that steamer when it came in. It would take me all the way down the fjord then across the sea to places I had only ever imagined.

'Did you hear that, Dagny?' Lillian was saying, 'Proverbs. *Ill-gotten treasures have no lasting value, but righteousness delivers from death.* You do understand what righteousness means, don't you? Are you listening? You're not going to learn anything staring out of that window. I put you there to think, not to daydream.'

'She's probably thinking about a boy,' Selma whispered, giggling.

'Someone with the initials J.F.,' Hannah added.

'Jacob, Jacob, Jacob,' Selma said, her voice singing, 'won't you cross the Eternal Waterfall with me and be my one true love?'

'Shut up!' I snapped.

'Dagny!' Lillian said, 'young ladies don't use language like that. What will your father say when I tell him how rude you've been, and that you've broken our telescope?'

I clenched my teeth, felt the heat flood in my cheeks.

'She's only angry because it's true, Mor,' Hannah said, 'they're always together. Dagny doesn't play with girls.'

'Either they're sweethearts, or she is a boy herself,' Selma said.

I stared at the telescope, thought about the troll that lived on the mountain and wondered if he might come down in the night and eat the three Jevnaker girls for supper. If Christians were those the trolls most reviled, then the Jevnaker girls would be prime targets. But they'd taste too soapy. He'd probably spit them out.

'Yes, well,' Lillian said, pretending not to be enjoying her daughters' gossip, 'whatever she is, her father wants me to make a young lady of her. The Lord sends us our challenges and we must graciously accept them.'

'If the Lord had wanted Dagny to be a girl, Mor, why did he make her act like a boy?' Lovise said. She was the youngest of the three but old enough to know what she was doing.

'The Lord has His own way of working, Lovise,' Lillian said, 'I'm sure Dagny would benefit a great deal from listening to His teachings and from seeing how well you girls behave. We must be an example to her, you see.' She stood up and laid her bible neatly on the chair where she had been sitting. 'Four times the amount of Grandfather Jevnaker's telescope,' she said, casting her clear eyes on me again, 'how much do you think it will cost to repair it, girls?' She did not look back at them but continued to look at me.

'I didn't touch it,' I said.

Lillian bent her knees and with a perfectly straight back, she knelt down and scooped up the lens from the rug. 'You must pay for the damage, Dagny,' she said, 'as a lesson.' She knew I wasn't afraid of her, so she continued to embellish the punishment. 'You will take Pastor Jevnaker's telescope to Konrad Olsen and have him fix it. You will pay for that. And you will have him clean it. That, you will pay for too. I think the Lord would deem that a reasonable penance, don't you?' She smiled at me. The Jevnakers prided themselves on their composure and their godliness. Lillian concentrated as she evened out her voice. 'If Zacchaeus considered it appropriate to pay back four times as much, I think you ought to accept that amount too. You will have the telescope mounted on a new stand, a nice new tripod, and you will pay for that. And–'

'I don't have any money,' I said. 'I can't pay for all that.' I heard the girls shift uncomfortably on the sofa as I challenged their mother. 'And anyway, I didn't touch it! It was Hannah. She was trying to see heaven.'

'It was her!' Hannah said, scornfully, 'I told her that Far could see heaven with the telescope and she wanted to see it too. She was trying to see her mother, her dead mother!'

I bristled. My fingers clenched into a fist.

'You will take the telescope to Konrad Olsen,' Lillian said, 'go on, take it now, and you will pay to have it fixed and cleaned. How you raise the funds is a matter for you to discuss with your father.'

I grunted, picked up the telescope and snatched the lens from Lillian's hand.

'Don't be insolent, Dagny,' she said, sweetly, 'young ladies aren't insolent.'

I looked down at the telescope, saw the words *Admiral Hans Petter Jevnaker* at the eyepiece as I slotted the three sections of it together. I wanted to smash it in Hannah Jevnaker's face.

'Mor,' Hannah said, as I crossed the room, 'you're actually letting her take it? Won't Far be very angry if–'

'If it isn't polished and shiny?' Lillian said, 'Looking its best? Well, perhaps not exactly *angry*, dear, we don't get angry in this house, do we?'

'No, Mor,' Hannah said, 'but if she, I mean, if Dagny takes it to the...can she be trusted with it?'

'But Dagny must take it dear, don't you see?' Lillian said, 'I'm sure, if she knows what's good for her, that is, if she understands what the Lord expects of her, she will have the telescope repaired and returned to us within a few days. Won't you, Dagny?'

'I will,' I said, with an acerbic tone, feeling the warm metal slide against my hands. 'I'll have Konrad shine it up like new.'

'Yes,' Lillian said, touching the two sashes that hung from her belt. 'Very good.' Hannah, Selma and Lovise looked as if they were going to be sick.

'We should probably end for the day now,' Lillian said, 'let us pray, girls.'

The four of them bowed their heads while I stood by the door, my blood boiling inside my skin.

On the chime of 'Amen' I flew out of the room.

3

It was the first time I had run away from Lillian Jevnaker without being dismissed. She always made me thank her and give her a ridiculous bow, and said that's what girls who wanted to become ladies did. But all it did was humiliate and belittle me and remind me of my place in the world.

I ran to Jacob's house holding the telescope and the lens in each of my hands. I bumped into old Mathilde Olsen in the main street, she was out looking for Konrad. Her hands were clasped in front of her, swinging back and forth. 'You seen my baby?' she said.

'Up the mountainside,' I said, as I passed her, 'out wandering.'

'You children, always running,' she muttered. All the folds and creases in her face deepened as she grimaced and shook her head as though the entire world had just slipped from her hands. I didn't have time to help her and ran on.

Jacob's house was at the end of the main street down by the water, a simple hut that he shared with his grandfather, Bestefar Jørgen, who was blind. The old man had come to live with Jacob and his mother after Jacob's father died in an accident at sea when Jacob was still a baby. Kristine Fjellheim cared for her father and her baby for four years until she succumbed to pneumonia, leaving the blind man alone to look after the boy. It didn't take long for their roles to reverse and as soon as Jacob was capable he became Jørgen's eyes. The two of them had stumbled along together and somehow managed to make ends meet.

The small red hut had one window and one door at the front and back. I went to the back, stood on tiptoes and peered in. If Bestefar Jørgen was in his chair, Jacob was home. When Jacob was out, Jørgen sat at the table and cleaned and repaired things: pots, pans, cutlery. It made him feel useful.

Jørgen was in his chair so I tapped at the door and opened it.

'Bestefar Jørgen,' I said to the white whiskery face, 'it's only me.'

The old man looked up, gazed past my left shoulder. Jacob was clattering things at the stove. There was a smell of gammon frying.

'Hello Dagny,' Jørgen said, his voice as gentle as dust descending. 'What is it you've got there?'

'How did you know I had something?'

'Your knock was different. Got your hands full?'

'As a matter of fact I have,' I said, 'it's a telescope.'

'Aah!' his face brightened and he held out his hands, 'may I see it?'

I knelt before Jørgen on the sheepskin rug and handed him the Jevnaker's telescope. He took it graciously, as though taking a newborn baby from my arms, and began to gently caress its surface. 'Ah yes,' he said, 'very fine. It's engraved?'

'Yes.'

'And the lens is missing?'

'I have it here,' I said, nestling the glass into Jørgen's rough leathery palm.

'Mmm,' he said, cupping it and weighing it like it was a ripe apple, 'we can fix that.'

'What's that?' Jacob said. His was wiping his fingers on his trousers leaving greasy streaks across his thighs.

I looked at him, widened my eyes, nodded slightly.

'Dagny's found herself a telescope,' Bestefar Jørgen said, 'needs fixing.'

'Where d'you get that from?' Jacob said, gulping.

'It's the Jevnaker's,' I said.

He glared at me then. His eyes were all suspicious and questioning, *you stole it?*

I shook my head a fraction so the movement would not be discernable to Bestefar Jørgen. 'It's all Hannah Jevnaker's fault,' I said. 'She picked it up off its stand, said Pastor Jevnaker could see heaven with it and that she could too. Then she twisted it and the lens fell out, and when Lillian came in, she blamed me. They quoted all kinds of bible verses and said I had to fix it and clean it and get a new tripod for it and that the Lord would consider that sufficient penance.'

Bestefar Jørgen held the telescope up to his blind eyes. 'See heaven indeed?' he said.

'I said I'd take it to Konrad Olsen but he's off wandering again,' I said.

'It won't be any trouble,' Bestefar Jørgen said, rubbing at the engraving on the eyepiece. 'Does that say Hans Petter?'

'Yes, Hans Petter Jevnaker, he was their grandfather, it was his,' I said.

'Mmm,' Bestefar Jørgen said. Memories danced behind his eyes then he laughed gruffly. 'Ha! And they think they can see heaven with it! Put it on the table, Jacob,' he said, 'job for later.'

Jacob brought Jørgen his dinner – a plate of fried gammon and a boiled egg. Everything was cut into small pieces and Bestefar Jørgen rested his plate on a shelf he had made from a plank of timber that perched across the arms of his chair.

'Have you had dinner?' Jacob said to me.

I shook my head. 'Haven't been home yet.'

Jacob got a plate and shared his own food with me. We sat cross-legged on the floor and ate with our fingers. The gammon was thick and juicy. Me and Jacob devoured it, while Bestefar Jørgen ate painfully slowly. I watched him longingly, like a stray pup, wondering whether he'd notice if I swiped just a tiny piece of gammon from his plate.

'Jevnaker's got some new boy helping, hasn't he?' Bestefar Jørgen said, as I sat there salivating. He was referring to Eugen Mohr, the young pastor-in-training at the church.

'Mmm,' I said.

'How's he turning out?'

'He's a fairy,' Jacob scoffed. 'Prances about, all morals and *the Lord our God*, but doesn't know nothin'.'

Jørgen chuckled. 'And how would you know, son? When do you ever read the bible?'

'Can just tell,' Jacob grunted, 'saw him trying to open the doors the other day. He spent a good long while wrestling with the key and rattling the bolts, was on his knees at one point, peering through the keyhole. In the end, he had to ask Petter Bremnes to help him when he saw him passing. Don't get me wrong, I ain't no friend of Petter's, but it was a picture to see him single out the right key and unlock the door in seconds. If Eugen can't even open the door to the church, how's he going to get the keys to heaven?'

I laughed.

Bestefar Jørgen's blind eyes looked upwards. 'Perhaps young Eugen needs to borrow that telescope, to show him the way?'

We finished our gammon and Jacob brought in three hunks of bread smothered with redcurrant jam that Bestefar Jørgen had made. Before he lost his sight, he had been a fruit farmer. Making jam wasn't something Jørgen needed eyes for. I relished the sweet red jam, savouring its thick texture and crunching the odd pip in my teeth. Jacob gobbled his quickly. He wiped his mouth with his sleeve and then cleared away the plates.

Bestefar Jørgen rested his head back against the chair and closed his eyes. I sat quietly and didn't say anything else. I thought Jørgen might be dosing off. But then Jacob came back in and started talking to him. 'Tell Dagny, Bestefar.'

Jørgen smiled without opening his eyes. 'Tell her yourself,' he said.

Jacob pulled a chair out from the table but didn't turn it around. He straddled it and faced me, draping his hands over the back of it.

'Tell me what?' I said.

'The stories about the troll's staircase,' Jacob smiled. His eyes lit up and his face became animated. 'Bestefar Jørgen says there ain't no cabins up there, nothing beyond the troll's staircase, not that he ever saw, and he knows that mountain better than anyone.'

I glared at him. *You told him we'd been up that high?*

Jacob placated me with a smile. 'I told him Mats Ellefsen said that's where the trolls lived, the ones who come down at night and eat girls for supper.'

'That they do,' Bestefar Jørgen said, his eyes still closed.

'And he told me how only once before did a troll build a house on our mountain. Many years ago, before Bestefar Jørgen was born, a mean old stinker of a troll lived up there, and he came down the troll's stairs one night and swiped a young girl from the town, and her name was...her name was...'

'Sigrid Gundersen,' Jørgen said, earnestly.

'Sigrid Gundersen,' Jacob said, taking a breath then continuing. 'And young Sigrid, well, the troll didn't eat her, he took a liking to her, and he kidnapped her and took her to his cabin, and he waited for her to grow up. And when she did, he married her! Some trolls take troll wives and some take human wives against their will.'

'What happened to her? What happened to Sigrid?' I said.

'She never came back,' Jacob said.

'Did anyone try to rescue her?'

'The townsfolk,' Jørgen said, from the chair, 'they tried, but the men couldn't get near.'

'Even the ones who made it up the troll's stairs,' Jacob said, 'because some didn't make it. Some *died* on the troll's stairs. But even the brave men, even the strong men who got to the top couldn't help Sigrid. The stinker fended them off, every last one of them.' He waved his hand through the air with a sweep of finality then lowered his voice. 'Once a troll has a wife, Dagny, he guards her fiercely...fiercely.'

'And no one can get her back?'

Jacob shook his head. 'No.'

I didn't question Jørgen's story. Stories like that had been told for centuries and weren't to be doubted. But from their faces, I couldn't tell whether or not I was being played.

'But that was a long time ago,' I said, 'it would be different now.'

'How?' Jacob said.

'Because people are cleverer now, aren't they?'

Bestefar Jørgen cleared his throat. 'How so?'

'Well...just...maybe we could...I mean, maybe *people* could find a way to get past the troll? Maybe they could find a way to sneak into his house and rescue the girl that had been kidnapped?'

'They'd have to be very clever indeed,' Jacob said, winking and holding up the Jevnaker's telescope. 'They'd have to be able to see exactly where she was, without being seen by the troll.'

'Yes,' I smiled, 'they would.' And without saying another word, the agreement was made. Jacob and I were going back. We'd climb the troll's stairs again, we'd take the telescope, and we'd find out why that woman was in a cabin on our mountain.

Our house was a yellow cottage up on the high road, past the church on the hill. It had four windows that faced the fjord: eyes that were always watching me. When I got home, Far and the boys were already seated at the table.

40

'Oh, here it is,' Knut said, when I came in. 'You smell that, Hans?'

He sniffed the air. 'A bad smell. Cow dung mixed with rotten stinking fish heads.'

'Where've you been?' Far said, his blonde brows knotting. 'It's late.'

'Probably with Jacob,' Knut said, 'she's never with anyone else.'

'You eaten?' Far said.

I nodded.

'Then get to your chores.'

He ripped off a piece of bread and stirred something in his bowl then chomped down on the bread without looking at me again.

I went up to my cot – a small triangle in the eaves of the roof separated from the boys' beds by a thin curtain. Our house was bigger than Jacob's but there were five of us living there and it always felt cramped. Behind the curtain was the only private space I had – a mattress and a few belongings. I crept in, heaved off my boots and put on my clogs. I changed my apron and went down to make a start.

'Snow's melted,' Far was saying, ignoring me as I passed. 'Thor says it's getting warmer, the lakes are stocked with trout.'

'We should take a trip up there,' Jon said, 'Hans and Knut can man the boat while we're away.'

'Can't leave them to it. They're not strong enough,' Far said. 'And what about the girl?'

'She doesn't matter,' Jon said, 'she's only a girl. She'll look after herself.'

'Could take her with us, I suppose?' Far said.

'She'd never make it as high as the mountain lakes,' Jon said, 'she'd be a hindrance.'

'True,' Far nodded.

He couldn't have known that I'd already been much higher than the lakes.

They ate for a while. Sounds of chewing and munching and slurping. My eldest brother Jon was past twenty. He and Lars always talked man-to-man and the other boys knew not to interrupt when the men were talking.

'Thor's thinking about buying a new boat,' Far said.

'How can he afford that?' Jon said.

'Peder Skarstad's offering him a decent price for that trawler he built last year.'

'He's selling it already?'

'Says he's got work, business is booming, he's building two more now. Doesn't have the time to sail it himself anymore.'

I walked past the table with the pail in my hand. 'He must be doing all right,' I said, 'Truls says he and Roald have a private tutor now, at home.'

'Who asked you?' Knut said, seizing the chance to speak again.

'And Alma's getting lessons with him too,' I said, ignoring Knut and going to the back door.

'That's not all she's getting,' Jon said, winking at Knut. 'Everyone knows about Alma Skarstad and that Leonard Steineger.'

'Everyone except Peder,' Hans added, grinning.

'You really think he doesn't know?' Jon said.

'What, about his wife's *lessons* with Leonhard Steineger?' Far said. 'Man only thinks about himself. Doubt he'd pay any attention.'

'Maybe he's happy about it?' Jon said. 'Who knows what Leonhard might be teaching her. Maybe she's *improving*?'

They all laughed.

I went out to the well and pretended I hadn't heard them. When I came back in, straining to hold my bucket with both hands, Far glared at me. 'Come on then, Dagny, get a move on, will you? I want that floor done quickly. Those shirts need mending as well.'

'Not tonight though? You don't need them before Sunday, do you?' I blurted.

He smacked the top of my head. 'Damned insolence,' he said. 'Girls don't talk to their fathers like that. If I say the shirts need doing, the shirts need doing.'

Knut sniggered, delighting in my castigation.

'Bloody Lillian Jevnaker,' Far said. 'Woman's meant to be teaching you a thing or two, but you're not learning anything, are you? Don't see any difference at all.'

'She's ignorant, that's why,' Knut said.

'And that's enough from you too,' Far said, pointing at him. 'Clear the table.'

I went about my chores in silence, sweeping the kitchen floor and trying my best to sew the boys' Sunday shirts. I was sloppy with a needle and my stitches were big and uneven. The holes ended up becoming creases and ruffles, so I folded the shirts unnaturally to hide my handiwork. I was just about to pile them up on the chair by the fire when there was a hard knock at the door.

Far was at the table making notes in his receipt book. 'Who's that then?' he said, getting up.

I looked at the door, shrugged my shoulders.

Lars wasn't a graceful man. He stomped over to the door, his torso curving forward, his arms swinging heavily at his side. He grappled with the handle and pulled the door open firmly.

'Yes?'

'Hello Lars,' a woman's voice said, 'may I have a word?'

'Oh, Fru Jevnaker,' he said, stepping back. 'Are you coming in?'

'No, I'd better not,' I heard Lillian say, imagining her eyes darting about, worrying she might be seen at our house. 'I'll say what I have to say and then be on my way,' she said.

I dropped the shirts. They unfolded in the falling, hit the chair and then sank to the floor in a heap of crumpled arms and cuffs.

43

'You see, my husband, gracious as he is, said the Good Lord would not wish to punish the girl in such a way,' Lillian was saying, 'and we would like to take the treasured telescope back and have it repaired ourselves.'

'I see,' Far said, 'wait a minute, Lillian.' He turned back in to the house. 'Dagny!' he hollered. But I had scarpered away. My heart was thumping in my chest. The telescope. I didn't have it. Jacob and I needed it. We wouldn't be able to see into the cabin without it.

'Dagny!' Far called again. I was out the back door and running up to the well. My three brothers, alerted by Far's shouting, scrambled about to look for me.

'She's out by the well!' Knut yelled.

'Jon! Get her!' Far bellowed. 'Go on! Fru Jevnaker's waiting. Sorry, Lillian.'

My brother Jon marched up the back yard and before I had time to think about my next move, he'd grabbed me by my hair and then yanked my arm. 'Come on, Dagny. You're in trouble...again.'

'I ain't speakin' to Lillian Jevnaker!' I said.

My body was moving faster than my legs and I stumbled and lunged as Jon tugged me back inside. Far was waiting at the door, his face blazing with anger.

'Get over here,' Far said. 'What's this about a telescope?'

'I didn't do anything,' I said.

'The girls were quite sure of it, Lars,' Lillian said, her empty eyes falling on me. 'Both Selma and Hannah witnessed it.'

'Where is it?' Far said.

I wriggled, but Jon held me still with both of his arms. 'I don't have it,' I said.

Lillian gasped. 'But I left it with you,' she said.

'Where is it?' Far said, louder, his voice full of grit.

'I gave it to Konrad Olsen,' I lied. 'He is going to fix it.'

'Konrad is not at home,' Lillian said. 'He's been out wandering all day.'

'Well I met him in the street and I gave it to him then,' I said.

'Is that true?' Far said, pulling me forward to stand directly in front of Lillian.

I nodded.

'Is it true?' Far shouted.

'Yes,' I said. 'I gave it to Konrad.'

'I see,' Lillian squeaked, 'well, I will have to take it up with Konrad tomorrow then. Thank you, Lars.'

Far closed the door and Jon released me roughly.

'What in hell's name have you been up to this time?' Far screeched, slapping me hard across the top of my head.

'Nothin',' I said. 'I didn't do nothin'.'

'You'll pay for this, Dagny. Stealing people's things, breaking stuff.'

'That's not what happened. I didn't touch it. It was Hannah Jevnaker.'

'Enough!' he said. 'And Lillian Jevnaker taking you in like that, trying to teach you good ways, feminine ways.' He wrestled me back into the house. 'Finish your chores. And for as long as I say, you're not goin' nowhere. Not out with that Fjellheim boy. He's a bad influence on you. Not out after school. Not anywhere. You got it? Only school, the Jevnaker's on Wednesdays, if Lillian'll still have you, and here.'

'But what about—'

'Not another word!' he said.

I refolded the shirts to hide the mess I'd made of them, mopped the floors, wiped down the table and the stove, then went to bed. Knut was already lying on his mattress. I stepped over his legs and he tried to trip me up, kicking at my shins. I stuck my tongue out at him.

'You're in trouble now,' he sneered. 'Konrad Olsen doesn't have that telescope any more than I have gold teeth. They're going to find out, you know. They're all going to find out.'

I slipped behind the curtain and changed into my nightgown. At one end of my alcove was a diamond shaped window. I crawled across my sheets and pressed my face to the glass. Night had fallen and the sky was a deep black ink. My heart was sinking. Everything ached: my throat, my chest, my head where Far had smacked it. *Not out with that Fjellheim boy*. It was an order I knew I could not obey but only break and in doing so incite further punishments. I sighed, accepting my fate. I would endure a thousand punishments for Jacob.

I gazed out at the night. Shadows of trees were swaying in the breeze. Beyond the treetops loomed the mountain, higher than the sky itself, with all its power and all its secrets. I put my hand on the glass. 'Come and take me away, troll,' I whispered, 'take me away.'

A note suddenly rose up within me. The start of a tune. It climbed the back of my throat and filled my nose and face. A note so forlorn and sorrowful that it awoke my tears. There came another to follow it, lower, sadder. The notes were forming a familiar tune, a lullaby, so deeply rooted within me that I couldn't remember when I first heard it. I began to sing it softly to myself. *My mother lifted me onto her knee, danced with me to and fro*. I sang it again and again, every note wrapping silk around my heart. A choir of voices in my head joined in as I sang, getting louder, following me, singing hypnotically in a round. The notes jumped higher as the song rose above its desolate beginning, *dance then, dance then, so the baby will dance*. I looked up to the mountain, the sky, heaven, where God was resting Emma's soul. *Dance then, dance then, so the baby will dance*.

INTERLUDE

To rapturous applause, I run into the wings. It's dark. Herr Hansson is there. 'Marvelous Dagny.' He is clapping too, his big fat palms cupping together, 'simply marvelous.' I smile, thank him in whispers as the audience begins to settle and the ladies choir patters past me like a flutter of diaphanous wings. I slip in between the heavy black curtains following the glow of the lamplight at the other end, feeling my way. The fabric ripples as I pass through it. Stagehands, silhouettes, move to let me past and all around me shadowy spectres work stealthily in the dark. Out there, the gentle plucking of strings begins.

The light becomes brighter. I'm out of the wings and in the passageway. Harriet, my assistant, appears at my side and takes my elbow. 'You were wonderful, Miss Jensen.' She ushers me to my dressing room with a cocksure stride full of confidence and bluster. No one is allowed near me. Harriet would take a swipe at any unwarranted advances. She is young, takes her job seriously. I have to laugh. I cannot say I have earned such rigid protection. I'm only a singer.

'The reporter is here, Bergen Times,' Harriet says, untucking a clipboard from her armpit. 'He has a photographer with him. I've said three questions, no more, and only a few photographs. Your time is limited tonight.'

'Give me five minutes,' I say, as we reach the dressing room door.

Harriet looks at her wristwatch. 'Do you want me to send Ellen in?'

'No. No need. Not yet.'

I leave Harriet standing guard and close the door. I go to my dressing table and sit down. The naked bulbs shine in an arc around the mirror and thrust a crescent of light at me. There are flowers in vases, from friends and well-wishers, arranged neatly on the table. On an oval tray is a bottle of water, a pair of crystal glasses and a bowl brimming with shiny apples. Harriet's doing. Everything is laid out for me: hairbrush, comb, make-up, jewellery box, perfume. My gown for this evening hangs on the screen behind me. I look at it in the mirror. Deep blue satin overlaid in lace. It is appliquéd with hand embroidered flowers and foliage. The silk hangs and scoops luxuriously like thick cascading cream pouring from a glittering jewel.

I look at my face, lean in close. My stage make-up covers the flaws, the feathery lines that have slowly been appearing around my eyes. The eyeliner is dark, my cheeks are rouged, my lips a deep reddish pink. I am puzzled by my own reflection and this contradiction that I am: a Hardanger girl hiding inside an opera singer. My fingertips reach up for Emma's brooch and I feel all the small circles of silver that shimmer at my collar. I think of all the times I have worn it. I could probably count them on one hand. My hair is braided and pinned the way it used to be, the way Mor Utne taught me. I stare hard at the woman before me, this blend of people that time has magically linked together. I am Dagny *out there* and Dagny *in here*, and we are at odds with each other, yet we coexist with a kind of reluctant acceptance, like dogs and cats who share the same owner.

My eyes drift to the side of the mirror where Harriet has pinned the running order. I stand up and lean in to read it although I already know its contents. *An evening with Edvard Grieg, by Royal Command.* The show includes chamber music, vocal and choral pieces, orchestral music and concertos, all of Grieg's most eminent works interspersed with lesser-known folk songs and traditional Norwegian tunes. The entire programme is a story I know so well that it could have had a different title: *The Music of My Life, by Dagny Jensen.* I glance at the songs I am going to sing and the music that practically runs through my veins, the music that links Dagny *in here* with **Dagny** *out there*. It keeps me connected to her, that girl on the mountain.

There is a tap at the door and Harriet swings in. 'They're here, Miss Jensen.'

'Send them in,' I say, sweeping my skirt out straight and touching a hand to my hair.

Harriet beckons them and the men come in. The reporter cowers slightly as he stretches out his hand. 'Miss Jensen,' he says, with an obsequious bow. His stiff collar cuts into his jowls; he's a man unaccustomed to dressing in such finery. A clear film of perspiration glazes his brow and he promptly reaches for a handkerchief. 'Thank you for seeing us,' he says, as the photographer lumbers in behind him. 'Arne Onstad, Bergen Times. It is an honour to meet you, and all the more so on a night as remarkable as this.'

'Miss Jensen only has a few minutes, gentlemen,' Harriet says, curtly, 'you'd better get on with it.'

'Yes, of course,' Herr Onstad says. 'It must be an honour for you too, Miss Jensen, to be singing for the king and queen tonight. How do you feel about that?'

'Won't you sit down, Herr Onstad,' I say, offering him a chair and turning my own around to face him.

He props himself on the edge of the seat and stuffs his handkerchief back in his pocket. His fingers delve about inside his jacket and he retrieves a notepad and a pencil. 'To be singing for the royal family…'

'It is an honour, yes,' I say, thinking about the Danish prince and the British princess, the great Empress Victoria's granddaughter, plucked out of Copenhagen and adopted as our new Norwegian king and queen.

'That they asked for you, specifically,' Onstad says, 'in this defining moment for our city; a new theatre where Norwegian culture will flourish. How does that feel?'

'Nothing gives me greater pleasure than to sing, Herr Onstad,' I say, 'and if it gives others pleasure, no matter who they are, then it is all the more satisfying to me.'

'Would you say that you are a part of our new national identity, Miss Jensen?' he says, 'someone who defines an independent Norway…what it is to be Norwegian?'

I glance down at the buckles on my shoes. 'I was a simple girl from Hardanger, Herr Onstad, and as such, I am no more or less Norwegian than anyone else from this country.'

'Oh, but that's precisely my point, Miss Jensen, much of the music that is being played tonight was heavily influenced by the peasants and farmers from the mountains and valleys. Grieg collected it and preserved it. It is part of our cultural heritage, is it not?'

'Yes, it is.'

'Then surely you are the very definition of Norway? You must not underestimate your influence and reach, Miss Jensen. You are known all over the world. When people think of Norway, surely they think of Dagny Jensen? You have been dubbed the *Voice of Norway*, after all.'

'I would hope they think of Edvard Grieg and the music being played here tonight,' I say, 'that is what makes me think of Norway.'

'Time, Herr Onstad,' Harriet says, impatiently.

'Yes,' Onstad says, scribbling some notes and hurrying on. 'It is a well-known fact, Miss Jensen, that you are a protégé of Nina Grieg. Is she here tonight?'

'She is.'

'How important would you say the Griegs were to your musical education and career?'

'Without them, I would not be here,' I say. 'They gave me everything.'

'Your mother died when you were an infant, did she not? Some people suggest Nina Grieg was like a mother to you. Is that true?'

Inadvertently, my hand flies to Emma's brooch at my neck and all the silver pieces feel cool against my skin. A shiver travels the length of my spine and I subtly alter my posture.

'Miss Jensen will not be answering any questions of a personal nature, Herr Olsen,' Harriet interjects, 'that was made quite clear in our correspondence. A few questions pertaining to tonight's event, that is all.'

'It's all right, Harriet,' I say, standing up. 'Yes, she was. Nina was like a mother to me and I will forever be in her debt. You can print that.'

Onstad jots it down hungrily and I move across to the sofa on the other side of the room. 'What about here?' I say to the photographer, who is fumbling with his camera on a tripod. 'Next to the flowers?'

'Er…yes, madam,' the young man says, squinting.

'*Exalted opera singer in Hardanger costume,*' Herr Onstad says, lauding me up again, 'or, *Dagny Jensen, the indisputable Voice of Norway?*' he scratches his chin, '*Voice of Norway* or *Voice of a Nation?* What about, *Celebrated opera singer makes a nation proud?* Or, *Dagny Jensen, the pride of our nation?*' He wouldn't be quite so reverent if he knew the truth. '*Eminent Hardanger girl sings for the king?*'

'I am not a girl anymore, Herr Onstad,' I say, sitting down beside a large bouquet of lilies, 'I would have thought, from my picture, that would be blatantly obvious to your readers, making your headline rather ridiculous.'

'*Hardanger girl at heart,* then?' he says, '*Legendary Dagny Jensen: still a Hardanger girl at heart.*'

Legendary? Soon I will be legendary for all the wrong reasons. I want to suggest *infamous,* or *notorious, shamed,* something more fitting for a fallen hero. I smile for the camera in the pose I always adopt for publicity; back straight, shoulders down, chin lifted and head held poised, turned a trifle to the right. They can't see through that.

'That's very good, Miss Jensen,' the photographer says, 'hold it there please.'

'One final question, Miss Jensen, if I may?' Herr Onstad says.

'Quickly,' Harriet says, looking again at her wristwatch.

'Yes, of course,' he says, returning his notebook to his pocket, 'I'm curious; of all the music being played here tonight, indeed, of all of Grieg's works, do you have a particular favourite, Miss Jensen?'

The button on the camera clicks and the flashbulb pops. I hold my pose and try not to move. I grapple for an answer but it's like trying to pick your favourite type of pain. 'I'm not sure I can answer that,' I say, 'these pieces all mean different things to me, each has equal importance, each has equal merit, they're just, different.'

'Surely there must be one that stands out?'

'Very well,' I say, scanning my body for the one single piece of music that sings the loudest in my soul. It rushes to my chest the moment I summon it and threatens to release the intimate contents of my heart. I throw my hand to my breast to try to contain it, I can't have it all spilling out here, especially not with a journalist. 'You may be surprised, Herr Onstad,' I say, glancing casually at the lilies in the vase, 'but it is not a vocal piece, it's *Morning Mood*.'

'Oh, yes, *Peer Gynt*. And why is that piece in particular so significant to you?' he says.

For a moment, I cannot answer. Harriet looks agitated and taps at her clipboard.

'It achieves the impossible,' I say, getting up, 'Edvard Grieg was a genius.'

Onstad wants to press me for more and starts asking another question but Harriet cuts him off and wades in between us, waving her arm and herding them out with a brusque, *time's up, gentlemen*.

I shake their hands and Onstad bows again, unnecessarily, smothering me with flattery as he backs out of the room.

Harriet holds the door open and as the gentlemen leave, I can hear the choir singing on the stage. Their voices are chiming like bells, they are singing a cappella. *Gjendin-bån*, *Gjendin-bån*. It's a lullaby: *Gjendine's Lullaby*, the song that was

52

planted inside me before I was even born. I was never taught it as a child and don't remember anyone singing it to me, apart from Nina, but I always knew it. It circles in the air, calling from the stage, reaching me with its hypnotic ringing. *Dance then, dance then, so the baby will dance.* It soothes me like an opiate and I sink back into my dressing room and settle again on the sofa.

'A short break, Miss Jensen,' Harriet says, 'then I'll send the ladies in to help you change.'

'Thank you, Harriet, I'm a little tired,' I say, looking up at her. Her eyes are ebony, so dark it's hard to tell where the pupils end and the irises begin. Her cheekbones are high and pinched, her chin pointed. It is a face of efficiency and accomplishment. She is a capable assistant but I would not choose her as a friend if we were the same age. She wears a black dress and glides about like a chess piece, contemplating her every move with precision and deliberation. She leaves me alone, closes the door and resumes her position of guard outside.

I continue to hum the choir's tune, amused by the irony of singing a lullaby to myself, here, tonight, of all nights. *My mother lifted me onto her knee, danced with me to and fro.* In the morning, I will be on the front page of the newspaper. It must go well tonight, I must give them what they want to hear, the *Voice of Norway*, or Herr Onstad will change his story and I will be thrown to the wolves. These journalists can never be trusted. I lean back and rest my head against the velvety sofa. Kristian said he would come and see me here in my dressing room but I hope he doesn't. If I could put it off for just one more night. *Dance then, dance then, so the baby will dance.* I close my eyes. It's true, I am tired. My mind and body are in a tug-of-war. I must face Kristian, I must sing, I must be good out there. But I want to run. I want to escape to the mountain and hide in its thick forests. I want to feel the pine needles brush against my skin and smell the fresh mud as it squelches beneath my feet. I long for the freedom of nature, the mighty fjord, the vast living world to which I belong.

I breathe deeply, try to relax my shoulders. In my turmoil, I think about Herr Onstad's headline: *Legendary Dagny Jensen: still a Hardanger girl at heart.*

4

The schoolroom was empty when I arrived. I'd hardly slept. I got up with Far, made him coffee and breakfast and left the house when he and Jon went off to the boat. None of us said anything. No reference was made to Lillian Jevnaker or the telescope, or to Konrad Olsen. Knut had been told to keep his eye on me but he and Hans were still in their beds when I left, snoring like dogs.

I stood there in the empty room looking at the desks as if I could choose where I wanted to sit. But there was a hierarchy to it: younger ones at the front, older ones at the back. My brother Hans and Petter Bremnes were the eldest in the class and sat at the good seats at the back by the window. They would only attend school for another few weeks. After that, they would each have their confirmation, then they'd leave school and begin a life of permanent work. Petter would join his parents at the Bremnes store and Hans would be a fisherman, like Far and Jon.

The Utne school only had two classrooms and two teachers, so each class was mixed in ages, although all the students came from the same nine families. The well-to-dos: Jevnaker, Bremnes, Skarstad, Ellefsen; and the less affluents: Fjellheim, Jensen, Paulson, Dahlberg and Lund. Jacob was the only one who didn't have any siblings. He was the only Fjellheim and that made him special.

Our teacher was Julla Johnson, a young woman sent to us from Christiania. Her accent was different to ours, and she didn't wear the same clothes as we wore in Hardanger. She was deliciously exotic. Frøken Julla was quite the opposite of the headmistress, Camilla Petersen, who was a strict disciplinarian. Fru Petersen taught the younger class, as it was considered important to drum the principles of Christian education into us at an early age. We learned through rapped knuckles and smacked hands, and standing in the corner with our faces to the wall. This learning by rote, humiliation and, at times, violence, produced results, of sorts. Most of us could read and write and do basic arithmetic. The school had recently introduced needlework for girls and gymnastics for boys, however, Fru Petersen's handball lessons were only popular because the boys took the classes as an opportunity to throw the ball at her head. Her stiffly starched headscarf made an attractive target. Unbeknown to her, there was currently a substantial prize fund growing for the centre of its high peak.

I circled my desk, reluctant to sit down. I wasn't in the mood for school, couldn't concentrate on anything but the trouble I was in. At first I blamed Far, then Lillian Jevnaker, then Hannah, then Selma, and then I traced it all the way back to the mountain and the dark foreboding sense of curses and omens I had not been able to shake since we found the cabin. Perhaps it was because I knew there was a woman up there. Was she really living with a troll against her will?

'You're early today, Dagny.'

It was Frøken Julla. She came sweeping in brightly. When I looked at her, my first thought was of her hair. It was immaculately swept up and rolled back from her face with a broad braid running from front to back, and more braids, thinner and tighter, swirled and secured around the back of her head. The whole thing looked like a shiny golden crown.

'How do you do that?' I said.

'Do what?' she smiled.

'With your hair?'

'Oh,' she patted the back of her head, 'practice.'

'Do you believe in curses?' I said, without thinking.

'That's a funny question, Dagny. Why do you ask that?'

'Just...do you believe in trolls, Frøken Julla? Do you think they can put curses on people?'

'Trolls?' she said, scratching her cheek, 'I've heard the stories just the same as you have, we all know about the trolls that live in the mountains.'

'Do you believe the stories, Frøken Julla?' I pressed. 'Have you ever seen a troll?'

Frøken Julla sat down at her desk and took some books out of her satchel. 'My father used to tell me tales about Askeladden, the ash lad. He had adventures that involved trolls, didn't he?'

'But do you *believe* in them, Frøken Julla?' I persisted. 'Have you seen one, in the mountains?'

'I've never seen a troll, Dagny, no,' she smiled, 'but I don't have any reason not to believe in them.'

'What about curses?' I said. 'Can troll's put curses on people?'

'All I know,' she said, touching the top of her pile of books, 'is that trolls are big and hairy and stupid.'

I was dissatisfied with that. She couldn't see that my concerns were genuine. I lowered my voice. 'Do they really eat girls, Frøken Julla?'

'Dagny!' she said. 'What's the matter? Did you have a nightmare?'

'Sort of,' I said.

'Well,' Julla said, 'trolls turn to stone in sunlight, don't they? So I don't think you need to worry about there being any around here.'

'Only some!' a voice said.

I turned to see Mats Ellefsen wandering in with his sister, Ingeborg.

'They don't *all* turn to stone,' he said. 'Some can stand the daylight just as much as we can. The ones that live under lakes for instance.'

'Do they take victims?' I asked him.

'Course they do,' Mats said, getting into his stride. Ingeborg, who was older than us, lifted her nose to the air and drifted to the back of the room. 'They kidnap princesses and fair maidens and take them to their huts in the forest and force them to spin by day and scratch the troll's head by night.' Mats' face had taken a menacing air. His lips were curling downwards and his eyes were screwed up tight. 'And those ones, those angry ones who kidnap women, they can't be overpowered by no one. Even a hundred strong men can't beat those trolls, no matter how stupid they are.' His expression returned to normal then and he sighed heavily, as though he himself was defeated. 'The worst of them all though,' he concluded, 'is the Dovregubben.'

'What's the Dovregubben?' I said.

Someone else was standing behind me now. They leaned forward and whispered in my ear, 'the mountain king.'

I spun around to see Truls Skarstad clawing at the air with his fingers outstretched in a bid to frighten me. 'The Dovregubben is the king of the trolls,' he said, dropping his hands and assuming an authoritative voice, something he must have picked up from Leonhard Steineger. 'The Dovregubben is the vilest, most frightening troll of all.'

'And he has nine heads,' Mats chimed in.

'No he does not,' Truls said, 'he has one great big ugly head. He's a giant, and he eats humans.'

'Does he curse people?' I said.

'The Dovregubben can do whatever he likes, he is all powerful,' Truls said. 'No one can ever defeat the mountain king!'

'What if he dies?' I said, 'Of old age.'

'Trolls live for up to two thousand years, Dagny, so even if he did die, it would be long after you, and anyway, when the Dovregubben dies, his son inherits the title.'

'What if he doesn't have any sons?' I said.

'The Dovregubben always has sons,' Truls said, condescendingly, 'and the scariest thing the Dovregubben can do, is that he can change his appearance. He can shapeshift.'

'What do you mean?' I said.

'He can appear to look like anything or anyone, just a normal man, all quiet and unassuming.'

'To trick you,' Mats cut in, 'to trick you into following him to his mountain lair.'

'That's how he gets the maidens?' I said.

'He tricks them,' Truls said, 'tricks them into thinking he is just a normal man.'

'And then he keeps them captive for years,' Mats said, 'to spend their lives spinning and scratching his head.'

'Why the sudden interest in trolls, Dagny?' Frøken Julla said, attempting to diffuse the conversation before the boys got carried away.

'I was just...curious,' I said.

'She's just being a *girl.*' It was Jacob. He came striding in, his eyes gleaming. He broke up the group and pinched my arm teasingly. 'She's afraid, like all girls are.'

'I am not!' I said, rising to the bait.

'All right, sit down everyone,' Frøken Julla said, 'that's quite enough talk of trolls for one morning.'

I went to my desk and sat down as the rest of the class began to filter in. Grete Bremnes, in her ridiculous bonnet, had her books clamped to her chest. She was followed by her brothers Petter and Håkon, who were laughing at some private joke. Frida and Pernille Dahlberg, each as gormless as the other, wandered in looking as though they were lost and had never set foot inside the schoolhouse before.

Jacob plumped his satchel down on the desk beside mine. He grinned at me then leaned over and whispered in my ear. 'We go today,' he said.

'What?' I said.

'We do it today, after class.' He stroked the surface of his satchel and looked at me knowingly.

Hannah and Selma Jevnaker appeared. 'Good morning Frøken Julla,' they said in unison. I cringed at the sound of their voices. Their affectations and pretentions didn't fool me. I knew those girls were devious. Selma sat in front of me and Hannah behind. They each looked at me with the same antagonistic smile, a pinch of the lips that said *you are in trouble, Dagny, serious trouble.*

I turned back to Jacob and shook my head.

He nodded eagerly.

I shook my head.

We continued like this, silently arguing, until my brothers came in.

Knut walked straight up to me and stood over me, acting all gruff like Lars. 'Where'd you go this morning?' he said.

'Left early. Came here,' I said.

'You been with him?' he sneered and jabbed his chin towards Jacob without looking at him.

'No.'

'If you have, I'll tell Far.'

'I was here!' I said. 'Ask Frøken Julla if you don't believe me.'

'Hmmff,' he muttered, 'I'll be watching you.'

I scowled at him.

'All right everyone, sit down now,' Frøken Julla said, as the last of the students, a sad-faced Erik Paulson, slumped in. Petter Bremnes shouted some taunt at him but Erik didn't look up. He hardly ever spoke. He kept his head down and fiddled with his cuffs, pulling at his sleeves to hide his bruises.

'Take your books out please!' Frøken Julla said, and we all lifted our desks.

While mine was open, Jacob threw a folded square of paper at me, which landed on top of my text books. I snatched it up quickly and held it in my fist before anyone else had time to notice it. Later, while Pernille Dahlberg was toiling laboriously through a passage about the origins of the Napoleonic wars, I silently unfolded the note: *Bestefar Jørgen fixed it. We go today. Before they take it back. After school, we climb the troll's stairs. You can't say no.*

I met him at the gates. Knut was hovering at the other side of the schoolyard, his eyes kept flicking in my direction.

'I'll never get past him,' I said. 'They all know. Lillian Jevnaker came to the house last night. I said I'd given the telescope to Konrad Olsen.'

'What did Lars say?' Jacob said, turning his back on Knut to conceal me.

'Went mad,' I said. 'Told me I couldn't go anywhere or see you anymore. That I could only go to school, the Jevnaker's on Wednesdays, and home.'

'And?'

'And what?'

'That's it?'

'Yes.'

Jacob seemed taller. It was as though he had grown overnight and I had to lift my face a bit higher to meet his eyes. 'You ain't gonna let a little thing like that stop you though, are you, Dagny?' He smiled and my chest fluttered, and that uneasy serious feeling returned.

'What if I go first?' he said. 'You can meet me at the bridge, where the stream widens, by the Paulson farm.'

I glanced over to Knut. He was kicking a ball with Petter and Hans.

'All right,' I said. 'I'll do it. Go!'

I casually leaned against the wall while Jacob ran out through the gates. Knut looked back at me again, paused for a moment when he realised that Jacob had gone, and then returned to the ball. Petter Bremnes said something and the three of them laughed. I stood by the gates for a while, tracing circles in the dust with my foot, trying to look as absent-minded as possible. I started humming to myself – a tune I'd often heard Joakim Lilleberg play on his fiddle, a dance, lively and uplifting. Notes circled me, helped me gather pace and momentum. I tapped my foot, made a circle, tapped again, made a circle, and then when Knut and Hans and Petter's backs were turned, I disappeared.

My feet thumped the road as I sped away. The notes in my head kept circling and repeating, fueling my movements. I didn't think about Knut or Hans or even Lars anymore. The only person I could think about was Jacob. I ran up the hill to the Paulson's farm, sprinting hard with the sun on my back and my boots churning dust into clouds at my ankles. I kept going until I saw the bridge where the stream flowed down the hillside and the Paulson's fruit was growing on poles, making perfect lines in the fields.

Jacob was already moving, running slowly ahead of me. 'Come on!' he shouted, when he saw me, 'before they find us!' He twisted his body as he ran and reached out as if to take a baton from me in a race. I pelted towards him, stretching out my arm until our fingers touched. He grabbed me, pulled me, and I followed. We didn't stop until we were deep in the forest and concealed by the trees. I bent over and gripped my side, panting with exhaustion.

'You're such a girl, Dagny,' Jacob laughed. He'd hardly broken a sweat.

'Where is it?' I wheezed.

'In here,' he said, tapping his satchel. 'You want to see it?'

I nodded and tried to straighten up.

Jacob pulled up the flap and reached into the bag. He lifted out Magnus Jevnaker's telescope and handed it to me. The sheen on it was extraordinary. It shone in my hands like a beam of pure sunlight.

'He's fixed it up like new!' Jacob said. 'Try it!'

I extended the three sections of the telescope and held it up to my eye. The lens was secured tightly in place now and the eyepiece twisted so smoothly it felt as if it was made of butter.

'What did he do to it?' I said.

'Oiled it. Fixed it up.'

'It's beautiful,' I said.

'Well, what can you see?' Jacob said. He began jumping about apishly and waving his arms. 'Can you see me?'

I sniggered. 'No, you're too close. It's all blurred.'

'Then focus on something far away. Can you see heaven?' He stood behind me and I could feel him close. I lifted the telescope up to the sky and looked through the branches of the trees.

'I can see something,' I said.

'Is it God?' Jacob said.

'Not unless God is a bird,' I said.

'What kind of bird?'

'Big. Black. Looks like a raven.'

'You can see a raven?' Jacob said, 'It's a sign.'

'What do you mean?'

'Bestefar Jørgen says ravens are messengers from another world.'

'He does not,' I said.

'Yes, he does! You can ask him yourself if you don't believe me. Ravens help you see messages, warnings.'

'What do they warn you about?' I said, lowering the telescope.

'I don't know,' Jacob said, creeping up to my shoulder, 'but they are black and dark and they keep secrets.'

I could feel Jacob breathing softly against my neck. A ripple of nerves passed through my chest. I looked again through the telescope and tried to find the raven but it had flown away. I turned from side to side, then I saw something unexpected and stepped back abruptly, stumbling into Jacob.

'What is it?' he said, catching me.

'Someone is following us.'

'Who?'

'I don't know. I saw someone over there, behind the trees,' I said, pointing back down the way we came. 'Come on, we have to hurry. If my brothers catch me, I'm dead.'

I closed the telescope and tucked it into my belt as we ran further up the mountain tracks. Almost all of the snow had melted now and the ground was wet. Small clumps of yellow coltsfoot and some early mountain daisies had appeared since the last time we were here. Mother was throwing off her sharp exterior and bringing us signs of life, revealing a world of colour that had been hidden for so long. We continued to hike, constantly checking the track behind us, moving quickly and keeping our voices low. With no snow to wade through, the troll's stairs appeared sooner than I remembered.

'This is it,' Jacob said, examining the rocks, 'we're here.'

I stood still, holding my fingers around the telescope at my waist. 'Jacob,' I said.

'What is it, Dagny? You're not scared again, are you?'

'No.'

I didn't convince him.

'Think about that woman up there,' he said, 'we have to try, don't we? What if she's been kidnapped? What if the troll has her? If we save her, we'll be heroes. They'll tell stories about us,' he grinned.

'And sing songs,' I laughed.

'Yes, they'll write songs about us, and they'll sing them for centuries,' Jacob said, beginning to climb.

'And Joakim Lilleberg will play them on his fiddle,' I said, following him, 'and Hedda will dance and clap by his side.'

'And there'll be a verse about you and a verse about me.'

'And all your verses will be difficult to sing,' he teased.

'Why?'

'Because...'

'Because what?' I said.

He hauled me up to the ledge where I had frozen before but I didn't think about my fear now. It was easier this time.

'Just because...' he said, pulling me higher, lifting me from rock to rock.

I stopped talking when we climbed the mid-section of the troll's stairs. I had to concentrate hard on putting my feet precisely where Jacob's had been. The final stone was large and bulged out at an awkward angle. I had to bend my body to hold on and tighten every muscle in my feet. On the last rim, I stretched up sideways to feel for Jacob's hand. He grabbed my wrist and lifted me onto a narrow shelf in the rock. As my knees straightened and I came to stand next to him, he reached both of his arms around me.

'Tell me, then,' I said, 'why would my verses be difficult to sing?'

Jacob looked deep into my eyes, lifting again the veil that separated us.

'Because no one could capture you in a song, Dagny, no matter how sweet they sung it.'

I didn't know what to say. I wasn't used to talking like that. I clung to his body with my arms clasped around his waist. If I'd moved, we would have fallen off the ledge. I was thinking hard, trying to find the right way to reply. I wanted to say that he would be even harder to sing if he were a song. How could a voice, or a word, or a note, ever describe Jacob? How could a tune ever *be* him? How would it possibly sound? Soft, I thought, yet strong and steady, gentle as a whispering breeze, as old as time yet fresh and different, captivating, powerful, mysterious, like ravens with secrets. It would be true and shining and glorious and triumphant, and all things great and magnificent. Music like that was surely impossible to make?

As I stood there on the ledge gazing at him, his expression suddenly changed. He held me closer and gave a loud gasp. 'Dagny!' he said, as the blood drained from his cheeks. 'Don't move...don't move now. Just be calm. Don't move.'

'What is it?'

He patted my hips. 'Don't move, Oh God, don't move.'

'Jacob? You're scaring me.'

I'd hardly ever seen Jacob panic, but he was panicking now with no room to express it here on the ledge. I imagined snakes and bears and trolls and monsters. Had he seen something? My brothers? My father? He looked up to the sky, mouthing curses, then he pressed his hands around my waist again and patted my body, front and back.

'Jacob?'

He peered back over the ledge, looked at me with agony in his eyes.

'It's the telescope,' he said, 'it's gone.'

5

It was nowhere to be seen. Not lying on some out of reach ledge, not below us on any of the rocks, not even on the ground where we had started our climb. It had vanished, slipped from my belt without me noticing. It must have rolled down a crack in the stones, a crevice beyond our sight; swallowed up by the mountain. If it had been anywhere on the troll's stairs we would have seen it – a shiny bright object like that, but it was gone and there was nothing either of us could do about it.

We climbed the rest of the rocks and came to the plateau where we could at least panic safely. Jacob was still cursing. My head was jumbled and I couldn't think straight. What was worse – that I had lost the Jevnaker's telescope, or that we wouldn't be able to see into the cabin without it?

'Must have come loose,' I said. 'I didn't feel it happen.'

'I should have put it back in my bag,' Jacob was saying. 'It's all my fault.'

'No, no, it's my fault,' I said, slumping to a rock. 'What do we do now?'

Jacob walked in circles, thinking.

'We go,' he said, after a while. 'We still have to go. We've come this far.'

I nodded in agreement. We had to find out about the woman in the cabin. Given all the trouble I was now in, I would either be imprisoned or beaten when Lars got hold of me. We wouldn't get this chance again.

'We can look for the telescope on our way back down,' Jacob said, as the wind ruffled his white hair. He had his foot up on a rock and he was staring out across the plateau. He looked like an explorer intent on conquering some uncharted territory, like a Viking about to set sail.

He reached out his hand. 'Come on, Dagny. They won't sing any songs about us if we don't try.'

The ravine on the other side was not as steep as it had first seemed. The cabin sat tucked into the mountainside behind a cluster of trees. Its walls were made of thick timber, sturdy round logs piled up and hammered together. There were little windows with wooden shutters and on the grassy roof the chimney still puffed out smoke. It snaked into the air and I watched it spread and curl into wispy ribbons and imagined it was forming words. What were they saying? Was it a cry for help from the woman who was trapped there? Or a warning? Something the raven might have wanted us to know?

Jacob and I crouched at the top of the incline.

'There it is,' Jacob whispered. 'You think she's still there?'

'Mmm-hmm,' I said, nodding.

We watched and waited but when nothing happened, Jacob started to creep down the hill.

'What are you doing?' I said.

'We need to get a good view. Come on!'

I went after him, stumbling and crawling at first, then sitting on my bottom and sliding down the slope breaking my speed with my heels.

'Stay down,' I said, when we got close to the house. My throat was tight as I said it and my whole body felt strange and sandy, as though I might disintegrate. It was as if we had sunk to the bottom of the ocean and we were so deep down that there was nothing that could bring us back up to the surface again now.

Jacob pointed to the front window and tipped his head. 'There,' he said. He was going to look inside. I followed close behind him, reaching my hands out and touching his back for guidance. 'Hush, Dagny,' Jacob said, turning to me, 'do you hear that?'

I stopped, listened.

I did hear it. It was the last sound I expected to hear coming from a cabin on a remote mountainside.

'Music!' I said.

Someone was playing the piano. Quick fingers were running over keys and a lively tune was repeating, intensifying. Its tempo was like a dance. One, two, three; one, two, three.

'Can trolls play the piano?' I whispered, wondering how a hairy ignorant giant could have been playing this lively piece.

'Maybe it's her?' Jacob said, 'the woman?'

We were so spellbound by the music that all we could do was listen. The melody was becoming increasingly urgent, dizzying.

'Do you think he's trying to hypnotise us?' I said. 'Can troll's do that?'

'Maybe,' Jacob said. 'Let's see if we can see him.' He motioned forward and we started to move again, almost in time to the rhythm of the waltz. It was difficult to ignore the whirling beat of it. We took three or four steps, it couldn't have been more. Suddenly the front door swung open and we stiffened.

The woman who came out was waving and smiling. 'Hello there,' she said, 'you'd better come with me. He doesn't like people listening.'

She was petite, gentle. Her face was rather sweet and she had kind round eyes and short curly hair. She was not wearing Hardanger clothes. She wasn't from here. Her grey dress had proper frills and edges, like the ones Frøken Julla wore.

I looked at Jacob and he looked at me.

'It's all right,' she said, sensing our apprehension. 'Please, come in. I don't get many visitors.'

I gripped Jacob's arm and we slowly moved towards the woman while the music continued to play. It was as though we were in a fairytale, like Hansel and Gretl. Was she a witch? Was she trying to trick us? I tried to be rational about it. We weren't stupid enough to climb into any ovens, and if Jacob was with me we could fight her off, she wasn't that much taller than me.

'He gets very bothered about people listening to him work,' she said, still beckoning us inside, 'but you can come and sit with me in the kitchen. We can talk quietly there.'

We followed her into the house. If it was a spell or a trick it was too late for us now, there was no going back. I tried to be brave like Jacob.

We came into a small room with a low ceiling. The timber was painted a soft green on the inside and the ceiling was white. There was an enormous fireplace in the corner of the room where the fire roared. There were candlesticks and two irons on the mantelpiece, a copper kettle by the fire, but no cauldron. A rocking chair was placed close to the fire on a cowhide rug and a fleece had been pressed into it. Some candles burned on a small table covered in a heavy linen cloth, and around the table were four chairs. The chairs were beautifully carved in dark wood. They had curving edges and small heart-shaped cutouts in the back like the chairs I'd seen in picture books when I was younger. The room was cosy and snug with pretty curtains at the windows. Over in the corner I noticed a music stand, which seemed oddly out of place.

'We have some cocoa,' the lady said, softly, as the piano continued to play in an adjoining room. 'Would you like some? Did you climb up from Utne? I've heard it's a steeper climb on that side. You could come by the waterfall of course, but that can be treacherous in the spring. The stones get so slippery.'

I thought Jacob would have talked but he just nodded and I did too.

The little woman crossed to a shelf and reached down some cups, then she poured a milky drink from a pot on the stove.

'Please,' she said, directing us to the table, 'come and sit down. You must be tired after your hike.'

We sat next to each other on one side of the table. Jacob didn't lean against the back of his chair. His was rigid, ready for an attack. He sniffed the cocoa dubiously and didn't drink it. But the lady didn't try to hurt us. She just continued to talk incessantly, as though she hadn't talked for many years. I thought that must have been a curse he'd put on her, the troll who was playing the piano, that she had to be silent with him, unable to speak at all, living a life of complete silence while the music played. That must have been why she was so desperate to talk to us.

'Such a difference now the spring is here,' she was saying. 'The winter was so long, stuck up here, no friends to see. I do miss Bergen. We had such a busy social life there.'

I sipped some of her cocoa. It tasted delicious, rich and chocolatey, and gave me the courage to speak up.

'Who is playing the music?' I said.

'My husband,' she smiled.

'Is it a dance?'

'Yes,' she said, 'it's Anitra's dance.'

I wondered who Anitra might be. 'It's very...enchanting.' I said.

I was about to say more, but Jacob leaned forward and started whispering to the woman, talking hurriedly and earnestly.

'We can take you back to Utne with us,' he said. The lady stared at him and her mouth dropped open. 'You could make friends there, talk to people there, have visitors there,' Jacob said, 'you would be free.' He was rushing his words, afraid at any minute the troll would come in and find us. 'But you must hurry. You must come with us now.'

I gulped down my cocoa and prepared to leave. Jacob stood up and held out his hand to the woman. At first she laughed, then her round eyes stared at us in confusion.

'Do you plan to kidnap me?' she said.

'No,' Jacob said, 'we are here to rescue you.'

She laughed again and shook her head. 'My dears,' she said, 'I know where the door is. If I had wanted to leave, believe me, I would have.'

'Then why do you stay?' I said.

She sighed, closed her eyes for a moment, then held her hand to her brow. 'It is what women do,' she said.

'But...even against your will?' I said.

She pressed her lips together and shook her head. 'It's the music,' she said, 'it *binds* us.'

I listened to the notes dancing in the air. Circling, swaying, spinning around and around, building momentum, becoming heightened, tense, frenzied and giddy, then reaching a woozy crescendo, falling, and beginning again.

'What is your name, dear?' she said.

'Dagny.'

'Pretty.'

'And this is Jacob.'

Jacob smiled at her and she smiled back.

Then the music stopped. We all looked at each other questioningly.

'He's coming,' the woman said.

'We should go,' Jacob said.

'But we will come back and visit you,' I said, making my voice sound kind.

'That would be very nice,' the lady said, getting up from the table.

We heard the troll coughing in the next room and then the sound of footsteps.

'Dagny, come on!' Jacob said, running to the door.

We tore out of the cabin in a flash without looking back. We stumbled up the incline, pulling at each other's arms, dropping to our knees and dragging ourselves up again. We kept running all the way back to the top of the troll's stairs where we finally stopped to breathe. Only then did Jacob glance behind us. 'No one,' he panted, 'no one there.'

'Do you think he saw us?' I said.

Jacob shook his head.

We sat on the rocks.

'Why does she stay up here with him?' I said. '*It's what women do.* What did she mean?'

Jacob shrugged. 'She said something about the music?'

'It *must* be a curse,' I said.

'Or a spell or something,' Jacob said. 'It was very hypnotic.'

'Do you think he's put a spell on us too?' I said. 'Are we cursed now, because we went there?'

'Don't know. Maybe.'

We thought about it for a while.

'I feel like we need to go back,' I said. Something was already calling me. It was the music, the whirling force of it was tugging me back to the cabin.

'We can't go back now,' Jacob said, 'he'd see us. And anyway, we need to look for the telescope.'

We descended slowly, scouring the rocks for the Jevnaker's telescope. Jacob bent down, balancing precariously. I couldn't watch. He examined every crack and fissure while I clung on, my fingertips gripping the clefts that I remembered from before. I tried not to look down as we moved, tried to be confident and courageous like Jacob, but the troll's stairs were treacherous and ruthlessly unforgiving, there was no room for any wrong footing. If I faltered, I would die. Each time I hesitated, Jacob was there. His hand would grip my wrist, or I'd feel his knee in my back, pinning me in place. A slight tremble and his arm would be under my elbow to support it, or his whole chest would somehow be covering me and holding me in place. Occasionally, he would speak, a single word: *right, up, higher, below, wait, hold*, it was enough to assure me. Inch by inch, we came down from sky to earth.

'It's gone,' Jacob said, when we reached the bottom. He was shaking his head in frustration. 'Disappeared.'

'What am I going to tell them?' I said.

'We'll think of something.'

We walked back down to Utne with the afternoon fading all around us and the clouds crossing the sky above the trees, and our heads spinning with questions that neither of us could answer. We were altered, somehow, by the day's events. It was as though we had set something in motion, which we were now unable to stop and whatever happened next would be hopelessly out of our control. It made me feel queasy.

When we reached the Paulson's farm, Jacob urged me to go ahead. 'Go straight home,' he said. 'Tell them you were out looking for berries.'

I nodded. 'What about the telescope?'

'You'll think of something,' he said, brushing my arm with his fingers. 'Now go.'

I turned from him and hurried away.

Coming out of the trees I could see that the sky had blackened over Utne. A dark shadow covered the fjord and the water was grey and unsettled. The mountains on the other side had turned an unusual shade of purple. The air was cool and everything seemed tense, as though a storm was brewing and the wind and the rain were scoping the valley still trying to decide where to unload their fury.

The lines of fruit in the Paulson's field were bending over, cowering beneath the anticipated outburst. As I passed the hill, I saw Jens Paulson. He was out working on his own, standing by a pole, inspecting the young apple trees that grew all around it. There was a knife in his hand. He looked at me menacingly and swiveled the blade when he saw me. There were dark bags beneath his eyes and not a trace of a smile beneath that heavy moustache. I thought about Erik Paulson and his bruises, put my head down and hurried over the bridge.

I came down the hill, past the Bremnes' house. I always felt a sense of injustice when I looked at it – that such a beautiful house could be inhabited by such irritating people. It was white with pretty pale green trimmings around its windows and mid-section, as if a scalloped ribbon had been tied around it. It had a beautiful porch that framed the front door and its roof was made of diamond shaped slates that were weathered and speckled and sometimes glistened like marble. One of the net curtains twitched as I went by; Grete or Veslemøy, no doubt. I glared at the window and the curtain fell shut. They were watching me. It felt like the whole town was watching me.

As I rounded the bend and made my way home, I felt a pain in my stomach. Prickling needles jabbed inside my abdomen and I winced. I had to stop at the side of the road. The pain came again, sharp and tight, and this time I cried out. When it subsided, I plodded on. I was trying to think of what I had eaten that day, what might have caused me to feel so strange. It was only when I thought of the troll that I started to panic. The cocoa. It must have been poisoned. Why had I been so gullible? The woman had poisoned me and now I was going to die.

I ran the rest of the way home. When I came through the door I was sweating and groaning.

'What in hell's name?' Lars said, looking at me from the table.

'I'm sick,' I said.

'Where've you been?' he said, his rage somewhat subdued.

'Was looking for berries,' I moaned. The pain came again and I bent over, then crouched on the floor.

Lars got up and came over to me. He stood there gaping at me with his hands on his hips. 'What d'you eat?' he said, accusingly.

'Not much.'

'You eat berries that weren't ripe?'

'No,' I said. 'I didn't find any.'

'Better get to bed then,' he snapped.

'Mmm-hmm,' I said.

I blew out through my cheeks and got to my feet again. I couldn't tell him I'd drunk the poisoned cocoa that a troll's wife had given me. Couldn't tell him I was going to die.

'T'sup with her?' Knut said, as I went to climb the stairs.

'Sick,' Lars said. He seemed puzzled.

'Probably ate somethin' she shouldn't have.'

'I told you to watch her,' Far said.

'I did.'

'So how did she come to be out picking berries?'

'Gah, she went off after school. I lost her,' Knut said, 'she was on her own though.'

Lars grunted and went back to the table. He settled momentarily, then I heard his chair scrape across the floor. 'Hey! Dagny!' he shouted.

'Huh?' I called.

'Did Lillian get that telescope back?'

'I don't know,' I said.

'She'd better get it back,' he said, 'in one piece and properly repaired, or your life won't be worth living.'

I didn't answer. There wasn't much of my life left to live anyway. The poison was working. Soon I would be dead.

I crawled into my alcove and managed to remove my boots and socks. I untied my apron, took off my belt and my bodice, then I peeled off my blouse and got into my nightgown. I slumped down onto my mattress, curling onto my side and hugging my knees to my chest. I closed my eyes and prepared to die.

Outside, the sky rumbled. The thunder was coming; the storm was about to break. My abdomen gurgled and the pain gnawed on. All I could think about was how wise Jacob had been. He hadn't touched the cocoa. He would be all right. He would live. If I died before the morning came, I wouldn't be able to say goodbye to him. I thought about writing him a note, something they would find after I was gone. But my body was so heavy and the pain so intense that I couldn't move.

The rain began to hit the roof, a few heavy drops at first, knocking like fists above me. Then more came down and the banging grew louder and more insistent before it all merged into one constant swash. I closed my eyes and music immediately rushed into my head. It was the swirling, dizzying sound of Anitra's dance. Round and round my mind it went, lolling to and fro like waves on a rocky sea, as if the storm had brought it to me and I could not escape it. This was the curse. Now the poison and the curse were working together to kill me. I lay there with my eyes closed and the thunder crashing and my mind agitated by the unending torment of the music. I hoped that death would come quickly.

The next thing I remember was waking up in the hazy light of daybreak. The music had stopped. It was quiet and still. I wondered if I was in heaven. My stomach still felt engorged but the needling pain had subsided now. I looked at my hands, wiggled my fingers. They looked alive. I was still breathing. Through the diamond window I saw a bird skim past. I sat up in bed, propped myself back on my elbows. I thought about the troll and his wife and the cocoa and the music, and wondered if it had all been a dream. It certainly had a strange dreamlike quality to it. I smiled to myself. Jacob would laugh when I told him I thought I'd been poisoned by the cocoa. The notion of it seemed absurd to me now that I was alive again. The lady in the cabin had meant us no harm. She was just a normal lady. I was safe.

But my moment of peace was as fleeting as a breath. Something odd caught my eye. Red. I panicked, kicked my legs, pulled back my sheets. Red everywhere. And wet. Sticky wet. All over me, all over my clothes and all over my bed. It was blood, red and vivid. On my legs, it was thick and warm. I started crying and choking and coughing all at once, touching the red sticky mess. I had been a fool. I *was* cursed. I *was* dying. The troll had cursed me with his music and I was bleeding to death.

INTERLUDE

Ellen is re-pinning my hair. She is a quiet girl, softly spoken, not excitable like some of the young hairstylists I've met. I enjoy our moments together away from the spotlight and the audience and Harriet with her regimental pacing and her clipboard. Ellen takes pride in her work, she makes it all about the art, the performer, how I feel, rather than it being a showcase for herself. She is not sycophantic, doesn't feel the need to butter me up to gain acceptance, she simply does her job.

'Is that comfortable for you, Miss Jensen?' she says, as she slides a pin into the crown of my head.

'Can't feel a thing,' I say. I look at her in the mirror as she inspects her work, prodding the bun she has created to test its security. She understands a good performance is about confidence, and a singer can't breathe easily if she's riddled with worry that her hair might tumble out at any moment.

Ellen reaches over my shoulder and lifts a bunch of large silk oxeye daisies from a cup on the dressing table. She jabs the wires into the bun on my head and starts to weave them into my hair.

'The day's eyes,' I say, watching her work.

'Miss Jensen?'

'It's how they get their name. They open during the day and close at night.'

'Oh, the daisies,' she says, resting a hand on the back of my neck as she reaches out for more. 'These silk ones are giants compared to the real thing, much easier to work with. We used to make chains with them when I was a young girl, necklaces and garlands for our hair. We'd slit the tiny stalks with our fingernails. My grandmother told us they were for

79

purity and innocence,' she smiles, 'and secrets,' she says, tucking the flowers into my hair.

'What kind of secrets?' I say, grinning at her.

Ellen's cheeks flush softly. 'Secrets between people,' she says.

'Oh, *those* kinds of secrets, and did you have any of them when you were a girl?'

'My sisters and I had plenty,' she says, 'things the boys had said to us, pledges of love. They seemed so important at the time and we would swear solemn oaths to each other that we would never ever tell.'

Ellen is so gentle and good hearted. She is precisely the kind of person to whom I would want to confide my own secrets. 'And did you ever tell, Ellen?'

'Not to this day,' she says, 'we took our oaths very seriously.'

'Quite right,' I say, 'so did I. I once kept a whopping great secret about a troll on our mountain, one that had cursed me.'

Ellen pauses for a moment and looks at me in the mirror. Our two faces stare back at us as though we are separate to ourselves, listening to the conversation of strangers.

'You saw a troll, Miss Jensen?' she says.

'We did. And we kept it a secret from the whole village.'

'What was he like?' Ellen says.

'That's my secret,' I smile.

'But how did he curse you?'

'Do you believe in curses?'

'Not anymore,' Ellen says, 'although my grandmother used to tell some terrifying stories that would keep us all awake at night. She'd scrub us clean in the bathtub in front of the fire and tell us about the time God came to visit Adam and Eve when they had children of their own. Eve had only washed some of her children when God came. Ashamed of the dirty ones, she hid them away. Then God decreed that

80

those that had been hidden from Him would be hidden from all humanity, and those dirty hidden children became the hulders, the mysterious creatures who lived underground. My grandmother said children could be cursed by the hulderfolk, stolen from their homes if they misbehaved, turned to stone if they spoke a word of a lie, it frightened us to death, made us hide under our beds. But we lived in the centre of Bergen and my sister Lotta always said we were safely hidden from such things, that trolls and hulderfolk would never dare come that close to us, not in the city.'

'It's different in a small town like Utne,' I say, 'those stories are even more potent when you grow up as part of nature itself. Who's to say what's out there in the dark? Who knows what exists within the mystical power of those gigantic mountains and down in the endless depths of the fjord? Nature is a force so much greater than ourselves. That's why I believed I was cursed.'

'How old were you?'

'Almost fourteen. Not a child, not an adult. The events of my life were skewed by the unknown. I didn't have the experience and knowledge to fill in the gaps and make my world feel safe. We had a respectful fear of the creatures that might be lurking out there on our mountain and everything they might be capable of. Like curses, for example.'

'And what had the troll done to you?'

'Made me bleed,' I smile. 'You had sisters and a mother to explain such things to you, my only confidante was a boy. I don't know if you remember your first time, Ellen, but for a girl with no mother at the last frontier of her childhood, that simple female bodily function became greatly distorted by my fear, especially when the only context in which I could frame things was folklore and superstition, trolls and curses.'

'People do call it a curse though, don't they?' Ellen says. 'That's what my mother always said. It says so in the bible; that Eve defied God in the garden of Eden and, as a result, all women after her would be cursed with blood every month and painful childbirth.'

I wince a little at her words. My own birth had been so painful that it had killed my mother. The fragility of it scares me: life and death are so intricately weaved. 'Cursed by a troll or cursed by God, what difference does it make?' I say, 'How incredibly misogynistic it is to make us believe we are impure and shameful.'

'Not if we wear daisies though,' Ellen grins. 'There we are, we're done,' she says, gently caressing my hair, 'you are ready for spring.'

'Thank you, Ellen. Where are we now? How long do I have?'

'I'll check with Harriet,' she says, going to the door.

Ellen has created a wreath of spring flowers around my head. I twist from side to side to admire it in the mirror and touch it carefully in wonderment. The silk daisies have a tinge of blue in their petals and the gypsophila floats like tiny clouds, creating an aura around my head.

I get up and go to the rail where my gown is hanging.

'*Anitra's Dance*,' Ellen says, quietly, coming back in.

The moment she says it, I hear the rhythm of that tune, the triple time chant of the whirling violins and plucking cellos.

'Oh,' I say, and I grab her arm.

'Miss Jensen? Are you all right?'

'A little dizzy, that's all, queasy. It's just my nerves.'

'Come and sit down,' Ellen says, settling me onto the sofa.

I close my eyes and the music is there. *Anitra's Dance* finds me, even as far from the stage as this. It seems to be swimming through the theatre, casting its spell on me again. The dizzying repetition of it is relentless. It makes me afraid.

'It's silly,' I say, looking at her again.

Ellen pours a glass of water and brings it over. 'Here, drink this, take some deep breaths.'

'To still be nervous, after all these years.'

'You haven't sung for the king and queen before, Miss Jensen. You're bound to be a bit tense.'

I take a few sips. Ellen runs a facecloth under the tap at the washbasin. She wrings it out and folds it over then presses it lightly against the back of my neck. 'There, Miss Jensen, you're all right, you'll be all right.'

I exhale. 'Thank you, Ellen.' I try to bring *Gjendine's Lullaby* back to my mind, to override the vertiginous waltz, but the violins penetrate my concentration and all I can do is wish for it to be over.

'Ellen?' I say, as she presses the cloth against my skin.

'Miss Jensen?'

'What would you do if…?'

There are three sharp knocks at the door. Everything in triples. Harriet comes marching in.

'Oh,' she says, 'is everything all right?'

'Miss Jensen just needed some water, that's all,' Ellen says, gently.

Harriet is flustered by this diversion from the agenda. 'Right…well, Nora and Adele are ready now. We need to get you into your gown, Miss Jensen. Will you be–'

I inhale deeply, shake my head a little. *Come on, Dagny. You're Dagny out there tonight, not Dagny in here.* 'I'm ready,' I say, straightening my back and clearing my throat. 'Thank you, Ellen, I'm all right now.'

Harriet is nodding her head in relief. 'Good. Yes. I'll send them in then.'

'I'll be back later,' Ellen says, then she whispers in my ear. 'You're not cursed, remember you have daisies in your hair.'

I get to my feet and regain my balance. I don't have time for this tonight. I untie my robe and reach up for the gown that's hanging on the rail. It's a short-sleeved pink dress of silk faille, covered with ivory chiffon and tulle, embroidered with silk cordonnet. It has drapery across the neckline and a short train. In it, I am to appear like a vision of spring.

I stop and listen. *Anitra's Dance* is over now. I hear nothing but the sound of movement in the corridor and the whisper of hushed voices as they pass my door. Then footsteps and another knock, 'Miss Jensen?'

Adele and Nora are here to dress me and finish my make-up.

'Miss Jensen,' Adele says, 'we still have a full ten minutes.'

Adele is a robust woman who spent many years as a seamstress in Bergen and made a name for herself fitting all the wealthy ladies and their daughters. She has been hired as the resident costume manager at the new theatre due to her flair and her sense for the dramatic. Nora is the make-up artist. She has porcelain skin and auburn hair, which gives her appearance a classical quality. She takes the dress down from the rail. 'I'll get that for you,' she says, and floats to the screen where I am to change.

The ladies work quickly. I step into the dress and it feels light to the touch. Adele hooks it at the back of my neck while Nora fastens the buttons. My costume changes are carried out with military precision. I am a mannequin. I stand still with my arms out and let the women move me and dress me and tie and tuck and fasten everything into place. When they are finished, I return to the dressing table where Nora dabs at my brow and re-touches my rouge.

I look at my face in the mirror as Nora sweeps powder across my temples. I inhale deeply and blow air out through my cheeks, puffing out then sucking in again.

Nora senses my unease. 'It's going very well,' she says. 'Harriet said Queen Maud was dabbing her eyes after *Solveig's Song.*'

'For all the right reasons, I hope.'

'Your voice has that effect, Miss Jensen. It moves people. Such a gift. Even the queen couldn't hide it.'

'Thank you.' I rub my lips together. 'Do I need more colour?'

'Perhaps a touch,' Nora says. She lightly dusts my brow with her fingertips, blending any excess powder into my hairline. She returns the brush to the table and picks up the thin oily lip brush and makes a shape with her own mouth, which I am to copy.

I open my mouth and draw my lips out tight, still watching her in the mirror. Then over my shoulder I notice the door open without a knock. I expect to see Harriet but it is Kristian, poking his head in. I try to say *come in* with my mouth open but the words are indecipherable. I wave my arm.

I am surprised at how happy I am to see him now that he is actually here. The familiar face, the reassurance he provides. He is handsome in his dinner suit, although he is unaware of how good he looks. He's moving stiffly. His head is restricted by his taut collar and his chin is lifted as if to avoid contact with the white bow tie at his throat.

'May I come in, Miss Jensen?' he grins.

Nora finishes my lipstick and I rub my lips together and smile at him.

He presents me with an enormous bouquet of peachy white roses tied with a silk ribbon. 'It was beautiful,' he says, 'you are divine.'

'Thank you, darling,' I say.

He stands behind me with the flowers in his arms while Adele and Nora flutter about me making their final touches.

'I'm about to go on again,' I say, 'it's *The Last Spring*.'

'I wanted to come now,' he says.

I grow impatient for the ladies to be done. 'That's enough,' I say, brushing them off, 'It'll do.'

'Very well, Miss Jensen,' Adele says. 'We will be back later.' She gives Kristian a nod on her way out, 'Herr Kolstad.'

When they have gone, Kristian hands me the flowers and I take them from him, cradling them in my arms. 'They're beautiful. You shouldn't have.'

'You have to have flowers on your big night, Dagny. Really, you sounded magnificent,' he kisses my freshly powdered brow politely, his impeccable clothes restraining him and preventing him from touching me in the way he normally does. 'I'm so proud of you.'

'You can watch this one from the wings, if you like?' I say, 'as long as you steer clear of the crew.'

He nods, 'I will.'

'I'll get Harriet to find a vase for these,' I say, 'we seem to be running out.'

At the mention of her name, Harriet comes striding in. 'Two minutes, Miss Jensen.'

'Yes,' I say. 'I'm coming. Could you find a vase for these?'

She takes the flowers from my arms. 'Time to get into position now,' she says.

'Herr Kolstad will watch from the wings,' I say, 'will you find a place for him?'

'Of course, Miss Jensen.'

Kristian accompanies me to the stage and I slip my hand into the crook of his arm. I start panting and blowing again; *bah bah bah, pah pah pah*. I inhale. Exhale. Tighten my grip on Kristian's elbow. And then I'm thinking about how I'm going to tell him. I can't do it now. I must sing first.

'Are you all right?' he says.

'A few nerves, that's all,' I whisper. '*The Last Spring*. It makes me think of my father.'

'It will be wonderful,' he says, and squeezes my hand.

'Harriet will find a place for you,' I say.

I leave him and step into the black, into the void, the world in between worlds. I wait with anticipation and listen for my cue. I am neither Dagny *out there* nor Dagny *in here*. I stand completely still, as if I have a choice to make, as if I must now decide between the two.

6

I established that the blood was coming from between my legs, so intimate and secret a place that I would rather have been stabbed in the guts. I couldn't tell Far and definitely couldn't tell my brothers. None of them would know how curses worked or how long it would take for me to die.

I didn't get up. I covered the blood with a quilt and told Far I was still unwell. When they'd all gone, I took my sheets down and washed them. I ran out to the well cautiously, frightened of being seen outdoors in my nightgown. I heated the water on the stove and used salt on the stains. I bathed myself and found some rags to absorb the blood. It was worse when I moved, the flow of the blood was heavier and more uncomfortable then, although I did not find it painful, which surprised me. I washed my nightdress and found a clean one, and had to hang up all my laundry inside. I would tell Far I had been sick.

In fresh bedding, I lay down and waited again to die. It was a strange business preparing for death. I began to think about my mother and wondered what it was like for her. If she had expected me to kill her? If she knew, after I was born, that I had cursed her? If she had lay there, like I was lying now, just waiting for it to happen? She had probably been perfectly calm, despite her pain, everyone said she was that kind of person, so I tried to be calm like her. My mind danced in strange circles. One minute I was a young girl, playing with stones at the water's edge with Far standing behind me, keeping watch. Then I was older, and Jon was carrying me on his back on our way up to the lake. Then Knut and Hans and me, picking apples on the Ellefsen's farm. Old Mor Utne, showing me how to plat my hair. And Jacob, always Jacob, his voice, his laughter, his games. Jacob was the one I would miss the most when I died.

After a while, I got tired of waiting for death. Whatever the woman had put in her potion, it wasn't going to kill me quickly. I decided to get up. I would move carefully to slow the blood flow, and I would eat something, it might settle my stomach. I pulled on my skirt and blouse but left my belt and bodice in my alcove.

As I began to climb down the stairs there was a hard knock at the door. The heel of a palm slapping at the wood insistently. At first I thought it was Lillian Jevnaker but the banging was too heavy and rough for her, no matter how angry she was. Then I heard his voice.

'Dagny! I know you're in there. Let me in.'

It was Jacob.

I froze. How would I tell him I was dying?

'Dagny! I haven't got much time. Let me in!'

I hesitated. My heart began to throb all the way up to my ears.

'For heaven's sake, Dagny. It's me!'

'All right, all right,' I said, opening the door.

He came bursting in, heaving, as though he'd been holding his breath. 'Knut said you were sick,' he said. 'What's wrong?'

I went to the table, silently, and he followed me.

'Dagny? What is it?'

I sat down. He sat next to me.

'What's the matter, Dagny? Are you just being a girl? Or is it something real?'

I shook my head. My eyes were filling with tears.

'Dagny?' he said, exasperated. 'Tell me!'

I looked at him. His face was anguished. His voice was changing, alternating from high to low. 'You can't just...' he said. 'Why didn't you come to school?'

The seriousness was back. The veil was lifted. He reached over and took my hand. 'Dagny,' he pleaded, 'tell me what's wrong with you!'

I was lost in his eyes. His blue, blue eyes. They held me like an embrace.

'Please?' he said, finally, 'I won't tell anyone.'

I wiped my tears with my free hand. 'I'm dying,' I said.

He jumped back and stared at me.

'You're what?' he said. 'How? Why? I mean, you were fine yesterday.'

'It must have been the cocoa,' I said, 'I drank it. It must have been poisoned.'

He was shaking his head and blinking and searching desperately for some sense. 'What do you mean? How do you know?'

'I'm bleeding,' I said. 'It must be a curse.'

'Bleeding? Where? Show me!' he said, eyeing my body for injuries.

I shook my head. 'I can't.'

'Why not?' he said.

'It's too...it's just that it's...I can't show you, Jacob.'

He took my hand again. 'You can't be dying, Dagny,' he said, without lifting his face. 'You can't be.'

'How else do you explain it?' I said. 'I was stupid to drink that cocoa. You didn't drink yours and you're not dying. You're not bleeding, are you?'

He shook his head.

'She must have poisoned me. I had a pain in my tummy and then I started bleeding, down there,' I said, embarrassed. 'I will probably bleed to death.'

'I won't let you die,' he said, releasing me and standing up. 'We'll have to go back, back up and ask her, get her to remove the curse or something.'

'I can't climb the troll's stairs if I'm dying,' I said.

'I will carry you all the way if I have to,' Jacob said. 'You're not dying and that's the end of it. If she put a curse on you, she can just as easily take it off again.'

'What if it was the troll who cursed me?' I said, 'With his music?'

'Then we'll force him to un-curse you,' Jacob said, getting angrier. 'I'll fight him with my bare hands if I have to, Dagny. You're not dying!'

He stood behind me, breathing heavily, concocting a plan. 'We'll go today,' he said, 'I'll go home, pack bread and water.'

'Today? I can't go today,' I said.

'Why not?'

'I'm...well, I'm *dying* today.'

'You won't die today, Dagny, not unless it hits you all of a sudden.'

'It might,' I said, 'I don't know how curses work.' I got up and faced him, felt another trickle of blood between my legs as I moved. 'What if you take me up there and I die on the mountain? What then?'

'You won't die while you're with me,' he said, soberly. 'I won't let you.'

'But we can't go today,' I said, 'Knut and Hans will be home later. They'll tell Far if I'm gone. And you have to get back to school now, before they suspect anything.'

He paused for a moment, holding his chin while he thought. 'Tomorrow then,' he said, decisively, 'we'll leave early.'

'If I'm still alive in the morning.'

'In the stories they die quickly,' he said, 'they drink the poison and they die, just like that. They don't take days to do it, they die instantly. And you didn't die instantly, you're dying slowly, so it can't have been the cocoa. It can't be poison.'

'Must be a curse then,' I said, thinking about the rhythmical music that had pulled me so strongly.

'Look, stay alive until tomorrow and I will come and throw stones at your window after the boys have gone.'

'What about school?' I said.

'Bestefar Jørgen won't mind,' he said, 'it's almost summer now and soon there'll be no school anyway.'

'You should go,' I said, 'go out the back door so no one sees you.'

At the door, he turned back to me. 'Don't die, Dagny,' he said, 'they won't sing songs about us if you die.'

He opened the door and grinned at me in a way that made my heart leap.

I didn't die.

Knut came home, shouting at me the second he entered the house, even though I had gone back to bed and told him I was still sick.

'What did he ever do to you?' he said.

'Who?' I moaned.

'Konrad Olsen!'

'Nothing, why?'

'He's taking the blame for all your mischief,' Knut said, angrily.

'What do you mean?' I said.

'Hannah Jevnaker said...'

I rolled my eyes and groaned.

'She said her mother went to see Konrad when he got back from his wandering, asked him about that telescope that you broke, and do you know what he said?'

'What?' I said, blandly. There was something about the prospect of dying that took the sting out of the Jevnaker family.

'He said, *Dagny had a telescope.*'

I looked at Knut, tried to hide my surprise. 'And?'

'And then Lillian asked him where it was and he said, *Oh, I must have misplaced it.*'

I stared at Knut for a moment then nodded my chin. 'He must have misplaced it then,' I said.

'Come on, Dagny,' Knut continued, 'you know that man has the mind of a child. It ain't fair to blame him for all the bad stuff you do.'

'I never blamed him!' I said. 'Go away. I'm sick.'

'We all know it was you. The Jevnakers aren't buying Konrad's story. They will probably report this to Rolf Qvale as a theft. Then you'll be in even more trouble.'

I waved my hand at him. 'Go away,' I said, again.

I rolled onto my back and stared out of the window. I was dying slowly. I thought about it for a long time. And I thought about Konrad Olsen and wondered how he knew I had a telescope? If I could live long enough to break the troll's curse, I would set things right with Konrad. I'd take the blame for the telescope. Losing it was my fault.

I managed to survive the night. Far came and looked at me before he went to bed. Felt my head as I grumbled and groaned. Said there wasn't much wrong with me that he could see, but I hadn't told him about the bleeding. *One more day*, he said, *before I get Doctor Helland to come and look at you*. I must have fallen asleep shortly after that, and I lived until morning. When I woke up there was fresh blood on my sheets but it was less than it had been the day before. Did that mean I was going to die soon? I lay very still, silently clinging on to my life while Far and the boys got up and went about their business. It felt like they would never leave. I slowed my breathing, trying to preserve my energy, while they fidgeted about and talked and argued then ate their breakfast and clattered pots. They would not miss me if I died, I thought. They didn't need me for a single thing.

Finally, when Hans and Knut went off to school, I got out of bed and dressed. I was aware that it could be the last time I put my clothes on and I savoured my dressing. I smoothed out my dark woolen skirt, feeling it with an appreciation I hadn't felt before – it was just my old skirt, but this morning I noticed the softness of it and my big clumsy stitches where I'd darned it. I put on my white blouse and my red bodice and fixed my bodice insert into place. I had embroidered it myself one afternoon at the Jevnaker's, it wasn't fancy, just a simple Hardanger pattern that I'd cross stitched. I tied my apron around my waist and fixed my belt so that the sashes hung straight down at the front. I leaned down to pull on my stockings and boots and when I got back up again, a stone cracked against the window, followed by another.

I waved my hand. 'You'll break the glass,' I said, even though I knew he wouldn't hear me. He cast another stone and I looked out at him. He was smiling, no doubt relieved to see that I was still alive. I hurried my hair into plats and pinned them up around my head.

He had tucked himself into the door frame to hide and when I opened the back door he almost tumbled in on me. 'You're alive!' he said.

'Yes, but I'm still bleeding.'

'Then we must hurry. I will carry you if you can't climb all the way.'

'I'll do the first part,' I said, 'but we'll have to go straight out through the trees here where it's even steeper. It'll be a hard climb.'

'Come on, then,' he said, grabbing my arm. 'I will pull you.'

Jacob dragged me straight up through the trees behind our house. The grass was getting long and there was no clear path, so he flattened out the ferns with his feet to make it easier for me to get through. We didn't talk. I was worried I could die at any minute, either if the bleeding stopped or if it continued to its own natural conclusion. I still didn't know when it would end. Jacob wasn't scared. He forged ahead, pulling me with him through pine trees and rowans and hanging birches until we reached the path that we knew.

We stopped for a few minutes and Jacob gave me his bottle. 'You're still with me?' he said, 'Still alive?'

'I'm here.'

'You know, even if you are dying, Dagny, your cheeks are rosy red after that climb. Your face is glowing.'

'Is it?' I said, touching my cheeks.

He reached out his hand and brushed my face, looking at me as if he was seeing me for the first time under the veil. Perhaps I looked different to him beneath it, in all the seriousness. 'And your nose, the way it comes to a perfect point like that, and your hazely eyes, they flicker with yellow, did you know? And, come to think of it, your lips, I've never...I've never seen them so...' His voice trailed off and he looked up at the mountain looming above us. 'We must keep going,' he said, 'drink up.'

We pressed on through the trees and up to the lake where the sun beat down on us. Jacob swung my hand in his at the water's edge and I thought what a wonderful last day of life this was, walking on the mountain with Jacob. 'If I do die,' I said, 'I will be doing this in heaven...walking with you.'

'Don't talk like that, Dagny,' Jacob said, bringing me to a rock where we sat down to rest again.

We looked out at the lake, heard the birds calling in the trees. We didn't say anything else for a while. Then Jacob suddenly turned to me, flustered. 'I've been thinking,' he said, hurrying to get the words out, 'that with you dying and all, we should...' he cleared his throat to even out his voice, 'we should get married.'

'Should what?' I said, laughing.

'We should get married,' he said.

'Very funny, Jacob,' I said, 'we're too young to get married.'

'No we're not. They have child weddings at midsummer.'

'They're not *real* weddings, they're just for the festival.'

'Well, I will be fifteen soon,' he said, 'that used to be enough for kings and queens. Why shouldn't it be enough for us? If you are dying, I want to marry you now.'

Jacob often played games with me. He was cunning, had me believing a thing for a whole day before he finally cracked and told me he was kidding, making me feel stupid for having believed him for so long.

'Jacob,' I said, 'you can't joke with young ladies like that. It's not very nice.'

'I'm serious,' he said, and he looked serious too. His eyes were downcast and his mouth kept dipping as if he might actually cry. 'Dagny,' he whispered, 'don't you feel it happening too? Sometimes when I look at you, or touch your hand, it's like something's igniting and starting to burn inside me. And it makes me so...so confused and scared, but happy.'

I was suddenly sadder than I had ever been in my entire life. At least it felt like sadness – a great clench in my chest and tears gripping my throat. I was frightened of this thing, this serious thing that was now coming out into the open.

'I feel it,' I said, quietly.

He took my hand. 'Do you feel it now?' he said, inching closer to me.

'Yes, but it scares me,' I said.

'It scares me too because of its power,' he said, 'I feel like it's pulling me to some new place inside myself that I don't understand.'

'Me too,' I said, 'like it's wrong or bad or something.'

'I don't know what it is, Dagny,' he said, 'but it seems to me that if we both feel it, then it can't be so wrong or dangerous, can it?'

'I suppose not,' I said.

'So will you marry me?' he said.

I nodded, solemnly.

'And promise not to die until we're married.'

'All right,' I said, 'I'll try. But how will we get married? Pastor Jevnaker won't do it, not until we're both confirmed. That's another year.'

'Then we'll do it our own way,' Jacob said, 'in secret.'

I smiled at him, feeling lighter.

'Dagny,' he said, 'can I kiss you?'

'Here?'

'Don't see why not. I mean, if it's all right with you? I would like to try it, wouldn't you?'

'All right,' I said, 'try then.'

We turned our faces towards each other and in an instant, my loud, boisterous, fearless friend transformed into something soft and tender. He rested his hands on my shoulders, almost afraid to touch me, then slowly lowered his plump lips to mine. I closed my eyes. Felt his warm mouth pressing against me. Felt him breathe, felt him touching me. The kiss was as gentle as the brush of a feather, but it pierced the depths of my body and I felt an eruption of something strong within me.

I gasped a little and he pulled back.

'What? Did I do it wrong?'

'No,' I said. 'it was just so...'

'So mighty,' Jacob said, 'like this mountain?'

'Yes! Like this whole mountain is inside me and it's bursting from me and trying to get out. It makes me want to sing!' I said.

'Then you must sing, Dagny,' he said, 'you must sing!'

There was something about our recognising this seriousness that had been growing between us, admitting it to each other and somehow trying to name it, that made it less intimidating. We continued up the mountain, so happy that we almost forgot about the troll and the curse and the fact that I was dying. Jacob made me sing silly songs about *The Woman with the Stick*, and *Paul and His Chickens*. By the time we reached the troll's staircase we were laughing loudly and each song was getting sillier as we inserted the names of people we knew. Now Lillian Jevnaker was a clucking chicken and Rolf Qvale was Paul who couldn't face his mother because the fox had taken Lillian. We were so absorbed in our game that we hadn't noticed the clouds gathering or the sky growing dark, or even the squawking of the ravens. We had already begun our climb onto the rocks when the sky burst open and the rain began to pelt. Jacob

97

was above me and I was following him, clinging to the places that were now familiar, the ones that provided the best grip. There was a violent rumble of thunder as a great wash of rain dropped from the sky.

'Jacob!' I screamed, as small streams began to pour down the rocks. I looked up, got water in my eyes and mouth, felt like I was drowning in the sky.

'Hold on, Dagny,' Jacob shouted, through the deluge, 'just find a good grip and hold on.'

His hair was sticking to his face. My clothes were getting heavier and the weight of them was pulling me down. The wind picked up and threw torrents at us from every angle as we clung on. I felt water trickle down my back. It made me shiver. The rocks were becoming dangerously slippery now and the rain was doing its best to cast us off the rocks and send us plummeting to our deaths.

'I'm not meant to die here,' I said, but I knew Jacob couldn't hear me.

'It'll pass,' he shouted, 'hold on, Dagny.'

I held and gripped with intense concentration as the rain continued to hurl itself at us. Jacob's foot slipped and he stumbled. I let go to support him and almost toppled back myself. He clung and I clung, to the rock, and to each other. My fingers were wrapped around his ankle.

'Sing, Dagny!' he shouted down at me, 'sing about Lillian and Rolf.'

'*Rolf let Lillian run out on the hillside,*' I sang, '*over the hill she went tripping along,*' Water spattered my face as I sang. '*Rolf he knew by the way she was acting, the fox was out with his tail so long. Cluck, cluck, cluck Lillian was cackling, cluck, cluck, cluck Lillian was cackling.*'

Jacob was laughing. He bent down and reached out for me. 'One...two...three...' he said, and yanked my hand with such force that my whole body was carried up and my legs scrambled after, trying to find a foothold. We were back on the ledge again, with all the sluices of heaven pouring down on us. And Jacob was laughing, laughing so hard he couldn't stop.

7

When the rain finally abated, we crawled to the top of the troll's staircase like reptiles finding land for the first time, gasping for breath and shaking with cold. The air was damp and misty and strands of cloud hung around us, foggy and dense. Jacob had scratched his arm and I saw that it was badly grazed, but he didn't notice it. He took my hand and led me over the rocks and stones, guiding me without saying a word.

We stood at the top of the hill and looked down at the cabin. I was surprised to see it. Before, it had seemed dreamlike, almost fanciful, as if we had imagined it, as if Jacob had made it up in one of his stories. But now, in the aftermath of the rain, it had a sobering sense of reality to it. The grass on the roof was wet and the air was damp; mundane not magical. I couldn't decide if it was the cabin itself or Jacob and I who were altered? Did we realise then, as we stared down the ravine, that this had all been a game? Had we always known it was a ruse? Another adventure that only we were allowed to share? The cabin was our discovery, a place that only we knew. It was our secret. And so was the seriousness, the powerful thing inside us that was starting to emerge into reality. That was our secret too.

We edged our way down the slope. My clothes were wet and sticking to my skin. The dusty ravine had turned to mud in the rain and my boots were getting wet as my feet squelched through it.

'We'll tell her what's happened,' Jacob said, matter-of-factly, 'and ask her to get him to remove the curse. That's all we need to do, come on.'

We drew nearer, creeping timidly, afraid of making any sudden movements. We heard music again as we approached the cabin and it made us even more cautious –

he didn't like people listening to him play. But this time the music we heard was different.

'Listen!' Jacob said, as we ducked beneath the window. 'Do you think that could be her?'

The sound was as haunting as an elegy. I wondered if someone had died. I slumped beside Jacob in the wet grass as the sadness reached into my chest and squeezed something tender within me. I bowed my head and Jacob did too.

Someone was singing. The woman. Her voice was sweet and gentle and clear, but it was anguished and sorrowful at the same time, and the tune it sang was like a plea or a promise, a solemn pledge. The piano accompanying the voice wanted to bring some happiness to the lament but it kept returning to the black keys over and over again, the ones that sounded sad.

'It is,' Jacob whispered, 'it's her. I'm going to look.'

'Don't let him see you,' I said, as the singing continued to twist the tender place within me. I listened more carefully, she was singing of waiting, waiting for someone to return.

'It's a man, at the piano,' Jacob said, dipping down again, 'in the back room. Doesn't look like a troll at all.'

'Maybe he's the mountain king,' I said, indifferently.

'It could be him,' Jacob said.

'And it could be a normal man,' I said, as though the entire story we had been so invested in had suddenly disintegrated all around us.

'Either way, we have to face him,' Jacob said.

He was right. We needed to know. We had to discover where this entire adventure had brought us and now that we had come this far there was no going back.

We were about to stand up and go to the door, when suddenly the music stopped and there was a heavy disjointed bang on the keys.

'Not like that!' the man's voice said.

'That's how it *feels*,' the woman said.

'She isn't mourning!'

'But she is!' the woman said. 'She's waiting and waiting and it seems like eternity. Don't you know what that feels like? It feels like grief.'

'But I'm playing it with longing and love, why can't you put more love into it?'

'I am!'

'Well I can't hear it, Nina.'

'Maybe you're just not listening for it. Maybe you've forgotten what love feels like?'

'I'm trying to bring some hope to the piece; that he will one day return. This is her man, Nina, for God's sake, not her daughter.'

A door slammed.

Jacob and I looked at each other.

'What do we do now?' I whispered.

Jacob looked puzzled and shook his head.

Unable to know what to do next, we sat and waited for something to happen. There was more door slamming and some mumbling, then the front door opened and the woman came running out. She didn't see us. She went straight to the ravine we had just come down and rested her head against a tree trunk. She was weeping.

We stared at her.

'Don't move,' Jacob said to me.

We sat very still until my body began to ache. We were cold and wet and I was still sad after hearing the lady sing. She was weeping and Jacob was looking this way and that trying to work out what to do.

'I can go in while she's out here,' he whispered.

I shook my head. 'Not on your own. I'm coming too.'

We crept to our feet and tiptoed to the front door. Jacob reached out for the handle and began to turn it. He opened it quietly and we stepped inside. The door squeaked on its hinges and we stopped, held our breath.

'You know I miss her just as much as you do,' the man said. He was sitting at the table with his back to us. I peered in. He was holding his head in his hands. I could see a wave of thick brown hair. He was only a slight man, which both surprised and pleased me. Jacob and I would be able to fight him and have a good chance of beating him too.

'We want you to remove the curse,' Jacob said, keeping his voice clear and steady.

The small man at the table spun around with a fright. 'Who are you?' he said, shocked.

'We're friends with your wife,' Jacob said, calmly.

The man made no attempt to attack us. He sat there, wringing his hands together and shaking his head. 'Oh, I see,' he said. 'She went out...I'm not sure where...'

'I'm here,' she said, coming in behind us, sniffing and wiping her eyes. 'Hello, my dears.' She motioned for us to come inside and closed the door. 'Come in, children, come and sit by the fire,' she said, 'you're soaking wet.'

'Who are...?' the man said, getting up from his chair.

I took a step back but Jacob stood his ground. 'We need you to remove the curse you put on Dagny,' he said, fearlessly, glaring at the man.

If he was the Dovregubben, he didn't frighten us. He had a small face with a broad brow, deep set eyes and a moustache that seemed to pull his mouth down into a frown.

'They're my friends,' his wife said, 'and you'll welcome them into our home.'

'You're inviting children to come and play here? How am I supposed to work then?'

'Oh, ignore him,' she said to me and Jacob.

He looked at us and then shook his head disapprovingly. 'Honestly, Nina. This won't bring her back.' He went into the room where the piano was and closed the door.

'He's a miserable grump,' his wife said, sighing and going to the rocking chair. 'Come on and sit down by the fire, you two. Dagny, you look as if you're wet right through to your bones. Why on earth did you come up here on a day like this?'

'We had to get him to reverse the curse,' Jacob said, sitting down on a stool beside me.

'What curse?' the troll's wife said.

'The curse that he put on Dagny last time we were here.'

'Did Edvard put a curse on you? Is that what it felt like? It's a curse being married to him sometimes, I can tell you that much,' she said. 'Did I say that my name is Nina? I don't think I did, did I? You must forgive me, here I am giving you a seat by my fire and I haven't even introduced myself properly yet.'

I smiled at her but Jacob persisted. 'He's done something to Dagny,' he said, 'with his music.'

'What did he do?' Nina said.

'We don't know for sure,' Jacob said, 'but she's dying now, and it all started the day we came here.'

A dark shadow fell over Nina's face and she looked at me with a kind of piercing sadness and I thought she might weep again. 'Dying?' she said, gently. 'Dagny, dear, what is wrong with you?'

I looked at Jacob and he nodded firmly.

'I'm bleeding,' I said.

Nina looked at me and then looked at Jacob, and then she stared at the door to the other room.

'I see,' she said.

'Can he remove the curse?' Jacob said, 'Can you ask him to do it?'

Nina went over to the other side of the room. 'I'll make some cocoa, shall I? You two look like you need it.'

At the mention of cocoa my stomach briefly rippled with nerves, but I smiled politely as Jacob continued. 'Do you want me to go in there and fight him for you?' he said.

Nina raised an eyebrow as though she was seriously considering it. 'You think that'll help?' she said.

'That's how to beat trolls,' Jacob said, 'face them head on and slay them.'

'I can't say I haven't thought about it myself,' Nina said, 'sometimes, when he is so infuriatingly insensitive. But he is my husband, and my cousin. I don't think our family would be very happy with me if I slayed him, would they?'

'Your cousin?' Jacob gasped. 'Do you mean to say that you are...one of them...too?'

Nina brought a pot to the stove and hung it on the chain. 'Yes,' she said, 'his mother was a Hagerup and my father was a Hagerup.'

Jacob and I looked at each other. Neither of us knew what a Hagerup was.

Nina was smiling and, try as I might, I couldn't find anything threatening about her, so I came right out and asked her. 'What's a Hagerup?' I said.

She smiled. 'It's what I was,' she said, stirring the cocoa. 'I'm a Grieg now. We are musicians.'

'Magicians?' Jacob said, mishearing her.

'No, *musicians*. Edvard is a composer. I am an opera singer.' She went back to the shelf and fetched some mugs.

'You mean he isn't a troll then?' Jacob said.

Nina laughed. 'Oh sometimes he can seem like one,' she said, 'but no, Edvard isn't a troll.' She poured the cocoa into the mugs and handed us each a hot cup of chocolatey milk. 'Now listen,' Nina said softly and carefully, 'Herr Grieg is no troll and there is no curse, so you've nothing to be scared of.'

'But what about Dagny bleeding to death?' Jacob said, 'Didn't his music do that to her?'

'I suspect, my dears,' she said, looking at me, 'that Dagny is bleeding because she is becoming a woman. You are growing up. You're on the cusp of womanhood, and it is perfectly normal for you to bleed every month, every woman does, apart from when she is...' she hesitated and her round

105

eyes closed for a moment, 'when she is *with child*. Didn't your mother tell you about these things?'

I felt sad again and pushed my nose into my cup. I didn't know I had to bleed to become a woman.

'Dagny's mother died,' Jacob said.

'Oh,' Nina said, 'oh, my dear, you poor thing. You have no mother?'

'Only a father and three horrible brothers,' I said. 'It's worse for Jacob, his mother and father *both* died. He only has Bestefar Jørgen.'

Nina looked traumatised. She reached out and leaned one way then the other trying to wrap each of us in her small arms. 'No mother or father? How tragic.'

'We have each other though,' Jacob said, 'and we are going to be married.'

'Jacob!' I said.

Nina smiled then. 'How wonderful,' she said. She put her own cup down on the floor and stood up. 'Come with me,' she said, 'let's see if I can persuade Edvard to play something for you. I think it might do him good to play it for someone else.'

Jacob was cautious but Nina waved us over, creeping up to the door mischievously. She tapped three times.

Herr Grieg groaned. 'What?'

Nina opened the door. 'Edvard, you didn't say hello to Dagny and Jacob properly. They'd like to hear a piece, wouldn't you, my dears?'

We nodded, unconvincingly.

'You know I don't like having an audience,' he said.

'But Dagny and Jacob are special,' Nina said. 'They know how to keep secrets, don't you?'

'Yes,' I said, eagerly, 'we kept the troll...I mean, *him*, a secret from the whole town.'

Nina smiled. 'You see, Edvard? They won't tell anyone.'

Herr Grieg leaned back on the piano stool so that we could see him. He looked at us suspiciously.

'I think they need to hear the mountain king,' Nina smiled.

I didn't understand what she meant.

'I thought you said he wasn't a tr–' Jacob started to say, but Nina hushed him.

'Come and listen, children,' she said. 'They are unbiased and young and imaginative, dear,' she said to her husband, 'what better audience could you have?'

'It isn't finished,' he mumbled.

'Then play them what you've got so far.'

Grieg made a low *grrrr* sound, then waved us in. 'All right then. But you have to sit still,' he said, pointing to some chairs by the wall.

We came in to his music room. The piano was of the upright variety, a Steinway like the Jevnaker's would never have fit inside this small room. It was colder in here and the walls were bare, apart from a clock that hung above the piano. A staircase wound around the wall and up to a floor above us. There was a shelf with some books and pictures on it. The photographs were in silver frames. I saw Nina smile at one of them as her husband prepared to play.

'You must imagine an entire orchestra,' Grieg said, grumpily, resting his hands on the keys.

He took a breath, sat perfectly still. At first nothing happened. Grieg closed his eyes and lifted his head. It looked as though he had changed his mind, that he wasn't going to play anything for us after all. But then his eyes twitched open and his arm jerked suddenly and he hammered one single note. It sounded like a bell, calling out to us to make us listen.

And then it began.

He placed his hands on the lowest notes of the piano and played a dark rhythmic beat. It felt like something was creeping up on us as the notes vibrated around the room and I moved closer to Jacob. Herr Grieg's fingers worked up the keyboard in a menacing way. The thing, whatever it was, was getting closer. His fingers started to get faster and the notes

107

became higher, but the pattern of them stayed the same. It was a *pom pom pom* sound, aggressive and threatening but whirling like a dance. Grieg closed his eyes and his face contorted as though he was in pain, then he looked at his fingers again as they spread wide and thudded at the keys and the entire piece grew more fearsome. His long wavy hair fell in front of his face and his foot stamped down on the pedal below. His arms began to shake as his playing became more intense, and then, abruptly, he stopped.

'It isn't finished yet,' he said. 'It needs more work, blessed thing.'

'Don't stop!' Jacob blurted, 'it was just gaining momentum.'

'Maybe too much...' Grieg said, 'maybe too much.'

'It has to get faster and faster!' Jacob said, enthusiastically.

'What is the piece about, Herr Grieg,' I said, politely.

He turned and looked at me. 'You really want to know, child?'

I stared at him, willing him to speak.

His weary eyes drooped. 'The Dovregubben,' he huffed.

I gasped and held my hand over my mouth. 'So you *are* the Dovregubben?' I said.

Herr Grieg, who, up until now had been thoroughly miserable, began to laugh. His face altered and his moustache curled upwards and his eyes began to sparkle.

'You think *I* am the Dovregubben?' he said, as his laughter grew, 'Me? Oh! What a funny thought! I'm sure I was the last person on Ibsen's mind when he wrote it. No, no, I am sorry to disappoint you but I am simply a composer, nothing more.'

'So who *is* the Dovregubben then?' I said.

Grieg was still laughing. 'He is the mountain king! Peer Gynt is betrothed to the Dovregubben's daughter and he must marry the ugly troll girl in the Dovregubben's great hall. This music tells that part of the story.'

'Who is Peer Gynt?' Jacob said.

'A young lad, a bit like you,' Grieg said, 'it's not my story though.'

'Can you tell us the story?' I said.

'Not today. I must get back to work.' He glanced at Nina who was smiling at him.

'Come on, my dears,' she said, 'let's leave him to his work.'

Herr Grieg scratched his moustache and pushed all the bristles downwards, as though chastising himself for having been momentarily lighthearted. He turned back to the piano and picked up a pencil that was on the music stand and scribbled a few notes onto the manuscript that was sitting there. He didn't say goodbye.

Nina hugged us close to her chest. 'Thank you, children,' she said, as we returned to the front door, although Jacob and I had no idea what she was thanking us for. 'I hope you'll come and see us again soon. Don't worry about Edvard, his soul is troubled, but he isn't always like this. You must promise not tell anyone that he is here. He can't bear to have people around him when he works, sometimes not even me. You will promise, won't you?'

We both said yes at the same time and Nina smiled at us proudly. 'Thank you, my dears,' she said, 'thank you.'

Jacob and I skipped happily back to the troll's stairs. We were so light we could have jumped from the top of those rocks and flown back down the mountainside with ease. We were free. Free from curses. Free from trolls. Free from impending doom and death. We were alive. My skin buzzed and my heart stirred and in that moment, I felt that I would live forever. The sun was shining again, the mists had evaporated, and the stones were drying now. I held Jacob's hand and we hopped down from rock to rock as though we were dancing to the music that circled in our heads. I felt no fear. I wasn't dying anymore, I was living, and I was carrying two new secrets that made me feel special; that a composer

was living on our mountain, and that I was becoming a
woman.

INTERLUDE

Kristian is a kind man. His face is etched with kindness. It's in the soft curve of his eyebrows and the dimples that flash in his cheeks when he smiles. He is there, waiting, as the audience claps, holding out his arms in the dark, finding me, retrieving me from the abyss and guiding me back into the light.

'Absolutely enchanting,' he whispers, as he drapes his arm around my shoulders and takes me back to my dressing room.

Harriet marches ahead of us. When we reach the door, she addresses us like a headmistress. 'Fifteen minutes, Miss Jensen. Your next song is *Jeg Elsker Deg*. The only changes required are your dress and hair.'

'Yes, I am aware of that,' I snap. Harriet is beginning to irritate me. 'Please leave us alone. I need a few minutes to breathe.'

She looks at her clipboard, resumes her position with her back to the wall and says nothing more as we go in.

'You'd think I'd never performed in a theatre before,' I say, slamming the door.

'She's only doing her job,' Kristian says, calmly.

'Well she doesn't need to be quite so authoritarian about it,' I say, returning to my dressing table and pouring a glass of water.

Kristian reaches out and touches my shoulder and I flinch, shying away from him.

'What's the matter?' he says.

I sigh, shake my head. 'Just a little on edge, that's all. This music. It's so powerful. It makes me think of things. Things I had long put out of my mind.' I take a sip of water. 'Grieg was clever, you see. He found a way to put it inside us, make

111

it a living breathing thing. Tonight it's coming alive again, all of it.'

'I noticed you were crying,' Kristian says as I drink, 'there were tears in your eyes when you sang. You rarely cry. You get emotional, of course, that's the nature of it, but this time your face was actually wet.'

'I couldn't help it,' I say, 'it has that effect on me, that piece.' I put the glass down on the table. 'Here,' I say, turning my back to him, 'will you undo me?'

'Is there something else that's bothering you,' Kristian says, unbuttoning my dress, 'You seemed so reluctant to go on stage tonight.'

'It's just nerves,' I say.

'You have nothing to be nervous about. You are Dagny Jensen, for heaven's sake.'

'Perhaps that's the problem,' I say, stepping out of my dress and pulling on my robe. I return to the dressing table and sit down in front of the mirror. I take out the compact case and set to work on my face, dabbing busily at my nose with the pad.

'Dagny?' He delves in his inside pocket for a cigarette. 'Are you quite all right?'

I can't look at him. I lower my face and press the powder shut again, studying my fingers and turning the case around in my hand.

'Oh, I see,' he says, pushing the packet of cigarettes back down into his jacket. 'This is about my answer, isn't it?'

I look up and stare at him in the mirror. 'Don't.'

'Why not?' he says.

'Not here, not now. I have to go back on again soon.'

His chest heaves and he pulls up a chair. 'Now's as good a time as any.'

'No, it really isn't,' I say, 'for God's sake, Kristian.' I take another sip of water, wishing it was something stronger.

'Why not?' Kristian presses. 'You are always in a dressing room. If I didn't talk to you in your dressing room, I'd never talk to you at all.'

I shake my head. 'Later,' I say, 'can't we talk about this later?'

'Why put it off?' he says. All his handsomeness is dissolving in the anger that's brewing. His lip curls into a snarl and he fixes his eyes on me. 'There's always something in the way; a party, a dinner, an event, a rehearsal. Why not now, Dagny? Why not have this out with me now?'

'What are you doing?' I say.

We have picked the scab, entered into the wound. It won't close now. It won't heal over on its own. I'm forced into it and I feel myself closing up.

'Well, what's holding you back?' he says, frustrated. 'It's been six years. Is it so wrong that I want to marry you? Isn't it time?'

'It's not that it's wrong,' I say, pulling a silk daisy from my hair.

'Then what is it? Is it because of the girls?' he says, his voice cracking slightly, 'I can't give them up, Dagny, you know I can never give them up.'

'Don't be so insulting,' I say, 'of course it isn't about the girls. You know I love them.' I tug at my hair coarsely and throw another flower onto the table.

Kristian stares at me. His face is a multitude of questions. All the debonair polish is fading, everything holding it together is dismantling. There are creases in his brow and his lips are changing shape and his eyes are filled with confusion. 'Then tell me why, Dagny. What is it that you are so afraid of?'

I must tell him. I open my mouth and try to find the words but I flail, cannot say it, and instead make an arbitrary remark. 'There are things that have happened, that's all.'

'We all have a past, Dagny,' he says. 'You've told me about yours and I've told you about mine. Do you think it makes any difference to me that you were engaged before? Hell, I was married before and I have two children, but that doesn't change the way I feel about you. Why should it matter?'

'It's so easy for you,' I say, 'you're always so sure.'

'I'm not always sure, I'm just sure about this, about you.'

'But you have nothing to lose.' I wring my hands together and stare at the discarded daisies. I notice I have damaged some of them in the pulling. 'I don't want to talk about it now. I can't.'

'You can!' Kristian shouts, getting up from the chair and shoving it to the side. 'You have to! We can't have any secrets from each other. We can't have this distance between us. That's not the kind of relationship I want. Nothing to lose?' he says, pulling at his collar as if to free himself, 'Is that how you see it? What will you *lose* if you marry me?'

'I just mean...whether we were married or not, there would be...I mean, things have changed and either way the risk is there, we could each lose something, and would being married necessarily make us happy?'

'You think I would ask you to give up your career? Is that what you think you would lose? You think I would try to stop you from singing?'

'No, I know you wouldn't do that, but it's not as simple as that. We must be married, of course. I will marry you Kristian, and soon, but it's just...' I am useless at this. I am talking in riddles. I feel claustrophobic and the dizziness returns. I imagine trolls. Evil creatures somewhere out there, to be feared. I embroider the images with my own details. Great ugly monsters coming to take me away and hold me captive. What will they do to me? Will they curse me? Will they kill me?

Kristian has walked away. He is facing the screen where my dress for this evening hangs.

'Look, Kristian, I can't talk about this now.'

'Is it because you don't love me, Dagny? Because if it is, why don't you just say it?'

'Don't be silly, you know I love you.' I stand up and turn to face him.

'I don't think I can do this anymore,' he says, exasperated.

'Don't say that. I will talk to you, just not now.'

'Why can't you tell me?' he says.

'Kristian, look,' I try to speak calmly, 'I have to get ready, change my costume. Ellen and Adele will be in soon.' I straighten my spine and roll my shoulders back.

'Change then,' he says, pulling out a cigarette and opening his lighter. All the tenderness has left him. He holds the cigarette to the flame and the end of it burns and frazzles orange as his sucks it alight. He moves towards the door.

'I have to sing. I can't be all clogged up with this if I am to sing well.'

He says nothing and reaches for the door handle. I can't let him go. I feel as if I need to warn him, tell him of that thing that's out there, looming, waiting to ravage this relationship and leave it in tatters; the thing to be feared that is beyond my control.

'It's *Jeg Elsker Deg*,' I say, 'and I do, you know, I do love you.'

'But who will you be singing it for, Dagny?'

'Kristian, please.' I reach out my hands to him but he doesn't see me.

The door is opening and Harriet is there. 'We absolutely must dress you now, Miss Jensen,' she says, as Ellen and Adele come hurrying in behind her.

I try to catch Kristian's attention again but he doesn't turn. He slips out into the passageway and closes the door.

8

Our climb to the Grieg's cabin in the rain was enough to give me a chill and a legitimate reason to be in bed. Disgruntled, Far called for Doctor Helland who insisted I rest. After a few days, the bleeding stopped but I exaggerated the symptoms of my cold to avoid Lillian Jevnaker, who I didn't see again until Hans' confirmation the following Sunday.

I was sent to the eld house early. It was my job to help Hedda Lilleberg and old Mathilde Olsen make the krote cakes for the confirmation. The eld house was down by the hotel in front of the ice store, a small wooden hut that was used for cooking, baking, butchering, meat salting, meat smoking, beer brewing, and even laundry and bathing. The making of krote cakes wasn't simply baking, it was a social event. I'd been helping Old Mathilde for two years. When I was younger, I would watch her knead the dough and she let me help her cut away the excess pieces using the special Hardanger pin. Now I was the official biscuit maker because my hands were small and made perfectly formed dough balls. It was a role which was not to be taken lightly as each ball had to be exactly the same size and shape.

I ran down the hill while the sun was still hiding behind the fjord. Across the water on the Granvin side, the crags cut a deep V into the mountain as though a giant slice of cake had been slotted into its peak. The domineering giants were black and solid in the early shadows of dawn, and the water was grey and had a glassy sheen. On mornings like this, the fjord hit you with a volley of threats: *don't disturb me! Don't interrupt my slumber! Don't take another step closer!* The threats frightened me and I respectfully slowed my pace. When I rounded the bend, I crept past the Jevnaker house.

The magnificent white house stood proud and pious on the corner, a statement of cleanliness and godliness and perfection. Some pink geraniums stretched from the garden as though making a bold dash from the place, desperate to be free from Lillian's restraints. Gnarly fruit trees hung over the flowers longing to uproot and join the escape, but all they could manage were a few bending branches whose tips fingered the grass.

When I got to the eld house, Mathilde looked as though she'd been there forever. She was sitting at the baking table with the fire roaring behind her and the tools all laid out in a row. She was bent over a bowl, kneading a ball of dough with her knobbly old fingers. The air was thick with smoke and the room was already hot.

'Started early,' she said, as I came in. Her wrinkled skin was ruddy next to the white headscarf on her head. 'First batch is already done.'

I watched her hands, folding, kneading, folding, kneading, with a rhythm that came only from years of practice. I was hypnotised by the motion of Mathilde's fingers and roused from my spell only when Hedda Lilleberg came in.

'Dagny,' she grinned, 'you're early, love. You beat me to it!'

'I'm the biscuit maker,' I said, 'I couldn't be late.'

Hedda was a pretty lady, warm and comforting like a cake herself. She was married to Joakim Lilleberg, the fiddler, and she taught me songs and sang with me.

'And I'm the cook,' she said, wafting the air with her hands, 'looks like the fire's ready.' She loosened her blouse at the waist, tugging it out of her skirt. 'I'm not putting my finery on until later,' she said, rolling up her sleeves. 'Can't cook in my Sunday best.'

We worked in our ordinary clothes: white blouse, red bodice, black skirt, white apron. Married ladies covered their heads with white headscarves, which were propped up into a peak by a starched insert they wore underneath, and tucked back into folds at the sides and a flap at the back. Girls and unmarried women did not wear headscarves, so I didn't have one, but my hair was platted and pinned up. Later, we would change into fresh shirts, a better bodice insert, an embroidered apron and a finer belt, and we'd add jewellery: brooches and belt buckles and silver earrings. I was allowed to wear my mother's formal jewellery for the confirmation, a silver brooch at my collar and two special buckles for my belt. My mother had worn them on her wedding day. Far couldn't bear to look at them.

We set to work. I sat down next to Mathilde. Having made the dough, she would now be the roller and the cutter. Hedda stood by the grill and waited for our first batch. 'So your brother's coming of age,' she said. 'Little Hans, who would have thought it? I remember the day he was born.'

I sunk my fingers into the warm mound of dough and pulled off a handful. All I could think about was how Hans had not killed my mother. None of the boys had even made her ill. I rolled the ball of dough in my hands and then turned the edges down and tucked them into the middle underneath, making sure the top of the ball was smooth and the dimple was on the bottom. I laid it on the tray that Mathilde had floured to let it rest for a few minutes.

Hedda sensed my unease. 'Even you are growing up, Dagny,' she said. 'Your mother would have been so proud of you. God rest her soul.'

I looked at her as I grabbed my next handful of dough. 'Do you think so?' I said.

Hedda laughed. 'Think so? Look at you! Such a beautiful young lady.'

I sprinkled some flour over the dough and began to roll it in my hands. 'I think it's hard to grow up.' I said.

Hedda leaned her head over to the side and dug the poker into the fire. 'Why, dear?' she smiled.

'Just...' I folded the edges under and made a dimple. 'Hedda, did you bleed when you became a woman?'

'Oh,' she said, 'that's why you think it's hard. It's the curse. It's happened to you, has it?'

I looked at her in confusion. Nina Grieg had said it wasn't a curse and now Hedda was telling me that it was.

Hedda laughed. 'Oh, don't look so scared love, we all have to go through it, every month until...'

She turned away from me then, pausing in exactly the same place as Nina had when she explained it.

'Until we carry a child,' Mathilde said, slapping a ball onto the table and taking the rolling pin in her hands. 'Or until we get old, like me. Then it stops.'

I watched Mathilde roll the dough into a flat circle. 'Is the curse lifted when you get older then?' I said.

'You could say that,' Mathilde said. 'But then we suffer a new round of curses...just look at these fingers!'

Mathilde's knuckles were enlarged and she couldn't bend her fingers easily, but her swollen joints gripped the rolling pin nevertheless and she flipped the dough over and began to roll again with vigor as the circle grew larger and flatter.

'Well I have young hands,' I said, 'but I still can't do *that*.'

Mathilde smiled, although her lips turned down and her chin jutted forward. 'You can't get to my age without learning a thing or two,' she said. 'Blessings and curses.'

Hedda splashed a drop of water on the grill to see how long it took to boil off. 'Every age has them,' she said. 'Grill's ready.'

The bleeding definitely had something to do with children. Hedda and Joakim did not have any children. Mathilde had Konrad, who had been a child all his life. I hadn't thought about it much before, but I wondered if I would ever have children, and if one of them would kill me, as I had killed my mother. The road to womanhood seemed rather brutal and I returned my thoughts to baking.

119

I made a full tray of dough balls and Mathilde rolled them. When she was done with the smooth wooden rolling pin, she changed to a steel pin that had a series of grooves in it. There was a technique to this part that Mathilde did effortlessly. She firmly rolled the steel pin, which pressed creases into the round but didn't cut it because of the special grooves. She ran the pin once over the dough, then turned it and rolled it again at right angles leaving a cross-hatch pattern that sealed the surfaces.

We got into a rhythm of working and talking. I made trays of dough balls, Mathilde rolled them and then cut them with the pin. When they were ready, Hedda took the scored rounds from the table and tossed them onto the grill. It wasn't long before Hedda started singing as she worked, a song about springtime and sunshine and nature. *To springtime my poem I utter, that back to us he may flutter, both laden with fancies sweet, in friendly affection meet.*

'Come on, Dagny, sing it after me,' she said.

I copied her, listening to the notes and singing them as she did. After several rounds, I had learned the words and I sank into the tune, singing of the brightening sun, the bubbling brook, and the breath of the flowers. Mathilde nodded approvingly as she rolled and cut the dough, and Hedda and I looked at each other knowingly, the way people who make music do, as we shared our voices and found notes that complemented each other in gentle harmonies.

We sang and worked and the eld house filled with the sweet smell of baking and the sound of our voices. I kept rolling and Mathilde's old fingers kept working and Hedda kept cooking and stacking the krote cakes until the morning had passed and the dough was almost finished. I was just splitting the last piece in two when there was a brusque knock at the door. We stopped singing. I held two balls of dough motionless in my hands. Mathilde looked up from her rolling and Hedda turned away from the grill. The door opened and suddenly the small low opening was filled with the bulky body of Rolf Qvale.

'Ladies,' he said, 'a word, if I may?'

'Come in, Rolf,' Hedda said.

I squeezed the dough in my hands. My stomach flipped uneasily. It was about me. I knew this was about me.

Rolf Qvale closed the door behind him. I couldn't look at his face and instead began counting the brass buttons on his jacket.

'Dagny, Mathilde, I need to speak to you.'

'Well, get it out, man,' Mathilde said, sharply, 'we're working.'

'Yes, right,' he said, scratching at the whiskers on his cheeks. 'You see, it's about this telescope.'

I tightened my grip on the dough. My hands clenched into fists and the dough oozed out through my fingers.

'Lillian Jevnaker wants me to arrest Konrad.'

'Arrest my baby?' Mathilde said, 'what would she want to do that for?'

'Well, it is theft,' Rolf said, awkwardly, 'and it's a family heirloom. She's very upset about the loss of it.'

'Konrad said he'd misplaced it,' Mathilde said, dismissively. 'You know he does that sometimes. He can't help it.'

'Yes,' Rolf said. 'It's just—'

'Tell Fru Jevnaker it'll show up,' Hedda said, 'there's no need for this.'

Rolf shoved his thumb into his belt. 'But I need to ask Dagny a few questions. If you wouldn't mind, Dagny?'

I released my grip on the dough. It was sticking to my hands. I looked up at him. He was a big man with a chubby face. 'You can't arrest Konrad,' I said, scraping the dough from my fingers.

'Did you give him the Jevnaker's telescope?'

I nodded, and guilt slowly cloyed at my throat. 'That's what he said, wasn't it?'

'Mmm-hmm,' Rolf said, 'it's all he *has* said, that Dagny had a telescope and he must have misplaced it. That's it.'

'Then he must have lost it,' I said. 'He didn't *steal* it though. Konrad isn't a thief.'

'Far from it,' Mathilde said, 'my boy's a good boy.'

Rolf knew he was getting nowhere. He sighed heavily and patted the wall. 'I want you to try to remember exactly what you did with that telescope, Dagny. Maybe you didn't give it to Konrad? Maybe you thought you did, but you put it somewhere else? Maybe you were going to give it to him, but you forgot? Whatever you did, it's all right as long as you tell the truth.' He bit his bottom lip. This wasn't a stolen bonnet or a silly prank. This was a real crime and Lillian Jevnaker wouldn't leave it be until the telescope was returned to her. It was somewhere on that mountain and I would have to go and look for it to save Konrad from arrest.

'I'll see you at the church,' Rolf said, backing out of the eld house. 'You come and talk to me Dagny, if you remember anything.'

The afternoon was supposed to be a celebration for my brother and Petter Bremnes, but I was uneasy and couldn't settle for a moment. Emanuel Sørensen was the toastmaster. He worked for Mor Utne at the hotel and was a gifted speaker with a strong voice that carried well. Emanuel did all the weddings, funerals, baptisms and confirmations in Utne and Granvin, and even some in Ullensvang. He led the procession to the church with Joakim Lilleberg playing the fiddle behind him, and the two boys looking solemn and nervous, as the rest of the town marched behind them.

The ladies were dressed in their finest clothes and the parade was a dazzling display of colour. The bodices were made from a wide range of fabrics and patterns, and the inserts were intricately decorated – embroidered calamanco and silk velvet. Some were appliquéd with beads or pearls and waxed materials that gave a glossy finish. There were glittering gold ribbons and stunning needlework in the shapes of hearts and roses and other Hardanger patterns. The belts were embroidered or woven in golds and greens and reds, and all the colours gleamed against the crisp white shirts and white embroidered aprons and white headscarves. To add to the bedazzlement, jewellery sparkled from cuffs and collars and belts and buckles. Everything had been polished and buffed to perfection. The ladies draped long linen coverings over their hands because they were going to church. These were also gleaming white and decorated with ornate embroidery that had been handed down through the generations.

I was not quite so elaborate but I was neat and tidy and I wore my mother's brooch and belt buckles with pride. I followed behind Hans with Far and Knut and Jon. Next to us was the despicable Bremnes family. Veslemøy's bodice had rows of glittering diamond shapes embroidered into it. She wore it with such arrogance, mistakenly thinking the thing made her look beautiful. Sigurd walked beside her looking like he'd sacrificed his life for that bodice. Grete was as conceited as her mother and wouldn't look at me at all. Håkon Bremnes walked behind his brother in black knee-length trousers and woolen socks. He wore a berry-red waistcoat and a black jacket. His chin was held so high I was surprised he could see where he was going.

Emanuel Sørensen said a few words and led us into the church where Magnus Jevnaker was waiting at the altar. He was dressed in black with a white ruff around his neck, which made it look as though his head was separate from his body. His hapless young assistant Eugen Mohr was handing out towers of hymn books that were placed upside down and the wrong way around. I took one from him and as he bent down to hand it to me, he dropped three more onto the floor, apologising to no one in particular as I walked away. Joakim continued to play his fiddle as we all paraded into the church. He would have to wait outside until we came out again. It was a well-known fact that fiddlers bought their talents from the devil and they weren't allowed to enter the church under any circumstances.

I scanned the pews for Jacob but couldn't see him. Bestefar Jørgen was slow and they were always the last to join the parade. Far tugged me by the arm and made me sit next to Knut, which I sneered at. 'Can't I go and sit with...'

'Sit down,' he said, pushing me into place.

When everyone was settled and the two boys were ready at the front, I saw Lillian sit down at the piano and begin to play. We all stood to sing. I couldn't concentrate on the words and kept twisting back to search for Jacob. Far prodded me and tried to give me a hard glare, but he wouldn't look at Emma's brooch hanging from my blouse and he promptly looked away again. *Behave*, was all he said. During the prayer that followed, I turned to see Konrad Olsen sitting at the end of the opposite pew. He saw me looking at him and his worried expression altered as he tried to smile. His dark brown eyes were as innocent as the day he was born. His wave of brown hair stood straight up from his brow and his fingers fidgeted with the tassel at the top of his socks. Sharp twitches of guilt hit my chest.

Magnus Jevnaker began his sermon. He talked about this coming of age for Hans and Petter, how they were blessed by God and that God would strengthen them in their transition to adulthood. He said that baptism was God's gift to us, a sign of God's love and that God now confirmed the blessings He had given Hans and Petter on the day that they were christened. The boys stood with their heads bowed at the altar and Magnus asked them to kneel before him while he prayed for them. I wished he would pray for me. I needed it more than Hans did. I was a thief and a liar, and now I was going to let an innocent man-child go to prison for something that I had done.

Lillian plonked at the clanging keys and we all stood again to sing. The strength my voice had in the eld house had now vanished and I mumbled my way through the hymn, staring down at the tips of my polished shoes. There was another lengthy sermon on the subject of honesty and truth, which I was sure had been penned by Lillian. She sat on the piano stool with her back as straight as a rod and her ears twitching as if to check her husband had said all the right things.

When it was all over, Pastor Jevnaker raised the crucifix and blessed the boys and all our community and asked us to go in peace. But there wouldn't be any peace for me.

We all came spilling out of the church and as soon as Far was distracted I broke from him and looked about for Jacob. Joakim Lilleberg had struck up the fiddle again and he accompanied the congregation to the hotel where Mor Utne was hosting the reception. People were meandering down the hill and I rushed among them impatiently, checking all the heads for chalk-white hair.

I finally found him behind the ice house where Bestefar Jørgen had stopped to rest. Jacob was wearing his good trousers and shiny shoes. It was odd to see him looking so neat.

'Jacob!' I shouted, rushing to meet him.

'Dagny, what's the matter?'

'I need to speak to you,' I said, looking at Bestefar Jørgen whose blind eyes were gazing back up at the church tower.

'Speak then,' Jacob said.

'In private,' I said, 'I mean in private.'

Jacob turned to Bestefar Jørgen. 'I'll be quick,' he said, and Jørgen smiled and waved his hand to dismiss us.

We went around the other side of the ice house and huddled together at the corner where its broad beams crossed.

'What is it?' Jacob whispered.

'Lillian wants Rolf Qvale to arrest Konrad,' I said, 'she's saying he's a thief and he stole the telescope.'

'What?' Jacob laughed. 'He can't arrest Konrad! That would be like arresting a child.'

'I know. But he will if Lillian insists. I need to find it, Jacob. I can't let Konrad take the blame. He might have to go to prison.'

Jacob swept his hand through his hair then he squeezed his lips together in his fingertips as he thought. 'I'll go and look for it,' he said. 'I'll find it, Dagny. Even if I have to search every inch of that mountain, I'll find it.'

I looked at him and he must have read the fear in my eyes.

'Don't be such a girl,' he said, and he pinched my nose and made me laugh.

When I turned to go back around the ice house the crowds had thinned. Looking up towards the church, I saw a man pounding down the hill alone. It was Rolf Qvale. He was staring right at us. Jacob stood behind me and placed his hand on my shoulder. Behind Rolf came a woman who was surrounded by girls. She too, was looking directly at us. It was Lillian Jevnaker. She had a smug look on her face. We watched them approach. Rolf Qvale glowered at us, and Lillian and the girls giggled and twittered.

'Jacob, Jacob, Jacob,' Selma teased, as they passed, 'won't you cross the Eternal Waterfall with me and be my one true love?'

Bestefar Jørgen raised his hand to his brow as though shielding his eyes from the sun. 'Jacob, boy, I do believe I can see again,' he said, getting to his feet. 'Yes! I see a pack of unruly fools who cannot hold their tongues. It is a miracle indeed.'

Lillian Jevnaker pursed her lips and hurried the girls away.

Jacob and I melted into fits of laughter and Jørgen's blind blue eyes glinted with mischief as though he was just a child himself.

9

School ended and work began. In the summer, all the children in Utne were expected to help with the labour. The sheep were taken to mountain pastures, there was planting to be done in the orchards, fruits and berries to be picked, and most of us helped with the milking. Some days I worked at the hotel for Mor Utne, whose hospitality was quickly becoming legendary amongst the tourists. Each summer, the steam ships brought a growing number of visitors up the Hardanger fjord to experience the spectacle for themselves. They were astounded by our mountains and charmed by our customs and way of life. Mor Utne liked us to be dressed in our good clothes if we were meeting guests. Some of the tourists had started buying our embroidery and having bodices and belts made, souvenirs to take back to the big cities. Mor Utne made Joakim entertain the guests with his fiddle and sometimes she asked me to sing for them. I sang the folk songs that Hedda had taught me, songs that had been sung here since time began.

The summer gave me more freedom. I didn't have Knut watching my every move at the schoolhouse and I could come and go as I pleased. If I was back late, I told Lars that there had been more work that day and he asked no questions, he barely seemed interested. Soon I was back to spending all my free time with Jacob and no one noticed or cared.

Jacob was supposed to be helping at the Ellefsen farm but he sneaked up the mountainside as often as he could to look for the telescope. He searched the troll's staircase, clinging on by his fingernails, risking his life to find it, but always came back empty handed. I started to wish I'd never laid eyes on the stupid thing. It had brought nothing but trouble. Rolf Qvale gave Konrad two weeks to return it to the Jevnakers. After that, it would be up to Lillian to decide how she wished to proceed.

A crowd of German visitors came to stay at the hotel and Mor Utne was rushed off her feet. I was asked to stay so late every night that sometimes I didn't bother to go home. I slept in a tiny room on the top floor, squeezed in next to Thora Hagen, a grown woman who begrudged having to share her bed with me.

One night, after dinner, Joakim was playing and I was singing with Hedda, and all the Germans were so carried away with it that they pushed all the tables to the side and they were dancing in the dining room and drinking all the cider from the cellar, and clapping and singing boisterously, even though they didn't know the words. Mor Utne was so happy about all the kroner falling into the till that she couldn't bring herself to put an end to it and the festivities continued long into the night.

Joakim's arms were aching from holding the fiddle and bowing back and forth for so long. His black hair fell across his brow as he played. His eyes were always tightly shut. I kept looking down at the fiddle's patterned fingerboard and all the beautiful bone pieces that had been so carefully worked into it. The triangles and circles seemed to be moving on their own as Joakim played and the head that was carved into the top of the scroll was swinging from side to side, dipping and ducking, watching me as I sang.

Hours after midnight, when my feet were so sore and my eyelids were so heavy I thought I'd fall asleep standing up, I caught a glimpse of white in the crowd. It was moving about quickly – a white flash, like a woman's white headscarf disembodied from the head. At first I thought I was dreaming but then I realised it was Jacob's hair. He was weaving his way to me through the dancing guests.

He stood by the wall and watched me for a moment, listening to the song I was singing. His face was transfixed and he seemed to be enchanted by the music. Then he beckoned me to him. 'Come, Dagny!'

I tried to wave him away but he was insistent.

'Come!'

I glared at him, pointed my elbow at Joakim, trying discreetly to tell Jacob that I couldn't get away. Wasn't it obvious? But he kept waving at me and then Hedda noticed him, and after the chorus she started laughing and dismissed me with a nod.

'What is it?' I said, hurrying over to him.

'You sing like an angel, Dagny, do you know that? Come with me, I have something to tell you!'

'Have you found it?' I said.

'No. Come with me though.'

He dragged me from the hotel and out into the street. It was still light. The sky didn't get dark in the summer. The mountains were sleeping, a pastel shade of lilac. The water was still and smooth, disturbed only by a gentle breeze.

Jacob waited until we were half way up the hill before he said anything. Then he stopped and pulled me round to look at him. 'I went back,' he whispered.

'What? On your own?' I said, 'Without me?'

'I was hungry.'

'What happened?'

'He played me the tune again, that *pom-pom pom-pom pom-pom-pom* tune...the one about the Dovregubben.'

'Has he finished it?'

'No. But I told him he had to finish it soon, for you.'

'Me? Why?'

Jacob was grinning and his eyes were gleaming at me. 'Because I told him I wanted him to play it at our wedding.'

'Jacob!' I said, my mouth dropping open.

'What? What's wrong with that? I asked Nina if we could have the wedding reception at their cabin and she said yes. She said it was a wonderful idea, and she said we could eat

129

waffles and drink blueberry juice and because we didn't have a fiddler she would sing and the old troll would play.'

'You are mad!' I said, shaking my head. 'You've lost your mind!'

Jacob was laughing. He took my hand again and pulled me past the church. 'We are getting married though, Dagny. You said you would marry me, didn't you?'

'That was when I was dying,' I said. 'I'm not dying anymore.'

'But I want to marry you anyway,' he said, 'and I'll be fifteen next week. That's practically a grown man.'

'And how are we going to get married then?' I said.

'It's easy, just like Selma Jevnaker said, the Eternal Waterfall. Everyone knows that if a girl and a boy cross it together and they make it to the other side, then they are true loves.'

'Do you really believe that?' I said.

'Of course, I do. Everyone knows it's true. Every person has one true love and you are mine. Crossing the waterfall will prove it. And that will make us as good as married.'

He stopped laughing and we started to feel the solemnity descend all around us again and wrap us inside its cape. We changed direction to avoid being seen and kept going, walking without talking, to the mountain. Something serious was about to happen. I could feel it coming, and at once I was both afraid and excited.

'I don't know if I'm ready,' I said, when we were hidden by the trees.

Jacob put his arm around my shoulder and I leaned in towards his chest as we walked. I inhaled the smell of him. He was just like the mountain. He smelled as fresh as the air, laced with pines, and every part of his body was as solid as the rock. 'Don't worry, Dagny,' he whispered, softly, 'it's normal to be scared when you are in love.'

'How do you know?' I said.

'Nina said so.'

'Did she? What else did she say?'

'She said that people in love only feel scared because of the newness and the depth of the feeling. She said when it's powerful like that, like what we feel, you know...mighty...well then she said it's the most frightening feeling in the world.'

'Oh,' I said, 'so it's all right to be afraid?'

'Yes,' he nodded. 'She said it terrifies you because you know you would give your very soul to your one true love, and that's a big thing to give.'

'It is,' I said. 'Souls must be bigger than us, don't you think?'

'They must be.'

'Maybe they're so vast that we can't contain them in our own bodies,' I said, 'maybe they don't need our bodies, and that's how part of them keeps on living after we die?'

Jacob held me closer. 'And maybe that's why this feeling is so powerful? Because our souls are so big?'

We looked at each other and the air seemed to tighten around us. I tingled with anticipation, aware that I was responsible for my own actions and for whatever was coming next.

'She said it has great rewards too, being in love,' Jacob went on, his voice gaining confidence, 'like happiness, higher than these mountains. Happiness that could take you all the way up to heaven, like that stupid telescope!'

I giggled. 'That stupid telescope! Do you think we'll ever find it?'

He shook his head. 'I've tried my best but there's no trace of it.'

'We don't have much time left,' I said, 'poor Konrad. I'm going to have to tell Rolf Qvale it was me.'

'You can't do that!' Jacob said.

'Why not?'

'Because Lars would kill you, and he'd never let you see me again, and then we wouldn't be able to get married. It would ruin everything. And it's all arranged, with Nina and the troll.'

'He isn't a troll.'

'Grieg then, I have arranged it with Herr Grieg. The day after my birthday, you and me will be married.'

'What about Konrad though?'

'Qvale won't put him in jail, Dagny. It's *Konrad*.'

'Lillian'll make him suffer, though,' I said, 'she wants to punish someone.'

We came to a clearing in the trees. We had almost reached the lake. Jacob took me out to a rock that bulged from the mountainside and we sat down near the edge. It was so late that the light summer night had turned into morning and the tone of the sky was changing. From the cliff, we could see Utne and the water stretching out in all directions, and the pale lilac mountains, and the little red farmhouses scattered amongst the trees on the other side of the fjord, and the sky, brightening, lit by the furtive creeping of the sun.

'Do you think there is any more world than this?' Jacob said.

'It's hard to imagine,' I said, 'hard to imagine anything bigger, anything more.'

'Imagine all of this is inside us, and that's how big a soul is,' he said, 'makes you think, doesn't it?'

I looked out at the beauty of the fjord. It was my home, my world, all I had ever known. Jacob edged closer to me and we sat there looking out at our world, both of us seeing it from a new perspective, knowing that when we returned to it, it would be different.

Eventually, he kissed me. Without asking. Without saying anything at all. His expression was the most serious I had ever seen it. He looked like a grown-up man, as he said he was. He placed his hand on my cheek and turned my face to his, then he just sat there looking at me for a second and I looked at him, and his eyes kept me still and quiet, like we were making a pact that words would only break. Then he put his mouth on mine and we kissed.

I felt the warmth of his lips press against me and I liked it. This time I opened my mouth ever so slightly and our tongues brushed against each other, and something inside my body leapt and burned. I felt it everywhere: an aching and longing in my chest that made me want to cry out, and a tingling between my legs that made me want him to touch me there. The feelings were so dizzying and enslaving, so enormous. And I knew in that kiss that he was giving me his soul. All the beauty of it, the vastness of it, as deep as the fjord and as high as the mountains, all of it was contained in that single kiss, and all of it was now within me.

*

I went over to the red cabin in the early evening. Bestefar Jørgen was dozing in the chair but he opened his eyes when he sensed me at the window.

'Sorry to wake you,' I said, prising the door open, 'is he here?'

'Off on that mountain again,' Jørgen said. 'Can't think why he has to spend so much time up there. But he's a Fjellheim, I suppose it makes sense.'

'I have a gift I wanted to give him,' I said, 'for his birthday.'

'Put it on the table. He can get it when he gets back.'

'Oh...' I said, and my cheeks flushed, 'it's not that kind of a gift. Not something I can leave on the table.'

Bestefar Jørgen scratched his chin. 'Well, maybe you should stay here until he comes home then?'

'How long has he been away?'

'Hours.'

'So he should be back soon?'

'Reckon so,' Jørgen said.

133

I came to sit in the chair beside him. Bestefar Jørgen moved in his own chair, as if to make room for me.

'You been at the hotel?' Jørgen said.

'Yes, Mor Utne's busy with the tourists.'

'Ah, Torbjørg's put her life into that place,' Jørgen said, 'loves those visitors. I'm sure they come to see her more than the hotel.'

'There were Germans staying last week and British people staying there now. There isn't a single spare room,' I said.

'That'll keep her happy,' Jørgen said, 'and keep you girls busy, no doubt.'

I suddenly realised how tired I was. I'd been scrubbing laundry since seven, then later I'd helped in the kitchen to make and serve the dinner, and then Mor Utne asked me to sing for the tourists. I sang an old song about a fair-haired maid. I stood there with my hands on my apron and my chin lifted up, and Joakim playing his fiddle beside me with his eyes shut. They all clapped when I finished and said things to me in a language I didn't understand.

'Joakim closes his eyes when he plays,' I said. 'What do you think he sees?'

Bestfar Jørgen stared blankly at the opposite wall. 'The music,' he said.

'You think he *sees* the music?' I said, 'How?'

'There are many different ways to see something, Dagny. Just because I don't have my sight anymore, doesn't mean I can't see lots of things, quite vividly. I see pictures in my mind: my family, my wife, my daughter, the people dear to me. Even if I could see with my eyes, I would no longer be able to actually look at them. But they're always there inside my head. I see the people in this town, know what they're thinking and feeling by just the tone of their voices. And you can see like a feeling, too, you just sense it. That's what Joakim must see in his music, a feeling.'

'How do you see in feelings?' I said.

'We just do,' Jørgen said. 'You never heard one of those tunes that reach right into your chest and make you feel like you're grieving but you don't know what you're grieving for?'

I thought about Nina, singing her haunting lament and how it had twisted a tender place within me. 'Yes,' I said. 'I have.'

'Or when you hear one of those jigs, like the ones Joakim plays, and you know you have to leap up and dance and be joyful? Music does that, doesn't it? It gives us a picture of something, a sense of something, makes us feel feelings without saying anything. Sometimes it makes things even clearer than if you could actually see them with your eyes.'

I tucked my legs up underneath me and rested my head against the side of the chair. I hoped that Jacob could see things in music because my birthday gift to him was a song, a song about a mountain, because that's what Jacob was. I would sing it to him and he would feel it, and I wouldn't have to say anything else to him because the music would have said it all.

I closed my eyes and pictured the mountain, our mountain. Jørgen was right, I could see every single crevice and pathway, every rock, every stream, every tree – it was all there inside my mind. And I saw the troll's staircase, and Jacob climbing it, and I thought about the song that I would sing to him: *in the evening's glory lies the body of the mountains, in the light of the full moon the red rises up. In the valley all is dark and quiet, and the sweet springs kiss as they rise from the source.* The mountain in my mind grew taller, swelling outwards and upwards finding new places in the sky and the clouds had to part to make way for it as it kept rising higher, its snowy peak penetrating the heavens. And, one by one, all its mysteries were exposed, and the creatures who lived on the mountain began to fall from it, tumbling down its sides, head over heels, plunging into the water below.

I didn't realise I was dreaming until Jacob roused me.

'Wake up!' he said.

Bestefar Jørgen was snoring in the chair beside me. It was late but I didn't know what time it was. I panicked. Was Lars looking for me?

In the dim light, Jacob himself looked worried. His face was dirty, his clothes were torn.

'Wake up, Dagny,' he said again, shaking my shoulder. He crossed to the other side of the chair wincing a little as he moved. He was limping.

I rubbed my eyes and sat up quickly. 'What is it?' I said.

'I've found it...the telescope,' he said. His voice was a loud whisper. He looked frustrated, as though he'd just lost a fight.

'Where is it?' I said.

'Troll's stairs. Out of reach,' he said, pulling up a stool to sit on. 'I twisted my knee trying to balance across the crevice. We need some pincers or a stick or somethin'. If I had the right stuff I'd be able to reach it.'

'Then we'll find some tools and go back,' I said, 'we can go back tomorrow.'

'No. Not tomorrow,' Jacob said. He glanced at Bestefar Jørgen who was still snoring in the chair. 'Tomorrow's, you know...what I planned with...you know.'

'But that can wait, can't it?'

'No...it's all arranged.'

I wasn't in the mood to sing to him now. 'Happy Birthday,' I said, emptily.

Jacob nodded. 'I'll get it for you Dagny, but it'll have to wait a few more days. Let's hope Lillian can listen to the word of God or somethin', find somethin' in that bible of hers that'll make her leave Konrad alone for a bit longer.'

'I had a present for you,' I said, 'it was a song.'

'Will you sing it? You sing so beautifully.'

'I can't now, it's late. I have to go home. I said I'd come home tonight. Are you all right?'

He nodded again.

'You think Doctor Helland should have a look at that knee?' I said.

'No. It'll be fine. Meet me tomorrow at the Paulson bridge, as early as you can. I'll be waiting for you there.'

'What about work?' I said. 'What about Mor Utne?'

'Sneak away,' Jacob said, 'when no one's watching.' He pulled me to him and kissed my cheek and I smiled shyly, as if I'd only just met him.

I slipped from the hut without waking Bestefar Jørgen. The night was light and cool and I was drawn to the water's edge. I walked along the shore and the soft waves lapped at my ankles. I passed the schoolhouse, now all locked up for the summer, and the Bremnes' shop with its shutters drawn. I crossed the road at the hotel. All the lace curtains were hanging wearily in the windows, even the guests were sleeping now. I cut through the path by the eld house and the ice store, and went up the hill towards the church. When I reached it, I was shocked to see that the big red door was wide open, gaping like a rectangular mouth.

I approached with hesitation, wondering why Magnus Jevnaker would be there at this time. I got closer, holding my breath to listen for the slightest sound, but there was nothing, no voices at all, just an ominous silence. I was frightened of the church at night, even though it wasn't dark, there was something ghoulish about it with the door hanging open like that. It wasn't right. My footsteps were loud, crunching in the road. I tried to creep up to the church but I was still making too much noise.

I put my head inside the vestibule. Had it been daytime I would have called out, but my throat was dry and I was shaking. I stopped and listened again. I should have run away, gone straight home, but something was pulling me in. I reached for the door handle and quietly went inside.

In the muted light, I saw a man kneeling below the empty pulpit. He was alone at the altar. His head was bowed but I recognised him instantly. Confused and frightened, I

137

stood completely still, watching him. He turned around when he heard the door.

'Far?' I said.

He was wiping tears from his eyes. 'Dagny? That you?' he said.

'Far? Are you–'

'I'm all right,' he said.

I'd never seen my father cry before. And what was he doing at the church at this hour? I looked at him, on his knees with his eyes red and his cheeks stained with tears, and he lowered his head as though he was ashamed to have been seen. 'I come here sometimes,' he said, 'at night, when it's peaceful. Gives me a chance to...well, your mother, God rest her soul, to think about...I mean, sometimes I talk to her here.'

I inhaled deeply. 'What does she say?' I said.

He half laughed and half cried, his face seemed crumpled and hurt. 'She was a good woman, Dagny,' he said, getting to his feet. 'I never thought I'd lose her like that. Sometimes it's hard to know what to do without her. It's like half of me went with her. Half of me is gone now too.'

He pushed his hand through his wavy hair and his tufted eyebrows crept together.

'I'm sorry, Far,' I said.

He shook his head.

'I'm sorry for...'.

'It wasn't your fault,' he said.

We walked back up the aisle together in silence. I was stunned to have seen my father looking so vulnerable. We left the church and walked home without saying another word. My mother was walking beside us. Both of us could sense her presence but we didn't say anything about it to each other. Far closed the door and hung up his coat. I crept up the stairs, passed my sleeping brothers and went to my alcove. As I drew the curtain, I knew that my mother was still there watching me. *I'm going to marry Jacob tomorrow*, I whispered to her as I got into bed. *Jacob is my one true love.* My mother seemed happy with this. I sensed her calmness and her grace waiting at my bedside as I began to fall asleep.

10

We met at the bridge by the Paulson farm. It was still early. Thora had seen me start the laundry but she and Mor Utne were going out to the market at Kvanndal and had to catch the first boat. As soon as they left, I cast my apron onto the pile of bed linens and ran from the hotel as if it were ablaze. My stomach was a knot of nerves. What if Far saw me? What if anyone saw me? What would happen to me when they discovered I was gone? Lars would be enraged. Mor Utne would dismiss me. I tried not to think of it as my feet pounded the path and I fled to the bridge.

Jacob was ready. He was carrying a backpack with provisions. It would be a long hike. To get to the Eternal Waterfall we would take our usual path up the mountainside but when we got to the first plateau at the lake, we would turn left instead of right and climb up the other side.

'You made it!' Jacob said.

'You thought I wouldn't?'

'You are a girl. Thought you might chicken out.'

'Not me,' I said, 'if I can do the troll's stairs I can do a waterfall.'

We rushed into the woods with a feeling of excitement and release. We were already in a lot of trouble, which would only intensify when everyone discovered we'd gone, but as long as we were together none of that mattered.

In our excitement, we started off quickly and made light work of the hike through the long grass. It was an adventure, like the thousands of others we'd had before, and as I followed in Jacob's footsteps I forgot all about the seriousness between us and the gravity of what we were about to do. We were going to get married, make a vow to each other that would last a lifetime, but it felt like one of our usual exploits onto the mountain with Jacob telling his stories and me hanging on his every word.

I noticed he was still limping. Some rocks were steep and required a high step – on those he grimaced.

'That knee still hurtin'?' I said.

'It's nothin',' he said.

'You want to stop for a bit?'

'No.'

He shrugged me off every time I asked and continued to climb eagerly, as though it didn't hurt at all.

'It's this way,' he said, when we reached the lake, turning in the opposite direction and picking out a lesser trodden track. 'Hey, maybe we'll see the Fossegrimmen when we get there, and it's Thursday!'

'The Fossegrimmen? What's that?'

'You ain't heard of the Fossegrimmen?'

'Well, only that it has somethin' to do with fiddles,' I said.

'He's a creature,' Jacob said, and he started to tell me the tale, 'a man who sits naked under waterfalls, playing the fiddle. He plays the music of nature itself. The sound of the water and the wind in the trees, the fall of the rain, all of it comes from his music. I reckon Joakim must have come up here when he was younger. The Fossegrimmen teaches people how to play the fiddle, and no one can play the way Joakim can.'

I thought about Joakim and the way he closed his eyes when he played, and how Bestefar Jørgen said he was *seeing* the music.

'Folks who want to play the fiddle come to the Fossegrimmen and offer him a bit of food, stolen meat,' Jacob said, 'in secret, at sundown. It has to be a white goat, with its head dipped in a waterfall that flows northwards, or a piece of smoked mutton, stolen from the neighbour's stores on a Thursday after sundown.'

'Why Thursday?' I said.

'Who knows why, Dagny, it's what the legend says. And if there ain't enough meat on the bone, the Fossegrimmen will only teach a person how to tune the fiddle. Now, that can't have been the case with Joakim, can it? Must have been a good offering from him because Joakim plays like no one else in the whole of Hardanger. No, he must have given the creature a succulent joint, and in return, do you know what the Fossegrimmen does?'

'What?'

Jacob turned to me and spread out his fingers. 'He takes the pupil's right hand and draws his fingers along the strings until they all bleed. And after that he is able to play so well that all the trees will dance and the torrents of rain will stand completely still in the falling, and even the moon will sing and the tides will turn.'

'You think Joakim did that?' I said, 'Came to see the Fossegrimmen and had his fingers bleed?'

'No question,' Jacob said. 'When Joakim plays, grandmothers and grey-haired men, the blind and the lame, and even babes in the cradle start to dance. That's a true sign of the Fossegrimmen. People sell their soul to play like that.'

'Is that why the fiddlers aren't allowed into the church?'

'The good ones,' Jacob said, 'the best of them bought their skills from the Fossegrimmen.'

'Is the Fossegrimmen the devil then?' I said.

'He's a creature, Dagny, not human. May as well be the devil for people like Lillian Jevnaker.'

The sun grew stronger as we continued to climb and Jacob told me another story, one about a boy with an enchanted fiddle. Little Freddie had earned three pennies from a sheriff and then given his pennies away in exchange for three wishes. One of Freddie's wishes was for a fiddle, and that everything alive must dance when he played it because he loved to see people merry and happy.

'And he met the sheriff, and Freddie played the fiddle,' Jacob was saying, 'and the sheriff danced and danced. He danced so much that the thorns tore at him, and he danced and cried and pleaded until the rags flew off him and he had hardly a thread left on his back. And this made him so angry that he said the boy had assaulted him and robbed him, and nearly taken his life, so he ordered him to be hanged and there was no way out of it for Freddie.'

'So what happened to him?' I said.

Jacob was about to tell me the rest of the story when we heard the rumble of the waterfall. It was such a forbidding growl that we stopped talking and lifted our heads to listen.

'There it is,' he said, 'you hear that?'

We continued for a while in the shadow of the thundering falls. The mountain grew rockier, first gradually, then suddenly. Jacob was struggling to climb the steepest parts. His knee kept buckling and I had to hold out my hands to catch him and push him forward.

'We should stop,' I said, 'have a rest.'

'We can't rest now, Dagny,' Jacob beamed excitedly, 'we're nearly there!'

The roar of the falling water grew louder and the earth and the rocks and the air around us began to tremble as we got nearer. Soon we were following the sound alone, veering off any clear pathways and scurrying through shrubs and branches, finding the quickest way to the water.

Eventually we reached a clearing. Through the trees I could see a wall of white foam. The noise was so loud we had to shout at each other.

'There she is!' Jacob said, 'the Eternal Waterfall! Isn't it magnificent?'

It was. It was the most magnificent sight I had ever seen. A wall of vertical rock towered before us and a mighty rush of white frothing water came churning over the top of it, falling in a sheer drop and spreading like an avalanche down to the rocks below where mists sprayed up like drifting fog. We edged closer and looked down into the frothing spray and the moisture covered our faces and we had to wipe our eyes. Below us, the waterfall crashed into more rocks and finally dissipated into a winding river. Nothing came near the erupting water. No birds dared to fly across it, the trees turned their backs on it. There was nothing here but rock and water on a gigantic scale.

The huge waterfall hung over the mountain like a curtain. Behind it was the ledge that Jacob and I had to cross.

'It'll be easy,' Jacob shouted, already throwing off his backpack and rising to the challenge, 'come on!'

I followed him. The noise was a terrifying indication of the force contained in the water. Like the mountains, we were insignificant in its presence.

To get to the ledge we had to scale the rocks, which were wet and slippery on the incline. Jacob reached for me and pulled me up with one hand. His hair was getting wet and sticking to his brow as he pulled me in beside him. We clung to each other behind the barrage of water that was pelting us with droplets as it spewed over the cliff.

'Hold on to me!' Jacob shouted, 'Follow my feet!'

He started to move and I inched along beside him as the waterfall screamed at us, defying us to cross it.

'Jacob!' I shouted back, 'I'm scared!'

'We will make it!' he said, smiling as though he wouldn't have chosen to be anywhere else. 'We are true loves! And the true loves always make it across!'

I held his hand with one hand and his wrist with the other, gripping him so tightly I could almost feel the throb of the blood in his veins.

In the beginning, the ledge was wide enough for me to put two feet side by side and almost walk normally, but slowly the ledge started to recede and thin out, until we had to place our feet carefully one in front of the other and Jacob could only partially turn to talk to me.

I couldn't look down. The ledge was only a body wide. If we slipped or lost our balance we'd be caught up in the sloshing sheets of water and the waterfall would carry us

144

with it on its freefall dive to the rocks below. We were already drenched and the water was freezing. At one point, I had to stop and wipe my eyes. I couldn't let go of Jacob so I blotted the spray with my sleeve and carried on, painstakingly slowly, as we approached the middle.

Jacob twisted to the side and shouted back at me. 'We're nearly there!' he said.

Nearly there meant that we were too far across the falls to turn back. I had to keep going. The wall of rock we were creeping along was slightly concave, which allowed us to bend our bodies in towards it, but as it curved around to the other side it began to fill out, giving us less room to manoeuvre. Soon it started bulking out and it was clear that we would not be able to continue in our current position. Jacob's feet turned towards the water and he stood with his back pressing against the rock. 'We can't hold hands here, Dagny,' he shouted, 'you need both of your hands to hold on to the rock. You understand?'

I nodded, grimly. My heart was thudding in terror as I let go of Jacob's hand.

'Watch what I do, nice and slow,' he said.

I lifted my chin and tried to draw a long breath but my lungs were too scared to let any air in. Instead, I inhaled small spatters of water that clogged my nose and mouth. Too afraid to shake my head for fear of losing my balance, I closed my eyes then stretched them wide open and blinked repeatedly until I could see clearly again.

Jacob's hand slipped from mine.

'Nice and slow,' he said again, as he gripped the rock, crossed one leg in front of the other and swung his body around. I watched his feet as he did it. His soaking wet toes moved easily and, as he hung there with his back to the waterfall, clinging on to the mountain, he looked just as safe as he would if he were lying in his bed at home. He eased his way past the jutting ridge, finding handholds, anchors in the rock that kept him steady.

'It's all right, Dagny,' he shouted back to me, 'there's room on the other side! Come on!'

I briefly thought about my mother. Never had I felt closer to joining her in heaven. Perhaps that was why she came to visit me last night? Was she coming to take me to her?

'Don't be such a girl, Dagny! Make your body go soft!' Jacob shouted, knowing I had frozen in fear. 'Do exactly what I did! I am here for you! Your one true love, remember!'

It wasn't the first time I'd risked my life following Jacob. I reached for the cold wet rock and spun around in one semicircular swoop, just as he had. I closed my eyes. My face was slammed up against the stone and I forced my body to stick to the rock, throwing all my weight forwards and bending my back to get a secure grip. I felt my way along, with the water crashing at my back and the cold spray whipping my skin. I found a strong hold and prepared my body. My feet were the last part of me to move. I grazed my face as I slid along but I was too scared to lift my head up off the rock.

Inside my head I screamed his name. *Jacob! Jacob! Jacob!*

Although I hadn't said a word out loud, he answered me. 'I'm right here! Keep going!'

I exhaled through my mouth and sucked in fast gulps of air. A few more inches along, I found a new grip that was strong enough to hold me as I moved my feet.

'Open your eyes, Dagny!' Jacob shouted.

And then I saw him there beside me, grinning at me proudly. As soon as I was close enough, he grabbed my arm and led me to the safety of the ledge, which was wider again on the other side.

We stood there for a moment. I was shaking and panting but Jacob was as relaxed as a gull in a storm, winging through the ferocity of it with natural skill.

'Look, Dagny,' he shouted, taking my hand and pointing ahead. The other side of the ledge was much shorter than I had anticipated and we could see through the tunnel of water to the mountainside beyond. 'We made it!' he said.

The remainder of the ledge was wide enough for us to stand normally again and Jacob held me so firmly that I didn't feel scared anymore. I started laughing as we came to the end of it. Not only had I made it across the treacherous falls, but we had proven that we were true loves: a boy and a girl who had crossed the Eternal Waterfall together.

'We did it!' Jacob cried as we stumbled out onto the other side. 'I told you!' he said, 'I told you we were true loves!' He wrapped his arms around me and I squealed with laughter as the thundering water roared behind us.

Jacob was so happy he lifted me in the air and spun me around in his arms then planted me back down again in front of him.

'I have something for you,' he said, as his face turned serious and I felt the cloak of solemnity once again descending.

He delved into his pocket and rummaged around for something, then he pulled his hand back out with his fist tightly clenched.

He got down on one knee.

I looked at him. My heart fluttered and I felt tears begin to prick in my eyes.

'Dagny,' he said, 'my one true love.'

He held his fist up to me and I kept looking down at his blue eyes, knowing exactly what he was going to say.

He opened his mouth to speak again but his sore knee suddenly weakened and he stumbled backwards, losing his balance. He slipped on the wet rock and tumbled onto his side.

'Jacob!' I shouted, before I even realised the danger he was in.

He tried to get up again but the damaged knee had lost all its strength and as he stood up he keeled over, lurching and sliding with his hand still clenched in a fist to protect what he was holding.

'Jacob!' I sprang towards him, reaching out both of my arms. 'Here! Hold my hand!'

He was falling backwards now, his feet scraping helplessly across the rock and his balance tipping the wrong way. My fingers stretched out and brushed the tips of his, but his body was already over the edge and he refused to take my hand, knowing that if he did, he would take me with him.

'Jacob!' I screamed again, as panic and horror scraped at my throat. 'Jaaacob!'

He stared at me as he flew back, his mouth wide open.

'No!' I shouted, 'Jacob! No!'

He opened his fist and threw something at me as he plunged into the thunderous water. His hands and his feet were still pointing forwards and I hurled myself down on to the rock and hung over the edge with my arms grasping out for him. 'Reach for me!' I screamed, 'Jacob! Reach out!' I willed him to come back, hoping that the force of the water would thrust him back into my arms. 'Reach for me!' I cried again. But the water was too powerful. It didn't spit Jacob back out but pulled him down in its ravaging rush, plummeting to the rocks below.

At first I thought it was a joke, all part of Jacob's plan and that in a few minutes he would reappear, crawling up the side of the waterfall, grinning at me and calling me a girl. I wiped my eyes so that I would see him and gasped, spitting out the water in my mouth.

'Jacob?' I shouted.

I scoured the frothing swirls for a sign of him. But the water was blasting so furiously and bending everything, even the rocks, to its will. Downwards. Everything was spilling downwards.

Then I thought maybe he had landed safely in the pool below and that he would swim to the edge at the bottom and come out there. I'd seen him jump off rocks and dive head first into the sea before. He was an excellent swimmer and would dare all the Ellefsen boys to go higher and higher until they were all too afraid to jump and Jacob was the last one standing.

I called his name over and over again and peered down into the water for an answer.

After a while I got up and ran along the edge of the cliff to get a better view of the rocks below. But I couldn't see anything. No matter where I went, all that surrounded me was the fierce, terrifying rush of the waterfall.

I returned to the spot where he fell, hung back over the edge and screamed his name until my throat rasped. 'Jaacob!' I shouted, wheezing between screams as my head tried to comprehend what had happened. Eventually, I lay face down on the rock, closed my eyes and whispered to him. 'Jacob! Please come back. I'm here. I'm your one true love and I'm here waiting for you.'

A long time passed. I fell into silence. I lay there, cold and wet, shivering on the rock. When I opened my eyes again, I saw something lying on the rock beside me, a glimmer of yellow through the mists and the spray. I reached out and touched it. It was a ring. I picked it up and rubbed at it with my thumb. It was engraved on the inside and I brought it up to my face to read the inscription. *Jacob Fjellheim* the writing said, *your one true love.*

I closed my hand around the ring and wept.

I sobbed and screamed until I couldn't remember anything else. Just darkness, and falling water, and Jacob.

I should have followed him.

INTERLUDE

Performing an entire evening of Grieg's music has opened a door within me from which comes spewing forth a great sadness I have not encountered for a long time. It seeps into my chest and spreads out until I can feel it in every part of my body, a low heavy ache. It's getting worse as the night wears on. It's as though my soul is exposed and all this music is examining every part of it, shining a light on the raw places within me that have never fully healed.

I sang *Jeg Elsker Deg: I Love You.* I sang it to Kristian. I stared out through the lights and tried to pick out his face on the front row. The music came bursting from that place within me as the fragile nerve was laid bare. I allowed myself to open and be vulnerable, right there on the stage with thousands of people watching me. They all felt my pain but there was only one heart I needed to touch. I sang it to him, as Nina had sung it to Grieg, but this time the meaning was my own, the sincerity of it undeniable. I can only hope that he felt the thread touch him and that he will reach out and grasp it as I need him to.

I always do this. I can't help it. Whenever anyone begins to retreat from me I have no other way of reaching out to them but music. The fear that I am going to lose them paralyses me and I am unable to move in any direction. It is impossible to do what is expected of me, to say the things they need to hear. It's as if I can only lie still, like I did that day on the mountain, and wait for them to return.

Kristian knows about my life in Hardanger and the events of that summer, all the things that damaged me, things that are almost too painful to say. He is a widower. Perhaps that's why I am closer to him than I have been to any of the others. He understands what it means to lose someone forever. To be left alone, frozen in fear.

I am sitting at my dressing table. My head is resting on my hands. Harriet is outside and the ladies have left. Soon it will be the interval and the room will be filled with guests. For now, it is quiet and in the silence, every sound in the theatre is magnified. I hear the rumble of the drums and the heavy strike of the keys. Falling minor second. Falling major third. It is the Piano Concerto in A minor. The anguished call of the wind and reeds orders us all to listen. Everyone in the theatre is hushed now. The music takes us like a giant wave and we are immersed.

I raise my head and glance again at the gown behind me hanging on the screen. Blue satin pooling like water. Water flowing, rippling, falling, like the music. It builds then fades. The orchestra softens, and the flute returns the attention back to the lone piano. The notes are played in a billowing flourish, so quiet and delicate they become dreamlike. First the music creates its own void, picking away parts of me, making holes, leaving me feeling utterly bereft and a deep unfulfilled longing takes hold of me. I sing the tune in my head, close my eyes and feel every soft fluttering note come floating like a greatly anticipated gift, falling gently into place like a snowflake, almost agonizingly slowly, until it finds the space it has created and settles once more where it belongs.

Inside the music I see waterfalls and ravens, the trees on the mountainside and the waves undulating across the fjord. How it aches within me. He wants me to ache, to re-live it, to have me stumble and wallow inside the pain. Grieg lost Alexandra. I lost Jacob. They are both here in this music. He lets me feel it, see it, forces me to go inside it, until the tears begin to well and I am brought to the edge of my anguish, almost broken. Then he hurls me out of it, in angry slamming notes. It is the same phrase, the same grief, only a different shade, a different tone, now measured, precise, furious and violent. But then almost as soon as he has taken me there, he forgives me, eases me out again, soothes me with the gentlest caress. The orchestra takes over, the strings provide the healing, create a space for the ruminating piano, and then, only when it is ready, does its voice return. Lightly, softly, a tune as compassionate as angels. It brings forgiveness. It brings peace.

I don't hear the door. I only hear his voice.

'Dagny?'

The piano is louder with the door open and the tune wafts in with him like a summer breeze. He comes to sit with me. Touches his hand to my shoulder.

'You're missing the concerto,' I say.

'I can still hear it.'

I turn to look at him and see the music in his eyes. He held the thread. He came back to me. I reach out, sweep my hand across his brow and tuck an imaginary hair behind his ear.

'He wrote it when Alexandra was born,' I say. 'I'll never forget the first time I heard it.'

Kristian tries to read my expression. He's looking at me with such yearning, wanting to know every detail of my pain, every note of it. He slumps back into the chair with a huff, knowing he must be the one to broach the subject, that I cannot do it.

'You've got to tell me, Dagny,' he says. 'If you will not be my wife…'

'I will be your wife. Didn't I say that?' I say, sliding my hand to his elbow. 'We must be married, very soon.'

'Then tell me what you are afraid of,' he says, 'why are you so reluctant? I don't understand why you are doing this to me?'

'Doing what?'

'Stringing me along. Making me believe that we have something real. Pretending that you love me when really you–'

'I do love you!' I say.

'Then why can't you bring yourself to commit to me fully? What have I done that is so terrible?'

'Nothing, you haven't done anything. I'm just...it's just that we lose the people we love, you know that.'

Kristian edges the chair closer to me. 'And that is what you are so afraid of?'

'That's part of it,' I say.

'We've all lost someone, Dagny,' he says, his voice leveling out again, 'but you can't stop living just because of that loss.'

'There's more to it,' I say, 'it isn't just that.'

'How do you expect me to understand if you won't tell me,' he says. 'We always end up here, with you saying nothing at all and me having to guess. It's wearing me out. I can't keep doing this, over and over again.'

There's a tap at the door and I hear Harriet calling out to me. 'Interval soon,' she says. She peeps her head in but as soon as she sees us and senses the mood she backs out again.

I open my mouth but it's hard to make another sound. There are heavy whisperings in my cheeks but words won't come. Fear grips me and refuses to let me say anything at all. I force myself to breathe but it takes some time before I am able to speak again.

'Kristian,' I say, 'there's a chance I might die.'

He stares at me, his face draining of colour. He gulps back a breath and shakes his head. 'What do you mean?'

'I should have said something earlier, much earlier, but I didn't have the courage.'

Kristian leans forward and reaches for my arm, his voice diminishes and becomes almost completely inaudible. 'What are you talking about? I don't understand.'

'That's one thing I'm scared of,' I hold my brow, 'dying. Not for me, but for you. You've already lost one wife.'

'Have you seen a doctor?'

'Yes.'

'But what is it? What is the matter with you, my darling?'

I am not being fair. I bite the inside of my cheek and look away from him. 'There's so much more to it,' I say.

'Tell me.'

'I will, I will.'

Just then, the buzzer rings, signaling the interval.

Kristian sighs and shakes his head.

'They'll be here in a minute,' I say, 'I must change. We'll talk after, all right?'

'But I need to know,' he says, 'I want to know every detail. There must be something we can do.'

'Yes, dear,' I say. 'Perhaps. For now, don't let it trouble you. Help me get through this night.'

'Of course,' he says, bewildered.

I don't know why I am putting him through it.

I really don't deserve a man like Kristian.

SECOND MOVEMENT
SILENCE

11

I stopped talking.

Jacob's name was the last thing I said.

A period of time passed, it is lost to me now. I remember so little of it. A pair of strong arms, being lifted, carried, only vague images. I later discovered it was Konrad Olsen who found me when he was out wandering. I had been lying there for almost two days. That evening, Rolf Qvale found Jacob's broken body on the rocks, lifeless, pummeled by the ferocious falls. The men had to attach ropes to their waists and wade into the water to get him out. They brought him back down the mountain to Bestfar Jørgen who had to feel Jacob's cold body to believe what Rolf was telling him.

Konrad carried me home. I remember being placed by the fire and all the boys being there but not saying anything and Far pacing back and forth. They tried to feed me but I wouldn't eat, tried to talk to me but I wouldn't speak. Days passed. People came and went: Hedda and Joakim, Mor Utne, Mathilde and Konrad. Everyone sorry, everyone praying. I spoke to none of them. Words of comfort didn't exist. Words of sorrow didn't exist. What good were words when Jacob was gone?

Magnus Jevnaker spent long spells in the afternoons carrying out his pastoral duties, visiting me, sitting with me, reading from the bible. I closed my eyes, pretended I was asleep, couldn't look at that man's face. Arrangements were being made for the funeral. Joakim would play his fiddle, Emanuel Sørensen would lead the proceedings. They thought I wanted to hear about it but I didn't.

On the fourth day, I ran to the church. I was taken by a compelling notion that Jacob was still alive. He spoke to me clearly. I heard him shouting for me, asking me to come. I shot out of the chair and fled, like a horse bolting from a stable. Far got up and called after me but I was gone before he had even crossed the room. I charged down to the church and rattled at the door pulling and turning the handle with all my strength.

Eugen Mohr finally opened it. 'Oh...Dagny,' he said, airily, 'how can I help you, child?'

I sped past him and rushed down the aisle to the transept where the coffin was waiting to be taken to Bestefar Jørgen. I touched the lid. It had not yet been sealed so I prised it open.

When I saw Jacob, my whole heart disintegrated. It fractured into tiny pieces and seeped up my throat in a giant swell of ache and despair. He lay there, still and cold. His beautiful face peacefully asleep. His brow was grazed and there were cuts on his skin, still bloodied but dry.

He seemed to be smiling, his lips were still so full and plump. I expected his eyes to flick open at any minute and for him to shout *boo!*

Jacob! Wake up! Wake up! But he didn't. I pushed the lid off the coffin and it clattered against the wall. I reached in and took Jacob's arm. He had been dressed in his fine clothes and was wearing his good shirt and jacket. I shook him. *Wake up! I'm here!* It made no difference.

'Dagny, dear,' Eugen was saying, 'one ought to leave the deceased to rest in–'

'Leave her!' I heard Lars shout from the door.

I squeezed Jacob's hand tightly in mine, then took each of his fingers and uncurled them one by one and pressed the palm of his hand to my mouth. I kissed him. *Wake up!* When that didn't work, I leaned over the coffin and kissed his mouth. I kissed hard, pressing the soul he had given to me back into his body. *Take it! Take it! Be alive!* But still he slept.

'Dagny, come on,' Far said, gently. He touched my shoulder but I wouldn't stop kissing Jacob. 'Let the boy go.' He pulled me back from Jacob's body and I hit the side of the coffin. 'Dagny, it's all right,' Far said, 'come on, now.'

I slapped and banged the coffin with my hands, then punched it and hit it so hard that Jacob's body shook.

'Dagny,' Far said, more sternly, 'let's go home.' He gripped my arm and I continued to hit, thumping Far's chest and face until he had to lock both of my arms away from him to avoid my swipes. I clenched my fists and tried to punch but Far was so strong I couldn't even bend my elbows.

Eugen Mohr sidestepped awkwardly behind me, 'Dagny, dear,' he said, reaching for my shoulder, 'we all understand you're grieving, but–'

'Don't touch her!' Far grunted, hauling me back up the aisle towards the door.

I was still writhing and wriggling. I wanted to go back to Jacob. I wanted to climb into that coffin with him and have Eugen slam the lid down on us so that I would be buried with him forever.

'Come on, Dagny,' Far said, trying to straighten me up enough to walk. 'It's the pain,' he said, 'it's the bloody pain. But this won't help.' He took me to the side of the vestibule and wrestled me into a crouching position. 'Breathe, girl,' he said, but I continued to squirm. 'Breathe!' he shouted. He got down behind me and wrapped his arms around my body and started breathing deeply himself as if he was teaching me how to do it. Hard exhales through his mouth were blasting in my ear. Eventually I picked up on the rhythm of them and took three or four deep breaths. I dropped to my hands and knees and Far released his grip a little. 'Breathe, girl,' he kept saying. The top of my head touched the floor and I rolled back until my brow was pressing against the flagstones. Hulking sobs retched out of me and I slapped the floor so hard my hands stung, then pounded my fists against the stones until my knuckles went numb.

Far scooped me up off the floor like a baby and carried me home.

He made up a bed for me downstairs by the fire. Went about the business of it mechanically without saying a word. He seemed to take great care, finding clean sheets and good pillows and a blanket he took from his own bed. It was summer, but he must have felt I needed heat.

'Get in,' he said, when he was done. Then he shouted for Knut to go and fetch Doctor Helland, who arrived shortly after with a big black bag.

Doctor Helland was an enormous man who seemed to take up the entire house. He was making a futile effort to be discreet as he came in. Far spoke to him at the door. 'For her nerves,' was all I heard him say.

Doctor Helland approached the bed and set his bag down on the floor. 'Hello, Dagny,' he said, 'you've suffered a terrible loss.'

I looked into the fire.

'We're all feeling it, dear,' he said, in his low gruff voice, 'the whole town's in mourning. He was a fine young man.'

I turned the ring on my finger.

'Do you think I could ask you a few questions?' the doctor said. 'I might be able to help. Give you something to make you feel better?' He smiled from behind his long black beard and asked if he could touch my brow while he was doing it. 'Don't think there's any fever, Lars,' he said.

Far was standing at the end of the bed with his arms wrapped around his body, hugging himself and looking at me strangely, as if I was a puzzle to be solved.

Doctor Helland took out a stethoscope and listened to my chest. 'Are you feeling lightheaded?' he said.

I stared at Jacob's ring.

'Any chest pains?'

'She doesn't talk, doctor,' Far said, 'hasn't spoken a word since it happened.'

'I see,' Doctor Helland said, 'not even a whisper?'

Far shook his head.

160

'Well, that's understandable, Dagny,' the doctor said, patting my arm. 'She'll come round again soon, Lars, when she's ready. I'll have Sissel make up some teas, chamomile and St. John's wort, and she needs rest.'

He stuffed his stethoscope back into his bag and Far accompanied him to the door.

'Give it a few more days, at least until after the funeral,' Doctor Helland tried to whisper, 'she'll be back to her old self again soon, once the initial shock wears off.'

Knut appeared again. He came and sat on the end of the bed and lifted one of his knees up to his chest. 'Dagny,' he said. He offered out a deck of cards with a conciliatory smile, 'you want to play?'

I rolled over onto my side and faced the back wall.

'All right, Knut,' Lars said, 'get to your chores now.'

My hands throbbed. My head throbbed. I thought of all the tiny fragments of my heart; a thousand pieces of sadness swimming inside my body.

I wished the blood would come again. I wished I was bleeding to death.

I didn't want to go to the funeral but Far made me. I curled up into a ball and shook my head every time it was mentioned. When the day came, I ran upstairs to my alcove and sat with my face pressed against the diamond window, watching the wind blow through the branches of the fir trees.

'You'll regret it forever if you don't go,' Far said. He spoke carefully as he pulled back the curtain, moving slowly and steadily in case I lashed out. 'We won't join the procession. We only need to walk from here to the church.' I didn't look at him. 'You sit next to me and your brothers. We will be your strength.' When that didn't move me, he used the only words that would. 'Jacob would have wanted you to be there, Dagny.' Far knew I would have done

161

anything for Jacob and I turned around and gave him a weak nod.

Lars even helped to dress me that day. He knelt before me and tied my belt, making sure the two lengths of it hung straight over my apron. And he took my mother's buckles and pinned them in place, and then he did the same with her brooch at my collar. It wasn't easy for his big fingers to fix all the clasps and he pricked his skin several times but didn't complain. He rested his hand for a second on Emma's jewellery before he told me he was done.

My brothers Hans and Jon flanked me like two great pillars and each of them linked their arms through mine, concerned that I might tussle with them. Far draped a white cloth over my forearms and he and Knut walked behind me to the church where the bells were ringing, calling the procession in.

The people came along the main road from Bestefar Jørgen's cabin. It was a sombre cortege and some were already crying. They were led by Emanuel Sørensen who was wearing a tall black hat. He had his head bowed before the cart, holding the horse's reins. Joakim was playing a sorrowful tune on his fiddle. The notes rose up into the air and laced everything with grief. Across the water the gigantic mountains looked on, turning a shade of dark blue, even though the sun was radiant. The coffin was covered in flowers that the women had collected. Bestefar Jørgen sat at the back of the cart, holding his hand against the coffin. A stick rested across his knee. He looked small and frail, his cheeks sunken and hollow. Who would be his eyes now?

I watched them come up the hill, trying not to look at their faces. Jon held my arm with both hands, he must have felt me trembling. They all huddled together at the church door: the Jevnakers, the Ellefsens, the Bremnes', the Olsens, the Paulsons, the Lunds, the Hellands, the Dahlbergs, the Skarstads, Rolf Qvale and Camilla Petersen the schoolmistress, all the people Jacob and I had been detached from. The two of us lived on the periphery, always skirting the edges of this. Now I was out here alone.

Emanuel Sørensen stood at the door and spoke a few words before they all went in. Two men were helping Bestefar Jørgen off the cart. The boys tried to guide me into the church but I dug my heels into the dirt and refused to budge.

'It's all right, Dagny,' Far said, behind me.

I shook my head. Then I lurched forward in the direction of the cart, and Jon and Hans allowed me only a little leeway, gripping me hard enough to avoid a scene. I scrambled to Bestefar Jørgen with my brothers restraining me, but when I reached the old man, they let me go. I threw off the embroidered cover and took Jørgen's hand.

'Dagny.' Bestefar Jørgen touched my face, felt the contours of my cheekbones with his thumb, then he put his hand on my shoulder and patted me there. 'Come,' he said, seeing me in a way that no one else did, 'you come with me.'

Far nodded to the boys and they let me go into the church with Bestefar Jørgen. I led him down the aisle to the front pew where we sat down together.

That's when I saw Lillian Jevnaker. She was sitting on the second row. Her hands were resting on her bible, which was placed squarely on her lap. She wasn't playing the piano today, a proper organist from Granvin was brought in to play at funerals. Lillian's face was partially shielded by her peaked headscarf but she lifted her chin when Jørgen and I sat down and she looked at me briefly with her vacant eyes and then looked away again. The three girls were all seated next to her, solemn-faced and perfectly turned out.

When Far and the boys had taken their places, Magnus Jevnaker went to the altar and the coffin was brought down the aisle. People were crying. I heard women stifling sobs and children sniffling, and some of the men were coughing.

163

Magnus began his sermon and asked us all to pray. I closed my eyes but didn't listen to the prayers, I just kept twisting the ring on my finger.

Magnus talked about Jacob but not as if he knew him. He could have been talking about any one of the boys in Utne and the whole sermon was full of inaccuracies. The only thing Magnus got right was the fact that Jacob had looked after Bestefar Jørgen all these years and was a devoted grandson, that he was. But he didn't mention anything about Jacob's sense of adventure, his wild storytelling, his bravery, or his humour. Instead he described an obedient boy who loved school and worked hard. *What do you know, Magnus Jevnaker?* What did any of them know?

I stayed seated through the hymns, wouldn't stand, wouldn't sing. Even old Jørgen got to his feet but I didn't move. Behind me, Hannah Jevnaker sang unnecessarily loudly as if she were trying to berate me.

There were more prayers and more hymns and I felt like the walls were closing in on me. I couldn't breathe. Finally, when it was all over, they took the coffin out to the churchyard and the bells began to ring again. I wanted to run from the church but I had to help Jørgen walk out. We came into the vestibule and everyone was looking at the two of us with pity and I tried not to meet their eyes.

Without turning, I could feel Hannah Jevnaker behind me again. She was moving slowly, her footsteps keeping time with mine. When we came to the front door, Mor Utne took Bestefar Jørgen's arm.

'Dear Jørgen,' she said, shaking her head, 'dear, dear, Jørgen,' then she looked at me but she couldn't say any more and covered her mouth with her hand.

I was just feeding Bestefar Jørgen's cane back into his hand when Hannah Jevnaker leaned over my shoulder and whispered in my ear. 'It should have been you,' she said, 'you dirty little thief. You killed your mother and now you've killed Jacob.'

I spun around. Hannah Jevnaker was taller than me but that didn't faze me. I reached up and lunged at her shoulders. She gasped as she stepped back, treading on Selma, who was standing behind her. Selma yelled. I shoved Hannah again, this time harder and she let out a scream. Everyone in the vestibule turned to see what the commotion was, but I didn't stop. I pushed Hannah again and again until she lost her balance and fell down at the feet of her mother, who was now staring at me, horrified.

'What in heaven's name...?' Lillian shrieked.

Hannah was squealing on the ground and Lillian quickly bent to help her up, affronted by the sight of her daughter rolling about on the church floor.

I went in to push her again as she struggled to her feet but Far and Jon came running from behind Lillian.

'Dagny, that's enough!' Far shouted.

'She just turned and pushed her,' Selma was saying, 'for no reason at all.'

'She's lost her mind,' Hannah sneered.

Far grabbed my arms and jostled me out. The entire congregation stared at us in shock.

Eugen Mohr was holding out his arms trying to shield us from view, but everyone was staring and whispering, almost unaware of the coffin being carried to the churchyard. Magnus Jevanker looked back in confusion, wondering why people weren't following on.

My brothers all gathered round but Far sent them away, told them to go and pay their respects. They peeled away from us and wandered after the coffin and, one by one, the rest of the congregation slowly drifted after them.

'Dagny, this has got to stop,' Far said, dragging me up the hill. 'You're angry and upset, but you can't keep hitting out at people like this. A girl like Hannah Jevnaker! What would you do that for? And of all days, today! Where's your respect?'

165

He flung me back into the house and told me to go and change and put my nice things away.

When I came down again he was sitting at the table with his head in his hands.

'Maybe I haven't known how to raise a girl,' he said, sensing me standing there, 'but in God's name, Dagny, this ain't right.'

I sat in the chair opposite him and he went to fetch some water. He sloshed it into a tin cup and slid it over to me. 'Drink,' he said.

I took a sip.

'You going to talk to me about this?' he said. 'I mean, I ain't a talker, but at some point, Dagny, you're going to have to speak.'

I looked into my cup, took another sip.

'I mean, I felt it...' Far said, '...when your mother...but I had you and the boys, I couldn't just...' He grabbed a clump of his own hair and pulled at it harshly. 'You can't just go crazy because they're gone.'

I pushed the cup away, left the table and climbed into the bed. I turned onto my side and faced the wall.

There was a gentle knock at the door and Far went to answer it.

'Yes, of course, come in, Sissel,' he said.

It was Doctor Helland's wife.

'The girl plainly needs something for those nerves,' she said, 'get some water on to boil, Lars, I brought teas.'

Sissel came to the bed and leaned over me. 'Dagny?' She put her hand on my arm and shook me gently. 'Dagny, dear, you must try...try to drink some tea.'

I rolled over. Sissel Helland was a severe lady with a harsh face and thin lips that wore a permanent frown, even when she wasn't angry. She was a practical woman who took no nonsense from anybody. 'Sit up, pet,' she said. She was still wearing her best clothes and the silver broach at her throat jingled as she patted my pillow. 'Now then,' she said,

166

'let me tell you this: for reasons known only to Him, the dear Lord has decided to take Jacob from us, God rest his soul,' she crossed herself, 'but you are still here, and you must live the life the Lord has given you. You understand?'

I touched Jacob's ring again and twisted it around my finger, thinking about his soul, restless like Emma's, and what could be done to pacify it.

'You must let us help you, dear,' Sissel said, 'you shut people out and you'll get lost in there,' she prodded at her temples, 'it's a dangerous place to be on your own.'

Far came with a teapot and Sissel emptied the contents of a muslin bag into the hot water. 'Make sure she drinks this four times a day,' she said, 'it's the strongest I've got.'

They let the chamomile steep and the fragrance of it bloomed on the air.

Far poured a cup full and handed it to me. 'Drink it, Dagny. It'll help.'

I took it reluctantly and held it in my lap, letting the heat of it burn my hands.

I didn't want Sissel's chamomile tea, didn't want any of them fussing around me. All I wanted was Jacob. I wanted him to come back to me and tell me stories. I wanted him to pinch my nose and tell me I was being such a girl. I wanted him to kiss me again and fill my entire body with his soul.

12

The summer dragged on. I drank Sissel's tea to keep Far happy and spent most of my days in bed, facing the wall. The visitors slowly ebbed away. I couldn't talk or engage with any of them and they ended up sitting there awkwardly, saying nothing either. After a while they stopped coming. Some would ask Lars to tell them when I started talking again making promises to return then, others simply didn't come back. There were a few exceptions, one of them was Hedda.

One afternoon, she brought a gift from Bestefar Jørgen. 'How are you, Dagny?' she said.

I was sitting up in bed. Far was out in the boat with Hans and Jon, and Knut was the only one home. His playing cards were scattered all over the bed, having tried again to tempt me into a game but eventually resigned himself to playing solitaire.

'Jørgen's worried about you,' Hedda said, sliding the cards away and sitting down beside me. 'He said he'd like a visit if you felt up to it?' She stroked my hand. 'He told me to give you this,' she said, handing me a book, 'it belonged to Jacob. It's his storybook.'

I took the book from her eagerly. The first thing I did was smell it. I held it to my face and fanned all the pages, breathing it in.

'Actually, it was originally Jacob's mother's,' Hedda said. 'Jørgen said he used to read those stories to her when she was a little girl.'

I brushed my fingers across the cover of the book then felt all the pages, knowing that Jacob's hands had held them too. On the cover was a picture of a princess sitting on a white bear. Her hair was so long and golden that it fell down her body and merged with the bear's white coat. Her crown was like a lily, perched on the top of her head, her eyes were downcast and she was holding a wreath in her hands. *Folk Tales*, it said, *by Asbjørnsen and Moe.*

Hedda watched me devouring it. 'Plenty of stories in there to keep you entertained,' she said.

I pressed the book to my chest and lowered my head. I wanted to thank her but I couldn't make a sound. I was too afraid to speak, even to Hedda. I could not fathom the layers of it, couldn't see then the crippling mix of guilt and fear and sadness and grief that kept my voice locked within me. I was holding on to Jacob with everything I had and in the process, I had swallowed my own voice.

'We all miss you, Dagny,' Hedda said, 'miss hearing that lovely voice of yours.'

I gazed down at the book.

'You let me know if you feel like visiting Jørgen and I will go with you if you like.'

She got up from the bed and asked me if I needed anything else. I shook my head.

When she had gone, I flicked through Jacob's book and found the story about the princess who was pictured on the cover. It was called *White Bear King Valemon* and it was about a princess who dreamed about having a golden wreath, which was so lovely that she couldn't live until she got it. I ran my finger along the page as I read and imagined the voice telling me the story was Jacob's. *But because she couldn't get the wreath, she began to pine and could not even speak for sorrow. One day, she caught sight of a white bear in the forest, which had the wreath she dreamed of in its paws. She wanted to buy it, but the wreath was not for sale, but the bear said he would let her have it in return for herself and so they agreed that he would fetch her in three days' time, which would be a Thursday.*

He took her to a castle where she was to live, and see to it that the fire never went out. The bear was away during the day but at night he was with her, and then he became a man. For three years all went well, but each year she had a child, which he took away from her as soon as it was born. So the princess became very sad and asked if she could go

169

home to see her parents, which Valemon allowed her to do, but he warned her to listen only to what her father said, but not what her mother wanted her to do. Her mother told her to bring a candle back to the castle so that she could see what the bear was like when he turned into a man at night, but her father said that would only do more harm than good. Nevertheless, the princess took the candle with her when she left and the first thing she did when Valemon had fallen asleep was light the candle and shine it on him. He was so handsome she thought her eyes would never tire of gazing at him.

I put the book down. My eyes were flooding with tears and the words had become obscured. I considered the possibility that Jacob hadn't died and had only turned into a white bear. If only I could find that bear, I could at least be with him at night when he became human again.

Knut interrupted my thoughts.

'Far said I should give you this,' he said, bringing me another cup of tea.

I waved it away.

'You've got to drink it, Dagny. They say it will help.' He put it down on the small table beside my bed. 'What you reading? Folktales? Did Hedda bring that?' He glanced at the cover. 'Oh, *White Bear King Valemon*. The one where the bear is a man cursed by a troll-hag? And the princess finds the cabins in the woods with the hungry children? And she feeds them with the magic cloth?'

I shook my head and glowered at him.

'Oh, you haven't got that far? Sorry.' He sat down at the end of the bed and picked up his cards again. 'It'll be harvest soon,' he said. 'I'm helping the Skarstads this year. Reckon it'll be a bumper crop, the fruit's already fallin' now. You want to come pickin' with me?'

I shook my head and returned to Jacob's book.

I finished the story. Knut was right. Valemon had been cursed by a troll-hag who wished to marry him herself, and the princess found him at the hag's castle after journeying through the forest and acquiring a magic cloth. She asked the troll-witch to let her sleep with the bear for three nights but the old hag gave him a sleeping potion so that he wouldn't wake up. On the third night, a worker at the castle told Valemon not to drink the potion and he only pretended to be asleep. He was reunited with the princess and together they disposed of the hag and then they retrieved their children from the forest and they lived happily ever after.

I closed my eyes. I couldn't imagine a happily ever after for me now, not ever. I couldn't even imagine a *happily*.

'You know it was actually quite funny,' Knut said, 'when you think about it.'

I opened my eyes again. He was still there on the bed.

'When you pushed Hannah, at the church. Lillian's still harping on about it. They're saying you're mad, Dagny, the Jevnakers.'

I slapped the book shut.

'But Lillian ain't doing nothin' about all that business with the telescope, not now. Whole town would never forgive her if she did, 'specially when it was Konrad who found you and saved your life. Did you really give it to him, Dagny? For fixin'? How did he manage to lose it then? I don't understand.'

I lay back on my pillows and stared at the ceiling until he stopped asking his questions and left me alone.

I must have slept. The next thing I remember, Far was home and sitting at the table again, talking to the boys. There was a smell of fish in the room.

'She might have a point though,' Far was saying. 'They said it was humane, not like those institutions you hear about. Dr Helland said he'd seen patients there make a full recovery.'

'How much is it,' Jon said, 'to send someone there?'

'A lot,' Far said, 'but that's where they've offered to help out.'

'Who have?' Hans said.

'The Jevnakers.'

171

'They've offered to pay for it?' Jon said.

'Well, because Dagny's been goin' there all this time, Lillian said she feels responsible and it would only be right if they helped her get treatment. But I don't like to take charity from church folk.'

'She's not mad though,' Knut said, leaping to my defense, which shocked me.

'No, I know that,' Far said, 'but it's the silence. She ain't talking at all, and how long has it been now? Too long. And there's the aggression. She has bouts of it. Keeps goin' for me for the slightest thing. She can't live her life like that, can she? Like an animal.'

I sat up in bed so that he knew I could hear him. 'You awake, Dagny?' he said. 'You want food?'

'Are you gonna tell her?' Jon whispered.

I looked from brother to brother.

'You have to tell her, Far,' Knut said, 'you can't just send her away.'

Far scuffed the top of Knut's head. 'I'm not just sending her away,' he said, coming over to me and handing me a plate with a slice of bread and a piece of fried cod. 'There now, Dagny, you tell me you don't want to go away and I won't send you.'

I glared at him.

'Tell me now,' Far said, 'say it! Say, *I don't want you to send me to the hospital in Odda*, and I won't take the money from Lillian and you'll stay right here.'

I jumped up to a kneeling position and Far stepped away from me with the plate, afraid I might attack him again.

My chest was pumping hard.

'I want you to get better,' Far said, softly, 'and this is your chance.' He rubbed his brow and then dragged his hand down his whole face to his chin. 'Teas ain't helpin' are they? Rest ain't helpin'. I ain't helpin'. What can I do, Dagny? Tell me what you want me to do?'

172

I rocked back and forth then twisted Jacob's ring round and round my finger.

'She doesn't want to go,' Knut said.

'Then tell me, Dagny!' Far shouted. 'Tell me that, for God's sake!'

I swallowed lumps of air, opening my mouth and then gulping back and shutting my lips again. I desperately wanted to speak but the fear prevented me from forming a single word. I blew out making shush-ing sounds in my cheeks, then I gave up in frustration, got out of bed and ran up the stairs to my cot.

Far came after me. He pulled the curtain aside and asked if he could come in. 'I don't want you to be frightened, Dagny,' he said, 'it might be just what you need. You'll get proper help to make you speak again. You'd be able to talk again. Don't you want that? What kind of a life would you have if you didn't talk?'

I lifted up the box that contained my mother's brooch and stroked my fingers across the lid. Far stared at me, his breath whistled in his nose as he waited for me to answer him.

'Maybe you're right,' he said, after a while, 'maybe I should go and ask Emma what she thinks, God rest her soul.'

He left me kneeling on the mattress with my mother's jewellery in my hands. I heard him leave the house. The door slammed and he stormed off to the church.

The next day I went and sat at Jacob's grave. It was late afternoon. Someone had laid fresh flowers; yellow roses arranged neatly in a glass bowl. I moved them to the side and huddled up to the wooden cross, curling up on top of the mound of earth. I leaned my head and shoulder against the cross and breathed against it as I slowly traced my finger around the letters of his name that they'd carved into it. *They want to send me away.* The wood was cold like the rocks on the

173

mountain and I felt the warmth of my own breath cloud about my face. I reached over and pulled a petal from one of the roses and spent so long ripping it into tiny pieces that its perfume began to cling to my fingers and fill the air all around me. I sprinkled the shredded petal over the mound of soil. *Far's lost his patience with me. Doesn't know what else to do.* I brushed my hands together as every last piece of rose petal fell, then I got back up and returned the bowl of flowers to the grave.

I didn't want to meet anyone and didn't want anyone to see me. I couldn't bear the way they all looked at me with such pity. They didn't know how it was, not really. I went up to the back of the graveyard, passing Emma's grave on my way. I brushed my fingertips across it. *Jacob's with you now.* I wondered if she already knew. Had she known the night that Far spoke to her in the church? When she had stayed at my bedside and I had told her that Jacob was my one true love?

I climbed over the wall and went back up the hill.

When I got home, I was horrified to find Lillian Jevnaker sitting at our kitchen table. She smiled at me when I came in. Her mouth curved upwards slightly but her eyes remained empty.

I stopped abruptly and stood there in the middle of the room, staring at her.

'Fru Jevnaker has come to talk to you, Dagny,' Far said, coming out of the kitchen, 'come and sit down.'

I knew it was a test. Lars was setting me up for a challenge.

'Hello dear,' Lillian said, curtly, 'how are you feeling?'

I turned for the stairs.

'Dagny,' Far snapped, 'I said come and sit down.'

I obeyed him.

'Now then,' Far said, 'the Jevnakers have kindly offered to help you, so what do you say, Dagny? Do you want to try this place in Odda?'

I looked from Far to Lillian. Far seemed certain the test was going to work.

'The care you would receive would be the best in all of Hardanger,' Lillian said, 'you can ask Doctor Helland.'

'You tell Fru Jevnaker, Dagny,' Far said, 'you tell her if you don't want to go.'

He knew I wanted to scream. I wanted to shout *NO! NO! NO!* so loud that the whole mountain would hear me. But I couldn't. My mouth opened but my lungs seemed to be pressed together as if there was no air left in them. I made the shush-ing sounds again in my cheeks but there was a terror inside me, a fear that had such intensity it wouldn't let me form words. I sucked at the air and filled my lungs again but no sounds came out. I couldn't physically use my voice.

'Tell her,' Far insisted, 'tell her if you don't want to go.'

Lillian looked at me and her eyes narrowed as she scrutinised my face. She could see the trap I was in. She knew I wouldn't say a word.

'It would appear Dagny is in favour of trying the therapy,' Lillian said, 'and quite right too, Dagny. I'm sure it will help.'

'Dagny?' Far said, 'Are you sure about that?'

'It's no trouble,' Lillian said, 'Magnus and I would be happy to help in any way we can.'

I grabbed the edge of the table and dug my nails into the wood. Far could see that I was about to pounce on Lillian Jevnaker and tear her hair out.

'Right then,' he said, 'it seems to be settled. Thank you, Lillian. We'll get her things together and have her ready to leave in the morning.'

Lillian gave me a hard stare and tapped her fingers against the tabletop before she left. 'Very good, Lars,' she said, 'we will meet you at the pier.'

When she'd gone, I threw my chair back and it hit the wall.

'You'll have to go,' Lars said. 'Unless you can calm down and start speaking to me, and show us you don't need any help, you'll have to go and see the doctors in Odda. You're giving me no choice, Dagny. You heard Lillian. We'll leave in the morning.'

I went to bed and faced the wall. The boys came back, they'd all been on the boat. Far clanged about in the kitchen and my brothers chattered, all of them talking at the same time.

'She definitely is,' Knut said.

'You're too young to know if she is or not.'

'I know what Truls tells me. She spends hours with Leonhard Steineger in the parlour with the doors *closed*.'

'Can't be true,' Hans scoffed.

'Peder *must* know then,' Jon said.

I cursed them for indulging in such gossip. Jacob was dead and I was being sent away. How dare they be interested in anything so trivial?

'It's all going on under his roof,' Knut said. 'He definitely knows.'

'All right, all right,' Far said. 'You're like a gang of old sailors. Quiet now. Dagny needs to rest. She's going tomorrow.'

'You're not sending her?' Knut said.

'She wouldn't tell Lillian she didn't want to go.'

'She doesn't have to,' Knut said, 'you know she doesn't want to go.'

'Enough!' Far shouted. 'She'll get the best care, the best treatment. They will help her there, so we have to try it.'

They all quietened down. My brother Jon came over to me and put his hand on my arm. 'Dagny? You sure you don't want to say somethin'? Not like you to hold your tongue when it comes to the Jevnakers.'

I hugged my knees up to my chest and locked my arms around them.

'Leave her be,' Lars said.

They stopped talking about Alma Skarstad and changed the subject to fishing but none of them seemed particularly interested in what they were saying, not even Far. I listened to them eat and talk and then clear their things away and tidy the kitchen, doing all the chores that used to be mine. Hans and Knut drifted away after a while, leaving Far and Jon talking in low voices in the armchairs. They didn't talk about me again, not that I heard.

In the middle of the night, when the house was finally still, I sneaked out of bed. I took Jacob's storybook and tucked it into my belt then crept over to the door as silently as I could, trying not to put my full weight on my feet. I avoided the two creakiest floorboards, picked up my boots and carefully unhooked the latch, sliding it in a controlled way, only a fraction at a time. I opened the door and quietly closed it again behind me.

At first I hardly moved. The stones would reveal me if I crunched them, so I inched along delicately until I was over the road and onto the grass at the other side. It was past midsummer now and the sky was darker at night. In the stillness of the shadows I ran down to the graveyard and sat with Jacob while I tied my boots.

I'm not going away to some hospital in Odda. I'm not goin' nowhere with Lillian Jevnaker. I pressed my hand against the cross and inhaled deeply, as if I was trying to draw some of Jacob's strength and fearlessness from it. I bent down and kissed his name, then I ran. I ran as fast as I could, past the Paulson's farm, over the bridge and up into the dark whispering pathways of the mountainside. The trees swallowed me into their arms and all around me were the sounds of the forest at night; the breeze crackling through the branches and night birds keeping watch. My feet pounded the earth as I jumped over roots and rocks and rushed through the grasses. I would have to climb the troll's stairs again. I had to climb them on my own, in the dark, before anyone found me.

INTERLUDE

There's a rush of activity out in the corridor. Voices are freed, no longer hushed, shouting out, emancipated. Kristian is looking at me incredulously, trying to piece my words together and make them fit into his reality. The thought of me, dying.

I've had one proposal of marriage before this, and there have been other men, but I am not good at relationships. I never meet the expectations placed upon me, never allow myself to return someone's love fully. The men in my past found me to be aloof and reticent, incapable of true love. And anyway, I had my work, my singing. I was hardly ever in the same place for long enough to settle down. I'm not housewife material. I'm like Nina in that respect.

What I have with Kristian is different. He makes space for me, like the orchestra to the piano. He sees me and allows me to be exactly who I am, making no demands, patiently fitting in to my unconventional life the way I want and need him to. I'm suddenly painfully aware of the fact that I might lose him too. I have been playing the same part in this relationship as I did with the others. It's all I know how to do. I have been taciturn, the Dagny *out there* for far too long.

'I will explain everything later,' my voice is encumbered with guilt, 'after the interval.'

It isn't long before the door swings open and people begin to filter in. Kristian and I wipe our faces, force smiles and pretend we are happy.

The first to enter is a tall handsome man in a finely tailored black suit. He's carrying a bottle of champagne.

'Well, you did it again, Dagny,' he says, striding over to me and planting the bottle on my dressing table, 'you did us proud!' It is my brother, Knut. He kisses my cheek. 'It was nice to see you in your Hardanger clothes again. Better than this thing,' he teases, ruffling the frills on my gown.

Knut's wife, Turid, follows behind him. 'You were spectacular, Dagny. Even King Håkon was crying, I'm sure I saw him wipe his eyes.'

'It's Grieg's music,' I say, 'it has that effect.'

'Don't be so modest,' Knut says, 'it's your voice, Dagny. It's your voice that does it.' He hunts about for some glasses and I leave him and Turid to reacquaint themselves with Kristian.

'You remember my brother?' I say, as other friends appear, people I have invited backstage for the interval. There are friends from the National Theatre in Christiania and people from the Royal Swedish Opera; singers, conductors, actors and musicians.

Kristian plays host to the guests and appears amiable and charming but he keeps looking at me with an agitated expression and every time I catch his eye I feel worse. It isn't a lie, not really.

Herr Hansson's round head appears at the door, sweat is beading on his brow. He looks over to me and I try to focus on his good eye. 'After the finale, you'll all line up on the red carpet.' He's told me this a hundred times. 'The royal guests will walk along the line. Curtsey, and don't speak to them before they speak to you, that's the protocol. After that, the motor cars will be waiting at the front door to take you to the reception. Yours is the third, Dagny. It's for you and Kristian and Nina. Where's Harriet? She does know all this, doesn't she?'

'Yes, Herr Hansson, undoubtedly,' I say.

'Good, good.' He smacks his hands together and dips out again.

I hear him talking to someone out in the passageway. I wait impatiently while they exchange pleasantries. 'Marvelous to have Miss Jensen here tonight,' Hansson is

179

saying, 'the king and queen requested her specifically, and she so encapsulates our nation, don't you think?'

'Yes, she does.'

'The Swedes had Jenny Lind and now we have Dagny Jensen. Everyone's calling her the new Nina Grieg. Your husband would have been delighted, I'm sure.'

'Unquestionably, he and Dagny were very close.'

There's a quiet tap at the open door and Nina is standing there smiling at me.

'Oh Dagny,' she says, reaching out her arms, 'Edvard would have been so proud of you.'

She is smaller than me, still petite and unassuming even in her satin evening gown. Her curly hair is white now but her eyes still twinkle mischievously. I bend down to embrace her.

'I wish he'd been here to see it,' I say.

'He would have been so pleased,' she says, squeezing my hands.

'He'd have been happier if you were singing out there.'

'Nonsense,' she says, shaking her head, 'I could not have done any better, my dear. You are simply captivating.'

'I'm trying to give them what they want,' I say, flustered.

'No need to try, Dagny. Just be yourself,' she rubs her thumbs across the top of my hands. 'Where's Kristian?' she says.

'Oh,' I glance across the room, 'he's with Knut.'

'Are you all right, my dear?' Nina says quietly, 'You seem a bit troubled. It's not the nerves, is it?'

'They must be getting the better of me,' I say.

'No need to be nervous, your voice is perfect tonight, simply perfect.'

'Well, I have you to thank for that,' I smile. 'It really should be you up there, Nina, not me.'

'No, no, it's not me they want to hear, it's Dagny Jensen, the Voice of Norway!' she grins.

'Gah! If I hear that one more time,' I shake my head with a smile.

Kristian is drinking champagne with Knut and Turid. I beckon him over.

'Look who's here,' I say.

'Fru Grieg,' he holds out his hand and kisses her on both cheeks, 'what a pleasure it is to see you again. We are all so proud of Grieg tonight. If only he'd been here to enjoy it.'

'He would have loved to hear Dagny sing,' she says, 'she brings his music so beautifully to life.'

'Not in the way you do,' I say.

'Oh, my voice isn't what it used to be. It hasn't been strong for many years,' Nina says.

'She is being modest,' I say, 'he only ever wanted Nina to sing his songs. She was the only one who could convey them and interpret them exactly as he wished them to sound. Did you know that Nina is the only soprano in the world who ever reduced Tchaikovsky to tears?'

'Did she, indeed?' Kristian says.

'He said her voice was a pool of sound that poured forth throughout the audience, and that he'd never met a better-informed or more highly cultivated woman.'

'Tchaikovsky said that?'

'He was flattering me,' Nina says. 'We had a mutual friend in Leipzig many years ago, Adolph Brodsky, the violinist. You remember Adolph, don't you Dagny? I would sing after dinner for their amusement. Edvard and Tchaikovsky were like kindred spirits. Each had such admiration for the other.'

'I wish I could have been at those dinner parties,' Kristian says.

'Yes, you could have played with Brodsky,' Nina says, 'he had a quartet.'

'With those geniuses in the room I would not have been able to play a single note,' Kristian says, 'I'd rather have hidden under the table.'

'Nonsense, you play very well,' Nina says.

'I'm afraid I should stick to banking, Fru Grieg, and the world of music will have to carry on without me.'

'Well it is all the poorer for it,' Nina says, 'I would love to hear you play again.'

Herr Hansson returns. He is pulling a watch from his pocket. 'Curtain up in five minutes. Everyone back to their seats please!'

Slowly the dressing room begins to clear amid kisses and smiles and words of commendation from my guests.

'I'll see you out there,' Nina says, stroking my arm as she leaves. 'You will be wonderful. Enjoy it, Dagny, no nerves, all right? Edvard never meant for you to be scared of his music.' She gives me a smile and I want to hold her and keep her with me so that I don't have to face Kristian alone.

Knut hugs me. 'Thanks for organising the tickets,' he says, 'what a night it has been! We won't forget it. You probably don't have time to see us later, all the dignitaries will want to talk to you and we wouldn't want to keep the king waiting, would we? My own sister, singing for the king,' he laughs, 'I still can't believe it.'

I hold him for longer than I expected to. 'I'll see you tomorrow,' I say, 'before you go back to Utne.'

They all float out, leaving Kristian and me alone again.

'You've never taken me to Utne,' Kristian says.

'You've never asked me to take you.'

'When was the last time you were there?'

'Oh, years ago. My father's funeral.' Lars was buried beside Emma in the graveyard on the hill, reunited with the wife he had loved and lost. I realise I have missed him tonight and I wonder what he would have made of all this. He's probably rolling his eyes at the mess I have made for myself. *You'll lose it all if you're not careful. Marry that man, and tell him the truth.*

'You should sit down, dear,' Kristian says. He drapes his hand around my shoulder.

'I have to go on again soon.'

'I will wait,' he says.

'No, you go out and enjoy it. I got you a front row seat, didn't I? Ellen will be in soon. She needs to fit my wig.'

'Yes,' he says, 'I'll go and find her for you.'

He kisses me lightly, still confused about where we stand and what is happening to me.

'We will talk later,' I say, 'I promise.'

'But will you be all right?'

'Yes dear, I'm fine.'

I watch him leave and feel a needle pricking my conscience. I have a task ahead of me. There is no way around it. It makes me think of Peer Gynt and the Bøyg, the character who is never seen but only heard, the shapeless monster that is Peer's self-outside-of-himself, the thing that tells him always to avoid, to go around, to beat about the bush. But at some point, we all must face ourselves and come to terms with this alternate identity we have. Dagny *in here*. Dagny *out there*.

It occurs to me that only women singing were able to defeat the Bøyg. Women's voices and church bells.

13

I faced the wall of rock. In the early hours of the morning it was difficult to see the crags and footholds but I pulled myself up and began to feel my way across the boulders. Jacob's book was knotted in my belt. I had tied a double loop around it. I wasn't going to lose it like I lost the telescope, which was here, hiding somewhere on the troll's stairs. I hated the blasted thing. If Jacob hadn't tried to retrieve it, he wouldn't have hurt his knee, and if he hadn't hurt his knee...I shook my head to stop myself from thinking about it and instead focused on the climb.

I balanced on the thin ledge and fumbled, searching with my fingers to find the best hold. The stones were cold and dark, and a chill breeze was blowing across the face of the rocks. I twisted my head from side to side, tested the holds, supported myself, and slowly moved upwards. I followed the same pattern I had followed with Jacob, reaching, holding, stepping. Soon I was climbing so briskly it was as though Jacob was there, hauling me up. *Relax your body, make it go soft.* I wasn't afraid of the troll's stairs anymore, even now, alone in the night. If I fell, I would be with him, and that made me fearless.

I quickened my pace, wondering whether Far had awoken yet and found me gone. It was still early but Lars had not slept soundly since the accident. He seemed almost as unsettled as I was. I often heard him pacing at night. The way he looked at me, with his finger hooked around his chin. I was the recurring puzzle he needed to solve. It must have plagued him even in his dreams. Now he'd given up trying to find the answer and he was letting Lillian Jevnaker take me off to an asylum.

The rocks levelled out and soon I was able to stand but the flatter terrain was harder to cross because I wasn't able to grab it with my hands. I tripped and stumbled, staggering over the uneven rocks and boulders, hurting my toes and ankles. Twice I fell and twice Jacob's book protected me from the jabbing stones that protruded from the ground.

When I finally got to the other side of the plateau, I stopped at the top of the ravine and stared down the mountainside with a feeling of disorientation. I couldn't see the cabin. In the semi-darkness, I couldn't find its walls and without the smoke rising up from the chimney there were no clues as to its whereabouts. I crouched down and scanned the valley, looking through the trees until I found a change in the shape of the mountainside, something manmade. It was the white paint at the windows that finally gave it away. There it was, hiding amongst the trees. I sank to the ground and wriggled my way down the hill, digging my heels in to break my slide.

I crunched twigs and swept my hands through the scree as I descended, sending small pebbles rolling off to the sides. I kept skidding until the ground evened out and there wasn't enough of a slope to propel me, then I got to my feet and ran to the cabin.

I threw myself at the door and hammered it with my fists. I tried to turn the handle but it was locked. I banged against the wood then moved around to the window and knocked hard against the glass. It seemed as though the cabin was deserted. There was no candlelight, no fire, no singing, no music.

I pummeled the timber again, this time more frantically. I felt my way around the side then the back and the other side, beating my fists against the walls as I went. I returned to the front door and kicked at it with the heel of my boot.

It was the sharp thud of my foot that woke her. I heard the sound of footsteps and then saw the orange glow of candlelight at the window.

'Who's there?' Nina shouted.

I knocked at the door again.

'Who is it?' she said.

This time I tapped gently so as not to frighten her.

Three taps. *Let. Me. In.*

I heard the rattle of the key in the door and the clunking thud as the door unlocked. The handle turned and Nina pulled the door open. Her eyes fell on me.

'Dagny?' she said, 'Dagny? Is that you?'

She was wearing a white nightgown and had a shawl draped around her shoulders. She came forward and reached out with both her arms. 'Dagny, dear,' she said, 'what are you doing here? At this time of night? Are you alone?' She pulled me inside and closed the door. 'Where's Jacob?' she said, searching for him. Then she pulled me hard into her arms. She could see on my face this was no wild adventure.

I shivered in her arms and she held me to her chest. 'You're cold, love.'

Without asking any more questions, she took her shawl from her shoulders and wrapped it around me, then she ushered me into the rocking chair and started gathering kindling and logs. She brushed away the ashes from the hearth and shoveled them into the pail, then lit a stack of sticks and blew on it to get it going. She layered the logs on carefully, giving each one enough time to burn before adding the next. Slowly the fire began to grow.

I sat in the chair and watched the flames lick the logs and listened to the soft hissing of the wood.

There were footsteps in the other room, the door squeaked on its hinges.

'What's all the commotion?' Herr Grieg said, appearing in the doorway holding a candle up in front of his face. He was rubbing his eyes.

'Edvard, it's Dagny,' Nina said.

'Lord, child,' he said, coming closer, 'have you climbed up here in the middle of the night? Where's the young man?' He looked about the room. 'Where's Jacob?'

'Jacob's not here, she's on her own,' Nina said.

'Has something happened?' Grieg said, holding his candle to my face. I glanced at him. His hair was an untamed mess of waves but his moustache was neatly trimmed. 'Well, tell us child?'

'Edvard, leave her.'

'If she's in trouble, we can't help her unless she tells us what it is,' he said, looking at me in the same way Lars did, as though I was a puzzle to solve.

Nina knew something serious had happened. She could tell by the look on my face, and the fact I wasn't talking.

'Go back to bed, Edvard,' she said, 'I will sit with her.'

She fetched a blanket and covered me, and continued to poke at the fire until it lit my face and made my cheeks glow. I lowered my chin and pulled Nina's shawl tighter around my shoulders. I shifted my weight, made the chair rock.

Nina piled more logs onto the fire.

Herr Grieg muttered something to himself as he turned and left.

'Don't mind him, Dagny,' Nina said, brushing my brow with the back of her hand.

'You look as if you should get some sleep. You can talk to me in the morning.'

She bolted the front door again and curled herself into the armchair on the other side of the room. I listened to the crackle and pop of the fire as Nina silently watched over me.

Gradually, I drifted into dreams.

There were voices, then the voices became notes on a piano. I was climbing again. There were rocks and waterfalls and a raven flying overhead. My dreams were of music. The images and events I saw were so intricately woven together with the tune I heard that the notes became living things; they were people, they were trees and mountains and rolling waves. They were a princess and a white bear, and a fiddler playing beneath a flume of water. Then the images began to fade and the notes became emotions whirling around me. At first they were calm and soothing, then they became disjointed and agitated, then they swelled into the highest trilling runs and became as soft as love, the gentle caress of fingertips. This lasted for a long time and I was wrapped up in a blissful state of peacefulness, but then the music changed. It sounded out like a horn as if to herald something coming. The notes turned to sadness, as raw as a wound. Mournful and aching. It grew, with the melody repeating like questions, building angrily, demanding an answer, then exhausting itself and finding its way back to sadness again. It was a sadness that burrowed into my chest and swam throughout my body, permeating every limb and organ. Sadness. Soul deep. It wallowed there, pitying itself and every creature capable of love. It seemed to know the sharp sting of loss, and the endless aching lament that remained when love was gone.

I woke up frightened, displaced. I didn't know where I was. Then Nina was there with a warm drink, and there was music playing in the other room.

'You've had a long sleep, dear,' Nina said.

I yawned and took the milky drink from her.

Something was cooking on the stove.

'Do you want a pancake? Edvard takes his break soon.'

The music from my dreams was calling to me through the wall, sadness echoing in circles, notes chasing after each other up and down the keyboard.

'He's very busy, buries himself in work.' Nina flipped the pancake on the grill and slid it onto a plate for me with a dollop of jam and sour cream. 'Eat something, Dagny.'

I tore pieces from the pancake. It was light and fluffy and sweet and melted on my tongue. I sipped the milky drink which tasted of malt and cocoa.

'Dearest,' Nina began, 'do you want to try to tell me what has happened?'

I took another sip and Nina waited expectantly as I cleared my throat. She pulled up a chair opposite me and leaned forward to give me all her attention. But when I didn't say anything, she retreated again and poked at the fire.

'I did wonder what happened that day,' she said, 'the day after Jacob's birthday. I had everything ready – a feast of waffles and blueberry juice. We waited up late but you never came. Did something happen, Dagny? It's just that Jacob was so determined, you were to have your little party here. I was even going to sing for you,' she smiled.

My eyes must have changed then because as soon as she looked at me, she stopped talking. She studied my face, trying to find the answers she needed.

'Something has happened, hasn't it?' she said.

I closed my eyes with a brief nod.

'Dagny, no. Has something happened to Jacob?'

When I opened my eyes again they were filled with tears and my body seemed to be eroding from the inside. The sadness of the notes from my dream were festering there like the symptoms of a disease.

'My dear,' Nina said, taking my hand. 'He isn't...?'

I nodded again and she covered her mouth with her hand. 'No,' she choked, her throat closing in anguish, 'but he can't be.'

Just then the music stopped. Herr Grieg came in. His fingers were clasped together and he was stretching them out in front of him. When he saw Nina's face, his hands dropped to his sides.

'What is it?' he said, quietly.

'It's Jacob, Edvard,' Nina, said, 'he's...I mean, something happened to him.'

'Something serious?' Herr Grieg said, coming over to the fire and sitting down beside us.

Nina nodded into her hand.

'Oh, goodness...I'm so sorry,' he said, '...but, how?'

Nina shook her head. 'I don't know. Dagny can't say.'

Edvard looked down at his fingers. 'No, words often won't say it, will they?'

The three of us gazed into the flames. Nina was crying heavily. It was as if the thought of losing Jacob had opened the door to another part of her, a place like mine, in the depths of her body where a never-ending sadness lurked. Edvard placed his hand on her back. 'There there,' he said. 'There there.' He turned to me again. 'He was a fine young fellow,' he said, wistfully.

Silence engulfed us.

After a while, I closed my eyes again. I heard Nina clearing things away and sniffing to herself. Then I heard Grieg whispering to her. 'She still hasn't said anything?' Nina must have shaken her head. 'Not a single word?'

'She's too distraught,' Nina said. 'Let her sleep. We will try again later.'

This cycle repeated itself several times: I slept and music haunted my dreams, I awoke, Nina fed me and they tried to talk to me again. *How did it happen? When did it happen? Was it an accident or did he get sick? When was the funeral? Tell us dearest, please, so that we can help you.*

Day turned to night again and night turned to day. Then Herr Grieg started getting agitated by my presence. 'What about her family?' I heard him saying. 'It's been three days now. They must be wondering where she is?'

'Let her sleep, Edvard. She needs to rest.'

'But she can't stay here forever, can she?'

'She can stay as long as she likes, as long as she needs to.'

'What if they don't know where she is?' he said. 'You can't hide her here without telling them.'

'She can *stay*, that's what I said.'

'Nina,' Grieg said, 'just because...well, you can't simply...it won't change anything.'

'She needs our help, Edvard. Can't you see that?'

'I'm just saying they need to be told, that's all.'

This conversation happened as often as the music.

One morning I woke up to find them both sitting at the table, their heads lowered in discussion. When Nina saw that I was awake, they invited me over to sit with them.

'You know, Dagny,' Nina said, 'you are welcome to stay here with us as long as you need to, dear.' She fidgeted with her lace cuffs.

'But,' Grieg cut in, 'we need to tell your father that you're here.'

I glowered at him.

'They'll all be worried about you,' he said, 'and what kind of people would we be to keep you here without telling them?'

I shook my head and started to stamp my feet.

'Edvard is right, dear,' Nina said. 'I will go down to Jåstad in the morning and get the farmer there to take me to Utne. I will have to tell your father where you are.'

I banged my fists on the table.

'What, dear?' she said. 'What is it that's so terrible about that?'

I opened my mouth and wheezed and gasped, then bit at the air, then pressed my lips together again. I couldn't say *Lillian Jevnaker*. I couldn't say *lunatic asylum*. I couldn't even say *Odda*.

'It isn't right for us to let you stay here unless your father knows about it,' Herr Grieg said. 'We can't keep you here without the consent of your father. It's as simple as that.'

I started to thump at my own temples.

'Dagny, dear,' Nina said, swiveling in her chair. 'Don't do that, my dear, you'll hurt yourself.'

I carried on punching at my skull, trying to block out the fear and find the courage to speak.

Grieg sprang to his feet and grabbed my arms. 'Dagny,' he said, sternly, 'stop it!'

'Come on, Dagny,' Nina said, 'calm down, dear.'

Herr Grieg was not a strong man, not like Far, but he pinned my arms down by my sides nonetheless and Nina wrapped her arms around my shoulders and pulled me into an embrace. 'It's all right, sweetheart. It's all right,' she kept saying.

Eventually, my frustration broke into a flood of tears and I sobbed against Nina's chest until all the strength had drained from me and Grieg let go of my arms.

I wondered what would happen to me. When Nina told Lars I was here, he would come and take me away and hand me over to Lillian Jevnaker who would see to it I was locked up and left to rot in Odda. I needed to learn how to speak again, but the fear and the guilt and the festering sadness simply wouldn't allow it. I didn't know how.

I ran back to the rocking chair and picked up Jacob's book. I took it to Nina and put it on the table. Flicking through it, I found the words I needed to say, the words I couldn't speak, and pointed to them. *Do.not.tell.him.I.am.here.*

'She's scared of something, Edvard,' Nina said, looking past me to Grieg, who sighed, although he wasn't defeated.

'Then at least tell him she's safe.'

The following morning, Nina went early and I was left alone in the cabin with Herr Grieg. He was a grumpy mumbling man who often seemed detached. Clearly uncomfortable being alone with me, he didn't speak to me at the breakfast table but when he retreated to his music room he looked at me and said, 'I have to work now. No disturbances, all right?'

I went back to the rocking chair by the fire. I flipped through Jacob's book and found the story he had started telling me about the boy called Freddie who had been given three wishes, made the sheriff dance with his enchanted fiddle and been sentenced to death. I read the story all the way through. One of Freddie's wishes was that no one would ever be able to refuse him the first thing he asked for. When he came to the gallows, he asked if he could be allowed to play one last tune on his fiddle before they hanged him. The sheriff begged them not to let him pluck a string, or else it would be the end of them all, but Freddie played and they all began to dance: deacon and parson, clerk and bailiff, sheriff and hangman. They danced and laughed and shrieked, some even danced until they lay stretched out as if they were dead. The sheriff danced next to a birch tree and rubbed patches of skin off his back, but no one thought to do anything to little Freddie and he could go wherever he wished with his fiddle and he lived happily the rest of his days.

There was an illustration of Freddie sitting at the top of the ladder leading up to the gallows, playing his fiddle as everyone below danced uncontrollably, hats and canes and shoes flying everywhere. I smiled. Jacob would have laughed. I put my finger on the boy playing the fiddle. As I touched the image a burst of music came from Grieg's room. It was like a warning, a panicked shouting sound. *Don't touch! Don't touch!* My finger jumped off the page and I turned to face the door with my heart beating hard. Then the music seemed to apologise. It slowed into a low rolling surge. I closed my eyes and tried to picture Herr Grieg's hands on the keys. The lower notes were rumbling in waves but there was one higher note that continued to sound, chiming like a bell. I tuned in to its rhythm, found myself swaying gently back and forth. This continued for a few minutes then suddenly it shouted out again, *don't touch! Don't touch!* I jumped out of my seat. Then I heard Herr Grieg shouting 'Damn it! Damn it!' and he threw something against the door. Then there was silence.

My curiosity was aroused. I wondered what was going on in there, how he could be having such an intense argument with no one but himself? I crept over to the door and pressed my ear up to it. There was a sniff, a slight cough and a tapping sound. I heard another snivel and then a choked gasp, then silence again. Was Herr Grieg *crying*?

He wasn't to be disturbed, but before I knew what I was doing, my hand was turning the door handle. I poked my head around the door. Grieg was slumped at the piano. His shoulders were shaking slightly. His fingers were thrumming against the lid of the piano and his wild mess of hair was hanging down in his face. I saw a pencil on the floor and picked it up. I crept towards him and he only became aware of me when I reached his shoulder.

Before he had a chance to berate me for having interrupted, I held the pencil out to him. He nodded his head and wiped his eyes and nose with his sleeve. He took the pencil and rested it on the ledge where his manuscript sat. I looked at all the scrawling notes that danced up and down the bars. There were crosses and errors, things blacked out, notes written everywhere.

'No need for the pencil,' he said, shaking his head. 'I'm not writing. The notes won't come.'

Hesitantly, I reached out and placed my fingertips on the keys, which seemed to be calling me to touch them. The ivory was cool and smooth beneath my fingers. I tried to think of the piece of music Jacob had wanted Herr Grieg to play for me, for our wedding. It was fast and lively and made a *pom-pom pom-pom* sound. I looked at Grieg, his face was pale and his eyes were heavy, the lids drooping and weary.

I dared to press the keys. *Pom-pom!*

Grieg looked at me, surprised, and I did it again, this time more urgently. *Pom-pom!*

At first, Herr Grieg was confused. I'd hit four high notes all at the same time and there was no tune to the sound that came out, just a high-pitched discord. But I repeated the rhythm of it. *Pom-pom! Pom-pom!* I looked at him and kept repeating it. *Pom-pom, pom-pom, pom-pom-poooom.*

Grieg returned his fingers to the keyboard. 'The Hall of the Mountain King,' he said, putting his left hand over the low notes and playing two of them, low and menacing. Then he played the melody with his right hand and the piece began to build. Something was creeping up on us and Grieg's fingers were bringing it closer. *Pom-pom, pom-pom, Pom-pom-poooom.*

He played it as he had before, with his face contorting and his teeth biting into his lip. His foot pressed down on the pedal as his playing became more intense. Then he stopped abruptly in the same place he stopped the last time, and he let out a sigh of frustration as the notes continued to resound around the room.

'And you two said that *I* was the Dovregubben,' he wiped his brow with the back of his hand. 'Perhaps I am, Dagny,' he said, 'perhaps I am...'

14

Nina did not return until late in the evening. I was tucked into the chair with a blanket over my knees. Grieg was at the table, writing in the dim light. Nina looked exhausted. Her curly hair had flattened against her head and she was moving slowly, as though every bone in her body radiated pain. She saw me looking at her when she came in and she nodded before taking her boots off. 'I didn't tell him,' she said, straightening up and clutching her back, 'only that you were safe, that was all.'

I felt a sudden twinge of guilt and regret, imagined Lars pacing the floor at night wondering why I didn't talk anymore. Far and I had never talked about our feelings. He barely knew I had any until Jacob died. Even then, he must have thought I was being willful and petulant. He couldn't have known the reason why I kept erupting with anger and acting out. I hardly understood it myself. Nor could he have known where I had gone or how he would get me back. Looking at Nina, it was like being on the outside of myself, seeing for the first time what it might be like for Far to be the one at home, the one responsible for me, trying to know what to do for the best.

'What did he say?' Grieg said, getting up from the table.

'He asked me how I knew she was all right,' Nina said, coming into the room and taking a chair by the fire.

'And?'

'And I said that I had seen her and I knew where she was, but that I couldn't tell him any more than that. Just that she was safe.'

'Didn't he want her back?' Grieg said, without looking at me.

'Of course he wants her back,' Nina said, 'but it seemed like it was enough for now to know that she was alive.'

'How did you find him?'

'The lady at the hotel told me where the house was.'

'Did you tell them who you were?' Grieg said.

'Oh don't worry, Edvard,' Nina said, bitterly, 'no one knows you are here.'

He picked up the poker and stabbed it into the fire, then he bent down and blew on the charcoal until it blazed and spat itself back to life.

'There was a letter from Hanchen waiting for me, down at the farm,' Nina said.

'Oh,' Grieg said, 'what news does she have?'

'She sent me some vocal exercises to try. But what use do I have for them stuck up here in this cabin with you?'

'What do you mean?' he said.

Nina looked at me and rolled her eyes, as if I was implicit in this tirade, as if I understood her inferences. 'I have no audience anymore,' she said, 'there's no one to sing to up here, is there? I don't even have any students to teach.'

'Nina, we agreed that we would come here for–'

'Yes, yes, yes,' she said, her mouth turning an ugly shape, 'we'd come to give you the peace you needed to compose, so that you could complete the music for Ibsen's play...so that you'd find...*yourself* again. But what about me?' she said, 'am I to lose myself while you find yourself?'

'Nina,' Grieg sighed.

'I have no one here, Edvard,' she said, 'no friends, no social life. I've lost everything I had in the city.'

'Is it friends you miss, or is it family?' he said, glaring at her, '*My* family...my brother?'

'Oh, don't bore me with that again,' she said, 'I won't rise to it. And you are a fine one to talk.'

'Just because John has children,' Grieg said, 'is that it? Six healthy children?'

'Stop it.'

'Both of my parents were *dying*, Nina. To think that you and John...under the same roof.'

197

'Stop it!' she shouted. 'You were away every day at Elsero. John and Marie were very kind to me. We were the ones who cared for your parents while you were gone, while you were *finding yourself* at the pavilion. Who else did you find out there, Edvard? Was Miss Schjelderup there?'

As their voices rose, I pulled the blanket up to my neck and drew my knees in closer to my chest. I was alone, disconnected from everything, isolated inside myself. I was used to Far shouting. When he shouted there was no bitterness in it, it was just his way. He was rough and coarse, barked and roared to instill some fear and ensure we obeyed him. The tension between the Griegs was worse. It was brimming with spite and resentment, as though they each blamed the other for a terrible thing that had happened and this thing, whatever it was, had driven a wedge between them that could never be removed.

'How can you make such accusations?' Grieg was saying, 'I was on my own. I had to play. I had to compose. I have to find a way to earn a living.'

'You ignored us all: me, John, Marie, your sisters, your parents. All you cared about was yourself. And now you are doing it again. You are turning your back on everything meaningful in pursuit of this ravenous self-indulgence.'

'So you don't want me to compose? To follow my life's purpose? You don't think that is meaningful?'

'Not if it must be done at the expense of your family.'

'I cannot talk to you,' Grieg said, throwing the poker into the fire. 'I thought that you understood. I thought you were the *only* one who understood, the only one who could interpret my music, the only one who knew how deeply I felt about my art. I thought you were my very soul, Nina!' He stared at her and all the anguish in his eyes frightened me. He marched away to the music room and slammed the door.

Nina tucked her feet up into the chair and sat there looking at the fire. I looked at it too, wondering if she could see some kind of an answer in the flames, some consolation that told her she had been right to challenge him.

'I told you it was a curse sometimes,' she said, after a while, confiding in me as if I were her friend, Hanchen.

I lowered the blanket to my waist. Grieg was playing the piano.

'Back to his music,' Nina said. 'I swear that's the only way that man can talk.'

Four notes sounded out, melancholic and spiritless. They made me feel abandoned, as though everything I had ever known was leaving me. I closed my eyes.

The four notes were repeating like a question. *Are you still there? Are you still there?* A flurry of higher notes came as if to bring more urgency, showing a memory of what the question was looking for. *Are you still there?* It changed key. A voice changing tone. Now serious, demanding: *are you still there?* Now quiet and calm: *are you still there?* Lighter, smaller notes, rushing, fluttering, *help help help*, notes so numerous and intricate it seemed that a thousand fingers were playing them. There was a gentle slowing and breathing, then a sudden rush of loud heavy notes. Anger. But always the question, the question repeating again and again. *Are you still there?*

The following morning the summer died. I woke up cold, my nostrils feeling the chill of the air as I inhaled. Nina was sleeping in the chair beside me. I wrapped my blanket about my shoulders and crept over to the fire. I brushed out the ashes and cleared away the mess; black lumps of charcoal the fire had coughed out, small knobs of wood that had refused to burn. I swept it all into the pail and stacked some kindling and fresh logs in the hearth. When I lit it, it began to hiss and pop. The noise woke Nina.

'Oh, Dagny, it's you,' she said. 'Have I been here all night?' She sat up in the chair, uncurled her legs and stretched them out. She yawned and rubbed her eyes as the

199

memory of the previous night returned and she remembered why she had not gone to her own bed. She got up without saying anything else and went about her morning activities in a perfunctory way: going out to fetch the water, splashing her face, setting the pot on to boil, making the coffee, slicing the bread. When Grieg came down, he brought with him an icy silence. They did not speak. Cups and plates were banged against the tabletop. Herr Grieg buttered his bread and took it with him to the music room. Nina read and re-read the letter she had received from her friend the day before. She did not engage with me or ask me any questions. I nibbled at a slice of bread then dressed hurriedly in front of the fire. I decided to go outside.

Until now, I had only been out to use the outhouse at the back of the cabin. I had been so terrified of moving, being found and being sent away, that I had hidden myself inside. Without Jacob, I had not wanted to look at the world, or at least what was left of it now that he was gone. I had focused all of my concentration inwards and withdrawn so deeply into myself that I had almost forgotten that anything existed beyond my own sadness. I was trapped within myself and couldn't feel safe outside the confines of my own body. But with the palpable tension that was growing between Nina and Grieg, I felt the need to get out. I craved wide open space. I had to reacquaint myself with the mountain that had taken Jacob from me.

There was a nip in the air and some of the birch leaves had fallen. I walked down the hill until I could see the valley dipping down to Jåstad and the fjord beyond. This side of the mountain was different to ours. The slope was gentler and a wide track led down to the farms below. I wondered how the Griegs had managed to get all their furniture up this high, especially Herr Grieg's piano. It must have taken a team of men and horses to drag it all up.

I trampled over twigs and stones and ran through the trees. Falling leaves brushed against my face and slid beneath my feet. The air was crisp and sharp; it had bitten the summer away and now it would only get colder. Mother was precise with her changes. She knew when it was time for things to move on. Everything succumbed to her wishes, without fail. It had no choice.

Soon I had gone too far. I wasn't familiar with this side of the mountain and I was scared I'd get lost. I turned back and headed up the track seeking out the familiarity of the cabin and the steep ravine. When I reached the top, I stood outside Herr Grieg's window and listened. There was no music, no song. Nothing but an eerie silence. I walked past the front door avoiding going back to the resentment that was simmering inside.

A crow cawed above me and I lifted my head towards the ravine. Looking up, I thought I saw a figure standing at the top, on the edge of the plateau. I raised my hand to shield my eyes from the sun. Somebody *was* up there. It was a boy. He was hovering at the edge, looking down at me.

I ran past the cabin and scrambled up the hill, stopping after a few paces to look for him again. The boy was stepping back now, moving away from the edge. I caught only his dark clothing. I didn't see his face.

I climbed higher, slipping on the loose stones as my feet dug into the shale. I reached for ropey roots and coarse shrubs, grabbing onto whatever I could to steady myself. I looked up again and scanned the edge of the plateau but the boy was gone.

I threw myself at the mountainside and clawed at it with my hands and feet, scurrying up the rocks like an animal, hurting my hands and soiling my clothes. When I got to the big boulders where the plateau evened out, I pulled myself up and scoured the landscape. There was nobody there. I started running back over towards the troll's stairs. No one else ever came up this high and Jacob was the only boy who had been brave enough to climb the rocks. I looked all around me, desperate to find a clue, but there was nothing. The boy had vanished.

When I came to the neck of the troll's stairs, I flung myself to the ground and eased myself over the edge to look down. Still I saw no one. The rocks beveled out, concealing the mountain below. All I could see were the treetops and the glimmering yellow leaves which soon would fall. Down the valley, Utne was hiding beyond the trees. It beckoned me: Far and the boys, Hedda, Mor Utne, Konrad and Mathilde, the life I had known before I lost Jacob. It seemed so far away, not just down the mountainside but in a different world, somewhere beyond the mountains and the sky.

I picked myself up and wandered back across the plateau and sat down on a rock. Soon my legs became cold and numb so I moved to another rock. I stared up at the sky and watched the changing shape of the clouds. I plodded about, picking up stones, casting them into the distance, looking back towards the troll's stairs then back towards the cabin, as though I was caught between two worlds.

I was hungry. The day had shifted around me. I could tell by the position of the sun that it was early afternoon. I searched again for the boy, checked the troll's stairs, searched the plateau, even looked up towards the peak of the mountain but there was no one else there. I was alone. I decided to go back to the cabin, still thinking about the boy I had seen. I was confused, couldn't find an explanation. The more I thought about it, the more afraid I became. I felt a presence then, as if someone was following me and I started running.

I came flying through the front door. Nina was sitting in the chair. Grieg was over at the table with his back to her. The hostility between them was palpable. Silent accusations and needles of blame hurtled through the air in a venomous crossfire.

'Dagny?' Nina said, as I thundered in, 'Where have you been, I was worried.'

I ran past her and past Grieg at the table.

'What?' Grieg said, 'You can't just...what's she doing?'

I opened the door to his music room and let myself in. Nina and Grieg came hurrying after me.

'What is it, Dagny?' Nina said.

I picked up the manuscript that was sitting on the piano and swiped the pencil from the ledge. I wrote the word firm and hard.

G.H.O.S.T.!

I pointed up to the mountain and tapped the pencil against the paper.

'She's having delusions,' Grieg said, 'she's upset.'

'Did you see him?' Nina said, looking at Grieg with a worried expression. 'Do you think you saw him, love?'

I nodded firmly and pointed back up towards the plateau. I started shaking.

Nina looked at Grieg again with that horrible expression on her face. 'Oh God,' she said, holding her hand to her throat. 'No, dearest,' she said, reaching out for me, 'it wasn't. It can't have been.'

I stabbed at the paper and shrugged her away.

My throat was making a choking sound and I gasped for air as I hit the paper.

G.H.O.S.T.S.? I wrote. *G.H.O.S.T.S.?*

Grieg held out his hand as if to ask for his manuscript back but I pressed it to my chest and shook my head.

'That's my work,' he said, 'it's important.'

I scowled at him.

'Leave her!' Nina shouted. 'Have you no heart? Do you not remember how it was with Alexandra?'

I held the manuscript up to them both again and thrust the pencil at it.

'No dear,' Nina said, gently, 'he's gone, love, he's gone. There are no ghosts.'

I jabbed my hand into the air and glared at them. They didn't believe me but I had seen a boy. I knew I had.

'You have to let him go, dear,' Nina said.

Their refusal to listen turned my fear to anger. I threw the manuscript and the pencil down on the floor and turned to the piano. I sank my fingers down on the keys and made loud chiming sounds, high notes and low notes, black notes and white notes. I banged and banged, thumping at the keyboard in frustration.

'Dagny, Dagny, that's enough,' Nina said. She tried to take my wrists but I shoved her away. I kept thumping at the piano, making every blow louder and more aggressive until the noise filled the room and filled my head and drowned out all the thoughts that taunted and terrified me.

Eventually, Grieg's hand came to rest on my shoulder. 'I understand,' he said, 'I understand.' He gently coaxed me to the piano stool and came to sit down beside me. 'I understand,' he kept saying, without any further explanation.

He calmly took my hand and placed it deliberately on the keys, spreading my fingers out and placing them on three specific notes. 'Play those,' he said. Then he started playing and he nodded at me to play too. *Pom-pom, pom-pom, pom-pom-pooom!* There was a rhythm to it. He played then I played, and somehow it all fit together. He gradually played heavier, faster and louder, encouraging me to play like that too. I felt him press his foot down on the pedal below and the notes became ringing and echoey. My three notes had their own place, their own voice, and Grieg was letting me shout as loud as I needed to. We played the same tune over and over again until my aggression lost its strength and I felt a sadness engulf me. Grieg seemed to sense this and he ended the piece with a definitive strike of the keys. But he didn't stop playing. He moved into a different melody and I watched his hands dance over the keys as the music spoke to me. It was sweet and calm, rolling like a mountain stream in summer.

Behind me, I felt Nina stepping forward. She placed one hand on Grieg's shoulder and one on mine. 'You do remember,' she said to Grieg. Gently, something within her broke and she began to sing. '*You are the single thought of my thoughts, you are my heart's first love. I love you, like no one else on this earth, I love you, for all time and eternity.*' Her voice was haunting, so sweetly melodic, so rich and smooth that it crept inside my body, burrowed into my chest and hid a little piece of itself in my heart. Grieg played and Nina sang, and tears sprang to my eyes. They fell when I blinked and somewhere inside me, a tiny fraction of something that had been ripped apart was magically sewn back together.

INTERLUDE

For my next piece, I am to be bundled into an ostentatious opera gown, a Baroque-style monstrosity with frills and petticoats and beaded loops across the bodice and front skirt. I feel like a walking chandelier and I look ridiculous in it for it does not fit the piece. It was Adele's idea to dress me in a costume that so many audiences are familiar with, to give the king and queen *Dagny Jensen, the opera singer.*

Ellen is fitting my wig. It is a tall white Marie Antoinette affair with ringlets and a towering bouffant. She has scraped and pinned my hair back into submission and covered it with a tight net. She lifts the wig carefully and lowers it onto my head.

'There we are,' she says, 'how does that feel?'

'Heavy,' I say.

She sets to work, pinning the enormous structure to my head, while Adele and Nora prepare the dress behind me.

There are four songs, all of which are in German. Grieg composed them when he was a student at the Royal Conservatory of Music in Leipzig. At eighteen, I was a student there myself. Nina and Grieg thought it the best place for me, despite their own frustrations with the Conservatory; its stuffiness and conformity to the old style had proved a constraint to Edvard when he was there. But they wanted me to learn technique and musical theory that they were unable to provide in depth themselves.

I had been living with Nina and Grieg in Bergen for four years. That spring, around the anniversary of her death in May, the loss of Alexandra was back to haunt them and the atmosphere had turned hostile again. As an escape, Grieg had resumed his flirtation with the painter Leis Schjelderup and was on his way to meet her in Paris when the Griegs' friend Frants Beyer intervened. Nina had no idea Grieg had actually been planning on leaving her for good. She presumed he was simply touring, going away to play a number of concerts. She only discovered the truth when Edvard returned to Bergen earlier than expected. Guilt stricken, he confessed everything.

With their marriage as brittle as it was then, I could no longer bear to be around them. I found myself hiding in corners, trying not be seen, while they scaled their attacks on each other at all hours of the day. I willingly agreed to take a place at the Conservatory. I needed to find my independence and it was time for me to do something on my own. Nina taught me a little German and I was sent to stay with their friends Adolph and Anna Brodsky who were based in Leipzig.

Stepping into the costume is like stepping back in time. My brain begins to think in German and I immediately picture Felix accompanying me, playing the piano while I sing. I see his curly mop of hair and his mouth fixed in concentration as he hammered at the keys.

Felix Weingartner was the first boy I was close to after Jacob, the first one I allowed in. He was a gifted musician, the same age as me. I was introduced to him one evening at the Brodsky's. He was a quiet and thoughtful young man who transformed when he played the piano. The others teased him, called him the *Austrian Philosopher*, because of his brooding nature and sullen disposition. He had come to Leipzig from Graz and initially studied philosophy but later changed direction because his musical talent was too great to ignore.

Felix was two people in one, which is probably what caught my attention. Music had such an acute effect on him that when he played, his solemnity dissipated and he became mellow and warm, his expression softened and his emotional depth became tangible and obvious. Like me, he was accessing that place within him, the raw and uncomplicated reservoir of emotion where the music was hidden. It made him blab things out unexpectedly, divulging thoughts he would ordinarily keep to himself. The first time we spoke, he had tears in his eyes. *Fräulein Jensen*, he said, *I don't believe I have ever heard a voice quite like yours.*

We were young, new to the city and neither of us had many other friends. My social circle was largely confined to Anna and Adolph's acquaintances who were mostly Russian, and although they shared my passion for music, they were much older than me and I found them intimidating. Felix was a student of Wilhelm Mayer, who insisted he attend the Brodsky's regular gatherings. Wilhelm had asked Adolph to take his young student under his wing.

At these musical soirées, Felix and I would drift to the music room on the second floor, finding an escape from the revelry below. He would play and I would sing. Softly, quietly, we sprinkled the air with music and the notes would dance about us, weaving a web of our own making.

I was impressed by this mysterious musician and fascinated by his mind. He took me seriously, and in my periods of melancholic contemplation about life and death, about souls and about Jacob, Felix listened, without judgment or derogation. He provided me with the vocabulary to discuss such things, explaining the complex ideas of philosophers such as Nietzsche and Kierkegaard. I didn't always understand, but Felix made it sound so profound, especially when he combined such thoughts with music. *And those who were seen dancing were thought to be insane*, he would say, as he waltzed me around the room, *by those who could not hear the music.*

Felix unlocked my pain and allowed it to bleed out. He showed me how to harness it, to embrace it rather than deny it and block it, to take ownership of it and use it to define the woman I was becoming. He encouraged me to find some meaning in the suffering of my past in order to truly live.

When I told Nina about him that summer, she smiled coyly and said, *That young man is in love with you, dear, don't you see?* As soon as she breathed the words something inside me closed up. *No, I don't see*, I said. I didn't want to see. When I returned to Leipzig after the break, Felix was invited to Weimar to study with Franz Liszt. I allowed the distance to open up a gulf between us. I was racked with guilt for having let him in. I felt like I had unwittingly invited something unwanted and, by doing so, I had betrayed Jacob. I let Felix go and I returned again to my familiar persistent belief: *we lose the ones we love*.

Ellen and Adele guide me to the door, handling me like a Christmas tree decked to the hilt. I am three times wider with the cage of the dress jutting out from my hips, and significantly taller with the elaborate wig stretching up above me. I move with caution, holding my chin up, as though I have a bucket of water on my head and must not spill a drop.

'She needs assistance getting to the stage,' Ellen is saying.

'Yes, of course,' Harriet says, 'I'll fetch Nora and the three of you can guide her to the wings.'

The women bundle me along, talking about me as if I am no longer there, as if the real Dagny is lost inside this caricature. Behind the façade I prepare to sing. The music is Grieg's, the lyrics were written by German poets: Heinrich Heine and Adelbert von Chamisso. It is the final song of the four, one of von Chamisso's that is repeating in my mind. *Was soll ich sagen* – what shall I say?

Nora clears the way ahead of me and I have to turn sideways to get up the ramp. I will enter from the back of the stage and I must be in position before the end of the preceding piece; Ingolf Schiøtt and the male choir are singing *The Great White Flock*.

'All right, Miss Jensen,' Ellen whispers, 'you're on.'

I shuffle along behind the curtain, sidestepping quietly until I am in place. There are stagehands standing by with ropes in the rigging, ready to lift the curtain in front of me and drop the one behind. When the lights come up, I will appear to have just descended a flight of steps in the garden of a magnificent château.

I think about Felix. I think about Kristian. Felix is now the director of the Vienna State Opera. He has had a glittering career: Director of the Königsberg opera, Kapellmeister in Danzig, Hamburg and Mannheim, the Royal Opera of Berlin, all places where I have sung. He is married for the second time now, but people say that Baroness von Dreifus does not make him happy and there are rumoured affairs with countless actresses and singers. He cannot be an easy man to be married to.

Then there is Kristian. Such an easy man to be married to, the kindest man. He is waiting for me, out there, worrying about me. What am I doing to him? As the audience breaks into applause and the choir exits into the wings, the words of the song I am about to sing grow in importance. The stage goes dark and the ropes of the rigging begin to hiss. *Kristian*, I am saying to myself, *Du heissest mich redden und machst mir's so schwer.*

You ask me to speak and make it so hard.

15

My head was filled with a void, a great chasm of silence. I started to worry that I couldn't even remember how Jacob's voice sounded or what he really looked like. Without being able to speak, it was as if he was being erased from my body. He was slipping away, and this frightened me. I would shake my head and smack my ears but I couldn't bring him back.

Grieg had given me discarded sheets of manuscript paper and I wrote in the spaces between the staffs in order to communicate. It was as though I was writing music with my words, a song I would have sung if I could. I pestered Nina with questions. She had not known Jacob particularly well but I became so tormented with fear that I wrote down questions continuously. *Jacob? Voice? Eyes? What colour? How tall?* She never brushed me off, always took me seriously and answered me patiently. *Well, his voice was starting to break, dear, that's what happens when boys become men. He was handsome. He had the deepest blue eyes and do you remember his hair? I've never seen hair so white.*

One morning I approached Nina with another question. She was twiddling the peg on the music stand, having decided to practice her vocal exercises again despite the absence of an audience.

'I may as well try,' she said, looking up at me, 'although it is quite frightening to think how quickly my voice has deteriorated. It has become so ugly.'

I shook my head. Nina's voice was the most beautiful sound I had ever heard. For such a small person, she was capable of immense depth and range. It had such a quality to it, finer even than Hedda's voice, it somehow managed to find its way straight into your chest and play all the invisible strings that were buried there.

'What is it, dear?' she said, reaching out her hand.

I gave her the note: *Rewards of love? What you said to him?*

'Oh,' she said, clearing her throat, 'yes, I remember. He was telling me how scared he was, you see, at the magnitude of it, the scale of the emotion, so vast he couldn't contain it. I told him not to be frightened because there were also great rewards to loving someone,' she looked over to the door of the music room and her voice faltered. 'Great rewards. Like happiness.'

I snatched the paper back out of her hand and wrote something else: *Happiness that could take you all the way up to heaven?*

'I think so,' she said, 'at least, *my* love stretches that high. Alexandra, she was only...' her eyes glazed with tears and she looked away. 'I'm sorry,' she said, turning back to face me, 'she was only a baby.'

My eyes searched the floor. I remembered the photograph I had seen on the shelf in the music room. It was a picture Nina often looked at; a baby wearing a bonnet and a shawl.

When I looked up again, my eyebrows pulled together shaping my face into another question.

'Our daughter, yes,' Nina said, then she shook her head. 'You're young. I'm sorry,' she said, weeping before me, 'I shouldn't be speaking of it with you. You have your own pain. But when you lose your own child...you can't imagine, Dagny...you just can't imagine what that does to a woman.'

I touched her hand and she allowed me to comfort her. She hunched over and leaned towards me, crying against my shoulder. I wished I could say something, just one word of solace, but even if I could have spoken it would not have alleviated her suffering. I sensed even then, that there was nothing I could have done to put right what was so emphatically wrong.

'I don't know the answer, Dagny,' she said, leaning back and wiping her nose on her sleeve. 'What kind of a God would take those we love so dearly away from us? And why must we only search in heaven to find happiness? What about here on earth?' she muttered, 'Why can't we be happy here?'

I was shaking my head. I didn't know. I thumped at my chest and pointed up to the mountain top. I tried to say *I* but I couldn't even whisper, tried to say *will ask Jacob*, but Nina didn't understand what I meant. Frustrated, I reached for Jacob's storybook and hurriedly flicked through it to find words. *I.find.out.*

I hugged her, then ran from her before she could stop me.

'Dagny? Where are you going? Dagny? Come back!'

I hurried up to the plateau, scrambling up the mountainside. When I got to the rocks, I knelt down and put my hands together as if to pray, although my thoughts were anything but pious. *Is there a God, Jacob? Do you know? Have you seen Him? Are you in heaven, or are you somewhere else? Why does God want you there? Can't He see that I need you more than He does? If there is a God, He must be mean and selfish. He took Nina's baby away from her and He took you away from me. Tell me where you are, Jacob? Are you in heaven? Is there even a heaven?*

I waited and listened but there was nothing, just the sound of the mountain, a quiet hum of desolation broken only by the occasional call of a distant bird.

I decided to go higher. Jacob and I had intended to climb up to the peak of the mountain that day in the spring when we found Grieg's cabin. If he had been with me he would be coaxing me into it, urging me to go to the top. He would have run off at a pace, telling me stories of brave men who'd slayed trolls, and I would have followed him.

If there was a heaven, I thought that if I climbed to the peak of the mountain I would be closer to it and, if Jacob was there, perhaps he'd hear me better from the top? I got up and started to run. I imagined Jacob running ahead of me. I saw flashes: his feet, his pale skin and the dirt smeared about his ankles. I followed his footsteps as I had so many times before. The terrain was stony grey, the rocks flatter and smoother than the boulders at the plateau. Here and there, pockets of snow interspersed the grey with circles of pure untouched white.

Before long, the air grew colder and I could see the peak of the mountain up ahead. The rocks at the top lay in a rumbling formation and their surfaces formed odd shapes. I saw the faces of trolls: hooked noses, sleeping eyelids, grimacing mouths. I found myself moving cautiously, careful not to wake them, stepping from nose to mouth, to ear, to eye, hopping from giant to giant. The highest rock was curled up like a sleeping cat at the foot of an angry troll. I followed the curve of the cat's spine, putting one foot in front of the other until I was there.

I stopped abruptly and took a great gasp. I was standing alone in the sky. All around me were the rolling peaks of endless mountains. I could see across the entire Hardanger fjord: vast ridges of rock, purple, blue and green; traces of snow, mists that mingled in the spaces between heaven and earth. I turned to see the familiar mountain formations at Granvin and Ulvik, recognised the deep V shape where the giant slice of cake slotted into the peak on the other side of the water. The colours changed from mountain to mountain, each of them had its own tone and texture, its own mood.

I didn't look up into the sky because I was already in it. Instead, I looked ahead, over clouds in the distance and between the ridges of the mountain peaks, staring and searching as the wind tousled my hair and brought a dry chill to my eyes. *Jacob? Can you hear me? Can you see me?*

I turned back on myself to see how far I had come. Below me, the plateau seemed small and insignificant. It was only a tiny piece of this gigantic world. The troll's stairs, too, were nothing but a notch on the mountain, and even the colossal mountain itself was only a part of something even greater.

I studied the plateau below and saw something moving. Dark, like a bird winging across the upland. I followed it, it wasn't fluid enough to be a bird, it didn't glide, it jumped and darted. It was definitely an animal but I was so far away that I couldn't get a sense of its shape. It stopped and then it ran. It was running to the edge of the plateau in the direction of the cabin. That's when I realised it was him again. It was the boy.

I scampered away from the summit and started running back down the mountainside. My feet slipped and I skidded down the rocks, holding my arms out to the sides to keep my balance. There were sudden drops, ditches and patches of snow but I wouldn't let myself fall. I came careening across the shale, gathering speed and momentum that was beyond my own control. My boots crunched on the small stones and my ankles strained as I jumped over rocks. I tried not to take my eyes off him but he moved so fast it was hard to keep track. Before I reached the plateau, I stopped. I looked all around me, from one side to the other, from the troll's stairs to the cabin, but the boy was nowhere to be seen.

I came bounding back down to the plateau where I walked slowly, combing every inch of it but I couldn't find him. I slid my way down the ravine and went back to the cabin. My steps were heavy, as though my pockets were filled with all the rocks I'd crossed. When I reached the door, I turned around and pressed my back against the wood. I slumped to the ground and sat in a heap with my head resting on my knees. I could hear the sound of Nina's voice. She was singing scales, changing the volume of every trill, turning it on and off at will. I listened to her for a long time.

Eventually, I lifted my head. I sensed there was someone watching me again. I turned back towards the ravine for one last look. The boy was standing up on the ridge with one foot up on a large boulder. He stood there for a second, looking down at me. I rushed forward, squinted against the

215

light to catch his face. He raised his arm and waved, then he was gone.

I didn't know if he was waving hello or waving goodbye.

*

That evening the snow fell. Mother was bringing her changes again and the rest of us had to succumb. The temperature dropped dramatically as winter crept around the walls of the cabin and squeezed us in its grasp.

Nina had made a make-shift bed for me in the corner of the living room but now she brought heavier blankets from upstairs and tried to move the little bed closer to the fire.

'You'll freeze down here on the floor,' she said, busily stacking up pillows and blankets as though preparing for an invasion, 'it's fairly coming down now.'

I went to the window. Thick flakes were cascading like feathers in the last of the evening light. It was already settling, covering the mountain tracks, laying down the first fragments of the deep white carpet that would conceal the earth until spring.

I stood and watched it, feeling the trees shiver as they braced themselves for the coming season. The birches were all stark and spindly now, standing like sticks in the emptiness of the mountainside while the thick green firs and spruces and pines were resolute, unperturbed by the snow. The air was sharp, restricted in its movement. Everything was slowing down, stopping. The streams would soon be motionless. The mountain world would be hushed and silent. Even waterfalls as wild and ferocious as the Eternal Waterfall would freeze, becoming solid needles of ice, stalactites suspended in time. The snow was blotting things out, slowly covering up all the traces of everything that had gone before.

'It will only get harder,' I heard Nina say, but she wasn't speaking to me.

Herr Grieg was over at the back window. 'I didn't expect to stay through the winter. Didn't think it would take me this long.'

'Then why don't we return to Bergen?' Nina said.

'No, I'm not ready.'

'You could take a break from it for the winter, Edvard,' she said, 'wouldn't that help?'

'I don't have time to take breaks. Ibsen's waiting.'

I heard Nina drag the music stand across the floor. 'We're going to have to go to the Jåstad farm and get supplies.'

'What about the girl?' Grieg said. 'We should take her back.'

I spun around to face him and he looked at me warily.

I was shaking my head.

'She doesn't want to go back,' Nina said.

'It'll be a harsh winter up here, Dagny,' Grieg said, 'you'd be better off back down in Utne with your family.'

I shook my head even harder.

'She'll need more clothes, warmer clothes than those she has,' he said.

'Then I will knit them for her,' Nina said.

'She'd be better at home,' Grieg said, 'with her people.'

'We are her people now. She will stay here as long as she needs to.'

'Her people?' Grieg said, 'Nina, she isn't *our* daughter. You can't just keep her here for your own sake. She doesn't belong here.'

'Can't you see anything but yourself for a single second, Edvard?' Nina snapped.

'Myself? I am thinking only of the girl. She would be better cared for by her own father. I'm sure they have fuel and plenty of food down there.'

'She doesn't want to go back,' Nina said.

'Why?' Grieg looked at me, 'why don't you want to go back, Dagny? We could take you down tomorrow, before the snow gets too deep.'

I opened my mouth and made a gasping sound. I wanted to form the words but my throat wouldn't work. I strained and tensed the muscles in my face. *You can't speak, Dagny,* my mind said, *if you speak, you will lose him forever.* Frustration brought tears to my eyes. Nina could see what was happening. She rushed to get my paper and pencil.

'Tell him,' she said, 'tell him why you don't want to go.'

I took the paper and slowly wrote down two words: *Lillian Jevnaker.*

Grieg looked at the page. 'Who's Lillian Jevnaker?'

Pastor's wife.

'And what does she have to do with this?' Grieg said.

Threatening to send me away.

'Where to?'

I looked at him. His skin was pale and his hair was messy and unkempt. His eyes were drilling into me impatiently. He wouldn't settle until there was some end to this, until I gave him a satisfactory answer.

Asylum. I wrote.

'Oh,' he said.

'What is it?' Nina said.

'Some woman's threatening to send Dagny to an asylum.'

'Whatever for?' Nina said.

'To make you speak again? Is that it?' Grieg said.

I nodded.

'And what does your father say about that? Does he agree?'

I nodded again and wrote some more.

Nina and Grieg followed my words as they appeared on the paper. I had run out of space and they were written across the bar like musical notes. It was a sad song: *Lillian will pay to send me away. Far thinks it will help.*

218

'I see,' Grieg said.

'Then she must stay here,' Nina said, 'she simply must. I won't let them send her away.'

Grieg pressed his lips together and sighed inwardly. 'And if you were able to speak again,' he said, after a pause, 'your father would have no cause to send you to an asylum?'

I nodded.

'Then Dagny is to stay here with us until she feels ready to speak again,' Nina said. 'I will help her.'

'You're not a doctor,' Grieg said.

'No,' Nina smiled and came to put her arms around me. 'I am a singer.'

'I don't see what difference that makes,' Grieg said.

'How can you not understand it?' Nina said. 'You of all people should know that there are more ways to speak than simply by talking. I will teach Dagny to sing.'

'Nina, have you lost your mind?'

'What do you mean?'

'Just because you miss your students, you can't make Dagny your student and think that you can help her. She needs specialists, doctors who know how to treat her. You aren't qualified for such a task.'

'Have a little faith in your wife, Edvard,' she said, 'Dagny, come with me.' She guided me into the music room and sat down at the piano. Grieg watched us, hanging at the doorway. Nina started playing scales. 'Stand there Dagny, nice and tall with your head up and your back straight.'

I did as she asked.

'Now breathe in, deeply, come on, inhale.'

I took a deep breath.

'And let it all back out again, but imagine it's coming from the pit of your stomach.'

I blew out.

'Now try it again, dear, only this time with an *aaahh* sound.' She sang a note herself. 'We'll start on the C, like this, *aaaaaahh*.'

She gave me a nod. I inhaled and breathed again, but no sound came out. Just the soft rush of my breath.

'That's all right,' Nina said, 'try it again.'

I inhaled and exhaled several times but my mouth could not make a sound.

Nina sang scales to encourage me but it didn't make any difference. The fear stopped me every time. Even when she held a hand to my belly and soothed me, I still couldn't make any noise.

The entire exercise made Grieg uneasy. 'Nina,' he kept interrupting, 'I told you, she needs doctors.'

But Nina wouldn't listen, she kept on asking me to breathe and she kept singing her scales to me with a determined perseverance. 'She's afraid to speak, aren't you, Dagny? We need to make it safe for her again.'

'Nina, it won't help,' Grieg was saying, 'let the girl go...stop it...come on, now.'

But Nina kept singing and I kept breathing.

Outside, the snow kept falling.

By the time I went to bed, it had covered the ground completely. A thick white blanket had quieted the earth. The snow was heavy, yet completely silent. The soft feathery flakes continued to float down from the sky and I watched them stick to the window and melt into trickles. I wondered if they were falling from heaven, and if a piece of Jacob was inside every single one of them. I opened the window and flung my hands out, reaching for Jacob, wanting him to touch me. I closed my eyes, felt the cold air prickle my skin and the gentle snowflakes land and melt in the palms of my hands. *I feel you, Jacob.* I pushed my head out of the window and lifted my face to the sky. The snow brushed against my cheeks and one large flake landed right on my lips. *Jacob? I know you're there.*

16

Nina knitted mittens. They were holey and too big. She was a city lady and didn't take to knitting or cooking like the women from Hardanger did. She was restless, hungered for entertainment and audiences to sing for. I was starting to see that singing was Nina's lifeblood. Without it, she was as lost as I was without Jacob. Like me, she was not a typical girl, and she did not fit the mould that society expected from her. I liked that about her. She wrote to her friend Hanchen – letters that could not even begin their journey until the farmer at Jåstad came with supplies. He trekked up the mountain with a horse and sled every few weeks. I always hid when he came. What if he knew Lillian Jevnaker? What if Lars found out I was here?

The farmer's name was Torgeir. He had a rough snapping voice that made him sound angry all the time but Nina was always pleasant with him. She said he was a kind man for making the trip up to the cabin, there weren't many who would. I overheard Torgeir say that he came on account of Herr Grieg's poor health and it was only after one of his visits that Nina told me Edvard had been ill when he was younger and now only one of his lungs worked properly. He'd kept it well hidden. Then again, I had never seen Grieg running or climbing or straining in any way. Perhaps that's how he kept it under control.

I usually hid in the music room when Torgeir came, especially if he stopped for a drink and some pancakes before returning to Jåstad. I would wait anxiously, cowering in the corner of the room until I heard the chair scrape across the floor and Torgeir grumbling about getting back while the light was still good. After he'd gone, I'd run outside and watch the sled drift away down the mountain again.

One day, I heard Grieg telling Torgeir that the piano had a sticking key. He needed a screwdriver to be able to get the key slip off and a shim to wedge in between the keys. I could tell from Torgeir's questions that Grieg was going to have to show him what he meant. They would have to come into the music room. To hide from Torgeir, I had no choice but to run up to Nina and Edvard's bedroom. Before I even heard the door handle turn, I was half way up the stairs.

I had never been in this part of the cabin before and knew that I was trespassing. It was Nina and Grieg's private space. I tried to find a hiding place without looking too closely at anything. Two small beds were fitted into the eaves of the roof, similar to my cot at home. There were two trunks covered in beautiful rose painting patterns and a table in between the beds where more photographs were displayed. I sat down on one of the beds and listened to the conversation below.

'You see, it's here,' Grieg was saying, 'the key slip must be too close. It's making this G stick.'

'Hmm,' Torgeir grunted.

'So I need a screwdriver to loosen this piece and then I need to slide a metal shim down into that space to keep it away from the keys. Do you see?'

There was a shuffling sound and Torgeir coughed. 'What size are your screws,' he said. His voice was muffled, his head was upside down. 'Right, I see, I see,' he said, 'I can get you that, yes, won't be back for a few weeks though.'

'No, that's quite all right,' Grieg said, politely, 'I highly doubt I'll be finished by then.'

When Torgeir left, Grieg stayed in the room leaving me trapped upstairs. He closed the door and started tinkling at the piano. I could tell by his sounds and movements that he didn't know I was there. I did not wish to disturb him but at the same time I didn't want to hide from him either, it was as though I was eavesdropping, intruding on his sacred work. Too much time passed while I was thinking, so I decided to wait until he took a break, then I would slip away and he would not notice that I had been there.

I kept as still as I could.

Grieg struck a chord then played it again.

He played a higher chord, then returned to the first. He repeated this pattern several times, and then he started playing a melody. It was a sweet rolling sound, like a bird calling or the ripples of sunshine shimmering across the surface of a lake. I closed my eyes and listened as something gradually began to emerge. The music was like shoots, even in winter, piercing the surface of the earth and finding their way up to the sun. It was a call, like the call of a bird winging and gliding on the air. The phrase repeated and swelled and Grieg somehow found a sprinkling of notes that perfectly supported it. The call mounted and grew and amplified until it burst with a heartbreaking peal of glistening sunlight.

I jumped up from the bed and ran down the stairs as if I had been punched in the chest. I was crying – I couldn't help myself. It was an automatic reaction to the music. I had never heard Grieg play anything like this before. It spoke to my heart. It was trying to tell me something.

I stood there on the bottom step with tears streaming down my face.

'Dagny?' Grieg said, pulling his fingers from the keyboard. 'What were you doing up there?'

I couldn't stop crying and I pointed at the piano.

'I'm working,' he said. 'Go and find Nina.'

I shook my head and kept pointing at the piano.

Grieg clasped his fingers together.

'I am working,' he said, more forcefully. 'Nina!'

She appeared at the door.

'I can't be disturbed like this,' Grieg said, pulling at his hair.

'Dagny, dear, what's the matter,' Nina said, coming to take me out. 'Have you upset her, Edvard?'

'Pah!' Grieg said, 'I haven't said a word. I'm trying to work, that's all. She's been upstairs all this time.'

'I'm sure she wasn't doing any harm. Come on, dear,' Nina said, 'Torgeir brought some smoked hams, would you like to try some? And we have cocoa out here too.'

She guided me out of the room with her pleasant chatter, although I was still in a daze. There was something about that music. It had seeped into my body and I didn't understand what it was doing there. It was like swallowing medicine and waiting for it to start taking effect, feeling strange sensations but not knowing where they would lead.

Nina sat me down at the table and put a plate of food in front of me. 'Torgeir's a good man,' she said, 'brought me some more wool. I thought I'd try another scarf for you,' she giggled, as we both remembered her first attempt – a long blue rope of varying widths, thick then thin, with a selection of large holes throughout. I wore it anyway. I'd never had good clothes.

I ate my food and drank a cup of cocoa.

'Let's try some exercises,' Nina said, 'you never know, they might help.'

We went over to the music stand and Nina started warming up her voice. She sang through scales and made strange smacking sounds with her lips and then blew air out heavily in puffs. 'The voice is an instrument,' she said, 'just as much as a piano or any other musical instrument. You have to care for it, tune it up.'

She had me stand next to her and she put her hands on me. She gently placed a hand between my shoulder blades to get me to straighten my back, then she lifted my chin, 'nice and open, it has to be open, that's it,' she said, then she touched my abdomen, 'from here, that's where it's coming from, Dagny, you have to use all your muscles here to support your voice, otherwise you'll strain your throat.'

When she was happy with my posture, she stood in front of me and indicated that I should mirror her actions. 'We won't worry too much about making a note,' she said, 'let's just whisper it, so that you can feel the air moving through your body.' She touched her hand to her own abdomen and inhaled. '*Ha ha ha ha ha ha haaaa,*' she whispered. 'It's a simple arpeggio. Try it, dear.'

I took a deep breath from the base of my stomach then opened my mouth. The air came out in one long rush.

'*Ha ha ha ha ha ha haaaa,*' Nina whispered, encouraging me.

I tried to repeat it but kept breathing in one breath as though my throat was afraid of making any sound that might resemble a word.

'It's all right,' Nina said, 'just keep practising your breathing. Make some of the breaths shorter and some of them longer.'

This, I could do. I breathed a long breath, then panted a shorter breath and kept alternating the breaths.

'Yes, dear, that's it,' Nina said, patiently. 'Try *ha ha haaaa, ha ha haaaa.*'

I managed to make the same rhythm Nina was making and we practised this for a while. Nina tried to get me to whisper the arpeggio again but whenever I tried, my breath would simply revert to a normal exhalation. She pushed me to repeat the breathing exercise but she sensed my frustration and suggested we stop before I gave up. 'We'll just keep trying,' she said, 'every day.'

I pointed to the door.

'Yes, you can if you like,' Nina said, 'a little more came down in the night so we need to clear the path again.'

I had taken to shoveling snow. I enjoyed the physical work and the repetitive movements helped to calm my mind. I borrowed Nina's coat – she was so small that her clothes practically fit me anyway. I pulled on all the holey knitted items she had made for me: mittens, scarf, hat, socks, and went out.

The air was fresh and the sun was cold and white. During these months, the sun provided only light, not warmth. The moisture in my nostrils stiffened as I breathed; a pinch of a chill that told me the temperature had dropped again. My feet tingled with cold – the socks Nina had made for me were not thick enough to keep me warm. I picked up the shovel and began to scrape and dig and clear away the fresh snow. The clanging of the shovel echoed all around me, as if I was the only living being on this mountain. The snow had silenced everything.

I cleared a path all the way out to the track where Torgeir brought his sled, throwing the snow out onto either side, building it up like a wall. I loaded and lifted, carried and dumped, bending low and stretching up again. I cleared another path to the outhouse, heaping up the snow and making my own mountains. When I had piled it all up, I threw the shovel down and plunged my hands into the snow. I knelt in it, grabbing handfuls in my mittens and patting it into snowballs. I could feel from the texture of it that it was what we called *kram* snow, a pliable snow that was easy to form – it stuck together when you pressed it. I made a snowball and tossed it from one hand to the other. It reminded me of a time last winter when Jacob and I had hidden behind the eld house and pelted every Bremnes or Jevnaker that passed. Jacob was ruthless. He aimed for the head. I would wait until they'd passed then hurl a snowball at their back. *You're such a girl, Dagny. If you're going to do it, you have to do it properly.* The best strike of the day was when Jacob hit Grete Bremnes' bonnet with such force that the snow splatted against its frills and plastered them flat against her cheek. We got into serious trouble, of course, but it was worth it to see the look on Grete's face.

I stood up and turned back towards the cabin. I hurled my snowball through the air without thinking about where it would land. It smacked against Grieg's window with a thud. I took a step back and waited to see what he would do.

When nothing happened, I bent down and picked up another handful, making a perfectly formed ball in my mittens. I took a deep breath and hurled this one directly at Grieg's window. It clapped against the glass with an echo and I smiled. The game became to see how loud I could make the snowballs hit. One after the other I threw them at the window, forming and hurling with increasing effort each time. *Smack! Smack! Smack!*

When Grieg finally came to the window, he was not amused. I was smiling, but he didn't see the fun of it. He waved his fist at me but he couldn't see Nina, who was watching from the other window. She was giggling and clapping her hands together like a child. She pointed at the snow and then at Edvard's room. *Do it again*, she mouthed.

I bent down and grabbed another handful of snow and shaped it into a ball.

Grieg was pointing at me now and shaking his head. Nina was grinning and nodding.

I lifted my arm and pulled it back, twisting my body for added power, then I threw the snowball directly at the centre of Grieg's window. It thumped so hard that it exploded on impact sending globules of melting snow across the whole window pane. Herr Grieg turned his back and walked away.

Nina came running out to join me. She was squealing and laughing and kicking up the snow. She was wearing Grieg's coat and a fur hat that completely covered her hair. She made a snowball and threw it at me, but it missed by a mile. I smiled at her and threw one back, which landed at her feet.

'Wooo-hoo! Dagny! You little monster!' she giggled, 'the Dovregubben is angry now!'

She ran up to me and lunged into the snow, throwing great sprays of it up into my face. I gasped and spluttered then threw a fountain of it back over her. We fought and played and Nina shrieked and howled as the snow got into her clothes and down her neck. 'You little monster!' she kept saying, 'I'll get you for this!' She reached out to grab me but stumbled as she moved, sending the two of us rolling into the snow. Nina screamed and laughed as the snow half buried her. She lay there on her back, panting and laughing as she wiped it from her eyes. I got up onto my knees and smacked my mittens together over her face. She snorted and hollered, 'Daaaaagny!' She reached out for me again but I rolled away. I'd had enough brawls and wrestling matches with Jacob and my brothers to know how to win a fight.

'I'll get you! I'll get you!' she said, scrambling to her knees, 'I'm coming to get you!'

I stood facing her, holding my arms out, ready to pounce or flee in a second.

'I will, you know,' she said, 'I'll get you!'

She approached me again, hesitantly, like a poacher, but I was too fast for an opponent like Nina. As she swooped, I dashed towards the outhouse, sending her reeling head first into the snow. 'Oh, Dagny,' she squeaked, getting up and spitting snow from her mouth. 'Dagny! Really!'

Just then, the snowballed window clunked open.

'In heaven's name!' Grieg shouted. 'How is a man supposed to get any work done around here?'

Nina was too buoyant to hear the tone of his voice. 'She's going to kill me, Edvard!' she shouted, 'I will be snowballed to death! Come and help me! I think we need an army to stop her!'

'I'm trying to work,' Grieg grumbled. 'Composers cannot work in zoos.'

Nina's face was bright red. Her hat was slipping off and her hair was poking free in odd places, making it look as though she had grown a pair of ears high up on her head. Her nose was dripping and her mouth puffed steaming clouds out into the air as she tried to get her breath back. She glared at her husband, the killer of our fun. She bent down and grabbed a handful of snow, making it hard and compact in her wet gloves, then she raised it up and slung it at him, only narrowly missing his eyebrow. 'You old troll!' she shouted.

He shook his head and disappeared back into his room.

'Don't pay any attention to him, Dagny,' Nina said, as she plonked herself down in the snow. Grieg's outburst had inadvertently called a truce, forcing Nina and I onto the same team. Game over, I came and sat next to her in the snow. We lay back and sank into it. There was so much of it. I scooped it up and threw it away, then scooped up more, digging into it with my hands and feet.

Nina was still panting. She lay there in the snow, staring straight up at the sky.

'It's all white,' she said, 'the earth, the sky, everything. It's like heaven and earth are the same place, isn't it?'

I gazed up at it. Everything was formless and shapeless. If the cabin or the trees weren't there, all I would have seen would have been white and the world would have had no perspective.

'It's really rather disorientating, isn't it?' Nina said. 'We could be anywhere, nowhere and somewhere all at once.'

After a while, it began to snow again. A fresh dusting kissed my eyelashes and cheeks and mouth.

'I'm getting cold,' Nina said. 'I should go and get these wet things off. Don't be long now. It'll be getting dark soon.'

I was happy to be left alone.

Nina tramped away, sniffing, and stamping her feet and clapping her hands together to shake off the snow.

I didn't move. I lay still and silent and let the snow cover me, wishing it would blot me out like everything else. Then I heard something. It wasn't Jacob's voice, but it was Jacob. It was a feeling of him. He was speaking to me but his voice was wrapped up inside musical notes. It was the call again, the flowing melody that sounded like sunshine. My chest began to flutter, and then the vibrations rose up towards my throat and I knew that Jacob was there. He was within me. His presence grew stronger with every note as it surged and expanded and intensified. It felt as though he was breathing inside me. And he didn't have to say anything at all because the music said it for him. The music *was* him.

I started to cry. Pain and love and loss all swirled inside my chest as the music rose and heightened and then built up into its dramatic crescendo. I wished Grieg would stop, and yet I wanted him to never stop playing. The notes reverberated within me. It was as if Jacob's soul was playing with mine and he was calling me to him. *Will you come to back to me? Will you come back to me? Will you come back to me, back to me now?*

He was pleading with me and I was pleading with him. Every note was more intense and more meaningful than words could ever be: the deepest longing to be with him, the most torturous lament. *Will you come back to me, back to me now?* I thought the yearning would kill me. When I could stand it no more, I jumped up out of the snow and ran straight into the cabin.

I was crying so hard that my throat was tight and my nose was streaming and the tears were blurring my vision. I rushed past Nina and burst into Grieg's room, hunching over and spewing out the pain, as though I had been attacked.

Grieg spun around and stared at me.

I stood there crying, with water pooling around me as the snow dropped from my coat and boots and melted on the floor.

'What in God's name...?' Grieg said.

I lifted my arm and pointed at the piano again. I wanted to tell him: *It's Jacob! It's Jacob! What you're playing is Jacob!*

But Grieg was too angry to even want to understand.

'I'm trying to work!' he yelled. 'Don't you see? Don't you understand that?'

I cried so hard that my throat started rasping.

'Get out!' Grieg shouted. 'Go on! Get out!'

'Edvard!' Nina screeched from behind me. 'Stop it!'

'Get her out of here!' he roared. 'Out! Out! Out!'

I didn't blanch but looked into his eyes, desperately trying to convey it: *What you're playing, it's Jacob!* Grieg's eyes blazed with fury. He didn't understand. Neither of them did.

No one did.

I wanted to scream. I was so cramped and contained, my voice so lost to me that I was suffocating myself. I couldn't breathe. It was strangling me. The music, the longing, the frustration.

I fled.

I ran from the cabin, out into the snow. Nina shouted after me but I paid no attention to her. I sprinted away from them, along the path that I had cleared, then up towards the ravine. My boots sank into the snow and I slipped and skidded as I climbed. But I didn't stop. I used my hands and elbows and knees to crawl up the mountainside, half climbing, half swimming through the freezing snow. It was in my mouth and eyes, and still it was falling from the sky. I scrambled to the top of the ridge. It was getting dark and night was descending all around me. My body was wet and cold but still I ran. I hurtled across the top of the plateau until I fell to my knees.

I'm here, Jacob. I lifted my face to the snowy sky. *Will you come back to me now?*

17

I could not feel my body. I heard my breath pumping inside my head but the rest of me was numb. It was dark and I was kneeling in the snow. I found myself there unexpectedly. I couldn't remember how I got there. I remembered the music, inside me, and Jacob's presence, and shouting and screaming at Herr Grieg, although I hadn't actually made a sound. And then here I was on the plateau, as motionless and unfeeling as a rock.

I was angry with Jacob. He'd abandoned me and left me in this desolate world of silence. I was afraid of everything: afraid of my own voice, afraid of being abandoned, afraid of being sent away, afraid of every day that lay ahead of me, my whole life. Without Jacob, it couldn't possibly have any meaning.

It continued like this for a while, the spiral of desperation that led from nowhere to nowhere else. I wrapped my arms around myself and keeled forwards until my brow touched my knees. The snow continued to fall and I felt it gather at the back of my neck. I started to accept the fact that I might die now, that's why I had ended up here. I had come here to die. Perhaps it was my time? Perhaps the mountain wanted me, too? Lars always said that animals ran away when they knew they were dying. They'd go and hide somewhere to be safe from predators. Running and hiding was their way of concealing pain and vulnerability. I had run away from Lars and I had hidden with the Griegs. Maybe the next part was for me to die?

I lifted my head and felt surprisingly calm. The sky had cleared while my face was lowered and the snow clouds had shifted to reveal a glittering array of stars. There must have been thousands of them, millions of them dotting the darkness like jewels glinting against black velvet. But there was something else drifting in from the north, a shimmering green smudge spreading out across the whole sky. It began to glow, shining down in rods like the sun's rays, rippling through the atmosphere as though a sail was billowing across the stars. The light moved and changed shape, twisting and flowing, floating on an invisible sea, then shooting, churning and fading again. I was captivated by it.

The green light intensified, splitting into lines, making pathways across the night. I watched it flash and glimmer, and I remembered a story Mathilde Olsen had once told us about the fires in the sky. *They're the souls of the dead. When the aurora blaze in the sky you should be very careful, keep quiet while they pass. If you whistle to them, you can summon them closer and they will whisk you away into the dark night forever.*

I rubbed my lips together and tried to whistle into the biting air. I wanted Jacob to hear me. I wanted the lights to take me away. I inhaled and blew out through my mouth but I couldn't make a sound, only empty puffing whispers. I summoned Grieg's melody back into my mind, the tune that was Jacob. *Will you come back to me? Will you come back to me? Will you come back to me, back to me now?* I blew and blew, but my lips would not whistle. I could feel the music move through me, I could sing it inside my head, but I could not make the slightest squeak. Not a note or a peep would come out of my mouth.

I could hear the soft tender song of Jacob's soul. It began to grow: the longing, the yearning, the question desperately seeking an answer. And then the giant gust of music, that painful burst of love rushed through my entire being as the green shimmering lights shone brighter and I wished for them to sweep me up and carry me away.

There were tears in my eyes again. They trickled down my cheeks and burned hot against my skin. I wiped my face. I didn't know how long I had been here. I tried to stand up but my body was so cold that all my strength had frozen inside my bones. I staggered about and reached for a slab of rock to hold myself up. The sky was still glowing green but as I found my feet again I became aware of another light. At first it was only a speck in the corner of my eye, a vague yellow glow. Then I turned my head and saw that it was growing, getting larger and brighter as it floated towards me.

Jacob? Is that you?

I focused on the ball of light. Was it a soul? Was it God? A golden chariot sent from the fires in the sky, the thing in which I was to be whisked away? It grew nearer and with it came a sound, a humphing grunting noise; a sound of struggle and effort. I tightened my eyes, trying to get a clearer image of it in the eerie green light that hung over me. Then I saw a hand attached to the yellow light, and then an arm, and then a face appeared. The light was a lantern and the face was Herr Grieg's.

'Daaaagny!' he shouted, 'Dagny? Are you there?' His voice was weak and he was wheezing and coughing. 'Dagny! It's me, it's Herr Grieg! Can you see me?' He lifted his hand to his brow and squinted his eyes. 'Dagny? Dagny, it is you, thank God!' he said. 'Goodness child, you will die out here in the cold!' He was carrying a blanket, which he threw around me. 'Nina is worried sick. We both are. Won't you come back?'

I lifted my eyes to the sky and sank against the rock.

'Dagny, honestly,' Grieg said, lurching towards me and clasping his chest, 'it's time to come home now.'

I didn't move.

'Look, I have an apology to make,' he said. 'I should not have lost my temper like that. I'm sorry.'

I continued to stare up at the sky.

'It's just...my work,' he said, realising the frailty of his words as he spoke them. 'Well, I'm sorry about it. I hope you can forgive me.' He lifted his head and scanned the strange green sky. 'Aurora Borealis,' he said, 'what a sight!' He put the lantern down in the snow and propped himself up against the rock. 'The Vikings believed they were

234

reflections of the Valkyrie's armour,' he said. 'The spears and shields and helmets of the warrior women flashing over the skies as they led fallen soldiers to their resting place at Valhalla.' Grieg pulled his hat down to cover his earlobes, he was shivering. 'But folklore says they are the spirits of children,' he said, 'children who died at birth.'

I turned to him. His blue eyes were watery, his face significantly weakened by the cold and the climb. His cheeks were withdrawn. He was trembling. 'I wonder,' he said, 'so many things we cannot explain.'

A breeze whipped up across the mountain and Herr Grieg wrapped the blanket tighter around me and rubbed my shoulders. 'You're freezing, Dagny.'

I had forgotten about the cold. I was so caught up in my desire to be taken away into the lights, to die.

'Did you come up here for a reason?'

I shrugged my shoulders.

'To be near him? Do you feel closer to him up here?'

I pointed at Grieg and with my mittened hands I mimicked playing a piano, then I pointed up to the green sky and pressed both my hands to my chest.

'The music?' Grieg said, 'You've been trying to tell me something about that piece, haven't you? About *Morning Mood*?'

My eyes brimmed with tears and I stared at him.

'It's supposed to depict the rising sun in a Moroccan desert.'

I thought about the burst of sunlight rippling across the lake and I nodded my head.

'Impossible to imagine that up here on this mountain,' he said, 'in the middle of winter. It's so hard for me to find it, Dagny, that part of me that I need to be able compose. I fear I have lost it. I fear I lost it all when we lost Alexandra. I think that part of me went with her.' He looked up, 'the spirits of children,' he said, 'maybe that's what they are?'

We stared up at the sky as the bitter night nipped at our faces, both of us searching for answers in the mysterious swirling light.

'She was only eighteen months old,' Grieg said. He rubbed at his arms but kept his eyes fixed on the sky. 'Encephalitis. Inflammation of the brain. I still can't understand why she was taken from us. My parents, well, that's hard enough, but my daughter, my sweet little girl. Do you think she is up there? Is she far away?'

I felt the pain of Grieg's aching heart bleed out into the mountain. He was as desperate as I was.

'Nina kept seeing her,' he said, 'for months after. In her crib. She wouldn't let me take it away. She'd reach into it with such tenderness. She'd smile at her and caress her, the baby that was no longer there. She got angry with me because I couldn't see her.' He stretched his neck out and scanned the stars above us. 'I don't think there can be a God, Dagny. Not a benevolent one. Why would He take them from us? Somewhere up there,' he said, 'in the blinking of the stars, that must be where they are.'

He picked up the lantern and urged me to come with him without saying another word. I reached out and took his hand. Then I lifted my face and I kissed him on the cheek. It was all I could offer him. I couldn't bring Alexandra back, or Jacob. Grieg and I knew they weren't coming back to us, we just couldn't accept that they were no longer here.

He slipped his arm around my shoulder and we trudged back through the snow together. We walked with a reluctant acceptance of the things that were beyond our control or comprehension, and together we shared a silent exchange of empathy, a small stitch that knotted us together. When we reached the ridge, I turned back and looked again at the sky. The vivid lights had faded now and only the faintest wisps of murky green mist laced the air. They hadn't taken me. Not this time. Not yet.

Nina was stoking the fire when we came in, despite its roaring flames.

'Heavens!' she said, 'Dagny, come and warm yourself. Where have you been, dear? I was so worried about you, going off into the night like that, you scared me half to death.'

'She's all right,' Grieg mumbled.

'Let me look at you,' Nina said, ignoring Grieg. She rushed at me, all hands and fingers, feeling my brow, feeling my neck, rubbing my arms and squeezing my shoulders. 'Come, come, come,' she said, pushing me towards the fire. 'Has he apologised?' she said, 'Has he told you he is sorry.'

I nodded.

'Good, and I should think so too. Lord, you must have a fever. You're shivering, look at your teeth chattering away.'

She made me stand in front of the fire as she peeled away all the wet layers of clothing that were sticking to my skin. 'There now, sit down, I have some soup. I'll bring you a bowl.' She looked at Grieg then, 'Edvard, you must come and get warm too,' she said. Her own iciness melted to sympathy when she saw that he was blue with cold and breathing heavily in cumbersome gasps. 'The Dovregubben indeed,' she said, patting his shoulder, 'a fine troll you would make.'

Grieg and I sat next to each other in chairs by the fire, supping Nina's meaty broth, snuffling and gulping as we began to thaw out.

'You should have seen the sky,' Grieg said to Nina after a while. 'It was sparkling like emeralds.'

Nina handed him a napkin, she seemed anxious. 'The Northern Lights?' she said.

'They were so bright.'

'The spirits of children,' Nina said, slumping to her knees on the rug, 'do you think she is near us?'

'I think she is always near us,' Grieg said. 'I just didn't realise it until I was up there with Dagny. Somehow she'd always seemed so far away but now she feels near. I can't explain why.'

I licked my spoon clean and tapped it against the side of my bowl making a tinging sound, as if I was about to hold a speech.

'What is it, Dagny?' Nina said.

I made the actions of writing with my spoon.

'Just a minute,' Nina said, fetching my paper and pencil. She took the bowl from me and placed the paper on my lap. 'You wanted to say something?'

Jacob is in Edvard's music, I wrote.

Nina read the note then handed it to Herr Grieg.

'That's what you were trying to say?' he said.

I wrote some more. *He is in that piece you are working on, the one about the sunshine. I feel him in it. It is him.*

'Really?'

I continued to write. *Isn't Alexandra in your music too?*

'Yes,' Grieg said, 'she is.'

Then that part of you that you were talking about, it is here, with you, in your music, not far away in the stars.

Grieg read my words. 'Is that how you see it?' he said.

Nina read it too. 'When she died, I was expecting another child,' she said to me.

Grieg reached down to her. 'It's all right, Nina,' he said, 'don't upset yourself again.'

'I lost that baby too, before it was even born. The doctors told us we couldn't have any more children after that.' She pressed her hand on top of Grieg's, drawing strength from his fingers. 'It's just that I never thought I would be given the chance again, Edvard, the chance to be a mother to someone, and Dagny has, well,' she stopped her tears with the palm of her hand, 'she has given me that chance.'

I slid down to the floor and crawled into Nina's arms. We leaned against Grieg's chair as the fire blazed and warmed all the parts of us that had been frozen. It was the first time I had ever felt a mother's love. It had such a comforting, healing quality. The only other love I knew was Jacob's, and that was so vast and deep and voracious that no amount of it could ever be enough. Nina's love was something different. It was calm and quiet. It asked no questions, it was gentle and soft, and whatever it was I seemed to be looking for, Nina's love had already found it.

She held me in her arms, rocking me gently until I began to fall asleep. Then she started singing, it was a lullaby, a song I had heard before. *My mother lifted me onto her knee, danced with me to and fro.* Nina's voice was like starlight, seeping into my body and relaxing every part of me. *Dance then, dance then, so the baby will dance.* She sang another verse. *The child is laid down in the cradle now, either crying or laughing. Sleep my child, sleep my child, may Jesus guard the sleeping child.* The song was calming and soporific, so familiar to me that it brought a quiet sense of belonging. Somehow it felt as though Nina had been singing it to me all my life.

My limbs sank, my jaw softened and my body was so heavy that I couldn't move. I felt Grieg's hands at my back and under my legs, and together they carried me over to my bed. 'Goodnight, Dagny,' Nina whispered, tucking me in. 'We should all get some sleep.'

I heard them blowing out candles and putting up the fireguard and tidying dishes and cutlery away. Nina was still humming the lullaby. I turned onto my side, listless but still awake. As the fire dimmed and the room became dark, I thought I heard Nina and Grieg kiss. They crept into the music room and I heard their footsteps on the stairs, then all went quiet and a peacefulness descended over the cabin.

INTERLUDE

I leave the stage, gliding off like a moving piece of furniture. My ladies catch me in the wings and lead me down the passageway as though I am blind. All I have to do is move my feet, which are pinched tightly in my Marie Antoinette slippers. When we reach the dressing room I kick them off impatiently, then I stand immobile with my arms held out to the sides like Christ at the crucifixion.

Ellen, Nora and Adele rush at me; six grabbing hands. Ellen reaches up and whips out the pins from my hair. She has to stand on a chair to remove the wig. Nora and Adele untie my strings and undo the hooks, undressing me in haste and peeling my clothes away from my body. I shake my arms free, glad to be liberated from the encumbrance of the costume. Adele loosens the enormous glittering bell of the skirt and starts working on releasing me from the hooped crinoline prison.

'That one brought the house down,' she says. 'There was even some whooping, did you hear it? The audience could barely contain their delight.'

'What a splendid night this is, Miss Jensen,' Nora says.

'Indeed it is,' I say, but I do not convince myself.

Ellen returns the wig to its stand and helps Adele pick through the laces and hooks at the back of my corset. After much undoing, the remains of the costume finally drop to the floor in a heap and I am able to step away.

I slip into my robe. Adele pours me a glass of water. 'Here, Miss Jensen, drink this,' she says, handing it to me as I sit at the dressing table. 'I'll be back later.'

Nora smears cream onto my face and wipes away the thick white powder, the beauty spot, the red lips, the penciled-on eyebrows. I slowly revert back to myself again with a sigh of relief. 'There,' Nora says, 'I'll give your skin a breather for a while. Can I get you anything, Miss Jensen?'

I shake my head. 'No, thank you. Just a few minutes of rest while Ellen does my hair.'

Adele and Nora leave. Ellen uncurls the net cap that grips my scalp, gently loosens my hair and starts combing. She has a smooth, light touch, gentle and serene. She combs in long soothing strokes and I no longer feel as if I am backstage at the theatre but instead I am at a resort in Eastern Europe or somewhere in the Mediterranean, taking the waters. I close my eyes as the tiredness returns and fills my entire body with fatigue.

I want to go home but I'm not entirely sure where that is. Is it Hardanger, or is it Bergen? My brothers, or Nina and Kristian?

I have always felt at home with Kristian, ever since we met. It was at a dinner party at the house of Consul Mohr, a close friend of Nina's. We were seated next to each other at the table.

Kristian was invited in the capacity of banker. I expected him to be grey and dull and I made a point of trying my best to ignore him at the table. I was rude and standoffish, and wasn't in the mood for small talk. When Consul Mohr stood up to announce a musical interlude between courses, we all smiled and expected Nina to go to the piano and sing, but to my astonishment, it was Kristian, the banker, who got up from his chair. He went to the end of the table where he was handed a violin. He took up his position in front of the piano and stood before us to play.

Kristian closed his eyes for a moment and while the pianist played the first few bars, *lento doloroso*, Kristian's eyebrows murmured with the briefest tremor; a memory, a mood, something painful crossed his mind. Then he tucked the violin under his chin and attacked the strings with his bow and the fluttering run of notes took us all by surprise. A sombre and beautiful lament followed, before the piece became fiercely upbeat. I watched Kristian's nimble fingers span the strings with such ferocity and decisiveness, racing up and down the neck of the instrument, and it made me think about Joakim Lilleberg. The entire piece felt as though it had flown in from the mountains. It had the familiar grit and lilt of the folk songs of my youth – those pounding parallel fifth chords.

It came to a dramatic and resounding end that had the entire party on their feet, thumping their hands together in appreciation amid cheers and shouts of *Bravo!* Kristian stood beside the pianist and bowed, rather humbly, then returned to his seat beside me.

'I had no idea bankers could play music like that,' I said, 'you must have sold your soul to the Fossegrimmen.'

He looked at me curiously and I told him the tale of the creature that resided in waterfalls and made the music of nature itself.

'I must tell that story to my daughters,' he said, 'they will like that.'

And so it began. He talked openly about losing his wife, Eleanor, and trying to pick up the broken pieces, struggling to make things work on his own as a father of two young girls. He had a sweet and endearing quality that was made all the more charming by the fact that he was unaware of it himself. He had lived enough of life and experienced enough pain to think less about what he needed for himself and more about what he could give to others. I liked that he was not impressed at all by Dagny *out there*, he was disinterested in all my accolades and cared far more about who I was as a person. I saw immediately that he needed someone to care for him. He deserved to be loved and I knew that I would be the one to love him.

With Kristian I found a ready-made family. I gave Lena and Iselin time, didn't want to rush anything or try to be their mother. What did I possibly know about that? I was surprised to find that they warmed to me at once and I liked having them there. They have always been my little friends and our relationship has been much the same as my own relationship with Nina. We have been happy these six years. Things have been solid, until now. Now I threaten to ruin everything, to change this contented quartet and throw it reeling into a realm of unknowns.

I open my eyes and look at Ellen in the mirror. She is dividing my hair into sections. She smiles at me, as if welcoming me back from a dream. I watch her braid my hair, her fingers moving deftly like machines as two platted ropes begin to form. 'One more to go, Miss Jensen,' she says.

'I'm so tired,' I say, 'I can't seem to shake it.'

'You'll be all right when you get out there,' she says, 'they love you.'

Adele and Nora return, followed by the call-boy. 'Twenty minutes, Miss Jensen,' he says.

'We have plenty of time,' Adele says, taking my Hardanger blouse from the rail and feeding it onto her arm.

Ellen drives pins into my head but I do not flinch. She tugs at the braids to make sure they are secure then gives me a nod in the mirror. 'There,' she says.

I stand up again and let them dress me. The blouse is thrown over my head and I step into my skirt. Nora bends down to fit my shoes. I breathe long deep inhalations and short puffing exhalations. I lift and drop my cheeks, tense and release my diaphragm, smack my lips together, waking myself up again. They fit the bodice and push the insert into place. I tie my belt myself, there's a technique, and I re-pin my mother's brooch as they are buttoning me up.

Nora does my make-up while I am standing. There is hardly any to apply for this costume. She powders my face to dampen down the shine, adds rouge to my cheeks and brushes on some pink lipstick. I look at the deflated chandelier dress in a heap on the floor and the blue evening gown hanging up on the screen as Adele pumps perfume from the bottle and it mists all around me. Looking in the mirror, I see Dagny *in here*, the young girl in her local costume, running on the mountain, wild and untamed like nature itself.

'Jacob?' I say. I stare hard in the mirror, leaning in closer.

Ellen looks at me strangely. She thinks I'm looking at her. 'Miss Jensen? It's only me.'

'Yes,' I pull back again, 'sorry, Ellen, I was miles away.'

I check the sashes of my belt, and suddenly think about Lillian Jevnaker and Rolf Qvale.

I smile to myself. '*Rolf let Lillian run out on the hillside, over the hill she went tripping along. Rolf he knew by the way she was acting, the fox was out with his tail so long. Cluck, cluck, cluck Lillian was cackling, cluck, cluck, cluck, cluck Lillian was cackling.*'

The three ladies gape at me as if I am demented and I laugh at their astonishment. 'Something I used to sing,' I say.

The door opens behind me and we all turn.

It is Kristian.

'Kristian?' I say, 'It's not the end yet.'

'No,' he says, quietly, 'but I had to talk to you and see if you were all right.'

The ladies stand awkwardly between us for a second before Adele leads them out. 'You will not be needing us again, Miss Jensen. Good luck.'

'Oh, but I will,' I say, pointing at my silk evening gown on the screen, 'won't you dress me for the reception tonight?'

They all nod eagerly. 'With pleasure,' Adele says.

Kristian and I are left standing face to face. It is a moment I have dreaded. It has all the hallmarks of that well-rehearsed scene; breaking point, where I say I cannot be a wife or give up my career, and the man standing opposite me says he will not live like this anymore, that I must commit to him fully. It is anguished and painful and hopeless, and yet I resign myself to it. But this time it is different. I cannot let Kristian walk away from me.

He looks at me. His eyes are full of fear. His heartbeats fill the space around us, priming the air with a quivering tenseness as if it is preparing to catch shards of glass. I too, am scared. I am terrified. I am afraid the terror will take my voice again and leave me mute. My heart screams.

Kristian reaches out to me and takes my hand in his.

'Please, my darling,' he says, 'tell me.'

18

I started spending more time with Herr Grieg, although I still did not speak. The silence was keeping Jacob close to me, as if I was clinging on to a ledge that bridged the gap between life and death and all of it was pasted together by the music. Grieg could see that I was curious. I had started sitting outside his room with my ear pressed up against the door, listening as closely as I could, trying to find Jacob in every note. I'd be there when Grieg came out, waiting like a dog waits for its owner. Soon, he started letting me in. *I think it would be more comfortable on the piano stool than it is on the floor, Dagny.*

He sat and worked and he let me watch and listen with intense concentration, without minding that I was there. It was as though my presence actually helped him to compose. He would mumble and mutter. Occasionally he'd stop and read parts of Ibsen's manuscript then return to the piano with new ideas. Slowly I began to piece together the story of *Peer Gynt*. It was just like one of Jacob's folktales: a young man from Gudbrandsdalen who tells tall tales and exaggerates to impress people, who goes on a journey and gets up to all kinds of mischief, but who never faces up to his responsibilities or listens to his own conscience. And all the time he is away, his true love, Solveig, waits for him.

'Here Dagny, this part,' Grieg said to me one afternoon, 'when the choir comes in, the trolls must be in uproar and swarm the stage in a frenzy, baying for Peer Gynt's blood. And the young trolls' lines, *let me cut off his fingers! Let me tear out his hair!* have to be said quickly, *bang, bang, bang,* and all the young trolls should run towards the Dovregubben, one at a time, and only say their lines when they get to the very front of the stage. That would heighten the dramatic effect, you see? They should all gather in front of the Dovregubben in anticipation, awaiting orders, until he roars: *Wait! Let your blood be ice water!* That's when the bass drum and the cymbals need to pound as hard as they can. It must be a giant boom at the end.' He hit the keys of the piano so hard that I jumped and he laughed. 'Precisely! The audience must be scared.'

He pushed up his sleeves. 'I've made this piece as overly Norwegian as I can, as frenetic and wild as possible, so much so that it's almost a cliché with its cow pats and pigs and oxen and ale, I can hardly listen to it myself anymore. But I hope the audience will see the irony. Ibsen's poking fun at all the Norwegian-ness of it, you see?'

I took my pencil and wrote in the corner of the page: *Why?*

'He's been out of the country so long. He is frustrated with it. I suppose all the artists and writers are. It's hard to get people to accept something new. Bjørnson and I have been trying to write a national opera. This country needs a flourishing cultural life with Norwegian themes. It needs an identity. But the musical culture in Christiania is in a sorry state. There's hardly even a full orchestra to speak of.'

As I listened to him, I started to sense that Herr Grieg might be quite an important man. I wrote: *are you famous?*

He laughed. 'My piano concerto was played all over Europe. Liszt played it by sight in Rome when I visited him. It was very well received, yes, but you see,' his voice drifted away and he returned to the piano, 'an artist is not simply one piece of music.' He played a few forlorn notes. 'And we need to eat, to pay the bills. That's part of the reason why I've ended up here with *Peer Gynt*. At first I thought it would be a simple case of writing a bit of incidental background music to cover the scene changes, but then when I read the text...it's so much more than that. You have to admire Ibsen's facetiousness. Although Bjørnson has fallen out with me for doing it, he thinks I've abandoned him.'

He returned to his work and I sat there watching his fingers move across the keys.

He continued to play, painting pictures with his music. I listened, imagining the trolls in the hall of the mountain king. As the music played I heard Jacob telling the story in his animated way, sticking his fingers out like claws and creeping up behind me, frightening me and then laughing at how easy it was to scare me.

Nina knocked at the door. 'It's Torgeir,' she said, 'back with provisions.'

Grieg got up from the piano. 'Good,' he said, 'now I'll be able to fix that G.'

They knew I always hid from Torgeir and I refused to come out of the music room. Nina smiled at me. 'If he has to come in here, you can go up and sit on my bed, Dagny,' she said, closing the door.

When they had gone, I looked again at the manuscript. Grieg had left the stack of paper on the piano stool. I picked it up and flicked through it. He had written notes on almost every page. When I heard Torgeir's surly voice bombarding the cabin, I picked up the manuscript and hurried up the stairs.

This time I paid more attention to the Griegs' room. It was cold up in the rafters. The beds were covered in matching checkered blankets and white sheets. Extra quilts were piled at the foot of each bed. Nina's nightgown was folded on one of the pillows. I sat down and slipped my feet under the heavy woolen blanket and leaned back. I looked at the photographs beside Nina's bed. One was a picture of Alexandra in a small oval frame, another was of Nina and Grieg. Nina was sitting at a writing desk and Grieg was standing facing her, his elbow resting against the desk. Nina was half smiling at the camera but Grieg had a faraway look in his eyes and his gaze was off to the side, as if he was looking at something else in the corner of the room. The last picture was not a photograph, it was programme in a rectangular silver frame. The programme was from *Herr and Fru Grieg's concert, at the Latin School in Drammen, Friday 2nd*

May 1872. There were six musical pieces listed in the programme, four of them were written by Grieg and two were by Mendelsohn. I looked at their names at the top of the programme; *Herr and Fru Grieg,* and I remembered something Nina said to us when we first met her: *It's the music, it binds us.*

I propped the thick manuscript up against my knees. *Peer Gynt, by Henrik Ibsen.* I flipped the pages, searching immediately for Solveig, the character I was most curious to know. Grieg had underlined certain lines and phrases and added notes in the margins. Some of them shouted out at me. The words seemed to lift off the page:

PEER GYNT: Be patient, my love. Long or short, you must wait.

SOLVEIG: I will wait.

One page had more notes and markings than any other, it was dog-eared and worn: *A hut in the forest. Its open door has a strong wooden bolt and there are reindeer horns above it. A handsome woman now middle-aged sits and spins outside the hut in the sunshine.*

SOLVEIG: The winter may pass and the spring disappear, the spring disappear.

The summer too will vanish and then the year, and then the year.

But this I know for certain: you'll come back again, you'll come back again.

And even as I promised you'll find me waiting then, you'll find me waiting then.

(She beckons to her goats; then, resuming her spinning, she sings again).

God help you when you're wand'ring your way all alone, your way all alone.

God grant to you his strength as you kneel at his throne, as you kneel at his throne.

And if you are in heaven now waiting for me, in heaven for me.

Then we shall meet again love and never parted be, and never parted be.

At the top of the page, Grieg had written *SOLVEIG'S SONG* in capital letters, and in the margin, he had written copious notes. *The actress must make the most out of characterising Solveig. If the actress is not able to perform the humming piece, a solo clarinet could take over and Solveig could be spinning for as long as that lasts? But it would not work for her to be spinning to a 3/4 tempo, because that's not the character of the song and because then the whole effect would be lost.*

I realised this must have been the song Nina was singing when Jacob and I had overheard the Griegs arguing and seen Nina crying – it was the haunting elegy that twisted the tender place within me, a woman waiting for someone to return.

I swept through the manuscript, needing to know if Solveig was ever reunited with Peer Gynt. And there, in the final pages, another line jumped out at me: *You have made my life a beautiful song.* Solveig cradles Peer in her arms and he buries his face in her lap as the sun rises in the distance. There were more scrawling notes: *I'm hoping to create a poetic effect here, using harmonies. Peer lies almost hidden in Solveig's arms while the light of the morning sun blazes across the horizon. The actress must be able to sing quietly and tenderly, but towards the end becoming louder and more intense. The beats must emphasise the beginning of the bar and quickly become pianissimo so that the entire scene is like a dream. The curtain must fall very, very slowly, while Solveig's head is bowed over Peer Gynt.*

The finality of it was chilling. The thought of a curtain falling made me sad. It brought the feeling of endings and the unavoidable emptiness that is left when someone is gone.

I heard the door below me open. 'It's safe to come out now, Dagny,' Nina called, 'Torgeir just left.'

I took the manuscript down to Nina and opened it at *Solveig's Song*. I hit the page with my finger then pointed at Nina and the piano.

'You want me to sing this?'

I nodded.

Grieg came in carrying a cup of coffee.

Nina looked at him and then at me. 'Now?'

I nodded again.

'Edvard, would you play *Solveig's Song*? Dagny wants to hear it.'

'It's the only one I've finished,' he said, putting his cup down on top of the piano.

I moved out of the way and Grieg sat down on the stool. Nina stood at his shoulder and he shuffled through his papers to find the score. As he began to play, I imagined the two of them performing together on a stage and it became clear to me that no matter how frustrated they became with each other they were meant to be together. Nina was right, the music did bind them.

Nina sang with such depth and grace. Not a single note was forced or strained. The music gently poured from her mouth and filled the room with a delicate and poignant tension.

She was so expressive, smiling, her eyebrows raised, her head slightly nodding then slightly shaking with conviction, her eyes lifting to the ceiling finding some far-off place. She had become Solveig herself. Grieg closed his eyes and his head shook at the same time as hers. His body bent over the keyboard and rocked to and fro, playing the notes so softly it seemed he was afraid to touch them.

The melody was utterly bewitching. Nina and Grieg had entered into their own secret place, an inner world. I hardly believed it possible for two people to be able to create something of such intense beauty. Each of them complemented the other. Each understood the other without any rehearsal or conversation. It simply came out that way. Beautiful, like all the beauty of nature, it was perfect.

When it ended, I was almost shocked to hear Nina speaking normally again.

'You look as if you understand it, Dagny,' she said. 'Do you? Do you feel it?

I nodded.

'Would you like to sing it?'

I stared at her. I wished with all my heart that I could sing *Solveig's Song* as beautifully as Nina did. I nodded gently.

'Then why don't we try?'

I shook my head and opened my mouth helplessly.

'Why not? Understanding the piece is half the battle. If it means something to you, in here,' she said, touching her own chest, 'then it becomes much easier to sing.'

She disappeared into the other room to fetch the music stand.

My lessons with Nina had not been fruitful. In all the weeks she had been working with me, all I had managed to do was breathe *ha ha haaaa* in a whispery inaudible breath. She had persevered but I failed to see the point in breathing lessons. I knew how to breathe.

'Right, there we are,' she said, setting up the stand and carefully putting the music in front of me, even though I couldn't read it.

She started off the way she always did. 'Breathe from your tummy, Dagny, as well as your lungs. Fill up your whole body, that's it.'

I started to breathe deeply, as she instructed, and she nodded encouragingly.

'Now dear, imagine a tiny thread at the base of your spine. Can you imagine me pulling that thread so that your tummy muscles pull inwards? Yes? Good dear, keep it going, that's it.' She kept smiling at me as I breathed in and out through my mouth.

'Try some *pah pah pah* sounds,' she said, 'with your lips.'

My mouth opened and closed, making empty sounds like a fish.

'Now look at me, dear,' Nina said, 'lift your chin and imagine it is your eyes that are singing, not your mouth. Good.'

She turned and gave Grieg a wink and he played a soft note.

'There, that's where we're starting. It's an E. Can you find that E in your head, Dagny?' I kept looking at her.

'Now, imagine another little thread, this one is in between your eyebrows. That's where we're going to pull the sound out from. Your eyes are singing, remember?' She came closer to me and placed her hand on my chest. 'It starts in your heart. Find it there, find it.'

I searched my heart and instantly felt Jacob.

Nina moved her hand to my stomach. 'This is where you give it power and strength,' she said, 'can you feel that, in your muscles?'

I kept staring at her. She knew I understood. She knew she had reached me.

'And then here,' she said, touching the bridge of my nose, 'this is where you express it. I'm going to pull that thread here. Now, breathe.'

I inhaled and sent air down through my whole body. Nina rested one hand on my shoulder and with the other she touched my chest and started singing the E herself. Then she touched her hand to my stomach and then moved it up to my nose. She pressed her thumb and index finger together and pulled, drawing an invisible thread out from my face. I opened my mouth.

'You're safe, Dagny,' Nina said. 'The E, find the E.'

I inhaled again. Nina moved her hand to my chin and lifted it higher. She was smiling with such love and tenderness. It was hard to feel anything but safe with her.

I kept my eyes on Nina and she twitched the invisible thread.

Grieg played an introduction. I relaxed and let go. I let go of the ledge. I exhaled.

I inhaled and exhaled.

Sound.

Nina kept smiling and nodding her head gently.

There was sound.

I kept inhaling and exhaling. It felt as though I was flying.

My chest filled with Jacob.

There was love and serenity, and there was sound.

Grieg didn't turn. He shook his head and rocked with the notes, just as he had with Nina.

Nina moved her hand as if to tell me to continue, that I was still safe, that she was holding me and we were flying together.

It took quite a few breaths for me to realise that the sound I heard was coming from me. It was my own voice.

I stayed inside the song, inside *Solveig's Song*, with Nina holding me and Grieg giving me all the musical cues I needed to know where to put the melody. I wasn't singing words, I was only making the tune with my mouth. It was an *aaahh* sound, rising and falling, high then low, soft then louder, then soft again.

When the song drew to a close, Grieg bowed over the final notes and stayed in that position until the resonance faded and ended, and all that was left in the room was Nina and Grieg and me, and somewhere, Jacob.

Nina threw her arms open wide and rushed to embrace me. 'Dagny! You were singing!' she said, hugging me tight to her chest. 'What a beautiful voice you have!'

Grieg turned around on the piano stool and then stood up. He came over to me slowly. His eyes were wet with tears but he didn't wipe them away. Nina stepped back and smiled at me, her entire face gleaming with pride, and then Grieg took me in his arms and held me to him. My head rested against his chest. He held me there for a long time then he kissed the top of my head.

'You found the place, my dear,' was all he said. 'You found the place.'

INTERLUDE

I stand there in my Hardanger clothes, trembling like the girl who once stood alone before the troll's stairs. I am facing the thing I have always feared the most, the unknown. Kristian waits patiently, keeping his eyes on me, doing his best to hold me even though what I am about to say might shatter him.

'We should sit down,' I say, stalling again.

'No. Here. Now. Just say it,' he says, through pinched lips.

'All right.'

He stares at me, waiting for me to start. I clear my throat. There is that moment of silence, just like the pause before a song, that intake of breath that unites us in anticipation; it is the edge of the precipice from which there is no return.

'Oh Kristian,' I say, shaking my head as pain and fear swell in my throat. The words come out in a whisper. 'I'm pregnant.'

He looks at me, opens his mouth. He's trying to say something but can't.

I glance nervously at the door.

He's staring at me so hard that I can't tell if he's angry or not.

'I will lose everything, don't you see?' I look over my shoulder and check the door again. 'What if anyone finds out about this?' I whisper, 'Even if we got married today this baby would be born less than nine months from now. What will people say? A baby outside wedlock? An illegitimate child? What will happen to Dagny Jensen then? I will be a public disgrace and I will bring shame on you too.'

He keeps staring at me without blinking.

'And it's so very dangerous,' I rush my words, 'haven't I told you that my mother died giving birth to me? I will most

256

likely die too. And where would that leave you if we were married? A widower for the second time – do you think I could do that to you? And alone with a baby, just like my father was, and no mother to look after it. You have already been through this before, Kristian. I couldn't put you through it again.'

He inhales fully and holds his hands motionless in the air at the sides of his face. 'You're pregnant?' he finally says.

'And even if I didn't die, the baby might. How would we cope with that? To be given that joy only to have it taken from us.' I touch the edge of my bodice and pick at the stitching. 'Look what happened to Nina,' I sniff, 'I couldn't bear...I mean, if you knew the agony it caused. The grief, it just broke them...I couldn't bear it, Kristian. I am so frightened.'

My fear finds its way out into the open and I feel a chill envelop me and seep into my skin. The cold of the mountain returns to my blood and I shiver at the memory of Grieg, gazing up at the green night sky, wondering if his lost child was near.

Kristian takes me in his arms and presses me against his body. 'You're pregnant,' he says again, with a fragile laugh.

'Kristian, there isn't a part of it that I can bear,' I say.

I feel his lips kiss the top of my head. 'You are expecting a baby,' he says, still trying to make sense of it.

'What about my reputation, and the shame of it all? What if people find out about my condition before we are married? I will be a pariah. There isn't a single member of that audience out there who would want to come and see me sing then.'

Kristian steps away from me. 'Dagny, is this the *only* reason you want to marry me now? Is it the only reason why you're suddenly so favourable to the idea? Because you have to?'

'What?' I see the fear in his eyes again, 'What? No...'

'Would you have married me anyway?'

'Of course.' I take his hand and breathe several times before I can say anything else. 'Look, I'll admit it, perhaps I have been putting this off, but that's just because of my own stupid fear, it has nothing to do with you or the way I feel about you. I would make such a dreadful wife, Kristian,' I hesitate, bite my lip, 'I'm not Eleanor.'

'No you are not, and I don't want you to be Eleanor either. I love you for who *you* are. That will never change.' He holds my face in his hands. 'No one's asking you to stop singing, Dagny.'

'I might have to now,' I say, swinging my arm out towards the dressing table, 'all this is lost to me.'

'You're not going to lose anything,' Kristian says, gently.

'I will lose everything. And I will bring such shame on you that you might lose everything too.'

'You couldn't possibly shame me, Dagny. Do you think I care about what people might say?'

'It would be in all the newspapers.'

'We'll find a way around it,' he says.

'How?'

Kristian cradles my head and gently holds me to him again. 'We can get you away for a while, cancel your concerts.'

'Away?'

'Away from Bergen, until the baby is born.'

'Where will we go? What about the girls? Your job?'

'You've never taken me to Utne before,' he says.

'You want to go and stay there?'

'I hear Nina has a little cabin we could go to, somewhere on the mountain,' he smiles.

'And you think I could do this there? What if I die?'

'You won't die, Dagny.'

'What if our baby died?' I gasp at the thought, 'What would that do to us? It almost destroyed Nina and Edvard. The bitterness and the blame gnawed away at them for years.'

'Dagny, darling,' he says, his voice quiet and patient, 'all this talk of death.'

'I can't help it,' I say, 'after everything that happened.'

'You are not your mother, and we are not Edvard and Nina Grieg. You must have some faith. This is not the catastrophe you think it is. It doesn't signal the end of things, only the beginning.'

I lift my face. He is smiling at me. The dimples flash in his cheeks. 'You're not alone. I will be here.'

'I thought you would leave me,' I say, wrapping my arms around him. 'How can we make this work?'

'We can start by getting married,' he smiles, 'we could do it in the morning, while your brother is still here.'

'Won't everyone think it suspiciously sudden?'

'Dagny, we have been together for years. I think they're more likely to think that it's about time.'

'I suppose you're right.'

Just then, Harriet batters at the door. 'Five minutes,' she shouts, abrasively.

'It is your encore,' Kristian says.

'*Solveig's Song*,' I nod.

He kisses me tenderly. 'I'll see you out there,' he says.

I stop him as he goes to the door. 'Kristian,' I say, pulling him back into my arms. 'I'm sorry.'

'No need to be,' he says. 'Now go out there and sing, Dagny Jensen. Show them who you are.'

He leaves me alone in the dressing room and I stand in front of the mirror and look at myself, finding again the young girl who hid at the cabin on the mountain that winter when so much was lost. *Solveig's Song* is the piece that brought my voice back, allowed me to speak again. So many winters have passed since then, so many summers, so many years. I stare at that girl. I summon the E and make it wait inside me. I bring the second verse to mind, whispering the words into the mirror to the boy I see over my shoulder.

And if you are in heaven now waiting for me, in heaven for me.

Then we shall meet again love and never parted be, and never parted be.

He grins at me, his chalk white hair glowing in the shadows. *You're such a girl, Dagny Jensen.*

Something ignites as he says it, a fighting spirit within me, and I feel the mountain calling me; I can smell its cold freshness and the waft of the pine trees, and I hear the call of the ravens inviting me home.

THIRD MOVEMENT
SONG

19

Nina, Grieg and I were in our own hidden world; a place detached from the lives we had known before. The little cabin was a mountainous nook of music and song, where our three souls could exchange the pain and loss we had suffered and somehow find redemption in the music we made. With the Griegs, I was as close to happy as I had come since losing Jacob. In the safety of their protection and with their gentle nurturing, I slowly began to use my voice again. I could sing, occasionally with strength and power, and I was gradually able to let go of the ledge and bring myself to talk in whispers to Nina and Grieg.

Nina and I sang every day. She taught me how to support my voice by using my diaphragm and how to efficiently control the stream of my breath. We talked about pitch and range and register. She showed me how resonance worked in my face and chest, and how smiling opened up the spaces in my cheeks and helped me create a fuller sound. She taught me about the physicality of singing, explaining the workings of my larynx and vocal cords and the interplay between these cords and the air from my lungs in creating sound.

I became consumed by music. My hunger for it was insatiable. I spent every waking moment singing, or studying, or listening, and asking endless questions. Grieg started teaching me how to read notes from the page and had me practice scales. He taught me about keys and chords, major and minor, and about octaves, variations and movements. I was absorbed by this science, it was a map, a route to the place where Jacob existed within me. Music occupied the same part of me that Jacob did, and singing gave me access to it.

When Christmas came, we gathered around the piano and sang hymns and carols. They were more wondrous than I had ever heard them sung before, sprinkled with the magic of Nina's voice and Grieg's delicate playing. Our harmonies reverberated through those rooms and imbued them with such serenity that we could no longer feel loss and separation, only unity and peace. Gradually, gently, a healing was taking place.

In January, I turned fourteen, but it felt as though I had aged a decade. My childhood had ended when I lost Jacob. Perhaps it was already over before the accident? I loved Jacob. We were young but it had never seemed like a childish whim or a game. We knew then that we were true loves. Maybe we'd always known, so what difference did it make how old we were?

At the beginning of March, I noticed that Mother was at work again. I would wake to the sound of dripping from the roof and, as the morning progressed, the sun would gain in strength. The heat had returned to its rays and in the afternoons Nina and I would sit outside the cabin wrapped up in blankets enjoying the warm beat of sunlight on our faces. I was always astounded by this contrast, how a day could be positively hot, yet everything was still covered in snow and ice. This exchange of snow and sun, cold nights and warm days, was a game Mother played almost behind our backs. Winter's grip slackened in increments and it took weeks to see how effective spring's early efforts had been. Then suddenly, small patches of green began to appear on the ground. Shoots were springing up. Life was once again returning to the mountain.

We weren't expecting Torgeir but one morning he arrived early with a horse and cart. There was not enough snow for a sled anymore. We heard the horse braying on the hill and Torgeir shouting for her to easy up.

'What's he doing here?' I whispered, getting up from the table and heading to the music room.

'I don't remember asking for anything specific,' Grieg said, 'did you, Nina?'

Nina was shaking her head. 'Maybe he's bringing the post? There might be letters from Hanchen?'

I left Nina and Grieg to ponder on it and took up my usual position in the music room. I closed the door and sat on the piano stool, hoping that Torgeir's visit would be brief. Nina and I had planned a morning of folk songs that I had promised to sing for her, the songs I used to sing for Mor Utne's guests with Hedda and Joakim. It would be the first time I had taught Nina something she had not heard before, the first time I would not be the student but the teacher.

I was trying to remember the songs Hedda and I were singing in the eld house on the day of Hans' confirmation: *to springtime my poem I utter, that back to us he may flutter, both laden with fancies sweet, in friendly affection meet.* It seemed fitting that we should sing that song today with the sun making its return to the mountain and the snowdrops peeping up through the slush below the trees.

I reached for a pencil to write down the words but a loud crashing sound out in the hallway distracted me and I dropped it again in fright.

The noise wasn't simply Torgeir's brutish voice, there was a sound of struggle and of furniture sliding across the floor.

'Where is she?' I heard someone shout.

'Really, Torgeir? What's going on?' Nina was saying. She was frightened and her voice had become high pitched.

'Dagny? Dagny?' the other voice roared.

I jumped up and flew up the stairs to Nina and Grieg's bedroom.

The poker from the fire was sent hurtling across the floor, there was a smashing sound and Nina yelped. I couldn't make sense of the commotion. Was Torgeir attacking them?

I heard Grieg protesting, then the chairs were scraping back across the floor.

'He says she's here,' Torgeir said, 'that she's been here for months. I told him there was no one here but you two, Herr Grieg, but...well...you can see...'

Then I knew. I pushed myself all the way up against Nina's headboard and pulled the extra blankets up over my head to cover me. It was Far. He was here, in the Grieg's cabin. He had come to take me away to the asylum.

He burst through the door to the music room. Nina screamed and I heard Grieg leading her away from the room. 'It's all right, dear, let him look.'

'Dagny! I know you're here!' Far screeched.

I heard him stomp around the music room, even the piano made a chiming sound as if it had been wrenched from the wall.

I pulled the covers tight over my head. It was shocking to hear my father's voice after so long, to hear such anger directed at me. I was shaking, praying the blankets would make me invisible but knowing all hope of hiding would be pointless if he came up the stairs.

It took him seconds.

I heard his feet thumping and the bannister creaking against the weight of his arms. 'Dagny!' he shouted. 'Come out! It's no use hiding. This is *over*! You're coming home with me, right now.'

'Leave her!' Nina shouted from below. 'Leave her alone! She's done nothing.'

My entire body tensed and I clung to the blankets, still hoping he wouldn't see me, but Nina's shouting had given me away and Lars would have been a fool not to notice the covered body on the bed.

'Right!' he said, whipping off the sheets, 'This is where you've been hiding then? Come on,' he said, grabbing my arm. 'We're going back!'

I resisted his hands and kicked him away but he was too powerful for me. 'That's quite enough, Dagny,' he said, wrestling me into his arms and forcing me down the stairs.

I was crying and fighting with my father as he dragged me along the floor.

'In God's name, leave her!' Nina squealed, rushing towards him and stealing my elbow from his grip.

'Please, let her go, let's talk about this,' Grieg said, calmly.

'Talk about it? Talk about it?' Lars flared. 'You people think you can kidnap a child and get away with it? This is my daughter and she's coming home with me, right now.'

I choked and snorted as I tried to writhe away from him and Nina kept pulling me from his arms.

'Just...talk to her first,' Grieg said, holding his hands up submissively. 'Let go of her, she isn't a doll.'

'Can't you see you are frightening her?' Nina said. 'Hasn't she suffered enough?'

Far seemed to listen to this. He backed away a touch and his grip loosened.

'You don't need to be so forceful,' Grieg said, gently, 'we understand how you feel, we do, but we didn't kidnap her. She came of her own free will. Nina came to tell you she was safe. Perhaps you should talk to Dagny?'

Torgeir was standing in the doorway, so shocked at the sight of me that he had to hold onto the back of a chair. 'I honestly didn't know, Herr Jensen,' he spluttered, 'I didn't know the girl was here.'

Far had me by the scruff of the neck and shook me. I felt the hairs at the nape of my neck spring free in painful pinches.

'All right,' he grunted, tossing me away.

'Let's sit down,' Nina said, backing off.

'Please,' Grieg said. 'A cup of coffee?'

Far nodded. He could barely look at me.

The four of them moved to the little table and Far sat down reluctantly.

'They're good people,' Torgeir said. 'I don't know what's gone on here, but I doubt they kidnapped your daughter.' He was still gawping at me in disbelief.

Nina hung the pot over the fire and we all waited in silence for the water to boil.

Then it struck me. How did Far even know I was here?

I glared at Nina. Had she betrayed my trust? Had Grieg?

'Dagny, dear?' She moved towards me but I stepped away, pushing the rocking chair between us. 'No,' she shook her head, 'no, no, no! I swear I didn't say a word.'

I looked at Grieg. He was shaking his head too, clearly disturbed by this violent intrusion.

Then I looked at Far. It was the first time our eyes had properly met. He hung his head shamefully as I stared at him.

'No,' he said, irked with himself, 'she came to tell me you were safe, that's all. She never told me where you were, although I pressed her and pressed her for an answer.'

I held my palms up and lifted my shoulders, drilling him with questions using only my eyes.

He looked away. A rush of air filled his lungs and he chewed the inside of his cheek.

'It was Erik Paulson. His father beat it out of him eventually. The boy came up here once or twice. Said he used to see you and Jacob run off past the farm and up the track, he followed you sometimes, knew about the rocks.'

I gulped back tears. The boy I had seen on the plateau had been Erik Paulson. It wasn't Jacob's ghost who had waved to me, it was Erik. He had known I was here all along, and he'd kept my secret for me until he'd had it thrashed out of him by his barbaric father. I thought about Erik, his timidness and his bruises. Now he would have more because of me.

I tightened my fists and punched the wall.

Nina flinched.

'We asked everyone,' Far went on, 'house to house we went, me and the boys. Day after day, week after week. Anyone that might know where you were? Anyone who knew the places you and Jacob used to go? No one did. The two of you were as cunning as foxes.' He wiped his brow and gave a sniff. 'You neither,' he said, looking at Nina, 'no one knew who you were, or where you'd come from, or how you knew Dagny. The whole thing was a mystery.' His voice eased a fraction as his aggression slowly dissipated. 'Did you ever think about me, Dagny? Night after night, pacing the floor, going crazy wondering where you were? Did you think about that while you were hiding up here? Did you? Not knowing what in God's name had happened to you. Not knowing if she was even telling the truth,' he said, waving his finger at Nina. 'You could have been anywhere for all I knew. Just upping and leaving in the middle of the night like that, without a word to your own father? You ever think about that? What that does to a man? Well, do you?'

His eyes were full of pain. Grieg and Torgeir stared at the surface of the table.

'A father could go insane,' Far said, 'but you didn't think about that, did you? And you two,' he said, glancing from Nina to Grieg, 'bet you don't have children of your own, do you? You can't imagine what it's like to lose one.'

I punched the wall again to quiet him.

The water was boiling. Nina brought it from the fire to the bench and set the coffee on to brew. She dutifully handed out cups to the three men and they all sat and looked at them as though they didn't know what to do with them.

'I see she's just the same,' Far said, then. 'Still mute. What's the point?' He swept his cup aside and ploughed across the room to grab me again. 'You're coming with me,' he said, 'we're going home.'

I backed up against the wall and reached my hands back, pressing my fingers against the wood to try to find a grip.

'Wait,' Grieg said, getting up. 'She isn't mute. Dagny can speak.'

'Then why the hell won't she answer my questions? Why won't she talk to me? Is it sheer defiance? Is that what it is, Dagny?'

He pounded towards me, reaching out with his big arms.

'Please, wait,' Grieg said again, 'my wife has been working very closely with Dagny, she sings rather beautifully. Did you know?'

'She'll be singing for her supper when we get home,' Far said, 'come on, we're going.'

'Herr Jensen,' Nina said, placidly, 'Dagny has made enormous progress while she has been here with us. She must feel safe before she is to talk, though. All this shouting and rattling, well, it's making her nervous. There's no way she will possibly sing or even whisper to you until her environment is calm. Please, why don't you have a seat? The coffee is ready now.'

She offered him the armchair and Far huffed into it.

Nina came over to me. She took me into her arms and kissed me lightly on the forehead. 'It's all right now, Dagny, my darling,' she whispered, 'no harm will come to you. You must trust me, dear.'

Torgeir handed Far a cup of coffee and he took a slurp. It burnt his mouth and he blew on it, wafting the steam out flat.

'You see, Herr Jensen,' Nina said, 'Dagny was very concerned that a woman named...'

'Jevnaker,' Grieg said.

'That a Fru Jevnaker was threatening to have her sent away to an asylum. That's why she came to us.'

'Yes, and it would be good for her,' Far said, 'look at her, she can't talk. Lillian was offering to pay for proper treatment, proper doctors. Who wouldn't take up an opportunity like that?'

'I don't believe locking her up in an asylum would do her the slightest bit of good,' Grieg said. 'She's suffered a terrible trauma, a loss so great that it has isolated her. She has been locked up within herself for a very long time. She has already been a prisoner, a prisoner to her own fear for far too long. Sending her away to an institution would only aggravate her condition and make things worse.

'I understand you are upset, as any father would be, and that you have been concerned about her welfare, and not knowing her whereabouts must have been truly painful for you. But I believe her time spent with us has been a form of therapy in itself. Dagny has a gift, you see, Herr Jensen, and here, with us, she has been able to use it to help herself get better.'

Far stared at him, bewildered. 'A gift?' he said.

Nina smiled. 'A beautiful gift. Won't you allow her to share it with you?'

'Far won't understand,' I whispered.

Far sat forward in his seat, almost spat out his coffee. 'Dagny? Did you just say something?' He wiped his mouth with the back of his hand. 'You can talk?' he said.

'But she sings with the strength of an entire orchestra,' Grieg said, then he turned to me, 'Dagny, I'm sure your father would like to hear you sing. Why don't we play for him? He would have no cause to send you away if he knew you could make the kind of sound you make when you sing.'

This convinced me. 'All right,' I whispered.

'Let's go through to the piano then,' Herr Grieg said, 'bring in some chairs Torgeir, would you?'

Nina guided me through, refusing to let go of me until Far had sat down at a safe distance. She fussed with the music stand and positioned me in front of Grieg at the piano.

'What about *The Last Spring*?' Grieg said. It was one of his pieces; an old man reflecting on his final spring days.

Nina had sung it with me several times before. It was only later I realised that Grieg had chosen it deliberately.

I nodded in agreement. I didn't look at Far, only glanced at Torgeir, who I'd hardly ever seen properly before. He was younger than I imagined and had black whiskers that gripped the sides of his face in large coarse triangles. He was still staring at me, trying to understand what he had become embroiled in.

Grieg started to play the introduction, a soft trill of the high keys, then, *andante espressivo*, a flowing build to bring me in on a C.

I inhaled and found a spot above the doorway to focus on. I tightened my stomach muscles, opened my mouth and began to sing. The melody was a sad, stirring tune in the key of A flat. It drifted from my body with soft intonation and at the end of the first line, as the accent fell on the mellow E, I unlocked the door to Jacob.

Once more behold from the earth day by day, the ice disappearing, snow melting fast and in thunder and spray, the river careering.

We were sitting on the mountain, side by side, looking out across our world in the pastel toned summer night when the light never faded, each of us trying to comprehend the sheer size of it all. The magnificent mountains that surrounded us, as high as the heavens, majestic and wild. *Do you think there's any more world than this?* The sun slowly creeping, finding its way up from the horizon, lifting the light and changing all the shades of blue in the water. *It's hard to imagine anything bigger, anything more.* My home. My world. *Imagine all of this is inside us, and that's how big a soul is, makes you think, doesn't it?* All I had ever known.

The music made me shiver. Those tinkling runs that Grieg was so good at, how he made the piano into a living being, an expression of every human emotion at its sharpest, its most tender, its most fragile.

I looked at my father. He was staring at me as though I had been brought to this room by an angel from heaven. His lips were trembling and his eyes were full of pain and awe. His white brows arched with the aching of it and tears were falling freely to his lips.

Once more I'm drawn to the Spring-gladdened vale, that stilleth my longing; there I find sunlight and rest without fail, and raptures come thronging.

All unto which here the Spring giveth birth, each flower I have riven; seems to me now I am parting from the earth, a spirit from heaven.

I gently coaxed the song from the place within me, my place, and infused it with all the love that hid there. Love for Jacob, for Nina, for Grieg, for my father and for my mother, whose presence I felt in the room.

Therefore, I hear all around from the ground mysterious singing; music from reeds that of old I made sound, like sighs faintly ringing.

Grieg's fingers on the keys were like messages that confirmed it all. My song asked questions and the piano answered them. Grieg held my hand with his notes, *yes it's true, Dagny, dear*, he reassured me, *you're right, it's true*. We were having a conversation without saying a word. It occurred to me then that Bestefar Jørgen had been right, music allowed people to talk to each other without having to actually speak. It was deeper than words; more genuine and undeniable, more expressive than talking.

Far listened more intently to my song than he ever had to my words and I knew that something somewhere had touched him. Even Lars could feel it, that's how powerful it was.

Grieg played the final few notes like the lament of a song that didn't want to end, it idled, repeated its last few clinks with regret and remorse as it timidly parted and said goodbye.

20

Far allowed me to stay with the Griegs until I felt ready to come home. The music had spoken to him and he couldn't argue with it. No one could. The cabin had become my home, the Griegs my family, and I did not want to leave. But the day was approaching. Grieg had almost finished *Peer Gynt*, and he and Nina would soon be returning to Bergen. The three of us saw it coming and resisted it as much as we could, making the spring days stretch out like one long note, a bar of tied semibreves all linked together. Nina would hug me for longer, knowing that her arms would not have the chance to hold me much more. And Grieg seemed to be faltering, even though *Peer Gynt* was long overdue.

It was not the tune of *In the Hall of the Mountain King* that had evaded him, for it was essentially a repetition of the same notes throughout. It was how to end it, how to bring it to its crescendo, how to tie all the instruments in the orchestra together to create the impact he wanted. On the day that he finished it, he came rushing to find me. I was out with Nina, stacking wood and filling the pails with water. He approached me hesitantly, almost scared to speak. 'It's done, Dagny,' he said, as though he was confessing some terrible crime. 'I've finished it.'

I set the buckets down and ripped off my gloves and three of us went inside. We gathered around the piano. Nina and I stood back to give Grieg the space he needed while he sat and looked at the keyboard as if he wasn't sure what to do with it. He studied it in silence, gazed at the keys, making some secret pact with them, as though they were discussing how the piece would be played, making adjustments, fine tuning their ideas. When it was all set, Grieg lifted his hands as if to scare the piano, then he gently placed his fingertips

on the notes and it began. *Pom-pom pom-pom pom-pom-poooom!*
It had returned, the thing that was creeping up on us.

Grieg's fingers cast shadows on the white keys and the dark lines rushed about like a panicked mob as the piece started to gather pace. Faster and faster the music swirled, climbing the keyboard, managing to escape, then being pulled back again into the Dovregubben's hands. Grieg's fingers were flicking up and down and his body was angled forward as his foot tapped at the pedal. The bass became more manic and frenzied as Grieg punched it out with his left hand and his right hand vibrated as it tried to keep up. Soon his fingers were a blur and what he was doing looked impossible, ten frenetic fingers hammering furiously at the keys yet still making a distinctive tune. His hair was shaking all about his face as he held on to this uncontrollable monster. Then it came: *bang!* The shout of the Dovregubben. Again: *bang!* Another run of his fingers then *bang!* and *bang!* A final *pom-pom pom-pom pom-pom* then an earsplitting *bang! bang!* He flipped his hand over and swept it across the keys in a great swoosh before he plonked the bass notes with one decisive strike to end it.

He hung over the piano, shaking with exhaustion as perspiration dribbled down his brow.

'It's marvelous,' Nina said, 'I could hear every instrument in the orchestra.'

'Especially the drums and the cymbals,' I said, 'when the Dovregubben shouts at the end.'

Grieg was out of breath.

Nina put her hands on his shoulders. 'Ibsen will be thrilled.'

It was the last time I heard Grieg play at the piano in the cabin. That night, we ate dinner at the table, knowing that our winter together was over, the season had changed, the snow had melted. Mother was urging me to go back. I could not hide away on the mountain forever.

'Listen, Dagny,' Nina said, fitting her knife and fork together on her plate, 'Edvard and I have been thinking.'

I looked at her, took a sip of water.

'You don't have to answer now, dear, but we were wondering if you would like to come to Bergen, to study music with us?'

'You are enormously talented,' Grieg said, 'I would hate to see talent like yours go to waste.'

'Bergen?' I said. It was one word, one question, but behind it there were so many. *Where would I live? What about school? What about Far? What about Utne and Hardanger? My home? My world? All I had ever known?*

'We thought perhaps you might come and stay with us?' Nina said. 'We would arrange for your schooling and your musical education. It would be an opportunity for you, dear, to sing, professionally, for audiences.'

'When I was young,' Grieg said, 'just a few years older than you are now, someone gave me an opportunity. A friend of our family, who was a famous violinist, heard me play and helped my parents send me to Leipzig, where I studied music for four years. Who knows what would have become of me if I had not had that opportunity.'

'We want you to have that chance,' Nina said, 'to use your gift.'

'What about Far?' I said.

Grieg smiled, 'I think if he had considered sending you to an asylum, then sending you to Bergen to study music might be a possibility.'

'We have written a letter to your father,' Nina said, 'explaining the precise details of how you would be educated and cared for. You can wait until after your confirmation if you like, but the offer is there. We would like to help you become a singer.'

She reached for my hand across the table and I squeezed her fingers.

'Thank you,' I said.

My voice was not a whisper anymore. It was steady and clear.

Our goodbyes were painful. Nina held me tight and found it hard to let go. She gave me a small backpack. It contained food and drink for my trip, Jacob's storybook, manuscript paper, music notes, my poorly knitted mittens, scarf, hat and socks, and the Griegs' letter to Lars.

'We will see you again,' Grieg said, patting me on the back as Nina released me. His mouth lifted into a rare smile and I caught a glimpse of what he might have looked like as a boy. 'Thank you, Dagny,' he said, 'thank you for running away to us.'

They watched me climb the ravine. The ground was moist and had that warm muddy smell of early spring. I pressed the balls of my feet into the stones and leaned my body forward. It was hard to climb the hill slowly, it needed momentum, so I scurried away, grasping at roots and clumps of shrubs that were limp and lame after their winter slumber. When I reached the rocks at the top of the ridge, I turned back and waved to the Griegs, just as Erik had waved to me. Their inner arms were wrapped around each other; their outer arms were lifted and waving. It looked as though they were one single being. I felt a deep crunch of sadness as I raised my hand. 'Goodbye Dovregubben,' I said, although I knew he could not hear me.

I walked across the plateau, reacquainting myself with its stones and rocks. There were special ones that had significant meaning to me: places where I had watched Jacob stand and think, where we'd sat together and he'd told me stories, and of course, the spot where Grieg and I had almost frozen to death under the green lights of the winter sky. The bright spring morning chased away the ghosts that haunted this place. I picked up pebbles and threw them across the rocky terrain waiting to hear the clinking thud when they landed. I looked up to the snowy peak then into the sky.

Wisps of cirrocumulus cloud formed a mackerel sky. The scales rippled in waves across the dazzling blue. Although I was at the top of a mountain, I imagined I was at the bottom of another world's sea, and if I jumped from the peak I would be able to swim to the surface of that other world.

I reached the troll's stairs, thinking about worlds connecting to other worlds, places that existed so far away that we couldn't see them, only the signs of them, like the ocean in the sky. I stopped at the top of the wall of rock, remembering how insignificant it was in the giant realm of the Hardanger mountains. It was a small step on my journey back to Utne. That's how I had to picture it.

The first part was easy. I stepped down over the boulders carefully picking my way through them until the drop became steeper and I had to use my hands. The stones were cold and a breeze was whining through all the cracks. I shivered. The descent went from steep to sheer in a matter of steps. I faced the rock, clinging to it in the way Jacob had shown me, with my face turned to the side and the flinty grey slab of stone digging into my cheek. I let my body go soft and curled my spine, fitting myself to the shape of the stone. I found bumps and crevices, places where I could wedge my fingers in and make a good grip. I edged my feet along the narrow ledges only a fraction at a time.

When I came to the mighty boulder with the perfectly flat surface, I felt for the clefts that Jacob had found. I stopped and rested my brow against the rock, concentrating on my next move. When I climbed up the troll's stairs alone, I had not cared whether I slipped and fell, it hadn't mattered to me whether I lived or died. This time it was different; I wanted to live. I wanted to sing, I wanted to go to Bergen, I wanted to have audiences, I wanted to live in my music and feel the power of my own voice.

I forced myself not to look down and reached my arms out so far that my armpits ached. I felt around for the crevice at the other side and, stretching out so wide I thought my body would split in two, I made the jump across the flat stone surface and my feet found the ledge on the other side. I wobbled for a second but quickly fumbled for a fresh grip and was able to lower myself down to the next step.

I stumbled down the lumpy rock, slipping on a stream of water that was trickling down the surface. I dug my nails into tufts of moss and clung on, pressing my chest against the wet stones while my feet readjusted. When I was stable again I took a deep breath. This time I looked down. I could see the slope of the mountainside below me and the treetops watching, swaying calmly in the wind.

I closed my eyes. I could hear music.

When I opened my eyes, I knew instinctively where to place my hands and feet. The next two rocks were easy to navigate and I slid over them nimbly, the way Jacob always did. I was just repositioning my right hand, sliding it into the mouth of a small crevice, when I felt something metallic brush the side of my fingers. I yelped, as if the thing had hurt me, but it wasn't painful, it was only the shock that had hit me. The metal was bronze, the object was shiny. I reached in further and grasped it in my hand. I laughed as I pulled out Lillian Jevnaker's telescope.

'There you are!' I said. 'You were here all this time.'

I couldn't understand how it was so accessible to me. The way Jacob described it, it had been far beyond his reach. He told me we'd need pincers or some other equipment to get it. He'd had to contort his body so much to reach it that he had hurt his knee. Yet when I found the telescope, it was at the mouth of the crevice, almost protruding from it.

I tucked the telescope firmly into my belt and swung myself down the last remaining rocks until I was so close to the ground it wouldn't matter if I fell. When I reached the bottom, I took the telescope out again and laughed to myself, shaking my head in wonder. The telescope had not suffered from a winter spent on a mountainside. It had not rusted, and all the parts still slid smoothly when I extended it and pulled it out. It was just as shiny as it had been the day Jacob gave it to me, after Bestefar Jørgen had fixed it.

I ran my fingers across its glossy surface, saw the engraved name: *Hans Petter Jevnaker.* I wondered if old Hans Petter, long dead by now, had any idea of the trouble his stupid telescope would one day cause.

I lifted the lens up to my eye. Music again floated through my head. I swung the telescope up towards the sky and adjusted the lens until the patterns in the clouds came into focus. I studied the silver white scales, their perfect formations rippling in the sunlight as the music in my head grew louder. The words were no longer a question, but an answer. *You will come back to me, you will come back to me, you will come back to me, back to me now.* I combed the sky, turning my head from side to side, scanning the endless stretch of blue and the strips of cloud that painted it. Then I caught a flickering glimpse, a tiny snatch of something white; pure white, chalky white.

'Jacob?'

The music was soft, but strong and steady. It was as old as time yet fresh and different. It was great and glorious and magnificent. It was all the things I once thought were impossible to capture in music, but Grieg had done it. Every note of it was Jacob.

I kept the telescope fixed on the heavens. Inside me, the door to the music began to open and I felt myself attach to its very source.

Then I saw a smiling face up in the clouds: blue eyes, white hair, plump lips.

'I can see you!' I laughed, 'I can see heaven!'

Jacob was running. His hair was flapping and his cheeks were flushed.

'I can feel you. I know it's you. I can see you.'

He grinned at me, still running. I could see his feet now, his dirty heels and ankles, his pale skin hurtling through the clouds.

'I am going to be a singer,' I said. 'I'm going to sing so loud you will hear me in heaven!'

I lowered the telescope and started running with him. I ran down the hill with my arms outstretched and all the fresh mountain air rushing into my nose and mouth, and *Morning Mood* circling in my head, round and round, building and fading then building again. I opened my mouth and lifted my face to the sky. 'You will come back to me, you will come back to me, you will come back to me, back to me now!'

I kept running. My boots battered the mountain tracks and I came reeling down into the trees and onwards along the pathways to the lake. 'It's here!' I shouted, 'Jacob, it's all still here, just as it was.' I ran to the water's edge and found the place we had sat when Jacob first kissed me, the place where he asked me to marry him.

I was hot and thirsty. I bent down and scooped up a handful of water and splashed it all over my face and neck. I took a drink from my bag and crouched at the water's edge, watching all the ripples my hand had made circling on the surface.

I stayed at the lake. I didn't want to leave it. I ran up and down the shore, tossing stones into the water, listening to them plop and plunge at varying depths. I found flat stones and skimmed them across the clear surface, counting the times I could make them bounce. I climbed over the rocks and dallied in all the places I had been with him. I ate the lunch Nina had packed for me and drank all the water in the bottle.

I saw Jacob's feet again, scurrying away from me. He was running ahead, sprinting so fast the dust was clouding at his ankles now. He ran and I followed. I followed him back to the mountain pathways, through the trees where the fresh tingly scent of the pines sharpened the air, over the thawing earth as it softened and sweetened under spring's first caress. I followed him over bubbling streams and snapping twigs, all the way back down the hill to Utne.

21

Like the lake, the farms, the fields and the mountains, Utne was still there waiting for me when I returned. I came down past the Paulson farm, wondering if Erik could see me. Maybe he was watching from a window? I would speak to him soon. Tell him I saw him on the plateau, tell him I didn't blame him. At the side of the road, stubborn mounds of snow still remained. It would take the full strength of Mother's sun to shift them, unless we used the pickaxe. Sometimes we'd hack up the mounds impatiently, helping the sun to do its job, desperate to see the last of the winter.

From the hill, I could see my house and the church spire poking through the trees, and the peaks of the Granvin mountains in the distance, but it was the water that beckoned me the most. The dark blue velvet spread out like a carpet. Indigo met turquoise and teal met sapphire on the puckered surface that surged against the mountains rising up from its depths.

I cut through the apple orchards at the side of the Bremnes house, picking my way through the huts and stores and the lines of fruit trees preparing to face another season. The sweet tang of fruit laced the air even though nothing was ripe. It was as though the air here had memories and would only smell a certain way all year round. The sweetness turned pungent when I reached the shore and caught a mouthful of the sea air. The boat was coming in at the pier and the gulls were squawking and circling overhead.

I walked along the pebbled beach until I came to the small red hut at the end of the road. It was mid-afternoon and the light was bright on this side of the fjord. I patted my hand against the warm red timber and some flakes of paint fell away, surprised by my touch. I went around to the back, following the familiar path that time had worn away. I looked through the window, Bestefar Jørgen was sitting in the chair.

I tapped at the door.

The old man looked up – a face of whiskers and whiteness searching for the sound. 'Dagny?' he gasped, as I opened the door.

'How did you know it was me?' I said.

'Same as I know the boat is coming in at the pier.' He was starting to stand up. His back was bent into a curve and his hands and wrists looked weak as they gripped the arms of the chair and tried to bear his weight. He searched about for his cane but I reached out and took his hand so that he could balance himself on me instead.

'You're taller,' he said, his blind eyes looking over my shoulder. 'You been on an adventure?'

'I suppose so. I was on the mountain.'

'With a troll?'

I laughed. 'Yes, a troll who makes music. And his wife sings.'

'Wife? Did you rescue her?' Jørgen said.

'I don't know, but she rescued me.'

'Folks were saying you'd stopped talking altogether.'

'Mmm-hmm, I did.'

'What about that lovely voice of yours? You found it again?'

'Yes,' I said, 'I found it, and they taught me to sing with it.'

'You could sing already.'

'Nicer, I mean...better.' I eased him back into his chair. 'How've you been?' I said.

'Oh Dagny,' he said, his ancient blue eyes rimy with tears, 'makes no sense me living to this age.'

'And what age is that?' I said, kneeling down on the rug in front of him.

'I don't know? What am I? Two thousand years old?'

'Are you the Dovregubben?' I said, 'Truls Skarstad says the Dovregubben lives for up to two thousand years.'

Jørgen smiled. 'I've missed you.'

'Me too.'

I held his papery hands in mine.

'I knew you'd come back,' he said. 'They told me you'd run away, that you disappeared in the night, just like that. But I knew you'd be somewhere on that mountain, with him.'

'I've felt him,' I said, 'and I've seen him too.'

'He isn't far away,' Bestefar Jørgen said, 'I only wish he was here.'

'I am here now,' I said. 'I won't leave you again. Not yet.'

'Yet?'

'The troll,' I said, 'he and his wife, they asked me to go to Bergen, to sing.'

'Oh,' Jørgen said, 'and will you?'

'I think so,' I said, 'if Lars will let me.'

'D'you ever find that telescope?' Jørgen said, as though that's what he'd been thinking about all along.

'Yes,' I patted my hand against my bag, 'I found it today when I was coming back down the mountain.'

'Hmm,' Jørgen said, drawing a deep breath in through his nose. 'Hans Petter Jevnaker. He was in love with my wife.'

'Jacob's grandmother?' I said.

'That's right,' Jørgen smiled, 'she passed over an admiral for a poor fruit farmer like me.'

'I saw heaven with it,' I said.

'The telescope?'

'Yes.'

Jørgen lifted his eyes to the ceiling. 'Must have been the way I fixed it up,' he grinned.

I left him, promising to return the next day. He would need a pair of eyes again, and I said I would read him stories from Jacob's book, the way he used to read them to his daughter, and he looked me straight in the eyes, as though he could actually see me, and said I was an angel that God had blessed with light.

I went back up the hill the way I had come. I wanted to avoid being seen by the whole town and I wasn't ready to talk to anyone until I'd seen Lars. I was suddenly tired and my steps felt heavy as I hauled myself past the pretty Bremnes' house and onto the road at the top. I came round the bend to the chiming of the church bells. Carts carrying barrels and timber were coming up from the pier. The horses clopped slowly on, straining their necks under the burden of their hefty loads.

I crossed the road and looked up at our house, the small yellow cottage with its four windows facing the fjord. I wasn't sure if I was still welcome and I approached the door hesitantly, listening for the rumble and boom of my brothers' voices, but the house was quiet. All I could hear were the church bells chiming from the other side of the road.

I opened the door and went inside, shaking my backpack from my shoulders and hanging it on a peg.

'Knut? That you?' Far said. 'Trading done?'

He came out from the kitchen. He had a pencil behind his ear and a knife in his hand. The fire was out and the room was cool and damp and smelled of fish.

'Good God,' he said, 'Oh, merciful Lord! Dagny? You came back?'

I nodded, afraid to enter the room, afraid of how he might react.

He put the knife down on the table. 'Well come here then, let me look at you,' he said. He seemed as apprehensive as I was and he hovered by the table for a while, just looking at me. 'You've come home?' he said. 'I thought you never would.'

He came to greet me, holding out his arms as I stood there staring at him. I didn't know if he was going to hit me or hug me. 'Oh Dagny,' he said, reaching out for me, 'you really did come back.'

He wrapped me in his big arms and held me to his chest. His shirt was dirty and he smelled of fish oil and tobacco. My head slumped weakly against his body and he lowered his lips and pressed a kiss onto my head. 'Just like Emma,' he said. He stepped back and looked at me. The sunlight came flooding in through the windows and his fair lashes caught the glow of the light. 'When you sang,' he said, 'I mean when you sang. You sounded just like her.'

'She could sing?' I said.

'She had the finest voice in all of Hardanger.'

'Why did no one ever tell me?'

'Some things get hidden, I suppose,' he shrugged, 'left behind in the grief. She used to sing to you, all the time, before you were born, I mean, with her hand on her belly.' He brought me to the table and sat me down. '*Gjen-din-bån*,' he sang, '*Gjen-din-bån*. Like that, sang it over and over again, she did. You hungry?'

I nodded.

'The boys are down at the pier, trading. They'll be back soon.' He brought me a bowl and a bag of potatoes. 'Here,' he said, 'peel these, will you?'

I took the knife and began to scrape at the tough red skins, easing them back with the blade.

'You found your voice then?' Far said. 'Not just whispering anymore?'

'Nina helped me. They both did.'

'I was worried you'd be silent all your life,' he said.

'You were going to send me away.'

'I only wanted you to get better,' he said, 'didn't know what else to do. D'you know how important it is to have a voice in this world?'

'If I'd gone, I would never have come back.'

'Oh, I'd have fetched you,' he snapped. 'You think I'd have left you to rot in an asylum?'

I dropped a spiral of potato peel that had come off all in one go.

'I kept wonderin' what would become of you if you couldn't speak up for yourself,' Far said, 'what kind of life you would have had in the shadows, in the silence? It ain't no life at all. People can take advantage of someone who don't have a voice. That's not the future you were destined for, Dagny. Not with your singin' and hollerin' and fightin' with the boys. You have to use that voice of yours. God gives you a gift like that, you can't say, *well no thank you God, I ain't gonna use it*, can you?'

Nina and Grieg had also said my voice was a gift. I hadn't thought of it like that before, we all had voices, didn't we? It was the music that came through mine, that's what they meant.

'Far?' I said.

'Hmm?'

'What's it like in Bergen?'

'Hmm? City, just like any other,' he said, throwing down a pot full of water. 'Put them in there when you're done.'

'Far?'

'Huh?'

'I found the telescope.'

'What?'

'The Jevnaker's telescope, I found it.'

'I thought Konrad had that? Where d'you find it?'

'Just found it,' I said.

'Well, you should get it back to the Jevnakers then, shouldn't you? Put it back where it belongs.'

'Yes,' I said. 'Yes, I will.' I stood up and pushed my chair back and put the knife in the bowl.

'What? Now?' he said.

'May as well get it over with.'

'Right, well, *behave*. And don't go shoutin' at them girls, or Lillian, just because you've got your voice back again,' he winked, 'and you can tell your brothers to get a move on if you see them. There's plenty to be done here.'

I went to the door and slid the telescope from my bag. 'Far?'

'What?'

'Why are the church bells ringing?'

'Bloody Eugen Mohr. Practising all the hours God sends. Perhaps you can ask the good Lord, when you go by, why in hell's name Jevnaker's got a pansy boy like that in to do His work. Ringin' and chimin' til we're all demented.'

I laughed. 'I won't be long,' I said.

I came out of the house and wandered down the tracks to the road. I looked out across the graveyard. The trees cast shadows between the headstones as if they were pointing at them, making lines all the way up the hill. The mountains stood all around, guarding every side, making the wall and the headstones, even the tallest birches, look like children's toys crafted in miniature.

I went to Jacob's spot and sat down for a while by the stone that had now replaced the wooden cross.

I rested the telescope on my knees and played with the lens, twisting it around in my fingers, wondering what Jacob would have thought about Hans Petter Jevnaker being in love with his grandmother. Then I giggled to myself, thought about that silly song we used to sing: *Rolf let Lillian run out on the hillside, over the hill she went tripping along. Rolf he knew by the way she was acting, the fox was out with his tail so long. Cluck, cluck, cluck Lillian was cackling, cluck, cluck, cluck Lillian was cackling.* I laughed hard and sensed that Jacob was laughing too.

I got up and pressed my hand against his name. 'Time to face Lillian,' I said.

I went down the hill, following the curving road down towards the water. I thought about my voice and how I would use it. I had freedom, the power to say anything at all. I wasn't stuck inside myself anymore, suffocated by my own silence. I could speak, and what a luxury it was. I thought about Nina, and everything she had taught me, and began tuning up my instrument. I breathed deeply using my diaphragm, filling my entire body with breath. I tensed and flexed my stomach muscles, they would give me strength and power. I blew empty breaths out through my lips and took bites at the air to tighten and loosen my jaw and my cheeks.

I turned in at the vegetable plot behind the house and went through the garden to the front door. The window was open and a maid was clinking glasses, cleaning them or putting them away, I couldn't tell. I stepped up to the front door as if I was reaching the gates of heaven on Judgment Day, knowing I would be condemned and sent straight to hell. I stared down at the pots of pink geraniums that framed the entrance.

The maid, Berit Lindeman, opened the door. Her tight brown eyes popped wide when she saw me and I expected her to start shouting at me but she didn't give anything away.

'Yes,' she said, as if I was a complete stranger.

'I'd like to see Fru Jevnaker, please,' I said.

'Come in,' she said, with an odd formal bow, something Lillian must have instructed her to do. 'Wait here and I will see if Fru Jevnaker is available.' She crossed the hall and knocked at the door of the sitting room.

'Come in,' I heard Lillian say.

'Dagny Jensen is here,' Berit said.

'Oh,' Lillian said.

I heard whisperings and the sound of a man coughing.

'You'd better send her in then,' Lillian said.

Berit reappeared and beckoned me with her hand. I followed her to the door and she stepped aside to let me in. I held the telescope behind my back and entered the room.

Lillian was standing in front of the sofa, holding her bible in her hand. Hannah, Selma and Lovise were sitting together in front of her, all three of them looked identical with their perfectly braided hair and their immaculate clothes. Behind Lillian, I saw Konrad, down on his hands and knees on the rug. He was polishing the Steinway. In the window was the empty tripod stand.

'Well,' Lillian said, as her glassy eyes fell on me. 'You are back? And what do you have to say for yourself?' she said.

'She can't say anything,' Hannah said.

'She can't talk,' Selma said, 'God has cursed her.'

I looked at the three hateful girls on the sofa and then again at Lillian. Her face was more severe than I remembered and her skin was powdery white, almost exactly the same texture as her headscarf.

'Have you come to your senses? Agreed to be sent to the hospital in Odda now?' Lillian said, changing her tactics.

I shook my head.

'Then what do you want?'

I brought the telescope from behind my back and handed it to her with a smile.

Her eyes widened when she saw it.

'Oh,' she said.

The three girls gasped.

Konrad stopped his polishing and looked up at me.

'It can't be the same one,' Hannah said, spitefully, 'she lost it.'

Lillian inspected the telescope, looking for the engraving. 'No it is,' she said, 'it's our telescope. It has Grandfather Jevnaker's inscription.'

'She said Konrad had it,' Hannah said, 'she lied.'

Lillian turned to Konrad and ordered him to get up. 'Well, Konrad, how do you explain this?'

Konrad fiddled with the rag in his hands. 'I misplaced it,' he said.

'And now Dagny has found it,' Lillian said, 'how convenient.'

She took the telescope over to the tripod and Konrad smiled at me while Lillian was distracted. I smiled back.

'Well it certainly looks as if you have made a marvelous job of it, Konrad,' Lillian was saying, 'it glides like a dream, and look at the shine on it. Magnus will be delighted indeed.'

Konrad nodded and his hair made a floppy wave on top of his head.

The girls laughed at him.

'You can tell your father the offer still stands,' Lillian said, coming back to me.

I stared at her.

I felt my voice waiting inside me, the power of it brewing from the base of my spine, filling my stomach, rising through my lungs and throat and penetrating my face and head. Its vibration pumped in every nerve, coursing through my blood with the beat of my pulse. It was as mighty as the mountains that surrounded us, a force so potent and intense that it seemed to well up from the very depths of the fjord. It was my gift, and I finally had the chance to use it.

'Still as dumb as you were before, girl?' Lillian said.

She stared at me and the three girls stared at me too.

My voice was ready to attack. I'd use it to my advantage. Show those stupid girls what it meant to really have a voice. It would pour all over them and the enormity of it would drown them out. I would silence them with it. I would give them no choice but to listen to me and me alone.

I caught the reflection of myself in the shiny surface of the Steinway. I thought about what Lars had said: *You have to use that voice of yours. God gives you a gift like that, you can't say, well no thank you God, I ain't gonna use it, can you?*

I stepped away from Lillian and gave her a pleasant smile. I nodded to the girls. Then I looked at Konrad and waved at him with the tips of my fingers. I turned my back on the Jevnakers and walked out. Lillian was spluttering about something but I wasn't listening. Berit Lindeman came gliding to the door to perform some exiting ritual, but she was too late, I had already let myself out.

I ran down to the water, past the crowds bustling at the pier, past the steam ship and the passengers disembarking, past the carts and the traders touting their fish. I went to the very edge of the fjord and the water came to meet me there, gently lapping at my toes. I lifted my face and stared out at the great hulking mountains all around me. I would never be able to fathom their size and their strength, their majestic beauty and their ever-changing colour and mood. How they soared above us, these breathtaking giants, how they always reminded us of how fragile we were. How they shaped us and made us, and how they dominated us, without ever saying a word.

ENCORE

I'm hurrying back along the passageway towards the stage with a sense that someone is following me. When I realise it's the Dovregubben, I smile to myself. 'There you are, Grieg.' *Pom-pom pom-pom pom-pom-poooom.* It's started. The bassoons and the bass are building the tension, setting the scene for *In The Hall of the Mountain King.* When I reach the wings, I find they are packed with trolls. It's tight and dark. Some of the little ones lift their masks to see where they're going. Grotesque faces, long curling noses and bulging yellow eyes sit on the tops of their heads. The pace picks up; the violins, the drums. I peer out to the audience and see the conductor's baton jabbing and poking at the air. The choir begins to chant. *Slay him! Slay him!* The trolls pull their masks down and storm the stage leaving me alone.

Again, I am standing here in the wings; a shadowland between two worlds in the dark folds of fabric that hide me. I wait in the void, standing completely still, wondering if I will ever get this chance again. Perhaps Kristian and I should go to Hardanger, to the Griegs' cabin on the mountain, and our baby will be born into the hands of Mother in the heart of the fjord. We could stay away long enough to avoid a scandal, long enough for people to lose count of the intervening months. Maybe I could have my career and my independence, as well as being a mother and a wife? Dagny *out there* and Dagny *in here.* Maybe this new Norway will allow me to be both?

The music is intense and powerful, the way Grieg wanted it to be. *Slay him! The Christian man's son has seduced the fairest maid of the Mountain King.* It grows louder and more febrile. *Let me cut off his fingers! Let me tear out his hair!* Then there's the bang of the bass drums, the crash of the cymbals and the Dovregubben's final cry: *Wait! Let your blood be ice water!* It ends with a boom and I feel the audience jump back in their seats, just as I had myself when Grieg played it to me on the piano.

When it is over, the theatre erupts with applause. The audience is cheering, some whistle enthusiastically. The stagehands pull on the ropes and the velvet curtains swish in from the sides. The trolls come pouring off the stage and I stand aside to let them past. Then I feel a hand on my arm. 'Miss Jensen,' a young man with a tiny oil lamp is standing beside me. 'Follow me, please.'

Guided by the light of his lamp, I am lead onto the stage. 'It will be dark for a minute,' he whispers. 'Are you all right?'

I nod, firmly.

Out there, the audience is still roaring with applause. There are shouts of *Encore! Encore!* and raucous cheering and whistling, as though they have all forgotten that the king and queen are present. Behind me, I hear the scenery moving as the crew clears the stage of every last trace of the Dovregubben's hall. I touch Emma's brooch then feel for the buckle on my belt as the clapping gradually subsides into a soft patter and that moment of complete silence approaches.

Then there's the tap of the baton and the music begins again. First the flute, then the clarinet and the violins. They are singing the tune that has haunted me from the day I first heard it, when I cried on the stairs in Grieg's cabin and I lay in the snow and let the snowflakes kiss my face.

I listen to this breathtaking piece, basking in this moment, alone on the stage in the dark, as though the orchestra is playing it just for me. Each note transports me and everything begins to fall away. The varnished floor beneath me becomes soft like the earth. There is light in the darkness, sunbeams twinkling on the surface of a lake. The air changes, becomes fresh and clear, the wind rushes in my ears, the soft tips of the birch leaves brush through my fingertips.

The flute gives way to the strings and in the agonising burst of longing, I spread my arms wide and feel the music unfurl, opening up like petals and flourishing in the intensity of the sunrise. *You will come back to me, you will come back to me, you will come back to me, back to me now.* I stretch up and spin around, reaching out to my mountain and finding myself again. I open my mouth and inhale it, I can taste it now, I can feel its power inside me and all around me. There is no separation, it is all here in the music.

I marvel at how Grieg could have imagined it, in all its glorious detail, every single instrument placed so perfectly, so harmoniously together. He had imagined it all up there in the cabin, knew exactly how it would sound when each instrument was played, and it is more beautiful than I could ever have hoped it would be, more like Jacob than any other music I have ever heard.

I twirl around and feel my skirt filling out in the rush of the fresh mountain air. I lift my face to the sunlight and see him there in heaven.

The flute returns, the clarinet follows. The final note hangs in the air and I savour every second of it, holding on to Jacob for as long as I can, gradually coming to a standstill once again.

There is a rumble of applause and then, once more, there is silence.

I see Jacob's feet before me, leading the way in the dark. Then as the curtains open and the lights shine in my face, I see my father, his white brows are lifted, his eyes are bursting with pride. *Just like Emma*, he says. I think about my mother's soul and what Jacob said about it living on through me, and I don't feel guilty about it anymore. We pass it on, the pieces of ourselves that we give to our children, they are melodies repeating down the generations.

I count my steps as I walk into the light.

The slide of bows on strings; soft, light, magical. The burst of longing and sorrow. The flute signaling the beginning; listen carefully now, something special is coming.

I inhale, find my E.

I extend the thread, send it out into the auditorium.

Four counts. Four people: Nina, Grieg, Jacob, Kristian.

The king and the queen in the royal box.

And me, waiting, as we all are, for that day.

Andante.

Slowly, I open my mouth to sing...

THANKS AND GRATITUDE

To my wonderful agent Bill Hamilton, for helping me develop this story.

To Jonathan Puddle, for honest help and guidance, and professional typesetting skills.

To Jason Anscomb, for creativity, understanding and infinite patience in designing the cover.

To Ben McGuire, for eagle-eyed editing and unending support.

To Heather Hepburn, for early reading and regular cheerleading.

To Janet Whitehead, for magic, inspiration, believing…this one's for you, Janet.

To all my friends and family who have supported me on this journey.

To Dagfinn, Sofie and Kristoffer, for consistently being the most amazing people I know.

To Layla Jane, my love, my companion, my cocker spaniel-shaped daughter, simply for being here in my life and giving us all so much.

CPSIA information can be obtained
at www.ICGtesting.com
Printed in the USA
LVHW020900100922
728014LV00004B/144